The Collector

ALSO BY DANIEL SILVA

The Collector

A Novel

Daniel Silva

HARPER LARGE PRINT

An Imprint of HarperCollinsPublishers

THE COLLECTOR. Copyright © 2023 by Daniel Silva. All rights reserved. Printed in the United States of America. No part of this book may be used or reproduced in any manner whatsoever without written permission except in the case of brief quotations embodied in critical articles and reviews. For information, address HarperCollins Publishers, 195 Broadway, New York, NY 10007.

HarperCollins books may be purchased for educational, business, or sales promotional use. For information, please e-mail the Special Markets Department at SPsales@harpercollins.com.

FIRST HARPER LARGE PRINT EDITION

ISBN: 978-0-06-283517-8

Library of Congress Cataloging-in-Publication Data is available upon request.

23 24 25 26 27 LBC 5 4 3 2 1

As always, for my wife, Jamie, and my children, Lily and Nicholas

We all want things we can't have. Being a decent human being is accepting that.

—JOHN FOWLES, *THE COLLECTOR*

And remember: you must never, under any circumstances, despair. To hope and to act, these are our duties in misfortune.

—BORIS PASTERNAK, *DOCTOR ZHIVAGO*

PART ONE
The Concert

1
Amalfi

It was possible, Sofia Ravello would tell the Carabinieri later that day, to spend the majority of one's
waking hours in another man's home, to prepare his
meals and wash his sheets and sweep his floors, and to
know absolutely nothing about him. The officer from
the Carabinieri, whose name was Caruso, did not take
issue with her statement, for the woman who had shared
his bed for the last twenty-five years was at times a perfect stranger to him. He also knew a bit more about
the victim than he had thus far revealed to the witness.
The man was a murder waiting to happen.

Still, Caruso insisted on a detailed statement, which
Sofia was all too happy to provide. Her day began as
it always did, at the dreadful hour of 5:00 a.m., with

the bleating of her old-fashioned digital alarm clock. Having worked late the previous evening—her employer had entertained—she had granted herself fifteen minutes of additional sleep before rising from her bed. She had brewed a pot of espresso with the Bialetti stovetop, then showered and dressed in her black uniform, all the while asking herself how it was that she, an attractive twenty-four-year-old graduate of the esteemed University of Bologna, worked as a domestic servant in the home of a wealthy foreigner rather than in a sleek office tower in Milan.

The answer was that the Italian economy, reputedly the world's eighth largest, was gripped by chronically high unemployment, leaving the young and educated little choice but to go abroad in search of work. Sofia, however, was determined to remain in her native Campania, even if it required taking a job for which she was vastly overeducated. The wealthy foreigner paid her well—indeed, she earned more than many of her friends from university—and the work itself was hardly backbreaking. Typically, she spent a not insignificant portion of her day staring at the blue-green waters of the Tyrrhenian Sea or at the paintings in her employer's magnificent art collection.

Her tiny apartment was in a crumbling building on the Via della Cartiere, in the upper reaches of the town of Amalfi. From there, it was a lemon-scented walk of twenty minutes to the grandly named Palazzo Van Damme. Like most seaside estates on the Costiera Amalfitana, it was hidden behind a high wall. Sofia entered the passcode into the keypad, and the gate slid open. There was a second keypad at the entrance of the villa itself, with a separate passcode. Usually, the alarm system emitted a shrill chirp when Sofia opened the door, but on that morning it was silent. She did not think it odd at the time. Signore Van Damme sometimes neglected to activate the alarm before turning in.

Sofia proceeded directly to the kitchen and engaged in the first task of her day, which was the preparation of Signore Van Damme's breakfast—a pot of coffee, a pitcher of steamed milk, a bowl of sugar, toasted bread with butter and strawberry preserves. She placed it on a tray and at seven o'clock exactly placed the tray outside his bedroom door. No, she explained to the Carabinieri, she did not enter the room. Nor did she knock. She had made that mistake only once. Signore Van Damme was a precise man who demanded precision from his employees. Needless knocks on doors were discouraged, especially the door to his bedroom.

It was just one of the many rules and edicts that he had transmitted to Sofia at the conclusion of the hour-long interrogation, conducted in his magnificent office, that preceded her hiring. He had described himself as a successful businessman, which he had pronounced *beezneezman*. The palazzo, he said, served as both his primary residence and the nerve center of a global enterprise. He therefore required a smooth-functioning household, free of unnecessary noise and interruptions, as well as loyalty and discretion on the part of those who worked for him. Gossiping about his affairs, or about the contents of his home, was grounds for immediate dismissal.

Sofia soon determined that her employer was the owner of a Bahamas-based shipping company called LVD Marine Transport—LVD being the acronym of his full name, which was Lukas van Damme. She also deduced that he was a citizen of South Africa who had fled his homeland after the fall of apartheid. There was a daughter in London, an ex-wife in Toronto, and a Brazilian woman named Serafina who dropped in on him from time to time. Otherwise, he seemed unencumbered by human attachments. His paintings were all that mattered to him, the paintings that hung in every room and corridor in the villa. Thus the cameras and the motion detectors, and the nerve-jangling weekly test of the alarm, and the strict rules about gossip and unwanted interruptions.

The sanctity of his office was of paramount concern. Sofia was permitted to enter the room only when Signore Van Damme was present. And she was never, *never*, to open the door if it was closed. She had intruded on his privacy only once, through no fault of her own. It had happened six months earlier, when a man from South Africa was staying at the villa. Signore Van Damme had requested a snack of tea and biscuits to be delivered to the office, and when Sofia arrived, the door was ajar. That was when she learned of the existence of the hidden chamber, the one behind the movable bookshelves. The one where Signore Van Damme and his friend from South Africa were at that moment excitedly discussing something in their peculiar native language.

Sofia told no one about what she had seen that day, least of all Signore Van Damme. She did, however, commence a private investigation of her employer, an investigation conducted mainly from within the walls of his seaside citadel. Her evidence, based largely on clandestine observation of her subject, led Sofia to the following conclusions—that Lukas van Damme was not the successful businessman he claimed to be, that his shipping company was less than legitimate, that his money was dirty, that he had links to Italian organized crime, and that he was hiding something in his past.

Sofia harbored no such suspicions about the woman

who had come to the villa the previous evening—the attractive raven-haired woman, mid-thirties, whom Signore Van Damme had bumped into one afternoon at the terrace bar of the Santa Catarina Hotel. He had given her a rare guided tour of his art collection. Afterward they had dined by candlelight on the terrace overlooking the sea. They were finishing the last of their wine when Sofia and the rest of the staff departed the villa at half past ten. It was Sofia's assumption that the woman was now upstairs in Signore Van Damme's bed.

They had left the remnants of their dinner—a few soiled dishes, two garnet-stained wineglasses—outside on the terrace. Neither glass bore any trace of lipstick, which Sofia found unusual. There was nothing else out of the ordinary save for the open door on the villa's lowest level. The likely culprit, Sofia suspected, was Signore Van Damme himself.

She washed and dried the dishes carefully—a single water mark on a utensil was grounds for a reprimand—and at eight o'clock exactly headed upstairs to collect the breakfast tray from outside Signore Van Damme's door. Which was when she noticed that it had not been touched. Not his typical routine, she would tell the Carabinieri, but not unprecedented, either.

But when Sofia found the tray undisturbed at nine o'clock, she grew concerned. And when ten o'clock came and went with no sign that Signore Van Damme was awake, her concern turned to alarm. By then two other members of the staff—Marco Mazzetti, the villa's longtime chef, and groundskeeper Gaspare Bianchi—had arrived. Both were in agreement that the attractive young woman who had dined at the villa the previous evening was the most likely explanation for Signore Van Damme's failure to rise at his normal hour. Therefore, as men, it was their solemn advice to wait until noon before taking action.

And so Sofia Ravello, twenty-four years old, a graduate of the University of Bologna, took up her bucket and mop and gave the floors of the villa their daily scrubbing—which in turn provided her with the opportunity to take inventory of the paintings and other objets d'art in Signore Van Damme's remarkable collection. There was nothing out of place, nothing missing, no sign that anything untoward had occurred.

Nothing but the untouched breakfast tray.

It was still there at noon. Sofia's first knock was tepid and received no answer. Her second, several firm blows delivered with the side of her fist, met with the same result. Finally, she placed a hand on the latch and slowly opened the door. A call to the police proved unnecessary. Her screaming, Marco Mazzetti would later say, could be heard from Salerno to Positano.

2
Cannaregio

W here are you?"

"If I'm not mistaken, I'm sitting next to my wife in the Campo di Ghetto Nuovo."

"Not physically, darling." She placed a finger against his forehead. "Here."

"I was thinking."

"About what?"

"Nothing at all."

"That's not possible."

"Wherever did you get an idea like that?"

It was a peculiar skill that Gabriel had honed in his youth, the capacity to silence all thoughts and memories, to create a private universe without sound or light or other inhabitants. It was there, in the empty quarter of his subconscious, that finished paintings had appeared to him, dazzling in their execution, revolutionary in their approach, and entirely absent of his mother's domineering influence. He had only to awaken from his trance and swiftly copy the images onto canvas before they were lost to him. Lately, he had regained the power to clear his mind of sensory clutter—and with it the ability to produce satisfactory original work. Chiara's body, with its many shapes and curves, was his favorite subject matter.

At present it was pressed tightly against his. The afternoon had turned cold, and a gusty wind was chasing around the perimeter of the *campo*. He was wearing a woolen overcoat for the first time in many months. Chiara's stylish suede jacket and chenille scarf were inadequate to the conditions.

"Surely you must have been thinking about something," she insisted.

"I probably shouldn't say it aloud. The old ones might never recover."

The bench upon which they were seated was a few paces from the doorway of the Casa Israelitica di Riposo, a rest home for aged members of Venice's dwindling Jewish community.

"Our future address," remarked Chiara, and dragged the tip of her finger through the platinum-colored hair at Gabriel's temple. It was longer than he had worn it in many years. "Some of us sooner than others."

"Will you visit me?"

"Every day."

"And what about them?"

Gabriel directed his gaze toward the center of the broad square, where Irene and Raphael were engaged in a hard-fought contest of some sort with several other children from the *sestiere*. The apartment buildings behind them, the tallest in Venice, were awash with the sienna light of the declining sun.

"What on earth is the point of the game?" asked Chiara.

"I've been asking myself the same thing."

The competition involved a ball and the *campo*'s ancient wellhead, but otherwise its rules and scoring system were, to a nonparticipant, indecipherable. Irene seemed to be clinging to a narrow advantage, though her twin brother had organized a furious counterattack among the other players. The boy had been cursed with Gabriel's face and with his unusually green eyes. He also possessed an aptitude for mathematics and recently had begun working with a private tutor. Irene, a climate alarmist who feared that Venice would soon be swallowed by the sea, had decided that Raphael should use his gifts to save the planet. She had yet to choose a career for herself. For now, she enjoyed nothing more than tormenting her father.

An errant kick sent the ball bounding toward the doorway of the Casa. Gabriel hastened to his feet and with a deft flick of his foot sent the ball back into play. Then, after acknowledging the torpid applause of a heavily armed Carabinieri sentry, he turned to face the seven bas-relief panels of the ghetto's Holocaust memorial. It was dedicated to the 243 Venetian Jews— including twenty-nine residents of the convalescent home—who were arrested in December 1943, interned in concentration camps, and later deported to Auschwitz. Among them was Adolfo Ottolenghi, the chief rabbi of Venice, who was murdered in September 1944.

The current leader of the Jewish community, Rabbi Jacob Zolli, was a descendant of Sephardic Jews from Andalusia who were expelled from Spain in 1492. His daughter was at that moment seated on a bench in the Campo di Ghetto Nuovo, watching over her two young children. Like the rabbi's famous son-in-law, she was a former officer of Israel's secret intelligence service. She now served as the general manager of the Tiepolo Restoration Company, the most prominent such enterprise in the Veneto. Gabriel, an art conservator of international renown, was the director of the firm's paintings department. Which meant that, for all intents and purposes, he worked for his wife.

"What are you thinking now?" she asked.

He was wondering, not for the first time, whether his mother had noticed the arrival of several thousand Italian Jews at Auschwitz beginning in the terrible autumn of 1943. Like many survivors of the camps, she had refused to talk about the nightmare world into which she had been cast. Instead, she had recorded her testimony on a few pages of onionskin and locked it away in the file rooms of Yad Vashem. Tormented by the past—and by an abiding guilt over having survived—she had been incapable of showing her only child genuine affection for fear he might be taken from her. She had bequeathed to him her ability to paint, her Berlin-accented German, and perhaps a modicum of her physical courage. And then she had left him. With each passing year, Gabriel's memories of her grew more diffuse. She was a distant figure standing before an easel, a bandage on her left forearm, her back forever turned. That was the reason Gabriel had momentarily detached himself from his wife and children. He had been trying, without success, to see his mother's face.

"I was thinking," he answered, glancing at his wristwatch, "that we ought to be leaving soon."

"And miss the end of the game? I wouldn't dream of it. Besides," added Chiara, "your girlfriend's concert doesn't begin until eight."

It was the annual black-tie gala to benefit the Venice Preservation Society, the London-based nonprofit organization dedicated to the care and restoration of the city's fragile art and architecture. Gabriel had prevailed upon the renowned Swiss violinist Anna Rolfe, with whom he had once had a brief romantic entanglement, to appear at the fundraiser. She had dined the previous evening at the Allon family's luxurious four-bedroom *piano nobile della loggia* overlooking the Grand Canal. Gabriel was only pleased that his wife, who had expertly prepared and served the meal, was once again speaking to him.

She stared straight ahead, a Mona Lisa smile on her face, as he returned to the bench. "Now is the point in the conversation," she said evenly, "when you remind me that the world's most famous violinist is no longer your girlfriend."

"I didn't think it was necessary."

"It is."

"She isn't."

Chiara dug a thumbnail into the back of his hand. "And you were never in love with her."

"Never," vowed Gabriel.

Chiara released the pressure and gently massaged the crescent-shaped indentation in his skin. "She's bewitched your children. Irene informed me this morning that she'd like to begin studying the violin."

"She's a charmer, our Anna."

"She's a train wreck."

"But an extremely talented one." Gabriel had attended Anna's rehearsal earlier that afternoon at Teatro La Fenice, Venice's historic opera house. He had never heard her play so well.

"It's funny," said Chiara, "but she's not as pretty in person as she is on the covers of her CDs. I suppose photographers use special filters when shooting older women."

"That was beneath you."

"I'm allowed." Chiara issued a dramatic sigh. "Has the train wreck settled on her repertoire?"

"Schumann's Violin Sonata No. 1 and the D-minor Brahms."

"You always loved the Brahms, especially the second movement."

"Who doesn't?"

"I suppose she'll make us sit through an encore of the *Devil's Trill*."

"If she doesn't play it, there's likely to be a riot."

Giuseppe Tartini's technically demanding Violin Sonata in G Minor was Anna's signature piece.

"A satanic sonata," said Chiara. "One can only imagine why your girlfriend would be drawn to a piece like that."

"She doesn't believe in the devil. Nor, for that matter, does she believe Tartini's silly story about hearing the piece in a dream."

"But you don't deny that she's your girlfriend."

"I believe I've been quite clear on that point."

"And you were never in love with her?"

"Asked and answered."

Chiara leaned her head against Gabriel's shoulder. "And what about the devil?"

"He's not my type."

"Do you believe he exists?"

"Why would you ask such a question?"

"It might explain all the evil in this world of ours."

She was referring, of course, to the war in Ukraine, now in its eighth month. It had been another dreadful day. More missiles directed against civilian targets in Kyiv. Mass graves with hundreds of bodies discovered in the town of Izium.

"Men rape and steal and murder all on their own," said Gabriel, his eyes fixed on the Holocaust memorial. "And many of the worst atrocities in human history were committed by those who were motivated not by their devotion to the Evil One but by their faith in God."

"How's yours?"

"My faith?" Gabriel said nothing more.

"Perhaps you should talk to my father."

"I talk to your father all the time."

"About our work and the children and security at the synagogues, but not about God."

"Next subject."

"What were you thinking about a few minutes ago?"

"I was dreaming of your fettuccine and mush-rooms."

"Don't make a joke about it."

He answered truthfully.

"You really don't remember how she looked?"

"At the end. But that wasn't her."

"Perhaps this will help."

Rising, Chiara made her way to the center of the *campo* and took Irene by the hand. A moment later the child was sitting on her father's knee, her arms around his neck. "What's wrong?" she asked as he hurriedly wiped a tear from his cheek.

"Nothing," he told her. "Nothing at all."

3

San Polo

By the time Irene returned to the field of play, she had fallen into third place in the rankings. She lodged a formal protest and, receiving no satisfaction, withdrew to the sidelines and watched as the game dissolved into chaos and acrimony. Gabriel attempted to restore order, but to no avail; the contours of the dispute were Arab-Israeli in their complexity. Having no solution at the ready, he suggested a suspension of the tournament until the following afternoon, as the raised voices were liable to disturb the old ones in the Casa. The contestants agreed, and at half past four, peace returned to the Campo di Ghetto Nuovo.

Irene and Raphael, bookbags over their shoulders, scampered across the wooden footbridge on the southern edge of the square, with Gabriel and Chiara a step behind. A few centuries earlier, a Christian guard might have blocked their path, for the light was dwindling and the bridge would soon be sealed for the night. Now they strolled unmolested past gift shops and popular restaurants until they came to a small *campo* overlooked by a pair of opposing synagogues. Alessia Zolli, wife of the chief rabbi, waited outside the open doorway of the Levantine Synagogue, which served the community in winter. The children embraced their grandmother as though it had been untold months, not three short days, since they had seen her last.

"Remember," explained Chiara, "they need to be at school tomorrow morning by eight o'clock at the latest."

"And where is this school of theirs?" asked Alessia Zolli archly. "Is it here in Venice or on the mainland somewhere?" She looked at Gabriel and frowned. "It's your fault she's acting like this."

"What have I done now?"

"I'd rather not say it aloud." Alessia Zolli stroked her daughter's riotous dark hair. "The poor thing has suffered enough already."

"I'm afraid my suffering has only begun."

Chiara kissed the children and set off with Gabriel toward the Fondamenta Cannaregio. While crossing the Ponte delle Guglie, they agreed that a light snack was in order. The recital was scheduled to conclude at 10:00 p.m., at which point they would repair to the Cipriani for a formal dinner with the director of the Venice Preservation Society and several deep-pocketed donors. Chiara had recently submitted bids to the group for a number of lucrative projects. She was therefore obliged to attend the dinner, even if it meant prolonging her exposure to her husband's former lover.

"Where shall we go?" she asked.

Gabriel's favorite *bacaro* in Venice was All'Arco, but it was near the Rialto Fish Market and their time was running short. "How about Adagio?" he suggested.

"A most unfortunate name for a wine bar, don't you think?"

It was in the Campo dei Frari, near the foot of the campanile. Inside, Gabriel ordered two glasses of Lombardian white and an assortment of *cicchetti*. Venetian culinary etiquette demanded that the small, delectable sandwiches be consumed while standing, but Chiara suggested they take a table in the square instead. The previous occupant had left behind a copy of *Il Gazzettino*. It was filled with photographs of the rich and celebrated, including Anna Rolfe.

"My first evening alone with my husband in months," said Chiara, folding the newspaper in half, "and I get to spend it with *her*, of all people."

"Was it really necessary to further undermine my position with your mother?"

"My mother thinks you walk on water."

"Only during an *acqua alta*."

Gabriel devoured a *cicchetto* smothered in artichoke hearts and ricotta, and washed it down with some of the *vino bianco*. It was his second glass of the day. Like most male residents of Venice, he had consumed *un'ombra* with his midmorning coffee. For the past two weeks, he had been frequenting a bar in Murano, where he was restoring an altarpiece by the Venetian school artist known as Il Pordenone. In his spare time, he was chipping away at two private commissions, as the parsimonious wages paid to him by his wife were insufficient to keep her in the manner to which she was accustomed.

She was pondering the *cicchetti*, deliberating between the smoked mackerel and the salmon. Both lay on a bed of creamy cheese and were sprinkled with finely chopped fresh herbs. Gabriel settled the matter by snatching the mackerel. It paired beautifully with the flinty Lombardian wine.

"I wanted that one," said Chiara with a pout, and reached for the salmon. "Have you given any thought as to how you're going to react tonight when someone asks whether you're *that* Gabriel Allon?"

"I was hoping to avoid the issue entirely."

"How?"

"By being my usual unapproachable self."

"I'm afraid that's not an option, darling. It's a social event, which means you're expected to be sociable."

"I'm an iconoclast. I flout convention."

He was also the world's most famous retired spy. He had settled in Venice with the approval of the Italian authorities—and with the knowledge of key figures in the Venetian cultural establishment—but his presence in the city was not widely known. For the most part, he dwelled in an uncertain realm between the overt and covert worlds. He carried a weapon, also with the approval of the Italian police, and maintained a pair of false German passports in the event he found it necessary to travel pseudonymously. Otherwise, he had shed the accoutrements of his previous life. Tonight's gala, for better or worse, would be his coming-out party.

"Don't worry," he said. "I'll be perfectly charming."

"And if someone asks how it is you know Anna Rolfe?"

"I'll feign sudden hearing loss and make a dash for the gents."

"Excellent strategy. But then operational planning always was your strong suit." A single *cicchetto* remained.

Chiara nudged the plate toward Gabriel. "You eat it. Otherwise, I won't be able to fit into my dress."

"Giorgio?"

"Versace."

"How bad is it?"

"Scandalous."

"That's one way to secure funding for our projects."

"Trust me, it isn't for the benefit of the donors."

"You're a rabbi's daughter."

"With a body that won't quit."

"Tell me about it," said Gabriel, and devoured the final *cicchetto*.

It was a pleasant ten-minute walk from the Campo dei Frari to their apartment. In the spacious master bathroom suite, Gabriel quickly showered and then confronted his reflection in the looking glass. He judged his appearance to be satisfactory, though marred by the raised, puckered scar on the left side of his chest. It was approximately half the size of the corresponding scar beneath his left scapula. His two other bullet wounds had healed nicely, as had the bite marks, inflicted by an Alsatian guard dog, on his left forearm. Unfortunately, he couldn't say the same for the two fractured vertebrae in his lower back.

Faced with the prospect of a two-hour concert followed by a multicourse seated dinner, he swallowed a prophylactic dose of Advil before heading to his dressing room. His Brioni tuxedo, a recent addition to his wardrobe, awaited him. His tailor had not found it unusual when he requested additional room in the waistline; all his trousers were cut in that manner to accommodate a concealed weapon. His preferred hand-gun was a Beretta 92FS, a sizable firearm that weighed nearly two pounds when fully loaded.

Dressed, Gabriel wedged the gun into place at the small of his back. Then, turning slightly, he examined his appearance a second time. Once again, he was mostly pleased by what he saw. The elegantly cut Brioni jacket rendered the weapon all but invisible. Moreover, the fashionable double vent would likely reduce his draw time, which, despite his many bodily injuries, remained lightning-strike fast.

He strapped a Patek Philippe timepiece to his wrist and, switching off the lights, went into the sitting room to await the appearance of his wife. Yes, he thought as he surveyed his sweeping view of the Grand Canal, he was *that* Gabriel Allon. Once he had been Israel's angel of vengeance. Now he was the director of the paintings department at the Tiepolo Restoration Company. Anna was someone he had encountered along the way. If the truth be told, he had tried to love her, but he wasn't capable of it. Then he met a beautiful young girl from the ghetto, and the girl saved his life.

The deep thigh slit and absence of shoulder straps notwithstanding, Chiara's black Versace evening gown was by no means scandalous. Her shoes, however, were definitely a problem. Stiletto-heeled Ferragamo pumps, they added ten and a half desirable centimeters to her already statuesque frame. She gave Gabriel a discreet downward glance as they approached the pack of press photographers gathered outside Teatro La Fenice.

"Are you sure you're ready for this?" she asked through a frozen smile.

"As ready as I'll ever be," he answered as a barrage of brilliant white flashes dazzled his eyes.

They passed beneath the blue-and-yellow Ukrainian flag hanging from the theater's portico and entered the multilingual din of the crowded foyer. A few heads turned, but Gabriel received no excessive scrutiny. For the moment, at least, he was just another middle-aged man of uncertain nationality with a beautiful young woman on his arm.

She squeezed his hand reassuringly. "That wasn't so bad, was it?"

"The night is young," murmured Gabriel, and sur-

veyed the shimmering room around him. Faded aristo-
crats, magnates and moguls, a smattering of important
Old Master dealers. Tubby Oliver Dimbleby, never one
to miss a good party, had made the trip down from
London. He was comforting a French collector of note
who had been burned to a crisp by a recent forgery
scandal, the one involving the late Phillip Somerset and
his fraudulent art-based hedge fund, Masterpiece Art
Ventures.

"Did you know he was coming?" asked Chiara.

"Oliver? I heard an alarming report to that effect
from one of my many sources in the London art world.
He's under strict instructions to give us a wide berth."

"What happens if he can't help himself?"

"Pretend he has leprosy and walk away as quickly as
possible."

A reporter approached Oliver and solicited a comment, about what, heaven only knew. Several other
journalists were gathered around Lorena Rinaldi, the
minister of culture in Italy's new coalition government.
Like the prime minister, Rinaldi belonged to a far-
right political party that could trace its lineage to the
National Fascists of Benito Mussolini.

"At least she didn't wear her armband," said a male
voice at Gabriel's shoulder. It belonged to Francesco
Tiepolo, owner of the prominent restoration company

that bore his family's famous name. "I only wish she'd had the decency not to show her photogenic face at an event like this."

"Evidently, she's a great admirer of Anna Rolfe."

"Who isn't?"

"Me," said Chiara.

Francesco smiled. An enormous, bearlike man, he bore an uncanny resemblance to Luciano Pavarotti. Even now, more than a decade after the tenor's death, autograph-seeking tourists flocked to Francesco on the streets of Venice. If he was feeling mischievous, which was usually the case, he indulged them.

"Did you see the minister's interview on RAI last night?" he asked. "She vowed to purge Italian culture of wokeism. For the life of me, I hadn't a clue what she was talking about."

"Neither did she," said Gabriel. "It was just something she overheard during her most recent visit to America."

"We should probably take the opportunity to pay our respects."

"Why on earth would we do that?"

"Because for the foreseeable future, Lorena Rinaldi will have the final say over all major restoration projects here in Venice, regardless of who's footing the bill."

Just then the lights in the foyer dimmed and a chime

sounded. "Saved by the bell," said Gabriel, and escorted Chiara into the theater. She managed to conceal her displeasure when settling into her VIP seat in the first row.

"How lovely," she said. "I'm only sorry we're not closer to the stage."

Gabriel sat down next to her and made a small adjustment to the position of the Beretta. At length he said, "I think that went rather well, don't you?"

"The night is young," replied Chiara, and dug a thumbnail into the back of his hand.

4

Cipriani

The Schumann was wondrous, the Brahms searchingly beautiful. But it was Anna's incendiary performance of Tartini's *Devil's Trill* that brought the audience to its feet. Three dramatic curtain calls later, she bade them a final farewell. Most of the patrons filed into the Corte San Gaetano, but a select few were discreetly escorted to the theater's dock, where a flotilla of gleaming *motoscafi* waited to ferry them to the Cipriani hotel. Gabriel and Chiara made the journey with a delegation of agreeable New Yorkers. None appeared to recognize the famous retired spy in their midst. The same was true of the attractive, clipboard-wielding hostess at Oro, the Cipriani's celebrated restaurant.

"Ah, yes. Here you are, Signore Allon. Table number five. Signora Zolli is at table one. The head table," the hostess added with a smile.

"That's because Signora Zolli is much more important than I am."

The hostess gestured toward the entrance of the restaurant's private dining room, and Gabriel followed Chiara inside. "Please tell me they didn't seat me next to her," she said.

"The minister? I believe she had to rush off to a book burning."

"I was referring to Anna."

"Play nicely," said Gabriel, and set off in search of his table. He arrived to find four of the New Yorkers from the water taxi. They were outliers, the Americans. The rest of the crowd was decidedly British.

Gabriel located his assigned seat and, resisting the urge to drop the place card into the nearest shredder, sat down.

"I didn't catch your name earlier," said one of the Americans, a ginger-haired specimen of perhaps sixty-five who looked as though he ate too much red meat.

"It's Gabriel Allon."

"Sounds familiar. What do you do?"

"I'm a conservator."

"Really? I was afraid I would be the only one here."

"Conservator," repeated Gabriel, stressing the final syllable. "An art restorer."

"Have you restored anything recently?"

"I did some work on one of the Tintorettos in the church of the Madonna dell'Orto not long ago."

"I believe I paid for that entire project."

"You *believe*?"

"Saving Venice is my wife's hobby. To tell you the truth, art bores the shit out of me."

Gabriel checked the place card to his right and was relieved to see that he had been seated next to the heiress to a British supermarket fortune who, if the London tabloids were to be believed, had recently tried to murder her philandering husband with a butcher's knife. Curiously, the card corresponding to the seat on his left was blank.

Looking up, he spotted the heiress, a well-preserved woman in a striking red gown, approaching the table. Her chemically enhanced face displayed no trace of surprise—or any other emotion, for that matter—when he introduced himself.

"For the record," she said, "it was only a paring knife. And the wound, such as it was, required no sutures." Smiling, she took her seat. "Who are you, Mr. Allon? And what on earth are you doing here?"

"He's a conservator," interjected the American. "He

restored one of the Tintorettos in Madonna dell'Orto. My wife and I paid for it."

"And we're all very grateful," breathed the heiress. Then, turning to Gabriel, she said, "Who do I have to kill around here to get a Beefeater and tonic?"

Gabriel started to reply but fell silent when a swell of applause rose from the neighboring tables.

"The enchanting Madame Rolfe," observed the heiress. "She's mad as a hatter. At least that's what they say."

Gabriel allowed the remark to pass without comment.

"Her mother committed suicide, you know. And then there was that terrible scandal involving her father and those paintings that were looted by the Nazis during the war. Anna's life went off the rails after that. How many failed marriages were there? Three? Or was it four?"

"Two, I believe."

"And let's not forget the accident that almost ended her career," said the heiress, undeterred. "I'm afraid I can't recall the details."

"A hillside gave way in a rainstorm while she was hiking near her home on the Costa de Prata. Her left hand was crushed by a falling boulder. It took months of rehabilitation for her to regain use of it."

"It sounds to me as though you're an admirer, Mr. Allon."

"You might say that."

"Forgive me, I hope I haven't spoken out of turn."

"Oh, no," said Gabriel. "I've never had the honor of actually meeting her."

There seemed to be some confusion over where Anna was to sit. Each of the eight seats at the head table was occupied. So, too, was every other chair in the dining room—with one exception.

No, thought Gabriel, glancing at the blank place card. She wouldn't dare.

"Well, well," said the heiress as the world's most famous violinist approached the table. "It looks as though this is your lucky night."

"Imagine that," replied Gabriel, and rose slowly to his feet.

Anna accepted his outstretched hand as though it belonged to a stranger, then smiled mischievously when he spoke his name. "Not *that* Gabriel Allon," she said, and sat down.

"How did you manage this?"

"In lieu of my usual exorbitant appearance fee, I made a single nonnegotiable demand regarding the seating arrangements for tonight's après-concert soirée." She offered an overbright smile to a patron at a neighboring table. "God, but I hate these things. One wonders why I agreed to this."

"Because you couldn't resist the opportunity to cause problems in my home."

"My intentions were honorable, I assure you."

"Were they really?"

"Mostly." Anna lowered her eyes apprehensively toward the plate that a white-jacketed waiter had placed before her. "What in God's name is it?"

"Cuttlefish," explained Gabriel. "A local delicacy."

"The last time I ate an uncooked creature from the lagoon, I was paralyzed for a week."

"It's divine."

"When in Rome," said Anna, and tentatively sampled the dish. "How much money did we raise tonight?"

"Nearly ten million. But if you play footsie with that wealthy American on the other side of the table, twenty million isn't out of the question."

Presently, the wealthy American was staring wide-eyed at his phone.

"Does he know who you are?" asked Anna.

"I have a feeling he does now."

"What do you suppose he's thinking?"

"Why is the retired chief of Israeli intelligence sitting next to Anna Rolfe, of all people?"

"Shall we tell him?"

"I'm not sure he would believe the story."

It began when Gabriel accepted what he thought was a routine commission to restore a painting at the Zurich residence of the immensely wealthy Swiss banker Augustus Rolfe. The tragic ending took place some months later, when Gabriel walked out of the villa in Portugal where Herr Rolfe's famous daughter had taken refuge from her family's deplorable past. He had always regretted his conduct that day—and the twenty years during which he and Anna had exchanged not a single phone call or email. Familial complications notwithstanding, he was pleased she was once again a part of his life.

"You might have warned me," she said suddenly.

"About what?"

She directed her gaze toward the head table, where all eyes were on Chiara. "Your wife's astonishing beauty. It was quite a shock last night when I met her for the first time."

"I believe I mentioned a vague resemblance to Nicola Benedetti."

"My dear friend Nicola wishes she looked like Chiara." Anna sighed. "I suppose she's perfect in every way."

"She's a much better cook than you. And better yet, she doesn't practice the violin at all hours."

"Has she ever hurt you?"

Gabriel pointed out the faint red mark on the back of his hand.

"I never stood a chance of getting you back, did I?"

"You made it abundantly clear when I left Portugal that you never wanted to speak to me again."

"I suppose you're referring to the lamp I accidently knocked from the end table."

"It was a ceramic vase. And you hurled it directly at my head with your remarkably strong right arm."

"Consider yourself lucky. The gentlewoman seated next to you would have come after you with something far more lethal."

"She swears it was only a paring knife."

"There were photographs." Anna nudged her plate toward the center of the table.

"You don't care for it?"

"I'm flying to London first thing. I'd rather not take a chance."

"I thought you were staying in Venice for a few days."

"Last-minute change in plan. I'm recording the Mendelssohn next week with Yannick Nézet-Séguin and the Chamber Orchestra of Europe, and I desperately need a few days of rehearsal."

"The children will be disappointed, Anna. They adore you."

"And I them. But I'm afraid it can't be helped. Yannick was quite insistent I come to London straightaway. I'm thinking about having a disastrous affair while I'm there. Something that will get my name back in the gossip columns where it belongs."

"You'll only get hurt again."

"But I'll play better as a result. You know me, Gabriel. I never play well when I'm happy."

"You were magnificent tonight, Anna."

"Was I?" She squeezed his hand. "I wonder why."

5

Murano

It was Chiara, on something of a dare, who had suggested that Gabriel paint a copy of *Reclining Nude*, Modigliani's controversial masterwork that in 2015 fetched $170 million at Christie's auction house in New York. Pleased by his effort, he had then executed an altogether convincing pastiche of Modigliani's original—a change of perspective, a subtle rearrangement of the woman's pose—if only to demonstrate his ability, were he ever so inclined, to earn his living as an art forger. On the morning after the gala, he awoke to find both canvases awash in the morning light slanting through the tall windows overlooking the Grand Canal. It was dull and gray, the light, much like the pain between Gabriel's eyes. It had nothing to do with the red wine he had drunk with his midnight supper, he assured himself. Rainy mornings in Venice always made his head ache.

He rose slowly, so as not to wake Chiara, and surveyed the damage from last evening's postgala proceedings. A trail of hastily discarded Italian formalwear and other assorted furnishings stretched from the doorway to the foot of the bed. A Brioni tuxedo and shirt. A strapless evening gown with a deep thigh slit by Versace. Stiletto-heeled pumps and patent-leather Derby oxfords by Salvatore Ferragamo. Gold studs and cuff links. A timepiece by Patek Philippe. A 92FS 9mm pistol by Fabbrica d'Armi Pietro Beretta. The act had been completed swiftly, with little regard for preliminaries. Chiara had gazed down at Gabriel proprietarily throughout, a half smile on her face. The rival had been vanquished, the demon exorcised.

In the kitchen, Gabriel filled the *automatico* with Illy and bottled water, and reviewed the coverage of the gala in *Il Gazzettino* while waiting for the coffee to brew. The paper's music critic had found much to admire in Anna's recital, especially her encore, which had somehow managed to eclipse her legendary performance of the same piece two decades earlier at the Scuola Grande di San Rocco. In none of the accompanying photographs was there any evidence of Gabriel's presence at the event, only a single image of his right shoulder, upon which rested the hand of Chiara Zolli, the dazzling general manager of the Tiepolo Restoration Company.

She was still sleeping soundly when Gabriel returned to the bedroom with two cups of coffee. Her position was unchanged; she was supine, with her arms above her head. Even unconscious, thought Gabriel, she was a work of art. He tugged at the duvet, exposing her heavy, rounded breasts, and took up his sketchpad. Ten minutes elapsed before the scratching of his charcoal pencil awakened her.

"Must you?" she groaned.

"I must."

"I look awful."

"I beg to differ."

"Coffee," she pleaded.

"It's on your bedside table, but you can't have it yet."

"Don't you have a painting to restore?"

"I'd rather sketch you."

"You're already behind schedule."

"I'm always behind schedule."

"Which is why I should fire you."

"I'm irreplaceable."

"This is Italy, darling. There are more art restorers in this country than waiters."

"And the waiters earn better wages."

Chiara reached for the duvet.

"Don't move," said Gabriel.

"I'm cold."

"Yes, I can see that."

Chiara returned to her original pose. "Did you ever paint her?"

"Anna? Never."

"She refused to sit for you?"

"Actually, she begged me to paint her."

"Why didn't you?"

"I was afraid of what I might find there."

"You don't really believe she needs to rehearse the Mendelssohn violin concerto."

"She can play it in her sleep."

"So why is she leaving?"

"I'll show you in a few minutes."

"You have exactly ten seconds."

Gabriel snapped her photograph with his Israeli-made Solaris phone, the world's most secure.

"Reprobate," said Chiara, and reached for her coffee.

One hour later, showered and dressed and cloaked in oilskin coats against the gentle rain, they stood side by side on the *imbarcadero* of the San Tomà vaporetto stop. Chiara's San Marco–bound Number 2 arrived first.

"Are you free for lunch?" asked Gabriel.

She fixed him with a stare of reproach. "You can't be serious."

"It was the sketch."

"I'll think about it," she said, and boarded the vaporetto.

"Well?" he called out as the vessel drew away from the dock.

"I might be free at one."

"I'll pick up something to eat."

"Don't bother," she replied, and blew him a kiss.

A Number 1 was approaching San Tomà from the direction of the university. Gabriel rode it to the Rialto, then hiked across Cannaregio to the Fondamente Nove, where he quickly downed a coffee at Bar Cupido before boarding his next vaporetto, a Number 4.1. It made a single stop along the western flank of San Michele, the island of the dead, then headed for Murano. Gabriel disembarked at Museo, the second of the island's two stops, and walked past the glass shops lining the Fondamenta Venier to the church of Santa Maria degli Angeli.

There had been a Christian place of worship on the site since 1188, but the current structure, with its listing bell tower and khaki-colored brick exterior, dated to 1529. In the late eighteenth century, a philosopher and adventurer who associated with the likes of Mozart and Voltaire had regularly attended Mass there. It was not faith that drew the man to the church, for he had none. He came in hopes of a fleeting encounter with a beautiful young nun who resided in the adjoining convent. The man, whose name was Giacomo Casanova, had many such relationships—hundreds, in fact—though he carefully guarded the identity of his secret lover from the convent. In his memoirs, he identified the woman, rumored to be the daughter of a Venetian aristocrat, only as M.M.

There were others like her at the convent, daughters of the republic's wealthiest citizens, so the abbess was rarely short of funds. She nevertheless balked when a popular painter who would one day be known as Titian demanded five hundred ducats for a depiction of the annunciation that he had produced for the church's high altar. Offended, Titian gave the painting to Isabella, wife of Charles V, and the abbess hired Il Pordenone, a ruthlessly ambitious Mannerist who had been accused of hiring assassins to kill his brother, to produce a replacement. Pordenone undoubtedly leapt at the opportunity, for he viewed himself as Titian's most serious artistic rival in Venice.

Titian's original altarpiece disappeared without a

trace during the Napoleonic Wars, but Pordenone's lesser work survived. At present it was secured to a purpose-built wooden armature in the center of the nave. On the wall behind the high altar was a black rectangle of corresponding dimensions where once the canvas had hung—and where it would hang again when the extensive restoration of the ancient church was complete. Adrianna Zinetti, perched atop a towering scaffold, was removing a century's worth of dust and grime from the ornate marble frame. She wore a zippered fleece jacket and fingerless gloves. The interior of the church was cold as a crypt.

"*Buongiorno*, Signore Delvecchio," she sang as Gabriel switched on a portable space heater. It was the cover identity he had used during much of his previous life—Mario Delvecchio, the standoffish, temperamental genius who had served his apprenticeship in Venice with the great Umberto Conti and restored many of the city's most famous paintings. Adrianna, a renowned cleaner of altars and statuary, had worked with Mario on several major projects. When not trying to seduce him, she had loathed him with a particular intensity. "I was beginning to worry about you," she said. "You're always the first to arrive."

"Late night," he replied, and scrutinized his work trolley. The telltales he had left behind the previous afternoon remained undisturbed. Still, one never knew. "You didn't touch anything, did you?"

"Everything, Mario. I put my grubby little fingers all over your precious flasks and solvents."

"You really have to stop calling me that, you know."

"A part of me misses him."

"I'm sure he feels the same about you."

"And what if I *had* touched your things?" she asked. "Would the world have come to an end?"

"It might well have, yes." He removed his coat. "To what shall we listen, Signora Zinetti?"

"Amy Winehouse."

"How about Schubert instead?"

"Not the string quartets again. If I have to listen to *Death and the Maiden* one more time, I'll jump."

Gabriel inserted a disc into his paint-smudged CD player—Maurizio Pollini's classic recording of Schubert's late piano sonatas—and then wound a swatch of cotton wool around the end of a wooden dowel. Next he dipped the swab into a carefully calibrated mixture of acetone, methyl proxitol, and mineral spirits, and twirled it gently over the surface of the altarpiece. The solvent was strong enough to remove the yellowed varnish, but not Pordenone's original work. The acrid smell invaded Adrianna's workspace.

"You really should wear a mask," she admonished

him. "In all the years we've worked together, I've never once seen you put one on. I can't imagine how many brain cells you've killed off."

"My missing brain cells are the least of my problems."

"Name one problem you have, Mario."

"An altar cleaner who insists on talking while I'm trying to work."

Gabriel's swab had turned the color of nicotine. He discarded it and prepared another. A fortnight into the restoration, he had cleaned nearly the entire lower third of the painting. The losses were extensive but hardly catastrophic. It was Gabriel's ambition to complete the final stage of the restoration, the retouching, in four months' time, at which point he would turn his attention to the remaining works adorning the nave.

Antonio Politi, a longtime employee of the Tiepolo Restoration Company, had already begun work on one of the canvases, *The Virgin in Glory with Saints* by Palma il Giovane. It was nearly half past ten when he sauntered into the church.

"*Buongiorno*, Signore Delvecchio," he called out.

From atop the high altar came the sound of laughter. Gabriel removed the disk from his CD player and inserted a recording of Schubert's String Quartet No. 14 in D Minor. Then he pulled on his oilskin coat and, smiling, went into the damp morning.

6

Bar al Ponte

The parcel that arrived at the Naples office of the Carabinieri on a stifling August morning in 1988 was by all outward appearances harmless, which was not the case. It contained a small but powerful bomb assembled by a member of the Calabrian criminal organization known as the Camorra. The addressee, General Cesare Ferrari, had been targeted several times before, most recently after the arrest of one of the Camorra's highest-ranking figures. The mail room attendant nevertheless delivered the package to the general's office. Ferrari would survive the explosion but lose his right eye and two fingers from his right hand. A year later he personally escorted the camorrista responsible for the attack into Poggioreale prison and bade him a not-so-fond farewell.

There were some who considered him ill suited for his next assignment, and perhaps a touch too brash, but General Ferrari thought otherwise. Brazenness, he insisted, was precisely what the Art Squad required. Known formally as the Division for the Defense of Cultural Patrimony, it was the first of its kind—a police unit dedicated exclusively to combating the lucrative trade in stolen art and antiquities. The first two decades of its existence had produced thousands of arrests and a string of high-profile recoveries, but by the mid-1990s, institutional paralysis had set in. Manpower had dwindled to a few retirement-age officers, most of whom knew little or nothing about art. It was said by the unit's legion of detractors, not without some justification, that they spent more time debating where to have lunch than searching for the museum's worth of paintings that went missing in Italy each year.

Within days of assuming command of the Art Squad, General Ferrari fired half the staff and replaced them with aggressive young officers who knew a thing or two about the objects they were attempting to find. He also sought authority to tap the phones of known criminal operatives and opened offices in the parts of the country where the thieves actually stole art, especially in the south. Most important, he adopted many of the techniques he had used against the Mafia during his days in Naples, targeting big fish rather than merely street-level hoods who dabbled in art theft. His approach quickly paid dividends. Under General Ferrari's leadership, the Division for the Defense of Cultural Patrimony had regained its lost luster. Even the art sleuths of the French Police Nationale were the first to admit that their Italian brethren were the best in the business.

They were headquartered in an ornate yellow-and-white palazzo in Rome's Piazza di Sant'Ignazio, but three officers were based in Venice. When not searching for stolen works of art, they kept a close eye on the director of the paintings department at the Tiepolo Restoration Company. Lately, he had been taking his midmorning coffee break at Bar al Ponte, so named because of its proximity to one of Murano's busiest bridges. He arrived there to find General Ferrari, in his blue-and-gold Carabinieri finery, occupying a table in the back corner of the room.

He smiled at Gabriel over that morning's edition of *Il Gazzettino.* "You've become a creature of habit."

"My wife tells me the same thing," replied Gabriel, and sat down.

"She made quite an impression at last evening's gala." The general laid the newspaper flat on the table and pointed to a photograph in the Cultura section. "But who's that out-of-focus chap standing next to her?"

"An afterthought."

"I wouldn't go that far. It's safe to say your presence in Venice is no longer a secret."

"I couldn't hide forever, Cesare."

"How does it feel to be a normal person again after all these years?"

"Let's not get carried away. I'm not exactly normal."

"You certainly have interesting friends. I'm only sorry I wasn't able to attend Signora Rolfe's performance."

"Don't worry, the minister of culture was good enough to put in an appearance."

"You behaved yourself, I hope."

"We got on famously. In fact, she invited me to next week's Leni Riefenstahl film festival."

General Ferrari's smile was courtly and brief. As usual, it had no influence upon his prosthetic right eye. "I'm afraid that our politics are no laughing matter. One hundred years after the rise of Mussolini, the Italian people have once again handed power to the fascists."

"The Fratelli d'Italia consider themselves to be neo-fascists."

"What's the difference?"

"Better uniforms."

"And no castor oil," added General Ferrari, then shook his head slowly. "How in God's name did we come to this?"

"'Things fall apart,'" recited Gabriel. "'The center cannot hold.'"

"Did Virgil write that, or was it Ovid?"

"I believe it was David Bowie," quipped Gabriel.

The barman delivered two coffees to the table and, for Gabriel, a small glass of white wine. General Ferrari pondered his wristwatch. "You Venetians really do know how to live."

"Too much coffee makes my hands shake. A few drops of *vino bianco* counteract the effects of the caffeine."

"You never struck me as the sort to have shaky hands."

"It happens from time to time. Especially when I have the nagging sensation that an old friend is about to impose on me for a favor."

"And if he were?"

"I would tell him that an altarpiece awaits."

"Il Pordenone? He's beneath you."

"But he pays the bills."

"And what if I were to offer you something more

interesting?" The general adopted the meditative countenance of Bellini's *Doge Leonardo Loredan*. "There was a spectacular wave of art heists here in Europe a few years ago. The newspapers referred to it as the summer of theft. The first took place in Vienna. The thieves recruited a disgruntled security guard at the Kunsthistorisches and made off with *David with the Head of Goliath* by your old friend Caravaggio. I'm sure you recall it."

"It rings a distant bell," replied Gabriel.

"The very next month," General Ferrari continued, "they stole *Portrait of Señora Canals* from the Museu Picasso in Barcelona. A week later *Les Maisons (Fenouillet)* vanished from the Musée Matisse. And then, of course, there was the textbook smash-and-grab job they pulled at the Courtauld Gallery. Once again, they helped themselves to but a single painting."

"*Self-Portrait with Bandaged Ear* by Vincent van Gogh."

Ferrari nodded. "As you might imagine, my European colleagues have been searching high and low for these irreplaceable works of art, without success. Now, quite unexpectedly, it appears that one of them has resurfaced."

"Where?"

"Here in Italy, of all places."

"Which one?"

"I'm not at liberty to say."

"Whyever not?"

"The painting was discovered late yesterday afternoon by another division of the Carabinieri. If it is indeed the work in question, I will contact the relevant authorities and begin the process of repatriation."

"Is there some doubt?"

"It certainly *looks* like the genuine article," said General Ferrari. "But as you know, the art market is awash with high-quality forgeries. Needless to say, it would be most embarrassing if we were to announce the rediscovery of a missing painting only to have it turn out to be a fake. We have our reputation to uphold."

"What does any of this have to do with me?"

"I was wondering whether you knew someone who could assist us. Someone whose expertise runs the gamut from Caravaggio to Van Gogh. Someone who could walk into an art gallery in, say, Paris and spot several forgeries within a matter of minutes."

"I know just the expert," said Gabriel. "But I'm afraid he's rather busy at the moment."

"I would advise him to find time in his schedule."

"Is that a threat?"

"Just a friendly reminder that you are a guest in this country, and I am the innkeeper."

It was General Ferrari, in his capacity as chief of the Art Squad, who had arranged for Gabriel to receive a *permesso di soggiorno,* a permanent Italian residence permit. Revocation of the document would threaten his livelihood, not to mention his marriage.

"A simple authentication? That's all you require?"

Ferrari shrugged noncommittally.

"Where is the painting now?"

"In situ."

"*Where* in situ?"

"Amalfi. If we leave now, you'll be home in time for a late dinner with Chiara."

"Will I?"

"Probably not. In fact, it might be wise to pack a bag."

"Gun or no gun?"

"Gun," said General Ferrari. "Definitely bring a gun."

7
Amalfi

While crossing the *laguna* in a Carabinieri patrol boat, Gabriel considered how best to explain the morning's developments to Chiara. He reflected upon the matter further while changing into suitable attire and tossing a change of clothing into his overnight bag. In the end he decided to employ a version of the general's original fiction, that the Art Squad required his connoisseur's eye to authenticate a recovered stolen painting. He spun this tale by text message because he no longer possessed the ability to lie convincingly to his wife using any other form of communication. She accepted his story without question, including his false assertion that he would be back in Venice in time for a late dinner. If anything, she seemed relieved that her hopelessly amorous husband would be away for a few hours.

The patrol boat ferried them next to the airport, where they boarded an AgustaWestland AW109 helicopter. With a cruising speed of 285 kilometers per hour, it covered the distance down to Naples in just under three hours. They made the winding trip over the hills of the Sorrento Peninsula, with its nausea-inducing switchbacks and hairpin turns, in a Carabinieri Alfa Romeo, piloted, surely, by an aspiring Formula One driver. It was half past two when he turned through the open security gate of a palatial cliffside villa overlooking the Tyrrhenian Sea. Three additional Carabinieri cruisers were parked in the forecourt, along with a crime-scene van.

"Nice crib," said Gabriel.

"Wait until you see the interior."

"Who's the owner?"

"A South African named Lukas van Damme."

"What does he do for a living?"

"Until recently, Signore Van Damme was in the shipping business."

"I'm obviously in the wrong line of work."

"That makes two of us."

Gabriel followed the general through the villa's grand entrance. A luminous gallery stretched before them, lined on both sides with pedestaled vases and vessels and Greek and Roman statuary. On the white-washed walls hung a remarkable collection of Old Master paintings of every school and genre. At the opposite end of the gallery, a doorway was open wide to the freshening afternoon breeze. The sun had yet to begin its descent toward the turquoise sea.

Gabriel approached one of the antiquities, an Etruscan terra-cotta amphora, and consulted the Art Squad evidence tag dangling from the handle. "The Paris Painter?"

"So it appears," said General Ferrari. "That piece belongs in a museum rather than a private residence. Thus far, we've been unable to determine where Signore Van Damme acquired it."

"Where is he now?"

"Naples."

"In custody?"

"More or less," said the general with an apathetic shrug.

Adjacent to the amphora was a large Bacchic scene that bore the hallmarks of the French Baroque artist Nicolas Poussin. And next to the Bacchic scene was a landscape that might or might not have been painted by the hand of Claude Lorrain. Both were in immaculate condition, as was the rest of the collection.

THE COLLECTOR · 59

"There are paintings and objets d'art of similar quality throughout the property," said General Ferrari. "Some better than others."

"Where might we find those?"

The general indicated a pair of ornate lacquered doors. Beyond them lay the spacious, light-filled office of a man who quite obviously held himself in high regard. Two Carabinieri officers were rifling through the contents of the desk, and a third was downloading files from a computer onto a remote storage device. It was this officer, when prompted by General Ferrari, who pressed the concealed button that initiated the motorized outward swinging movement of two solidly built bookcases. Behind them was a stainless-steel door, like the door of a bank vault, and a keypad.

"The better ones?" asked Gabriel.

"I'll let you be the judge."

The experts had long called into question his very existence. There was no such thing, they said, as the mysterious wealthy collector who acquires illegally what he cannot purchase legitimately on the open market. He was a fantasy of fertile Hollywood imaginations, they claimed. A myth. They even had a name for him; they called him Dr. No, the cartoonish title character of Ian Fleming's spy thriller featuring British secret agent James Bond. Gabriel, however, had never fallen victim to such misconceptions. Yes, many art thefts were carried out by common criminals who had no idea how to profitably dispose of a painting once it was in their hands. But there was also a thriving black market for stolen art that catered to men who were driven to possess the unpossessable. By all outward appearances, Lukas van Damme was such a man.

His vault was approximately three meters by four and decorated in the formal manner of an exhibition room at a commercial art gallery. There was a single Eames chair, which was oriented toward the room's only painting—*Self-Portrait with Bandaged Ear*, oil on canvas, 60 by 49 centimeters, by Vincent van Gogh. Of more interest to Gabriel, however, was the empty frame and stretcher, 70 by 65 centimeters, give or take a centimeter or two, leaning against one wall. Twenty or so copper-plated canvas tacks littered the floor.

He looked to General Ferrari for an explanation.

"We believe it was stolen two nights ago, but we can't say for certain. It appears as though the thief gained access to the vault by hacking into the villa's Wi-Fi network. The entire security system was disabled, and all of the video has been erased."

"What makes you think it was two nights ago?"

"More on that in a moment. The question is," said

Ferrari, "why would a thief steal *that* painting and not one of the most famous works of art in existence?"

"I can think of two possible explanations."

"The first?"

"The Van Gogh isn't a Van Gogh."

"That fact that it's hidden in a vault would suggest that it is."

"So stipulated."

"And the second explanation?"

"The Van Gogh is a Van Gogh, but it wasn't worth stealing."

"And why would that be?"

"Because the other painting was more valuable." Gabriel lowered his voice. "Much more."

"How much, hypothetically speaking, of course, would *Self-Portrait with Bandaged Ear* fetch at auction? Two hundred million? Two hundred and fifty?"

"In the shade."

"Is there another missing painting worth more than that?"

"Only one."

"First things first," said General Ferrari. "Is it, or is it not, *Self-Portrait with Bandaged Ear* by Vincent van Gogh?"

Gabriel placed a hand to his chin and tilted his head to one side. It was the right ear, of course, that was encased in the heavy dressing. Vincent had taken a razor to it on the evening of December 23, 1888, following a heated quarrel with Paul Gauguin in the Yellow House in Arles. He had produced the self-portrait after his release from the hospital in January 1889. In his haste to complete the work, he had failed to apply paint to portions of the canvas, including a patch beneath his cheekbone and another where the collar of his woolen coat fell against the side of his neck. The bare spots on the painting before Gabriel were identical to the ones on the painting that had been stolen from the Courtauld Gallery. They were Vincent's bare spots, thought Gabriel. So were the brushstrokes.

"Well?" asked General Ferrari after a long moment.

"I should probably have a look at the back of the canvas just to be certain."

"But it isn't necessary?"

"No," said Gabriel, and turned his attention once more toward the empty frame and stretcher leaning against the wall—and the twenty or so copper-plated canvas tacks littering the floor. No razor for this thief, he thought. It was the mark of a professional. And a cool one at that.

He reached for the stretcher.

"Don't," said General Ferrari. "Not unless you'd like us to take a set of elimination prints from you."

Gabriel withdrew his hand.

"How old is it?" asked Ferrari.

"The stretcher? Twenty years, maybe less. It's laminated pine, with a five-eighths setback. Quite common. It could have come from any artists' supply shop in Europe."

"The measurements suggest it was custom-made to someone's exact specifications."

"Seventy-two-point-five by sixty-four-point-seven centimeters?"

Ferrari nodded. "You wouldn't happen to know a missing painting of those dimensions that's worth more than *Self-Portrait with Bandaged Ear* by Vincent van Gogh, would you?"

"Only one," said Gabriel.

"I thought so, too." The general smiled. "Would you like to go back to Venice now? Or should we have a look at the rest of the crime scene?"

8

Amalfi

Upstairs, Gabriel stood at the foot of Lukas van Damme's bed and extended his right arm. "Bang," he said softly.

"Actually," said General Ferrari, "there were two shots. And the killer undoubtedly used a suppressor."

Gabriel lowered his arm. "Caliber?"

"Nine-millimeter."

"Shell casings?"

"None."

"Where was the victim shot?"

"The victim," repeated the general, "was shot twice in the head. The first round was recovered from the wall behind the headboard. The trajectory indicates the killer was standing exactly where you are now."

"And the second shot?"

"Point-blank."

"Just to make sure?"

"So it would seem."

"Time of death?"

"Sometime between midnight and four a.m."

"Sign of a struggle?"

"No."

"Defensive wound to the hand?"

The general shook his head.

"He was sleeping?"

"The forensic experts think he was."

"Toxicology report?"

"Not yet."

Gabriel gazed down at the blood-soaked bedding. "Theory of the case?"

"Thief kills Van Damme, thief steals painting."

"How did thief get into the villa?"

Ferrari smiled. "Thief was invited to dinner."

At a table outside on the immense terrace, with the sea rising and falling against the base of the cliff below, General Ferrari popped the latches on his attaché case and withdrew a manila file. Its contents included a surveillance image captured by a security camera at the nearby Santa Catarina Hotel. A dark-haired woman in her mid-thirties was seated at a table at the hotel's popular bar. She was conversing with the late Lukas van Damme.

"She arrived in Amalfi in September and took out a six-month lease on a villa." Ferrari rotated a few degrees in his chair and pointed out a small dwelling, white as bone, anchored to the cliff above Van Damme's property. "In case you're wondering, she paid in cash. Called herself Ursula Roth. Said she was German. Told her housekeeper and anyone else who would listen that she was working on a novel. The night before last, she accepted Van Damme's invitation to dinner."

"Did the forensic team find any evidence of sexual activity?"

"None."

"What about hair?"

General Ferrari shook his head.

"Not to belabor the point," said Gabriel, "but there's no evidence of sexual activity and no evidence the woman was ever in Van Damme's bed? Is that what you're suggesting?"

"That appears to be the case."

Gabriel looked down at the photograph. "Is this the only one?"

"It's the best we've found so far. She seems to have a knack for avoiding cameras. And for cleaning up after herself," added Ferrari. "She wiped down every surface of her villa before leaving. There are no fingerprints here, either. At least none we've been able to find."

"What about a vehicle?"

"A Volkswagen Passat estate car, Munich registration. We were able to track her movements on the autostrada. She reached Florence shortly before sunrise yesterday and promptly disappeared from the grid."

"The sun rose at approximately seven thirty yesterday, if I'm not mistaken."

"You're not."

"And it's a five-hour drive from Amalfi to Florence, which means she probably left around two in the morning."

"Well within the window of the estimated time of death."

"But there's just one problem with your theory of the case, General Ferrari."

"And what's that?"

"Art thieves rarely kill people. Especially an art thief who charms her way into the victim's home and allows herself to be seen by his household staff."

"In that case, who killed Van Damme?"

"The man with a silenced nine-millimeter handgun who entered the villa after the thief left. As for the painting in the vault room," said Gabriel, "you can return it to the Courtauld Gallery with complete confidence that it's the missing Van Gogh."

"Actually, I'm inclined to retain possession of it for the foreseeable future."

"But surely you plan to tell the Metropolitan Police that you've found it."

"Not anytime soon, no."

"Why not?"

"Because alerting the British authorities will only make it harder for you to find the painting that the thief so carefully pried from that custom-made stretcher measuring seventy-two-point-five by sixty-four-point-seven centimeters."

"Isn't that your job?"

"Finding stolen paintings? Technically speaking, yes. But you're much better at it than we are, especially in cases involving thieves who aren't Italian. If I were you, I'd start by showing that photograph to some of my contacts on the dirty side of the art trade." The general paused, then added, "The dirtier, the better."

Gabriel did not bother to refute General Ferrari's assertion regarding his links to certain unsavory elements of the art world. In his previous life he had sometimes found it necessary to associate with such creatures and, on occasion, to commit crimes against art himself, some spectacular, others less so. In the process, he had

managed to recover numerous stolen or looted paintings, including Caravaggio's *Nativity with St. Francis
and St. Lawrence.* He had made certain that General
Ferrari and the Art Squad received the credit.

"And if my contacts prove unaccommodating?"
asked Gabriel.

"You will squeeze them until they see the error of
their ways. And you will do it quickly," added Ferrari.
"The fact that she left behind a Van Gogh would suggest that she stole the painting at the behest of a wealthy
client. Which means you have a limited amount of
time to find it before it disappears again. A few days
at most."

"How much leeway do I have to make a deal?"

"Considerable."

"How considerable?" pressed Gabriel.

"In order to recover one of only thirty-four surviving works by one of the greatest painters who ever
lived? I'd be willing to overlook almost anything."

"A dead body?"

General Ferrari shrugged. "Lukas van Damme was
hardly a pillar of our expatriate community."

"Anything specific?"

"A close business relationship with a certain notorious criminal organization based in Calabria."

"'Ndrangheta?"

Ferrari nodded. "As you know, the 'Ndrangheta are the primary European distributors for the South American drug cartels. And for the past decade or so, LVD Marine Transport has served as the transatlantic conveyor belt."

"Wonderful," said Gabriel. "Is there anything else you'd like to tell me before I begin my investigation?"

"Thief killed Van Damme, thief stole painting."

"Not a chance."

"All right," said Ferrari. "Let's hear *your* theory of the case."

Gabriel looked down at the photograph of the woman sitting at the terrace bar of the Santa Catarina Hotel. "Thief didn't know the score when she took the job. Thief is in over her pretty little head."

9

Rue de Miromesnil

There was an ITA Airways flight to Paris leaving Fiumicino at half past eight. With General Ferrari's assistance, Gabriel was permitted to sidestep the body screeners at security. He rang Chiara from the departure gate.

"You'll never guess where I am."

"I know exactly where you are, darling. More important, I know where you're going."

"How is that possible?"

"I just got off the phone with the general."

"You're not angry?"

"A little," she admitted. "But I'm prepared to grant you a few days' leave to pursue the matter. Unpaid, of course."

"How generous of you."

"You will be careful, won't you?"

"I promise not to visit any art galleries."

"You're staying somewhere dreadful, I hope."

"Actually, I was planning to borrow a friend's pied-à-terre."

The friend was the Swiss billionaire venture capitalist Martin Landesmann, and his luxurious pied-à-terre was located on the Île Saint-Louis. Gabriel had utilized the apartment—as well as the services of Martin's ethically challenged Geneva-based firm—during his last major operation as chief of the Office.

"How long do you need it?" asked Martin.

"Two nights. Three at the most."

"Not a problem. I'll have my property manager stock the fridge. I believe there's a bottle or two of Château Pétrus in the wine cooler. Your life will never be the same."

Gabriel drank a glass of the extraordinary Pomerol wine late that evening with the *poulet roti* and *haricots verts* he ate for his supper. He passed a restful night in Martin's guest room, and at nine fifteen the following morning he was walking along the pavements of the rue de Miromesnil in the Eighth Arrondissement. At the northern end of the street was a shop called Antiquités Scientifiques. Its proprietor, a man named Maurice Durand, was drinking a café crème across the street at Brasserie Dumas. Gabriel joined the Frenchman uninvited and, signaling the waiter, ordered a coffee for himself.

Durand folded his copy of *Le Monde* with inordinate care and placed it on the table. He wore a tailored suit, undertaker gray, with a striped dress shirt and a lavender necktie. His bald head was polished to a high gloss.

"What an unpleasant surprise, Monsieur Allon. I didn't realize we had an appointment this morning."

"It must have slipped your mind, Maurice."

"I'm quite certain it didn't." With a pair of small, dark eyes he watched the pedestrians filing past the window. "Do your friends in the Police Nationale know you're in Paris?"

"I certainly hope not."

"As do I."

Just then the door of the brasserie opened, and in walked Angélique Brossard, owner of a nearby shop that sold antique French crystal and glass figurines. The table she chose was on the opposite side of the room—as far away from Durand as possible, noted Gabriel.

"You're not fooling anyone, Maurice. The entire

arrondissement knows that the two of you have been involved in the longest *cinq à sept* in French history."

"A slanderous rumor, I assure you."

"When are you going to marry her?"

"Angélique is married. Just not to me."

"And when she tires of you?"

"I'm confident she won't. You see, I'm rather good at what I do." Durand smiled. "As are you, Monsieur Allon."

"I'm an art restorer. And you—"

"Are a dealer of antique scientific and medical instruments." He pointed toward the shop across the street. "It says so in the window."

But Maurice Durand was also one of the greatest art thieves who ever lived. These days he operated solely as a broker in the process known as commissioned theft. Or, as Durand liked to describe it, he managed the acquisition of paintings that were not technically for sale.

"What brings you to Paris?" he asked.

"An interesting development in a high-profile case."

Durand accepted Gabriel's phone and examined the photograph displayed on the screen, his expression inscrutable. At length he asked, "Do you think it hurt when he did it?"

"He's lucky he didn't die. The razor severed an

artery in his neck. There was blood in every room in the Yellow House."

"But the result was a masterpiece. And to think it's gone forever." Durand gave a slow shake of his head. "A tragedy, truly."

"But with a happy ending, as it turns out. You see, Maurice, that photograph was taken yesterday."

"*C'est impossible.*"

"The painting was discovered at a luxury villa on the Amalfi Coast. The owner is a man named—"

"Lukas van Damme." Durand lowered his gaze toward the screen of Gabriel's phone. "Where is he now?"

"An Italian morgue."

"What a pity."

"I take it by your entirely disingenuous expression of grief that you and Van Damme were acquainted."

"We were introduced by a common associate."

"When?"

"Let's call it five years ago."

"Let's be precise instead."

Durand made a show of reflection. "I believe it was the autumn of 2017."

"Van Damme wished to utilize your services?"

Durand nodded.

"What was he after?"

"A Van Gogh."

"Anything in particular?"

"*Bedroom at Arles.*"

"Which version?"

"The third."

"The one at the Musée d'Orsay?"

"A *bastille*," murmured Durand. "I told Van Damme the job was out of the question and suggested several other Van Goghs that were more readily attainable. When he ruled out those paintings, I suggested *Self-Portrait with Bandaged Ear.*"

"Which you had pinched from the Courtauld six years earlier."

"Approximately."

"On behalf of a client from the Arab world," added Gabriel.

"The identity or nationality of the original buyer is of no consequence. All that matters is that I offered him a chance to sell the painting at a profit, and he agreed. Monsieur Van Damme was so pleased with the arrangement that a few months later he approached me with another commission."

"What was he in the market for this time?"

"Dutch Golden Age."

"But not just any Dutch Golden Age," said Gabriel.

"*Non.* Van Damme wanted something specific. A

genre piece, musical in nature, painted in the city of Delft in 1664."

"Oil on canvas? Seventy-two-point-five by sixty-four-point-seven centimeters?"

"*Oui*," said Maurice Durand. "*The Concert* by Johannes Vermeer."

10
Rue de Miromesnil

For a few brief years, he enjoyed a certain modest celebrity, at least in his hometown. But by the autumn of 1672, with Holland locked in a protracted and economically ruinous war with France, he was no longer able to find buyers for his paintings. His death in December 1675 left his wife, Catharina Bolnes, and their eleven surviving children destitute. In a petition to her creditors, she declared that her husband's inability to sell his work had plunged him "into a frenzy" and a state of "decay and decadence." His end, she wrote, was swift. "In a day and a half he went from being alive to being dead." She inherited nineteen of her husband's paintings, more than half his oeuvre. She immediately sold two of the canvases, for the sum of 617 guilders, to the baker Hendrick van Buyten, to whom she owed a substantial debt.

A court-ordered inventory of his studio—it was located on the second floor of his mother-in-law's spacious house on Oude Langendijk in Delft—listed two chairs, two easels, three palettes, ten canvases, a desk, an oaken table, and a cupboard filled with "rummage not worthy of being itemized." The trustee's document made no mention of his costly pigments, especially his beloved lapis lazuli, or the maulstick he used to steady his hand while painting. Also absent was any reference to a camera obscura or camera lucida, optical tools that some later scholars would insist he utilized.

Where he learned his craft—or even whether he was properly trained at all—is not known. Indeed, with few exceptions, the details of his brief life went with him to his grave in Delft's Oude Kerk, where his coffin was laid atop those of three of his children who had died in infancy. Even the exact date of his birth in 1632 is unclear, though according to surviving Reform Church records he was baptized on October 31 and christened Joannis, perhaps because his parents found it more fetching than the conventional Jan. His father, an innkeeper and art dealer, was called Reijnier Janszoon Vos—Vos being the Dutch word for fox. Sometime around 1640, however, Reijnier began to refer to himself by a contraction of the surname Van der Meer, or "of the sea." His son also took the name, which was Vermeer.

Within a few short years of his death, his reputation had fallen into such decline that Arnold Houbraken, in his indispensable 1718 anthology of the Dutch Golden Age, scarcely saw fit to mention him. But on May 22, 1822, a painting called *A View of Delft* sold at auction in Amsterdam to a representative of the Mauritshuis museum in The Hague, which was where, twenty years later, it caught the eye of Théophile Thoré-Bürger. So enchanted was the noted French journalist and art critic that he resolved to track down the artist's surviving works and rescue him from obscurity. An 1866 essay—it was entitled "Van der Meer de Delft"—listed more than seventy potential paintings, though even Thoré-Bürger was convinced the actual number was perhaps forty-nine. Later scholars would whittle it down to just thirty-four.

Most were painted in one of two rooms in the house at Oude Langendijk and featured the same furniture and the same women as his models. He portrayed them as mistresses and maids, as writers and readers of letters, as drinkers of wine and makers of lace. And in 1665 he dressed a young woman in an exotic gown and turban and produced his masterpiece. The work would eventually derive its name from the girl's large, pear-shaped earring. Whether it was actually a pearl is now a matter of some dispute, with at least one scholar suggesting it was likely fashioned of tin instead.

During that same period, he executed a musical scene that would become known as *The Concert*. Precisely where the painting went when it left his studio is unclear, though it is widely assumed it was once in the collection of Pieter van Ruijven, his longtime patron. What is known for certain is that on December 5, 1892, *The Concert*, lot 31, oil on canvas, 72.5 by 64.7 centimeters, changed hands for 29,000 francs at the Hôtel Drouot auction house in Paris. The seller was none other than Théophile Thoré-Bürger; the buyer, a wealthy American heiress and art collector named Isabella Stewart Gardner. She took the painting to Boston and in 1903 placed it in a new museum she built in the city's marshy Fenway area. Which is where it remained, in a room on the second floor, until the early-morning hours of Sunday, March 18, 1990, when it disappeared without a trace.

It was security guard Rick Abath, a Berklee School of Music dropout and keyboardist in a local rock band, who, at 1:24 a.m., unwittingly admitted the two thieves into the museum. Dressed in what appeared to be authentic Boston Police Department uniforms, they claimed to be investigating a disturbance in the neighborhood. Abath saw no reason to question their story. Nor did he find it suspicious when the shorter of the two men asked him to step away from the watch desk. The intruder immediately forced Abath against a wall and cuffed his hands behind his back. Randy Hestand, who was working the overnight shift for the first time, was handcuffed a moment later, when he returned to the watch desk after making his rounds.

"Gentlemen," announced one of the thieves, "this is a robbery."

With the guards subdued and the museum's security cameras disabled, Isabella Stewart Gardner's remarkable collection of art and antiquities lay defenseless. For more than an hour, the thieves attacked without mercy, beginning with a pair of Rembrandts in the second-floor Dutch Room: *A Lady and Gentleman in Black* and *The Storm on the Sea of Galilee*, the artist's only seascape. The marauders slashed both works from their stretchers. They also attempted to steal Rembrandt's iconic *Self-Portrait, Age 23* but left it leaning against a cabinet, helping themselves instead to a postage-stamp-size Rembrandt etching. Two works they managed to remove from their frames without resorting to undue violence. One was *Landscape with Obelisk* by Govert

Flinck. The other was the Dutch Room's most valuable painting: *The Concert* by Johannes Vermeer.

After snatching an ancient Chinese vase, they headed next to the Short Gallery, which yielded an imperial French finial and five sketches by Edgar Degas. The last painting seized was Édouard Manet's *Chez Tortoni*, from the first-floor Blue Room. The immense size of the haul required the thieves to make two trips to their waiting hatchback on Palace Road, the last at 2:45 a.m., when they made their escape. The total time of the robbery was eighty-one minutes. The estimated value of the thirteen stolen artworks was an astonishing $200 million, making it the largest heist in history.

By midday the FBI had assumed control of the investigation. Led by twenty-six-year-old Dan Falzon, it would be hampered by an unusual lack of forensic evidence such as fingerprints, footprints, hair, or cigarette butts. Agents interviewed witnesses and scoured the museum's employment and maintenance records for possible links to the robbery. Security guards Abath and Hestand were subjected to repeated interrogations as Falzon and his agents probed their accounts for inconsistencies. They found it suspicious that Abath, while making his rounds earlier that evening, had opened and closed the museum's side door. Agents were troubled, too, by the fact that the motion detectors in the Blue Room—from which Manet's *Chez Tortoni* was taken—showed no intruders during the eighty-one minutes of the robbery.

With an annual budget of only $2.8 million, the Gardner Museum could not afford to insure its collection. But with the help of the auction giants Sotheby's and Christie's, it was able to offer a $1 million reward for information leading to the recovery of the stolen works. Falzon and his team pursued thousands of leads and tips from the public, including one from a man in Charlestown who claimed to have seen *The Concert* hanging on a neighbor's wall. The neighbor invited FBI agents and museum officials into her home and showed them a high-quality print of the painting. A report that *The Storm on the Sea of Galilee* might be in Japan proved no more accurate. It was not Rembrandt's masterpiece that Falzon and Japanese police found hanging on the wall of an eccentric collector, but a crude paint-by-numbers version instead.

Four years after the theft, the museum received an anonymous typewritten letter promising to facilitate the return of the stolen works in exchange for $2.6 million. Gardner director Anne Hawley considered it the most promising lead to date, but like all the others it quickly went nowhere. Desperate, Hawley increased the size of the reward to an astonishing $5 million.

In the Dutch and Blue Rooms, patrons gawked at six empty frames. A psychic claimed that the museum's founder, in her grave since 1924, had told her the missing paintings were hidden in the ceiling of the restoration lab. Security chief Lyle Grindle dutifully climbed a ladder to have a look for himself. The paintings, of course, were not there.

In May 2017, the Gardner Museum's board of trustees doubled the reward to $10 million, the largest bounty for stolen goods ever offered. Still, the thieves refused to part with their loot. But who were they? And for whom were they working? There was no shortage of suspects, most of whom were connected to Boston's thriving Irish and Italian criminal underworld. But there were other theories as well, some laughable, others merely implausible. And it was there that Maurice Durand, perhaps the greatest art thief who ever lived, picked up the thread of the story.

11

Rue de Miromesnil

y favorite was the one about the shadowy Vatican operatives."

"Mine, too," admitted Gabriel.

"Why would the Vatican, which has more paintings than it knows what to do with, want to steal more? And who are these so-called shadowy Vatican operatives?"

"You'd be surprised."

Durand raised an eyebrow. "Are you saying it's possible?"

"I'm more interested in your opinion, Maurice."

He appeared to give the question serious consideration before answering. "In my opinion, the thieves were almost certainly local Boston hoodlums who were connected to larger criminal networks. Generally speaking, these networks are quite good at stealing art, but they haven't a clue how to bring it to market. As a result, the paintings end up being used as underworld cash. Criminal travelers' checks, if you will. They move from gang to gang, usually as collateral, sometimes as tribute and trophies. Because paintings are easily smuggled, they often travel long distances. Across oceans, in fact."

"Where did the Vermeer end up?"

"Monsieur Van Damme had been told by one of his associates that it could be had in Dublin."

"From whom?"

"The Kinahan cartel. Ireland's most powerful criminal organization. He wanted me to travel there on his behalf and negotiate a deal."

"What was your response?"

"Thank you, no. This business is dangerous enough without getting mixed up with Irish gangsters."

"How much did it cost to get you to yes?"

"My memory is a little fuzzy on that."

"Put your back into it, Maurice."

"It might have been twenty percent of the final sale price."

"Highway robbery," said Gabriel.

Durand placed a hand over his heart. "The negotiations included blindfolds and several long journeys in the trunk of a car. I consider myself most fortunate to have survived."

"Who was the man on the other side of the table?"

"Let's refer to him as Monsieur O'Donnell. A connoisseur he was not. He allowed me to see the painting only once. For all I know, I was in Belfast at the time."

"And?"

"I do not pretend to be the last word on Dutch Golden Age painters, but I was confident it was the Vermeer."

"Did you get a second opinion?"

"Monsieur O'Donnell wouldn't allow it."

"What was the final sale price?"

"Fifty million," said Durand. "The handover took place in Barcelona a week later. I was lucky to survive that as well. I delivered the painting to Amalfi the next day, and Monsieur Van Damme paid me my commission."

"Mazel tov, Maurice." Gabriel removed a manila file folder from the zippered pouch of his overnight bag. Inside was the photograph that General Ferrari had given to him in Amalfi. He placed it before Durand and said, "I assume you recognize the man."

"*Oui.*"

"What about the woman?"

Durand shook his head.

"She called herself Ursula Roth."

"German?"

"So she said."

"What can you tell me about her methods?"

"Evidently, she sweet-talked her way into Van Damme's villa and broke into the vault after dinner."

"The lock was very secure."

"She seems to know her way around safes and computers."

Durand slid the photograph into the file folder. "And if I'm able to find her?"

"I will return *The Concert* by Johannes Vermeer to the Isabella Stewart Gardner Museum in Boston. And against all better judgment, I will once again overlook your deplorable conduct."

"And if my inquiry proves unsuccessful?" asked Durand.

"I'm quite confident it won't."

"How long do I have?"

"How long do you need?"

"A week, at least."

"In that case," said Gabriel, "you have exactly seventy-two hours."

12
Skagen

The custom-made Pinarello road bike, the envy of Jutland's thriving cycling community, leaned against the exterior of Norden Bar & Café on Havnevej. Ingrid Johansen, in a Gore-Tex jacket and full-length leggings, sat at a nearby table, phone in hand. The town around her, with its quaint buildings painted Skagen yellow, was bathed in the intense golden sunlight that had drawn a circle of painters to the little fishing village in the late nineteenth century. Ingrid scarcely noticed it; she was distracted by an article she had stumbled across in the Naples daily *Il Mattino*. The one about the murder of a wealthy South African expatriate living on the Amalfi Coast.

Rising, she swung a leg over the sloping top tube of

the Pinarello and set off along the empty street. At the southern edge of the village, she rounded a traffic circle and eased onto the bike path bordering Primærrute 40. With the wind at her back, she covered the thirteen and a half kilometers down to Hulsig in twenty minutes. Then she headed west, across tabletop-flat farmland, to Kandestederne.

In the gorse-covered dunes was a colony of holiday cottages occupied mainly in summer. Ingrid's modern dwelling, with its soaring windows overlooking the North Sea, was a few paces from the beach. The lock on the front door was electronic, with a hard fourteen-digit passcode that she changed frequently. She typed it into the keypad, then wheeled the bike into the entrance hall and silenced the bleating of the commercial-grade alarm system. The information screen showed no intrusions during the two hours she had been away.

She removed her cycling shoes and in stockinged feet padded into the great room. The floors were pale wood, the furnishings were Scandinavian and modern. Luxurious, yes, but with the exception of her reference-level Hegel audio system there was nothing to suggest that Ingrid might have access to hidden sources of wealth. The government was under the impression she was a well-paid freelance IT professional, which was indeed the case. Her company, Skagen CyberSolutions, had taken in more than four million Danish kroner in 2021. Her legitimate earnings were down slightly this year, though she had more than made up the shortfall with her illicit income, which had soared to record levels.

Her annual winter visit to the ski resorts of Switzerland and France had proven especially profitable. There was the wealthy but guileless couple from Connecticut—he worked for a hedge fund, she in corporate public relations—whose suite at the Badrutt's Palace Hotel in St. Moritz had yielded a double strand of Mikimoto pearls and a diamond bracelet by Harry Winston. And the libidinous Russian tycoon who awoke after a night of heavy drinking in the clubs of Courchevel to find that both Ingrid and his million-euro Richard Mille wristwatch had vanished without a trace. And the minor Saudi prince, a distant cousin of the future king, who somehow managed to misplace an attaché case stuffed with cash while on holiday in Zermatt with his three wives and twelve children.

The jewelry alone had fetched a half million on the black market in Antwerp. Ingrid spent the summer relaxing at her villa on Mykonos, one of the few places in the world where, for the most part, she kept her hands to herself. It had been her intention to return to Denmark in September, but her plans changed after the phone call she received from Peter Nielsen, an antiquarian book dealer who disposed of rare manuscripts that Ingrid occasionally found lying around unoccupied European villas and châteaux. Peter had received an unusual request from one of his clients, a request that involved a painting that hung in a villa on the Amalfi Coast. The offer was too lucrative to turn down. Five million euros up front, another five million on delivery.

Ingrid's office was located on the second floor of the cottage. The painting was locked in a storage cabinet, hidden inside a leather document tube. She removed the canvas and unfurled it onto her desk. Unframed, it appeared somehow ordinary. Still, she felt honored to be in its presence—and guilty as well. Cash and jewels could be replaced, but *The Concert* by Johannes Vermeer was part of the Western canon, a sacred object.

The previous evening, while under the influence of Miles Davis, she had given serious consideration to quietly placing the Vermeer in the hands of the proper authorities—perhaps in the Dutch town of Delft. That, she reasoned, would provide a fitting and dramatic finale to the painting's story. But it would also put Ingrid sideways with Peter Nielsen and his client. After all, she had accepted five million euros of the client's money, a significant portion of which she had already donated anonymously to charity.

And then, of course, there was the article in *Il*

Mattino. Ingrid was quite certain that Lukas van Damme had been alive and well—and sleeping soundly thanks to the liquid ketamine he had ingested with his Barbaresco—when she left his villa at 12:45 a.m. Breaking into the South African's vault room had required all of thirty seconds. Ingrid had been taken aback by the presence of an iconic painting by Vincent van Gogh but had resisted the urge to steal it. Her instructions had been specific. The Vermeer and only the Vermeer. Besides, removing the canvas from its stretcher had taken longer than she anticipated.

Just then her phone pulsed with an incoming encrypted Signal message. It was Peter Nielsen, wondering when he might take delivery of the world's most valuable missing painting—or words to that effect. Ingrid had no choice but to deliver the Vermeer as promised. If nothing else, it would give her the opportunity to clear up one or two small details about the events in Amalfi. Specifically, she wanted to know what sort of mess her friend had got her into.

Ordinarily, she delivered stolen goods to Peter's shop, but present circumstances called for discretion. Vissenbjerg, located on the island of Funen, was about halfway between Skagen and Copenhagen. There was an auto plaza just off the E20. A Q8 petrol station, a convenience mart, a little café. What was the name of it? Jørgens? Yes, that was it. Jørgens Smørrebrød Café. They could meet there.

But not right away, thought Ingrid, reaching for her phone. She wanted to spend another day or two with the Vermeer before letting it go. Thursday sounded about right, but come to think of it Friday would probably be more convenient—Friday at 6:00 p.m. at Jørgens Smørrebrød Café. Peter was to come alone and with five million euros in cash. No money, no painting, typed Ingrid.

Or words to that effect.

13

Île Saint-Louis

Gabriel left Martin Landesmann's apartment on the Île Saint-Louis at one the following afternoon and lunched in the shadow of Notre-Dame. Afterward he walked along the Seine embankments to the Musée d'Orsay and was relieved to find *La Chambre de Van Gogh à Arles* still hanging in the Galerie des Impressionnistes. His next stop was the Richelieu wing of the Louvre, where he paid a visit to Vermeer's *The Astronomer*. Like *The Concert*, the painting had once been stolen—not by ordinary criminals but by the Einsatzstab Reichsleiter Rosenberg, the official art looters of Nazi Germany. It had survived its wartime ordeal largely intact, though with the addition of a small swastika stamped in black ink on the back of the canvas.

Gabriel's final destination was Brasserie Dumas on the rue de Miromesnil. There, at five fifteen, he observed Maurice Durand switching the sign in his shop window from OUVERT to FERMÉ. Angélique Brossard departed thirty minutes later, followed soon after by Durand himself. The Frenchman joined Gabriel for an aperitif.

"She's a good old-fashioned cat burglar, your girl. Likes to get close to her targets, then robs them blind. She prefers cash and jewelry, though on occasion other valuable *objets* have been known to attach themselves to her sticky fingers."

"Is she German?"

"That depends on whom you ask. Apparently, she's something of a chameleon. Some say she's German or Swiss, others say Dutch or Scandinavian. Everyone agrees she's quite skilled when it comes to disabling security systems."

"How is she with a nine-millimeter pistol?"

"She might carry one, but she would be loath to use it. That's not her modus operandi."

"Is this the first time she's strayed onto your turf?"

"Evidently."

"The impertinence."

"My feelings exactly."

"Jewelry is easier to unload than paintings," observed Gabriel.

"Much," agreed Durand. "Luxury wristwatches have to be resold intact, of course. But gold can be melted down, and diamonds can be incorporated into other pieces."

"All of which would require a fence."

"As usual," said Durand, "I am one step ahead of you."

Next morning Paris awoke to a barrage of thunder and lightning, the opening salvo of a freak autumn storm that dumped a month's worth of rain on the city in less than an hour. Gabriel monitored the rising waters of the Seine from the comfort of Martin's sitting room, with one eye on *Télématin*, France 2's breakfast television program.

Elsewhere, the news was little better. On the opposite side of the English Channel, a British prime minister was fighting for her political life after signing off on a disastrous tax cut plan that had disrupted British debt markets and driven the pound to record lows. Not to be outdone, Russia had launched yet another murderous air assault against civilian targets in war-torn Ukraine, this time using drones supplied by the Islamic Republic of Iran. Almost unnoticed was a warning by a leading American security expert that the war had brought Russia and the West closer to a nuclear confrontation than during the Cuban Missile Crisis. The world, thought Gabriel, was careening dangerously out of control. One more shock to the system—another financial meltdown, a disruption of the food supply, a resurgence of the pandemic—might well spell the end of the project known as the postwar liberal order.

By late afternoon the deluge had eased, and life in Paris had returned largely to normal, at least on the rue de Miromesnil. "What's next?" asked Maurice Durand as he stared gloomily out the rain-spattered window of Brasserie Dumas. "A plague of locusts?"

"Frogs," murmured Gabriel.

"I wouldn't mind frogs, so long as they're edible, of course."

"Plague frogs aren't edible, Maurice. That's why they're plague frogs."

Durand frowned. "Something bothering you, Monsieur Allon?"

"Besides the imminent collapse of Western civilization?"

"*Oui.*"

"I'm a bit miffed that my confidential informant found time for his daily rendezvous with his mistress but hasn't been able to determine where my girl is fencing her stolen jewels."

"Antwerp," said Durand. "Where else?"

It made sense, thought Gabriel. Eighty percent of

the world's diamonds passed through Antwerp. And Belgium, with its weak central government and largely incompetent national police force, had a well-deserved reputation as Europe's destination of choice for criminals looking to buy or sell goods on the black market.

"Do you know the fence's name?" asked Gabriel. "Or should I just go door to door in the Diamond Quarter?"

"I believe there are at least twenty-four hours remaining on my deadline clock."

Gabriel spent most of those hours locked away in Martin's apartment, reading a French-language edition of *Charlotte Gray* by Sebastian Faulks. He finished the novel while sipping a glass of excellent Côtes du Rhône at Brasserie Dumas. Maurice Durand joined him at six thirty, wearing a glassy-eyed expression of incredulity and, it seemed to Gabriel, utter defeat.

"Why so blue?" he asked.

"Angélique," muttered the Frenchman.

"She's unwell?"

"In love." Durand paused, then added, "With someone else."

"After all these years?"

"I asked her the same thing."

"How did she possibly find the time?"

"Trust me, I asked her that as well." Durand handed

Gabriel a slip of paper. On it was written a name and an address. "He's connected to the European branch of the Armenian mafia. They have anger-management issues, the Armenians. Therefore, I would be grateful if you didn't mention my name when you speak to him. I have enough problems."

Outside, Gabriel bade farewell to his lovelorn confidential informant and returned to the apartment on the Île Saint-Louis. He rang the owner and requested another favor.

"How much are we talking about?" asked the Swiss financier.

"Enough to turn the head of a dirty diamond dealer in Antwerp."

"He's not one of yours, is he?"

"Armenian, actually."

"I'm sure he'd find Monique's jewelry to his liking." Monique was Martin's glamorous French-born wife. "She only keeps a small collection in Paris, but everything is quite valuable."

"Diamonds?"

"My darling Monique doesn't set foot outside the house unless she's dripping with them."

"Where might I find them?"

"The safe in our dressing room."

"Combination?"

"I'm surprised you need it." Martin recited three numbers. "Just to be clear, you *do* intend to return everything, don't you?"

"Barring some unforeseen development."

"These things add up, you know. A million here and a million there, and pretty soon you're talking about real money."

"I need some of that, too."

"There's a couple hundred thousand in the safe," said Martin with a sigh. "Help yourself."

14

Funen

The Coalition for a Green Denmark was founded in 2005 by Anders Holm and nine other students from Aalborg University's department of politics and society. The group's primary objective, spelled out in its grandiose charter, was a carbon-free Danish economy by the year 2025. It created a website that no one visited, organized symposia and marches that no one attended, and obtained signatures on lofty petitions that few people in positions of power or influence bothered to accept, let alone read.

Which led Anders Holm, two years after the Coalition's formation, to undertake a shift in tactics. The days of pamphlets and petitions, he declared, were over. The group would now embark on a campaign of provocative direct action, a campaign that included a series of embarrassing hacks and denial-of-service attacks on the computer networks of Denmark's largest emitters of greenhouse gases. The Danish police were never able to apprehend the hacker responsible, in part because only Anders knew her identity: Ingrid Johansen, a brilliant student from the university's department of computer sciences.

Ingrid was proud of the hacks she had carried out for the Coalition, but it was the druglike rush of breaking into supposedly secure computer networks that she found most exhilarating. She carried out a few more jobs for Anders—against polluters and powerful businessmen and even a government minister—but soon her skill at the keyboard alone was not enough to satisfy her addiction. It was too easy, too safe. Feeding her habit required the assumption of greater risk.

Like most thieves, she honed her skills by shoplifting. Before long she was picking locks and pockets, especially in the bars of Aalborg, where her victims were often addled by alcohol. She learned to be outgoing and flirtatious, which did not come naturally to her, and to welcome the advances of men—older men in particular, as they generally carried more cash and other valuables and were easily flattered by attractive young women. Ingrid's looks, she discovered, were an asset.

The face of crime in contemporary Scandinavia bore little resemblance to hers.

She left the university at the end of her second year—on the pretense of starting her own IT consultancy—and embarked on a one-woman crime wave that stretched the length and breadth of Denmark. She stole her first diamonds in Copenhagen and sold them for a fraction of what they were worth to a Serbian gang in Frankfurt, a transaction she had been lucky to survive. It was then that she bought her gun, a Glock 26 subcompact, from a member of the Black Cobras street gang in Malmö. The Cobra, whose name was Ibrahim Kadouri, taught Ingrid how to use the weapon and how to sell stolen jewelry without getting killed in the process. Ibrahim knew an Armenian in the Diamond Quarter of Antwerp, a reputable fence, if there was such a thing. Ingrid returned the favor by giving Ibrahim ten thousand kroner in cash and two hundred stolen credit cards for which she had no use.

By the time she turned thirty, she was taking in upwards of a half million euros a year as a thief in addition to the legitimate income she earned from her consulting business. She purchased the cottage in Kandestederne and, after a particularly productive summer in Saint-Tropez, her villa on Mykonos. She stole only from the wealthy—they were the ones with the money and the valuables, after all—and kept only what she needed to finance her admittedly comfortable lifestyle. The rest she donated to charity using anonymous wire transfers or DHL parcels stuffed with cash.

Through it all, Ingrid remained a committed environmentalist and climate activist. Her homes were carbon-neutral, and her car was a plug-in hybrid Volvo XC90. At half past four on Friday afternoon, it was moving southward down the Jutland peninsula on the E45. Ingrid wore a fashionable Rhanders beanie and lightly tinted sunglasses, rendering her all but unrecognizable. Her Glock was in her handbag, which was resting on the passenger seat. The leather document tube containing *The Concert* by Johannes Vermeer was in the Volvo's forward trunk.

The skies over Jutland had finally cleared after forty-eight hours of torrential rain and wind. Ingrid crossed the Little Belt Bridge at 5:00 p.m. and headed eastward across Funen on the E20. The sun was still shining brightly when she reached the auto plaza in Vissenbjerg. She attached the Volvo to a charging station at the Q8 and, taking only her handbag, entered Jørgens Smørrebrød Café.

Two tables were occupied, one by an unhappy-looking Danish couple of late middle age, the other by a man of perhaps forty who was wearing a dark business suit beneath a car-length overcoat. Not Danish, thought Ingrid. A Finn, perhaps. Maybe an Estonian or Latvian. Good shoes, nice wristwatch, probably a few hundred in his wallet. Not an easy mark, though. He looked confident, sure of himself. He also seemed to have no interest at all in Ingrid, which was rare. Most men couldn't help but cast at least a glance of appraisal in her direction.

She ordered coffee and a chicken salad smørrebrød from the girl behind the counter and carried it to a table against the window. The unhappy Danish couple departed the café first, at 5:45 p.m., followed ten minutes later by the man who might or might not have been from Finland or one of the Baltic states. Outside, a man in his mid-sixties was filling an E-Class Mercedes sedan with petrol. With his tweed jacket and beige rollneck sweater, there was no mistaking him for anything other than an antiquarian book dealer from Copenhagen—and a crooked one at that.

He returned the nozzle to the pump and eased his Mercedes into a space in the car park. When he entered the café, he was carrying a cheap-looking attaché case. He purchased a coffee and, with both hands occupied, approached Ingrid's table. Rising, she embraced him warmly and plucked the phone from the patch pocket of his tweed coat.

He sat down and placed the attaché case on the chair next to him.

"When are you going to get rid of that car?" asked Ingrid as she slid Peter's phone into her handbag.

"It's only three years old."

"Which means you'll get a very good trade-in price when you switch to a hybrid or electric model."

"I like the feel of a gas engine."

"And how will you *feel* when the rising seas inundate your beautiful bookshop on Strøget?"

"I'm on the second floor," replied Peter, and held out his hand.

Frowning, Ingrid surrendered the phone.

"You've lost your touch, girl."

"The painting in my car would suggest otherwise."

"It belongs to my client."

"Not yet," said Ingrid.

"You're not thinking about doing something stupid, are you?"

"Like what?"

"Attempting to sweeten your end of the deal."

"It never entered my mind. But now that you mention it . . ."

"Forget it, Ingrid. My client is angry enough as it is."

"About what?"

"The needless bloodshed."

"That makes two of us."

"Was there really no other way to get the painting?"

Ingrid raised her coffee to her lips. "I didn't kill Van Damme," she said quietly. "Someone entered the villa after I left. I was wondering whether you or your client might know who it was."

"I can assure you, my client had nothing to do with it."

"Who is he?"

"You know the rules, Ingrid. You don't know the identity of the client, and the client doesn't know you." He peered out the window toward Ingrid's Volvo. "The damn thing is locked, I hope."

"To tell you the truth, I'm not sure."

"What kind of shape is it in?"

"Remarkably good."

"Maybe I should have a look at it."

Ingrid glanced at the attaché case. "First things first."

She unplugged the charging cable from the Volvo and slid behind the wheel. Peter lowered himself into the passenger seat. With the attaché case balanced on his thighs, he worked the combination locks, then popped the latches.

Ingrid removed two bundles of newly printed five-hundred-euro banknotes and examined them by the overhead light. "Five million, right, Peter?"

"Have I ever shortchanged you?"

He hadn't, but they had never done a deal of this scale. Besides, this was likely to be the last money Ingrid would earn for some time.

She returned the bundles of cash to the attaché case, and Peter closed the lid. "Are we good?" he asked.

Ingrid started the engine and pressed the release for the forward trunk.

"You might want to keep some of that for yourself," advised Peter, and climbed out. A moment later he was carrying the leather document tube across the car park toward his Mercedes, unaware of the fact he was no longer in possession of his mobile phone. Ingrid switched off the device and slipped it into the Faraday pouch she carried habitually in her handbag. So much for losing my touch, she thought, and set out for Kandestederne.

Peter Nielsen was halfway across the Storebæltsbroen, the eighteen-kilometer bridge linking the islands of Funen and Zealand, before he realized that Ingrid had once again taken his phone. He supposed he had it coming. The remark about her skills decaying had been out of line; his friend was as sharp as ever. The painting resting on the floor of the backseat was proof of that.

It was too late to go chasing after her now. He would drive to Skagen in the morning after delivering the painting to the client. He only hoped that Ingrid didn't manage to unlock his phone in the interim. It contained encrypted correspondence he did not wish her to see, correspondence regarding the client's identity and the amount of money he had paid Peter to acquire the Vermeer. Yes, Ingrid had been well compensated, but the split had hardly been equitable. In a few hours' time Peter would be a very rich man indeed.

As usual, the wind was howling through the Great Belt. Peter drove with both hands fixed to the steering wheel. Even so, he labored to keep the Mercedes within its lane as he traversed the towering suspension portion of the bridge. He never enjoyed crossing the Storebæltsbroen, especially at night, when the sensation of being airborne above the black water always made him slightly sick to his stomach. And what about that guardrail? Less than a meter high, it was. Would it really save him if a sudden blast of wind were to send his car out of control? Unlikely, he thought. He would plunge to his death and sink slowly into the abyss, undoubtedly in the deepest portion of the strait. And there he would lie for all eternity, with *The Concert* by Johannes Vermeer at his side.

His mood improved as he began the long descent toward Zealand's western shoreline. He sped through the express lane of the toll plaza and an hour later reached the fringes of Copenhagen. His bachelor's apartment was on Nansensgade in the trendy district of Nørrebro, about a ten-minute walk from his shop. He slid the Mercedes into an empty space outside his building and switched off the engine. Then he reached a right hand toward the floorboard of the backseat and grasped the leather document tube containing the world's most valuable missing painting.

He maneuvered the document tube carefully over the headrest of the passenger seat and opened the door and climbed out. Only then did he notice the man walking toward him along the pavement with his hands thrust into the pockets of a car-length overcoat. Peter was certain he had seen the man somewhere before—and recently.

But where?

The gun brought a sudden end to his deliberations, the large semiautomatic pistol that the man drew with shocking elegance from the interior of his overcoat. When pointed toward Peter's face, the weapon emitted two bright flashes but scarcely a sound. And down he went, into the black water, into the abyss. *The Concert* by Johannes Vermeer did not make the journey with him; the man with the gun had taken it. The man whom Peter had seen at 5:55 p.m. that very evening, leaving the café in Vissenbjerg. He needed to warn Ingrid that her life was in danger, but he couldn't. Ingrid had taken his damn phone.

15
Diamantkwartier

O nly a man of Martin Landesmann's immense wealth would have used the word *small* to describe the astonishing collection of jewelry that Gabriel discovered when he opened the safe in Monique's dressing room. There were more than a hundred pieces in all, including a diamond solitaire pendant in a platinum setting, about twelve carats in weight. Gabriel stole wisely but judiciously, taking only what he needed—including a hundred thousand euros in walking-around money—and made his escape in his victim's car, with his victim's usual Paris driver behind the wheel. It was midnight when he entered the appropriately named Sapphire House in central Antwerp. A Diamond Suite had been reserved in his name. His victim's investment firm was picking up the tab, including incidentals.

The hotel was on Lange Nieuwstraat, not far from Antwerp's stately old town. With its narrow streets and plentiful shops and cafés, it was a perfect place for a leisurely surveillance-detection run, which Gabriel conducted after a light breakfast the following morning. It did not take him more than a few minutes to establish that Belgium's crack internal security service did not realize that the former director-general of the Office was staying at one of the city's better hotels.

He headed next to Meir, Antwerp's main shopping street, for a wardrobe change: formfitting black jeans, a black pullover, zippered ankle boots, a leather overcoat, an oversize gold wristwatch, a gold necklace, a pair of yellow-tinted glasses. He donned the clothing in his suite at the Sapphire House and emerged at half past twelve looking thoroughly disreputable and not a little dangerous. He was, after all, a criminal, a master thief who had recently pinched more than a million euros' worth of jewelry from an apartment on the Île Saint-Louis in Paris. Several of the pieces were concealed in the pockets of his overcoat, including a twelve-carat diamond solitaire pendant. The rest of his loot was stashed in his room safe, along with his Israeli passport and Israeli-made mobile phone, reputedly the world's most secure. His 9mm Beretta pistol was wedged into the waistband of his trousers at the small of his back. Unlike many of his ilk, he knew how to use it.

Downstairs, the concierge regarded him with distaste as he crossed the lobby and went once more into Lange Nieuwstraat. This time he turned to the right and set out toward Antwerpen-Centraal railway station, widely regarded as one of the world's most beautiful. Its imposing western facade overlooked the Diamantkwartier, a compact district of retail shops, jewelry manufacturers, and brokerage houses through which 234 million carats' worth of diamonds flowed annually. Gabriel arrived to find much of the neighborhood shuttered and deserted. It was a Saturday, the Jewish sabbath, and much of Antwerp's diamond trade remained in Jewish hands.

But many recent arrivals in the Diamond Quarter chose to keep their shops open on Saturdays while their Jewish competitors were observing their religiously mandated day of rest and prayer. One such entrepreneur was a certain Khoren Nazarian, the Armenian-born owner of the Mount Ararat Global Diamond Exchange, located at 23 Appelmansstraat. On the opposite side of the street was a trattoria called Café Verde. Gabriel greeted the hostess in Italian and, despite his suspect appearance, was shown to a coveted table in the window.

There he quickly reached the conclusion, based in

large measure on instinct and hard-won experience, that his old friend Maurice Durand had once again pointed him in the right direction. Perhaps it was the discretion of the firm's entrance, with its opaque glass door and easily overlooked brass placard. Or the furtive demeanor of the two men—one of whom appeared to be carrying a concealed weapon—who requested admission to the premises at one fifteen. Or the steroid abuser, he of the shaved head and tree-trunk neck, who showed the two callers into the autumn afternoon some twenty minutes later with a smile that suggested their meeting had gone well.

Had it involved only precious gemstones, or was the Mount Ararat Global Diamond Exchange a front for other criminal activity? Narcotics, say, or illicit firearms. All Gabriel wanted was a name—the name of the woman who had stolen the Vermeer from Lukas van Damme's villa in Amalfi. It was his ambition to acquire this piece of information with a simple business transaction, one that safeguarded his identity, thus the small fortune in jewelry hidden in the pockets of his atrocious coat. And if that didn't work, he supposed he could always resort to violence. He hoped it didn't come to that. Belgium was one of the few countries in Europe where he had no friends in government or law enforcement. Besides, his back was giving him fits.

But what would he call himself? He decided, while placing several crisp banknotes atop the bill for his lunch, to borrow his son's name, which rivaled his own for hipness. He would be Raffaele. No surname, just Raffaele, like the painter. He was a thief from a hardscrabble village in Calabria who was connected to the violent criminal syndicate known as the 'Ndrangheta. His bosses were looking for a woman who had recently pulled a big heist on the Amalfi Coast. Tribute was owed, honor was due. It was a language every organized criminal understood, especially when a member of the 'Ndrangheta showed up at his door unannounced.

Which was precisely what Gabriel did at the stroke of two o'clock. He pressed the call button on the intercom panel and, receiving no response, pressed it again.

At length a metallic male voice asked, "*Ja?*"

Gabriel answered in English, in a pronounced Italian accent. "I'd like to speak to Khoren Nazarian."

"Mr. Nazarian is unavailable."

"I'll wait."

"Who are you, please?"

"My name is Raffaele."

"Raffaele who?"

Gabriel raised the large-carat diamond solitaire toward the security camera.

The dead bolts opened with a thud.

16

Appelmansstraat

The steroid abuser was waiting in the cramped foyer, arms folded across his inflated pectorals, feet shoulder-width apart. The carpet beneath him was beige and threadbare; the lights above his head were harsh and fluorescent. Behind him was another locked door and another camera. Wordlessly, he thrust a hand in Gabriel's direction, with the palm facing up. Gabriel grasped the appendage and gave it a genial squeeze. It was like shaking hands with a block of concrete.

"The diamond," said the Armenian.

Gabriel dangled it like the pendulum of a clock.

"Where did you get it?"

"It belonged to my late mother, may she rest in peace."

"She had good taste."

"And a rich husband." Gabriel returned the pendant to his coat pocket. "I'm interested in selling it. A few other pieces as well."

"Are you carrying a gun?"

"What do you think?"

"Let's have it."

Gabriel surrendered the Beretta butt first to avoid any possible misinterpretation of his motives. Ordinarily, he would have cleared the weapon as well, but members of the 'Ndrangheta were not known for their adherence to basic gun-safety etiquette. "May I speak to Mr. Nazarian now?" he asked in his pitch-perfect Italian-accented English.

The Armenian lifted his eyes toward the security camera, and the dead bolts of the next door gave way. Beyond it was an empty waiting room decorated with outsize photographs of glittering diamonds and the rugged mountains of Armenia from which they had purportedly come. More than fifty diamond-cutting companies operated in the former Soviet republic, and diamonds accounted for a quarter of the country's exports. Khoren Nazarian handled a small portion of those stones. He had no mines or factories of his own, and no retail operation. He was merely a broker, a middleman. He purchased diamonds from one party and sold them to another, hopefully at a profit sufficient enough to keep a roof over his head. It was not an easy way to make a living, thus his willingness to occasionally handle stones of uncertain provenance.

He received Gabriel in his office wearing a crisp gray suit and open-necked white shirt with diamond cuff links. He was a slender, sharp-featured man in his mid-fifties, with an aquiline nose and thinning hair combed close to his scalp.

He regarded Gabriel speculatively over an unlit cigarette. "I didn't catch your name earlier."

Gabriel repeated it. One name only. Like the painter.

"And what sort of work do you do, Signore Raffaele?"

"I'm involved in a number of charitable endeavors. Widows and orphans, mainly. I'm also quite active in the Church."

"How noble." Nazarian coaxed an elegant gold lighter into flame and touched it to the end of his cigarette. "And in your spare time?"

"I work for an international conglomerate based in Calabria. We did about sixty billion last year, mainly in pharmaceuticals and real estate development."

Nazarian cast an anxious glance toward his associate, and an exchange of quiet Armenian ensued. Gabriel, who neither spoke nor understood a word of the language, used the opportunity to take inventory of the items arrayed atop Nazarian's desk. A crystal paperweight in the shape of an oval-cut diamond. A vintage brass message spike. A Harald Schneider professional jeweler's loupe. A cushioned countertop display pad. A weighty ceramic ashtray overflowing with cigarette butts. A calculator. An open notebook computer.

The room's only window overlooked a deserted courtyard. The glass was gray-green, one-way, and shatterproof. And bulletproof, thought Gabriel suddenly, though he certainly hoped it didn't come to that. After all, he was not in possession of his firearm. Fully loaded, with a round lodged in the chamber, it was in the giant Armenian's coat pocket. The left pocket, to be precise.

Nazarian placed his cigarette in the ashtray. "May I see the diamond, please?"

Gabriel took note of the Armenian's use of the word *please*. They were off to a good start.

He placed the solitaire pendant on the display pad. Nazarian examined the stone with the loupe while the steroid abuser examined Gabriel. He didn't look quite so sure of himself any longer.

"My compliments," said Nazarian after a moment. "This stone is quite extraordinary."

"Yes, I know." Gabriel tossed the rest of the pieces

onto the display pad with deliberate carelessness. Four diamond necklaces, six diamond bracelets, four pairs of diamond earrings, and two diamond rings, the larger of which was six carats. "Those aren't bad, either."

Nazarian examined them slowly, stone by stone. "Where did you get these, Signore Raffaele? And please let's skip the part about your sainted mother. I've heard that one many times before."

"I acquired them in Paris."

"How recently?"

"Yesterday evening."

"Cartier? Piaget?"

"An apartment in the Fourth Arrondissement."

"Does the owner know they're missing?"

"Not yet."

Nazarian reached for the calculator and spent a moment nimbly fingering the keys.

"How much?" asked Gabriel.

"Diamonds of this quality would be worth nearly four million euros on the legitimate market."

"And at the Mount Ararat Global Diamond Exchange?"

Nazarian worked the calculator again and frowned. "I might be able to do two hundred thousand."

"My associates in Calabria will be disappointed."

"I'm sorry, Signore Raffaele. But I'm afraid it's the best I can do under the circumstances."

"Perhaps we can come to some other arrangement," suggested Gabriel.

"What sort of arrangement?"

"I will pay you ten thousand euros in cash, and you will tell me where to find a woman I'm looking for. Mid-thirties, quite pretty, maybe German or Swiss, maybe Dutch or Scandinavian. She likes to get close to her targets and then robs them blind. She's especially fond of fine jewelry, which you fence on her behalf. She had a big score on the Amalfi Coast recently. My associates would like their cut."

"And if I knew this woman?" asked Nazarian after a moment. "Why would I betray her for a mere ten thousand euros?"

"Because my offer expires in exactly ten seconds."

"And then what?"

"Things are liable to get ugly."

Nazarian placed the loupe to his eye. "You're right, Signore Raffaele. They are indeed."

Gabriel turned to face the steroid abuser. "After you."

The Israeli martial arts discipline known as Krav Maga is not known for its gracefulness, but then it was not designed with aesthetics in mind. Its sole purpose is to incapacitate or kill an adversary as quickly as possible. Nor does it value fairness. In fact, instructors encourage their students to use heavy objects in their assault, especially when confronted with an adversary of superior size and strength. David did not grapple with Goliath, they are fond of saying. David hit Goliath with a rock. And only then did he cut off his head.

The only rocks in Khoren Nazarian's office were the diamonds, but even the twelve-carat solitaire would have bounced off the Armenian bodybuilder like a pebble hurled at a speeding truck. Gabriel wisely reached for the glass paperweight instead. It struck the Armenian in the left eye and, judging by the crunching sound of the impact, fractured one or more of the seven bones of the orbit.

Gabriel was tempted to make use of the brass message spike, but delivered a devastating kick to the shin instead, followed by a knee to the exposed testicles and a Phoenix fist to the larynx. The elbow to the temple was probably gratuitous, but it facilitated the recovery of the confiscated Beretta. Aiming the weapon at Khoren Nazarian proved unnecessary. Having just watched Gabriel pulverize a man twice his size and half his age, all in a matter of seconds, the diamond broker was suddenly quite loquacious.

Yes, he admitted, he knew the woman in question

and where she might be found. And, no, under no circumstances would he attempt to warn her that a member of the 'Ndrangheta was looking for her. He asked only that her life be spared, an assurance Signore Raffaele refused to provide. He was, after all, a thoroughly dangerous man.

With the jewelry once more in his coat pocket, he saw himself out and returned to the Sapphire House. This time the man who emerged from his suite was a respectable-looking figure of late middle age clad in hand-tailored Italian trousers, a cashmere jacket, stylish suede loafers, and a woolen overcoat. At half past four he was aboard a train bound for Hamburg, the first leg of a journey that would eventually take him to a picturesque fishing village in the far north of Denmark renowned for the quality of its light. A part of him was actually looking forward to it. If nothing else, it would give him a chance to spend a few days by the North Sea. There were, he thought, far worse ways to find the world's most valuable stolen painting.

17
Kandestederne

It happened at 9:17 p.m. Of that, the Danish police were certain. Also beyond dispute was the number of shots fired, which was two. Both had struck the victim, sixty-four-year-old Peter Nielsen, owner of an antiquarian bookshop on Copenhagen's Strøget, in the head. A passerby recalled seeing muzzle flashes but heard no gunshots, suggesting to police that the killer had utilized a suppressor. He had made his escape on a BMW motorcycle, which had been parked outside the victim's apartment building. Traffic surveillance cameras indicated he entered neighboring Sweden shortly after ten o'clock. As yet, Swedish authorities had been unable to ascertain his whereabouts.

Police were perplexed by numerous aspects of the

killing, beginning with the fact that it happened at all. Denmark was statistically one of the world's safest countries, with far fewer murders each year than the United States typically saw in a single day. The motive for the killing appeared to be robbery, though investigators were at a loss to explain why the perpetrator's weapon, a 9mm pistol of indeterminate manufacture, had been fitted with a suppressor. Ordinary street thugs rarely bothered with such niceties, at least not in Copenhagen. It was the mark, police concluded, of a professional.

But a professional *what*, exactly? And why had he targeted a rare book dealer, of all people? Yes, there was a fair amount of mischief in the trade, but Peter Nielsen had many prominent clients and had never been the subject of a complaint to the police. Was he embroiled in a business dispute? Always a possibility. Had he happened upon a book of great value? Something for which a powerful man might have been willing to kill? An intriguing notion, though it seemed unlikely. After all, the gunman had made off with a storage device better suited to rollable objects—objects such as architectural drawings or, perhaps, a work of art.

The police were likewise confounded by their failure to locate Peter Nielsen's mobile phone, one of several key facts they withheld from their initial statement, which they released at 7:15 a.m. on Saturday. Because it was a weekend, the Copenhagen press was slow off the mark. The tabloid *B.T.* had it first—beneath a sensational headline, of course—but it was nearly noon before the story finally appeared on the website of the more reputable *Politiken.*

Ingrid noticed it at half past one after returning to her cottage from a three-hour training ride. The headline declared that a rare book dealer had been murdered in Nørrebro. Surely, she told herself, it was a different dealer. But the story's second paragraph identified the street where the murder had taken place, and in the next paragraph appeared the name and age of the victim.

The remaining details were sparse. There was no mention, for example, of a leather document tube containing a long-missing painting by Johannes Vermeer. The suspect, though, was described in some detail—a man in his late thirties or early forties wearing a business suit and a mid-length overcoat. As it happened, Ingrid had seen a man matching that description approximately three and a half hours before Peter was murdered.

He had been sitting in Jørgens Smørrebrød Café in Vissenbjerg.

For the moment, at least, Ingrid was more alarmed by the prospect of arrest as an accessory to Peter's murder. She was, after all, in possession of the victim's mobile phone. Stored in its memory was GPS location data that could be used to pinpoint the device's whereabouts at 6:00 p.m. the previous evening. But even without the phone, police would have little trouble reconstructing Peter's movements during the final hours of his life; he had used his credit card to purchase fuel and a coffee. Surveillance video would show him meeting with a woman in her mid-thirties. A woman who had given him a leather document tube in exchange for a briefcase filled with five million euros in cash.

Unless, of course, there was no surveillance video.

Upstairs in her room, Ingrid stripped off her cycling gear and hastily pulled on jeans and a fleece and a pair of suede boots. The Faraday pouch containing Peter's phone was in her office. She shoved it into a nylon backpack along with a laptop. She would ditch the phone somewhere on the way to Vissenbjerg. Somewhere deep and wet where it would never be found. Fortunately, there was no shortage of such places in the island nation of Denmark.

Outside, she slid behind the wheel of her Volvo. A few kilometers south of Aarhus, she turned off the E45 and headed for Mossø, the largest freshwater lake in Jutland. On the eastern shore was a deserted car park. She carried Peter's phone to the water's edge and tried to calculate how far she could hurl the thing, this 174-gram rectangle of silicon, aluminum, potassium, lithium, carbon, and reinforced glass that might well contain the information necessary to identify Peter's killer. Penetrating its defenses was beyond Ingrid's capabilities. Better to be rid of it, to never think of it again.

But not here, she thought. No, this wouldn't do.

She walked back to her car and returned the phone to the Faraday pouch. Her navigation system forecast an arrival time of 5:45 p.m. She only hoped she wasn't too late.

She nearly tossed the phone out her window as she was crossing the Vejle Fjord Bridge—and again, twenty minutes later, as she was spanning the Little Belt. Both times she returned the device to the Faraday pouch. It was tucked into her backpack when she entered Jørgens Smørrebrød Café. A different woman stood behind the counter. She was approximately the same age as Ingrid, mid-thirties, with magenta hair and too much makeup around her coal-black eyes. The name tag affixed to her Roxy Music shirt read KATJE. Something about her face was familiar. Ingrid was convinced she had seen it somewhere before.

She ordered a shrimp-and-egg smørrebrød and a coffee, and sat down at the same table near the window. This time the seating area was deserted. She removed the laptop from her backpack and scanned the list of available wireless networks. She ignored the café's free Wi-Fi service and selected a private network called Q8VSBJ instead. A password was required for admission. Ingrid cracked it with a brute-force attack, and she was in.

The rush hit her instantly. She remembered to eat some of the smørrebrød and, realizing she was famished, devoured half of it. Then she located the security system and got to work.

There were ten surveillance cameras—two over the petrol pumps, two inside the convenience mart, four in the car park, one over the door of the café, and another behind the counter. All ten of the cameras were connected wirelessly to a display monitor and recorder in the convenience mart.

The weak link in the system was its remote access. Ingrid checked the output of one of the cameras and saw a woman, mid-thirties, jeans, a fleece pullover, sitting alone in the smørrebrød café before an open laptop computer. It was no matter, she thought. The woman would soon be forgotten.

The recorder was capable of storing continuous video for twenty-five days, a typical interval for security systems designed for homes and small businesses. Ingrid reset the time code for the camera to 6:05 p.m. the previous evening and saw the same woman sitting at the same table with an antiquarian book dealer from Copenhagen. On the chair next to him was an attaché case.

She reset the time code again, this time for 5:40 p.m., and Peter vanished. Two other tables were now occupied, one by an unhappy-looking Danish couple of late middle age, the other by a man of perhaps forty who was wearing a dark business suit beneath a car-length overcoat.

Ingrid advanced the time code to 5:55 and watched the man's departure from the café. The camera behind the counter captured his left profile; the camera over the door, the back of his head. Both cameras, however, had a perfect view of his arrival, which had taken place at 5:18 p.m.

Ingrid downloaded the video onto her hard drive, along with footage from a camera in the car park that showed the man climbing into a dark-colored Toyota hatchback. Then, with a single click, she erased twenty-five days' worth of video from the recorder.

Outside, two men in uniform were climbing from a

Volkswagen Passat bearing the markings of the Police of Denmark. Ingrid calmly finished the last of her shrimp-and-egg smørrebrød. Then she slipped the laptop into her backpack and walked out.

It was nearly 10:00 p.m. when she arrived home. In the kitchen she brewed a pot of coffee and carried it upstairs to her office. "Well, well," she whispered as she opened her laptop. "Who do we have here?"

The image on her screen was of an overcoated man stretching a hand, his left, toward the door of a café. The camera angle was downward, the lighting shadowed and subdued. Even so, certain critical aspects of the subject's features were visible. The slope of the forehead and the distance between the eyes. The shape of the cheekbones and nose. The contours of the lips and chin. Ingrid enlarged the image and filtered out some of the graininess. She did the same to the shot captured by the camera behind the counter. Here the lighting was better, and the subject's face was animated by speech.

Ingrid decided to use the second shot for a facial recognition search. She expected it to produce numerous additional photographs of the man—from social media, for example—that she might use to discover his name. At which point, the floodgates would open, and his life would be laid bare. His home address. His email address. His mobile phone number. His nationality. His marital status. The name of the football club he supported. His politics. His sexual preferences. His darkest desires.

Unless the subject of the investigation was not a normal person. Which was the conclusion Ingrid reached after eight different search engines failed to exhume even a single photograph. Indeed, had she not laid eyes on the man herself, she would have questioned whether he existed at all.

By the time Ingrid closed her laptop, it was approaching 4:00 a.m. She shed her clothes and crawled into bed and lay there, wired and wide-eyed, until seven, when she switched on *Go' morgen Danmark*. The broadcast opened with the murder of a rare book dealer in the fashionable Nørrebro district of Copenhagen.

The story led the eight o'clock hour as well, but at nine it was displaced by the latest Russian crime against humanity in Ukraine. Ingrid, however, was distracted by an unsettling development closer to home. It was the arrival of a new tenant at the rental cottage up the lane. A well-dressed man of late middle age. Medium height and build. Very gray at the temples.

Definitely not Danish.

18

Kandestederne

The cottage had two bedrooms, a single bathroom, a cramped sitting room, a galley kitchen, and a small terrace sheltered by the eaves of the steeply pitched roof. Because no one of sound mind came to Kandestederne in autumn, Chiara was able to snag it for two weeks at a discounted rate. She settled the bill using a credit card linked to the Tiepolo Restoration Company and instructed the property manager to leave the cottage unlocked and the key inside. No, she said, laundry and maid service would not be necessary; the man who would be staying at the cottage would be working on an important project and wished not to be disturbed. Needless to say, she did not inform the property manager that the man in question was none other than the world's most famous retired spy—or that his project involved the recovery, by any means possible, of *The Concert*, oil on canvas, 72.5 by 64.7 centimeters, by Johannes Vermeer.

Gabriel had seen to his car and his provisions. The car, a Nissan sedan, he had rented in Hamburg. The provisions he acquired during a predawn raid on a SuperBrugsen in a town called Hinnerup. He placed the tins in the pantry, the perishables in the fridge, and three bottles of decent red wine on the countertop. Then he hung his wholly inappropriate city clothing in the closet of the larger of the two bedrooms. In violation of every rule of professional tradecraft, written and unwritten, he concealed four million euros' worth of borrowed diamond jewelry and one hundred thousand euros in cash between the mattress and box spring.

Returning to the kitchen, he brewed a pot of strong coffee and drank a first cup outside on the terrace. The view was westward across the dunes toward the sea, though it was saved from perfection by the large modern dwelling at the end of the lane. A Volvo XC90 was parked outside, and a light burned faintly behind drawn shades in a window on the second floor. The surrounding cottages were darkened and shuttered and gripped by an air of sudden abandonment. Indeed, from

Gabriel's vantage point, it looked as though he and his neighbor had the entire settlement to themselves.

A blast of frigid wind drove him inside. He lit a fire in the wood-burning stove and drank the rest of the coffee while watching a breakfast television program on Denmark's TV2. His Danish was only slightly better than his Armenian. Still, with the help of the video images, he was able to deduce that there had been a shooting death in Copenhagen, an unusual occurrence.

A weather forecast was next, followed by a political discussion. Gabriel couldn't make heads or tails of what the panelists were saying and didn't much care; he was watching a cyclist coming down the lane from the direction of the beach. She shot past the cottage a moment later, all but invisible beneath her winter-weight kit, her pedal stroke smooth and effortless, and vanished from view. A hearty soul to be heading out in conditions like these, thought Gabriel. But then he supposed she was used to it. She was Danish, after all. A bit of a chameleon, as was he. But definitely Danish.

The cottage had four windows, one in each bedroom, a third in the sitting room, and a porthole above the kitchen sink. The woodwork was weakened by age, the latches brown with rust. The lock on the only door was aspirational; Gabriel could have picked it himself in less than a minute. He engaged it nevertheless and, after wedging a tiny paper telltale between the door and the jamb, set off toward the cottage at the end of the lane.

It was the largest in the entire settlement. The newest as well, or so it appeared. Unlike its neighbors, which were sparingly furnished and occupied only during the summer months, it would doubtless have a proper security system. Sensors on the doors and windows. Motion detectors and cameras. But would the Danish police receive an automatic alert in the event of a break-in? Gabriel supposed that would depend on the quality of the owner's public-facing facade. According to Khoren Nazarian, she worked as a cybersecurity consultant in addition to her primary occupation, which was theft.

Her plug-in hybrid Volvo suggested she was also something of an environmentalist, as did the unkempt heather and gorse that grew wild on her property. Gabriel paused at the end of the sandy footpath that stretched toward the cottage's entrance. The door was solid wood, with a keyless entry system and a camera. A camera, he thought, that was recording his every move.

Turning, he followed the lane down to the beach and, alone at the tide's edge, weighed his options. A forcible entry and rapid search of the cottage was the most obvious course of action, though the chances of avoiding detection were slim, and there was no guarantee he would find the painting. There was also a risk, slight, that he would land in a Danish jail cell—or that he might meet the same fate as Lukas van Damme. No, the smarter move would be to take a page from her playbook. He would make her acquaintance, earn her trust. Then they would strike a deal, one professional to another. And with any luck, Gabriel would be back in Venice in time to save his job and his marriage.

But how to get close to her without tipping his hand? Office doctrine forbade direct approaches. An Office field agent boarded the streetcar *before* the target, not after. And he always, *always*, waited for the target to make the first move. But the field agent was permitted—encouraged, in fact—to prey on his target's weaknesses, to tempt his target with objects of great beauty or value. Especially if the target was a sticky-fingered cat burglar with a weakness for cash and jewelry. As luck would have it, Gabriel had an ample supply of both.

Lost in thought, he failed to notice the approaching wave that heaved itself onto the beach and washed over his handmade Italian suede loafers. Returning to the cottage, he composed a note, unsigned, business-like in tone, offering the target complete immunity in exchange for information leading to the recovery of *The Concert* by Johannes Vermeer. Then, in keeping with the finest traditions of his old service, written and unwritten, he carried it into the larger of the two bedrooms and stuffed it between the mattress and box spring.

There was a single hotel in Kandestederne, with an excellent restaurant that opened on weekends during the off-season. That evening Gabriel had the dining room to himself. Erika, his pretty young waitress, was glad of his company.

"What brings you to Kandestederne at this time of year?" she asked.

"A desire for solitude," replied Gabriel in his most neutral accent.

"Is this your first visit?"

Oh, no, he assured her. He had been to Kandestederne on two previous occasions. His last stay had involved the interrogation of a kidnapped Iranian intelligence officer, but he left that part out.

"Which cottage have you taken?" asked the waitress.

He raised a hand toward the north. "I couldn't possibly pronounce the name of the street."

"Dødningebakken?"

"If you say so."

"A friend of mine lives there. The large cottage by the beach. Don't worry, she won't interrupt your solitude. Ingrid enjoys the pleasure of her own company."

She rolled past Gabriel's cottage again at ten fifteen the next morning. This time, after allowing exactly five minutes to pass, he slid behind the wheel of the rented Nissan and set off after her. He spotted her just west of Huslig, sailing along at an impressive forty-four kilometers per hour. As he overtook her, she stared straight ahead, her knees pumping rhythmically. In the rear pouch of her Gore-Tex jacket, he noticed the distinctive outline of a firearm. Something small and ladylike, he thought. Something along the lines of a Glock 26 subcompact.

They both headed south on Primærrute 40. Gabriel accelerated and soon she was a speck in his rearview mirror. He drove to Frederikshavn, a busy port town on the Baltic side of the peninsula, and purchased hiking boots, thick woolen socks, base layers, undergarments, two pairs of corduroy trousers, a fleece pullover, an anorak, a traditional Danish zippered sweater, a waterproof coat, a pair of Zeiss Conquest HD binoculars, a French *plein air* easel, a palette, six canvases of various dimensions, twelve tubes of oil paint, four Winsor & Newton sable-hair brushes, a bottle of solvent, and a bag of painter's rags. His last stop was a bakery near the ferry terminal where he purchased two loaves of freshly baked bread. As he was leaving, he nearly collided with his neighbor, who was looking down at her phone and brushed past him with neither a word nor a glance.

It was nearly one o'clock when she returned to her cottage in Kandestederne. With the aid of his powerful Zeiss field glasses, Gabriel was able to make out much of the fourteen-digit passcode she entered into the keyless lock of her front door. She carried the bike inside and, upstairs, stripped off her cycling gear. Gabriel knew this because she opened the shade of her bedroom window before disrobing. He quickly lowered the binoculars and prepared his lunch, all the while wondering if her cabaret had been for him.

Later that afternoon, Gabriel erected the French easel on the beach and produced a rather good seascape he would later call *Kandestederne Strand at Sunset*. His neighbor observed his efforts from her terrace for several minutes before disappearing from view. The telltale was still in place when Gabriel returned to the cottage, but he nevertheless headed straight for the bedroom. The money, jewelry, and note were where he had left them.

He dined at home that evening with a bottle of red

wine and a Danish television newscast for company. An update on the Copenhagen murder case appeared in the second block of the program. Gabriel found the story online, translated it into English, and read that the victim was a rare book dealer, that he had been shot twice at close range with a silenced handgun, that his killer had escaped on a motorcycle, and that police believed the motive for this brutal, well-oiled assassination was robbery, though they had yet to determine what, if anything, had been stolen.

The next morning dawned cloudless and calm. Gabriel produced a work he called *Cottages in the Dunes*, then made the fifteen-kilometer hike along the beach from Kandestederne to Grenen, the slender spit of sand at the northernmost tip of the Jutland peninsula where the incoming waters of the North Sea collide with the outgoing current of the Baltic. He arrived there to find his neighbor, in Wellington boots and an anorak, standing alone at the tip of the headland.

Turning, she regarded him for a long moment without expression, then set off along the Baltic side of the peninsula toward the car park at the old nature center. Gabriel headed in the opposite direction and took his time walking back to Kandestederne. The telltale fluttered onto the threshold when he opened the door of the cottage, but the money, jewelry, and offer of immunity were nowhere to be found. The likely perpe-trator of the crime had left a note on the bedside table, handwritten, formal in tone, inviting him to dinner that evening at eight o'clock. It was addressed to "The Honorable Gabriel Allon." The salutation read, "With admiration, Ingrid Johansen."

19

Kandestederne

G abriel showered and shaved and dressed in corduroy trousers, the Danish wool sweater, and his
suede loafers, which somehow had survived submersion
in the frigid waters of the North Sea largely unscathed.
He deliberated over whether to carry his Beretta and,
recalling the gun in the pocket of her cycling jacket,
thought it wise. On his way out the door he grabbed a
bottle of red wine from the kitchen counter and, perhaps presumptuously, *Kandestederne Strand at Sunset*.
He didn't bother with the lock. He had nothing left to
steal.

Outside, the sky was cloudless and awash in hard
white stars—diamond-white, thought Gabriel as he
pursued his shadow up the lane toward her cottage.

The door swung open before he could ring the bell, and there she was again, in shimmering black pants and a black rollneck pullover. Her earrings were pearl, and the bracelets on her left wrist were gold. On her right wrist was a handsome tank-style watch with a band of black leather. She wore two rings on her left hand and three on her right.

But no diamonds, noted Gabriel. Not a diamond in sight.

Inside, she accepted the bottle of wine, then the painting. "Is it really for me?"

"I didn't have time to buy flowers. And thanks to you, I didn't have any money, either."

She feigned ignorance. Quite well, in fact. "What do you mean?" she asked.

"You removed a significant quantity of cash and jewelry from my cottage this afternoon when you left the invitation to dinner. Because none of it actually belongs to me, I'd like it back before we begin."

"I'm sorry to hear that you were robbed, Mr. Allon. But I can assure you, it wasn't me."

So that was the game she intended to play. It promised to be an interesting evening.

She left the wine on the table in the entrance hall and led him into the sitting room. The tall windows were opaque with reflected interior light, rendering the North Sea invisible, but the crashing of waves was faintly audible. It was the perfect accompaniment to the moody Scandinavian jazz that issued from her Hegel amplifier and Dynaudio speakers. Her furniture was modern, as was the art that adorned her walls. Gabriel was not ashamed to admit that much of it was a damn sight better than the hurriedly completed winter seascape she held in her hands.

She leaned the painting against a low coffee table and took a step back to admire it. "There's no signature," she pointed out.

"I don't often sign my work."

"Why not?"

"Habit, I suppose."

"You're working as an art restorer now, yes?"

"How do you possibly know that?"

"Your cottage was rented by someone from the Tiepolo Restoration Company in Venice." She lowered her voice. "Kandestederne is a very small place, Mr. Allon."

When he made no reply, she helped him out of his coat and in the process managed to determine that he was carrying a firearm. She was good, he thought. He would have to watch his step tonight.

She laid his coat over the arm of a chair and, bending slightly at the waist, drew a bottle from the marble wine cooler resting atop the coffee table. Her every movement was efficient and effortless and catlike in its smoothness. "Do you drink Sancerre?" she asked.

"Every chance I get."

She filled two glasses. Their toast was guarded, like two fencers touching foils at the outset of a match.

"How did you know it was me?" asked Gabriel.

"It was rather obvious, Mr. Allon. Even from a distance. But I confirmed my suspicions using facial recognition software."

"You took my photograph outside the bakery in Frederikshavn."

She smiled. "A trick of the trade."

"And what trade is that?"

"I own a small cybersecurity consulting firm."

Gabriel looked deliberately around the elegant room. "You obviously do quite well for yourself."

"As you know, Mr. Allon, it's a dangerous world. There are threats everywhere." She indicated the couch and they sat down. "Which is why it's so surprising to see a man like you in a place like this. What brings you to Kandestederne?"

"An investigation I'm conducting on behalf of the Italian police."

"What sort of investigation?"

"I'm looking for a professional thief who stole a

painting from a villa on the Amalfi Coast. I was told I could find her here."

"Told by whom?"

"A dirty diamond broker from Antwerp."

"I'm afraid you've been misled, Mr. Allon. Kandestederne is hardly a hotbed of criminal activity."

"The events of this afternoon would seem to suggest that's not entirely the case."

"This mysterious robbery, you mean?"

"Yes."

"Are you sure your valuables are actually missing?"

"Quite sure. The cash as well."

"How much cash are we talking about?"

"A hundred thousand euros."

"I see. And the valuables?"

"About four million euros' worth of diamond jewelry."

"The plot thickens." She tapped the rim of her wineglass thoughtfully. "Have you considered the possibility that the thief was trying to send you a message?"

"An interesting theory. What sort of message?"

"Could be anything, really. But it might have something to do with this painting you're looking for."

"Do you think she knows where it is?"

"I'm quite certain she doesn't. But she knows who had it last Friday evening."

"Who?"

"A man named Peter Nielsen."

"The rare book dealer who was murdered in Copenhagen?"

She nodded slowly.

"Does she know who killed him?"

"She has a hunch. She has a couple of decent video stills as well."

"What else does she have?"

"It's possible she has Peter Nielsen's phone."

"Why?"

She smiled sadly. "He said she had lost her touch, and she couldn't help herself."

20

Kandestederne

Dinner was a candlelit buffet of traditional Danish fare, served in her formal dining room. The jewelry and cash lay between them like a centerpiece, along with a dormant mobile phone, a slumbering laptop, and Gabriel's handwritten offer of immunity.

"How did you break in?" he asked.

"I bumped the lock."

Lock bumping was a technique that involved inserting a specially crafted key into a lock and tapping it with a small hammer or the grip of a screwdriver.

"That hardly seems sporting," said Gabriel. "Why didn't you just shoot off the lock instead?"

"Is that how you do it?"

"Lockpick tools. I'm old-school."

"I gathered that from the telltale."

"How did you spot it?"

"The better question is, how could I have missed it?"

She lowered her pale blue eyes toward the jewelry glowing softly in the candlelight. Her hair was the color of toffee and streaked with blond. Parted in the middle, it framed a face of straight, even features. There was nothing out of place, not a line or mark.

"You have very good taste, Mr. Allon."

"Your friend Khoren Nazarian told me the same thing."

"How did you convince him to betray me?"

"You know what they say about honor among thieves."

"Why didn't you simply go to the Danish police?"

He pointed out the offer of immunity. "I was hoping to settle the matter privately."

"Is that still your intention?"

"To be determined."

"By what?"

"Your level of candor in the next few minutes."

She added Sancerre to his glass. "It isn't really an actual crime, you know."

"What's that?"

"Stealing a stolen painting."

"It is when it involves shooting someone twice in the head at close range."

"I didn't kill Lukas van Damme, Mr. Allon." She returned the bottle to the cooler. "Or Peter Nielsen, in case you're wondering."

"What was the nature of your relationship?"

"Peter was a book hunter. Collectors hired him to track down volumes of great significance or value. And when their current owners refused to part with them . . ."

"He turned to you?"

She gazed at him through the candlelight but said nothing.

"How much did he pay you to steal the Vermeer?"

"Ten million."

"Kroner?"

"I wouldn't have touched it for that amount of money. The deal was in euros."

"How was it structured?"

"Does it matter?"

"It does now."

"I received half of the money up front. The rest I received when I delivered the painting to Peter last Friday evening at Jørgens Smørrebrød Café in Vissenbjerg." She opened the laptop and turned the screen toward Gabriel. "And this is the man who killed Peter three hours later outside his apartment in Copenhagen."

"How did you get the video?"

"Click, click, click."

"And Peter Nielsen's phone?"

She smiled. "Old-school."

They went through it once from the beginning. Then they went through it a second time to make certain there were no inconsistencies in her story. The date of Peter Nielsen's original offer. The nature of the information he had provided in advance. The circumstances surrounding the theft itself. The exchange of money and art at the café on the island of Funen. The man had been waiting there when Ingrid arrived. She reckoned he was in his late thirties or early forties, but Gabriel, after close examination of the video and still shots, concluded he was closer to forty-five, maybe a bit older. He also disagreed with Ingrid's assertion that he was a Finn or from one of the Baltic states. The eyes and cheekbones suggested his ethnic roots lay farther to the east. His physical movements, in Gabriel's learned opinion, were those of a professional—a professional whose photograph Ingrid could find nowhere online.

Gabriel asked her to run the photos through the search engines one more time, but once again there were no matches. Then they rewatched the video of the man's arrival at the café. It occurred at 5:18 p.m., forty-two minutes before Ingrid was supposed to deliver the painting to Peter Nielsen.

"How did you set up the meeting?"

"I believe we've covered that ground, Mr. Allon. Twice, in fact."

"And we're going to continue covering it until I'm satisfied that *The Concert* by Johannes Vermeer isn't in this house."

"Peter and I conducted sensitive business discussions over Signal. And even then we always spoke in code."

"And remind me, please, who chose the time and place."

"I did," she said with a sigh. "And in case you didn't hear me the first two times, I was the first to arrive."

"At half past five?"

"Yes."

"And you brought the painting into the café?"

"I left it in a leather document tube in the trunk of my car."

"The perfect way to transport one of only thirty-four known works by Johannes Vermeer."

"I handled the painting very carefully, Mr. Allon. It suffered no damage while it was in my possession."

"I don't suppose you took a picture of it?"

"That would have been a bit like keeping the bloody knife as a souvenir, don't you think?"

Gabriel smiled in spite of himself. "How did you get into Van Damme's vault room?"

"Easy peasy lemon squeezy."

"Can you be more specific?"

"Click, click, click."

"And the button under the desk that moved aside the bookcases?"

"I pushed it."

"How did you know where to find it?"

"The same way I knew about the existence of the vault room."

"The client told Peter?"

She nodded.

"And Peter never mentioned his name to you?"

"No, Mr. Allon. For the third time, he never told me the name of the client." She nudged Peter Nielsen's phone across the table. It was an iPhone 13 Pro. "But I have a feeling we might be able to find it here."

"Have you tried to crack it?"

"Newer-model iPhones are beyond my capabilities. But there's a zero-click malware called Proteus that should do the trick. It was developed a few years ago by an Israeli firm called ONS Systems. The licenses are rather hard to come by."

"Not as hard as you think," said Gabriel.

"Can you lay your hands on a copy?"

"A distinct possibility."

"How's your Danish?"

"Nonexistent. But Proteus has an auto-translation function."

"That software is dreadful. You really should have a native Danish speaker looking over your shoulder. Preferably someone who knew Peter well."

"You?"

She smiled.

"You seem to be forgetting that you were the one who stole the Vermeer in the first place."

"Who better to help you find it? Besides, if I stay here in Denmark, I'm liable to end up dead, too." She lowered her voice. "Please, Mr. Allon. Let me help you find the painting and the man who killed Peter."

He took up the phone. "Do you know what will happen when we turn this on?"

"It will pop onto the Danish network. Which means we have to do the work outside the country."

"How about Paris?" suggested Gabriel.

"Any particular reason?"

"A friend of mine would like his jewelry and money back."

"In that case," said Ingrid, "Paris it is."

Gabriel walked back to the rental cottage by the blue-green glow of his mobile phone. Inside, he hastily packed his clothing and toiletries. Then he stuffed his paints and solvents and rags into a plastic rubbish bag, along with the contents of the refrigerator and the undrunk wine. The French *plein air* easel, Winsor & Newton brushes, palette, and unused canvases he set alight in the wood-burning stove. *Cottages in the Dunes* he left behind as a small token of his esteem. If it belonged anywhere, he thought, it was here.

He loaded his things into the rented Nissan and drove the three hundred meters to Ingrid's cottage. She was stepping from her doorway as he drew to a stop. She entered the fourteen-digit passcode into the keypad, then started down the footpath, an overnight bag over her shoulder. Gabriel pressed the internal trunk release and climbed out of the car to help her. Which was when he heard the sound of an approaching motorcycle, the first motorcycle he had heard in Kandestederne since his arrival two days earlier.

He spotted the headlamp an instant later, moving at high speed down the settlement's main road. For a moment it looked as though it might be headed toward the hotel, but a hard turn to the right sent it careening directly toward the spot where Gabriel and Ingrid now stood.

The motorcyclist was controlling the bike with a single hand, his left. With his right, he was reaching into the front of his jacket. When it emerged, Gabriel saw the unmistakable silhouette of a gun fitted with a sound suppressor.

He seized Ingrid and drove her to the ground behind the Nissan. Then he drew the Beretta from the small of his back as two superheated rounds split the air a few centimeters from his right ear. He did not seek cover or even flinch. Instead, he poured four rounds into the motorcyclist's torso, blowing the man from the saddle.

Riderless, the bike continued along the lane. Gabriel sidestepped the machine, then walked over to the spot where the man was lying motionless on the pebbled concrete. His silenced firearm, a Makarov 9mm, had come to rest next to him. Gabriel pushed the weapon aside and removed the man's helmet. He recognized the face at once. In fact, he had seen it that very evening on the video from Jørgens Smørrebrød Café.

The front of the man's leather jacket was pierced with four bullet holes and soaked with blood, as was the black crewneck base layer he wore beneath it. The holes corresponded to the four in the center of the chest. Directly above the wounds was tattooed the letter Z. The bleeding was torrential. He didn't have long to live.

Gabriel snapped a photograph of the dying man's face. Then he asked, "Where's the painting?"

The man said nothing.

Gabriel placed the barrel of the Beretta against the side of the man's knee and fired another shot.

The man screamed in agony.

"The painting," said Gabriel. "Tell me where I can find it."

"Gone," was all the man managed to say.

"Gone where?"

"The collector."

"What's his name?"

"The collector," the man repeated.

"His name," shouted Gabriel. "Tell me his name."

"The collector," said the man a final time, and then he died.

PART TWO

The Conspiracy

21

Ben Gurion Airport

By rights, Gabriel should have phoned the Danish police, gone on the record, and washed his hands of the whole affair. Instead, he rang Lars Mortensen, the longtime director of the PET, Denmark's Security and Intelligence Service. He told Mortensen that an assassin on a motorcycle had just taken a couple of shots at him in Kandestederne. He indicated that the fellow was no longer alive. Mortensen knew he was getting about ten percent of the story, if that.

"What were you doing all the way up there at this time of year?"

"Painting," answered Gabriel, with at least a grain of truth.

"You're sure he's dead?"

"As a doornail."

"Any idea who he was?"

"The tattoo on his chest suggests he might have been a Russian. He's lying outside the cottage at the end of Dødningebakken. You can't miss him."

"I'll take care of it."

"Quietly, Lars."

"Is there any other way? But please do me a favor, and get the hell out of the country."

Gabriel killed the call, then dredged up a deceptively labeled entry in his contacts. He hesitated before dialing the number, for it rang in an anonymous building on King Saul Boulevard in Tel Aviv. His break with the Office had thus far been remarkably clean; he was all but forgotten. It was his abiding wish to avoid the pitfalls of rediscovery, but the Russian assassin lying dead at his feet had irrevocably altered the nature of his inquiry.

He brought down his thumb on the screen, and after a delay of several seconds a phone rang. He recognized the voice of the woman who answered, and doubtless she recognized his.

"Are you wounded?" she asked.

He said he was not.

"Do you have transport?"

"A rental."

"Can you get down to Schiphol?"

"I'm leaving now."

"How many in your party?"

"Two."

"The plane will collect you at the FBO tomorrow morning at seven. And don't worry about the car," the woman said before ringing off. "Amsterdam station will take care of it."

The plane in question was a Gulfstream G550 that Gabriel had acquired during the early days of the Covid pandemic, when he scoured the globe in search of ventilators, testing material, and protective medical clothing. It departed Amsterdam's Schiphol Airport at 7:15 a.m. and landed at Ben Gurion at half past twelve. Gabriel emerged from the cabin door to find Mikhail Abramov waiting on the tarmac. He was a tall, long-limbed man in his early fifties, with fair hair and pale, bloodless skin. His eyes were blue-gray and translucent, like glacial ice.

Smiling, he extended a hand toward his former director-general. He addressed him in Russian-accented Hebrew. "I was beginning to think we'd never see you again."

"It's only been ten months, Mikhail."

"Trust me, it feels longer. Things haven't been quite the same around here since you left."

Born in Moscow to a pair of dissident Soviet scientists, Mikhail had immigrated to Israel as a teenager. After serving in the Sayeret Matkal, the IDF's elite special forces unit, he joined the Office, where he specialized in a type of operation known as "negative treatment," the Office euphemism for a targeted assassination. His enormous talents, however, were not limited to the gun. It was Mikhail Abramov, at Gabriel's behest, who broke into a warehouse in a drab commercial district of Tehran and stole Iran's entire nuclear archives.

He glanced at Ingrid. "You haven't done something foolish, have you, boss?"

"I agreed to track down a stolen painting for the Italian police. Things went downhill from there."

Mikhail indicated the armored SUV idling nearby. "Your successor ordered me to personally escort you to your apartment in Narkiss Street."

"Actually," said Gabriel, "we have a little errand to run first."

They headed north to Mount Carmel, then east toward the Sea of Galilee. By the time they reached Rosh Pina, founded by thirty families of Romanian Jews in 1882, it was nearly two fifteen. The driver started toward the mountain hamlet of Amuka, then turned onto an unmarked track cut through a dense grove of cypress and pine. He slowed to a stop a moment later after coming upon four men in khaki vests, each clutching a Galil ACE automatic. Behind them was a chain-link fence topped with concertina wire.

"Where are we?" asked Ingrid.

"Nowhere," answered Mikhail.

"What does that mean?"

"It means this place doesn't exist. Which is why those four nice boys are about to shoot the former director-general of the Office."

Gabriel lowered his window, and one of the guards approached the car. "Is that you, boss?"

"Former boss," replied Gabriel.

"You should have told us you were coming."

"I couldn't."

"Why not?"

"Because I'm not here." Gabriel glanced at Ingrid. "And neither is she."

His real name was Aleksander Yurchenko, but like most aspects of his previous life, it was gone forever. Even now, five years after his coerced defection to Israel, he still referred to himself by his workname, which was Sergei Morosov.

He was a child of the old order. His father had been

a senior official at Gosplan, the masterminds behind the Soviet Union's Marxist command economy. His mother had worked as a typist at the headquarters of the KGB, the monsters who crushed anyone foolish enough to complain. Later, she would serve as the personal secretary to Yuri Andropov, the longtime KGB chairman who would eventually succeed Leonid Brezhnev as the leader of an empire that would soon be dead and buried.

Perhaps not surprisingly, it was in his mother's footsteps that Sergei Morosov chose to follow. He spent three years at the Red Banner Institute, the KGB's school for fledgling spies, and upon graduation was assigned to the German operations desk at Moscow Center. A year later he was posted to the *rezidentura* in East Berlin, where he witnessed the fall of the Berlin Wall, knowing full well the Soviet Union would crumble next.

When the end came in December 1991, the KGB was disbanded, renamed, reorganized, and renamed again. Eventually, it would be broken in two, with the Lubyanka-based FSB handling domestic security and the SVR, headquartered in Yasenevo, responsible for foreign intelligence gathering and other assorted special tasks. Sergei Morosov served in three declared SVR *rezidenturas*—first Helsinki, then The Hague, and finally Ottawa, where he foolishly tried to tempt the Canadian defense minister with a bit of honey and was asked to quietly pack his bags.

His last posting was in Frankfurt, where, posing as a Russian banking consultant, he stole German industrial secrets and ensnared dozens of German businessmen in operations involving kompromat, the Russian shorthand for compromising material. He also played a supporting role in the brutal assassination of the Office's most important Russian asset. Gabriel returned the favor by abducting Morosov from an SVR safe flat in Strasbourg, stuffing him into a duffel bag, and dangling him out of a helicopter over Syrian territory held by rabidly anti-Russian jihadists. The interrogation that followed had allowed Gabriel to identify a Russian mole at the pinnacle of Britain's Secret Intelligence Service, perhaps the crowning achievement of his career.

As for Sergei Morosov, he was now the lone prisoner of the same secret detention facility in the Biriya Forest near Rosh Pina where he had undergone his initial interrogation. He lived in one of the old staff bungalows, where he spent his days watching Russian television and his nights drinking Russian vodka. Lately, he had developed a taste for the wines produced by the vineyard on the other side of the ridge.

He had been in the process of removing a cork from a bottle of sauvignon blanc when Gabriel appeared on his doorstep unannounced, accompanied by the gray-eyed man who had handled some of the more unpleasant aspects of his interrogation. Their handshake was cordial nonetheless—warm, even. Morosov seemed genuinely pleased to see the two men responsible for his imprisonment. They had long ago made their cold peace. What happened between them was simply part of the game; there were no hard feelings. Nor was Morosov inclined to leave the secret camp in the Upper Galilee anytime soon. Beyond the concertina wire there was only the prospect of a Russian-style death.

"Are you sure you don't want to go back to Moscow?" asked Gabriel in jest. "I hear the Red Army is looking for a few good men to help turn the tide in Ukraine."

"There are no good men left in Russia, Allon. They've all fled the country to avoid the mobilization."

"You sound disappointed."

"That my country is losing this war? That my fellow citizens are being fed into a meat grinder? That they will soon be freezing to death because they don't have proper supplies? Yes, Allon, I'm disappointed. But I'm also afraid of what comes next."

They went onto the veranda of the bungalow—his dacha, as Morosov called it. He was wearing a V-neck sweater against the cool afternoon air. Gabriel thought he looked rather good for a Russian male who had recently celebrated his sixtieth birthday. It was unlikely to last. Old age tended to fall on Russian men like a brick from a window. They were a bit like poor Johannes Vermeer. Alive one day, dead the next.

From the dusty courtyard of the camp came a muted, rhythmic thumping. It was only Ingrid. Surrounded by the four heavily armed security guards, she was demonstrating her ability to keep a leather footbag aloft while her eyes were closed.

"Who's the girl?" asked Morosov.

"My bodyguard."

"She doesn't look Jewish to me."

"Was that a microaggression, Sergei?"

"A what?"

"A microaggression. A comment or action that subtly and often unconsciously expresses a prejudiced attitude toward a racial minority or otherwise marginalized group."

"Jews are hardly marginalized."

"You just did it again."

"Don't pull that shit with me, Allon. At this point, I've practically made aliyah. Besides, if anyone is guilty of prejudice, it's you."

"Not me, Sergei. I love everyone."

"Everyone except Russians," said Morosov.

"Are you referring to the people who massacred

more than four hundred and fifty innocent civilians in the Ukrainian town of Bucha? Who are deliberately firing missiles into shelters crammed with women and children? Who are using rape as a part of their military strategy?"

"We Russians know only one way to fight a war."

"Or to lose one."

"Volodya is without question losing this war," said Morosov. "But under no circumstances will he actually lose it."

Volodya was the affectionate-diminutive form of the Russian name Vladimir.

"And how will he manage that?" asked Gabriel.

"By any means necessary." Morosov refilled his wineglass. "You know your Russian history, Allon. Tell me, what happened after Russia suffered a humiliating defeat in the Russo-Japanese War?"

"The Russian Revolution of 1905 happened. There were worker revolts and peasant uprisings in every corner of the empire. Tsar Nicholas II responded by issuing the October Manifesto, which promised basic civil rights for Russian citizens and a democratically elected parliament."

"And when Russia suffered a series of battlefield disasters during the First World War?"

"The Bolsheviks seized power, and the tsar and his family were murdered."

"And what about our misadventure in Afghanistan?"

"The Red Army withdrew in May 1988, and three years later the Soviet Union was gone."

"The greatest geopolitical catastrophe of the twentieth century, according to Vladimir Vladimirovich. He won't lose the war in Ukraine because he *can't* lose it. Which is why I'm so worried about what comes next. As are you, I imagine."

"Worried, yes. But I'm retired now, Sergei."

"In that case, why are you here?"

"I was wondering whether you would be kind enough to have a look at a photograph." Gabriel handed Morosov his phone. "Recognize him?"

"Sure, Allon. I know him. His name is Grigori Toporov."

"What kind of work does Grigori do?"

"The kind of work that involves bullets and blood."

"SVR?"

"At last check. But it's been a while."

Gabriel reclaimed his phone. "Grigori said something interesting last night after he tried to kill me in Denmark. I was hoping you might be able to explain it."

"What did he say?"

"'The collector.'"

Morosov peered thoughtfully into his wineglass. "It's possible that he was giving you the code name of an asset. A Danish asset," added the Russian. "A very important one."

"The collector?"

"His actual code name is Collector. One word."

"How did he acquire it?"

"Rare books. He *collects* them ravenously. Nominally, he's an SVR asset, but the SVR doesn't really handle him."

"Who does?"

"The boss of bosses."

"Vladimir Vladimirovich?"

Morosov nodded. "Peace be upon him."

22

Biriya Forest

In the summer of 2003, the British oil-and-gas conglomerate BP paid $6.75 billion to acquire a fifty percent stake in the Russian energy company TNK. So monumental was the deal that the British prime minister attended the signing ceremony in London, as did the president of the Russian Federation. On his way back to Moscow, the Russian leader stopped in Copenhagen, where he presided over a similar corporate marriage, this time between Denmark's DanskOil and Russia's RuzNeft. The investment was smaller, a mere $3 billion, but it came with a pledge to assist Russia in exploiting its massive untapped reserves in the Arctic Sea.

The final details of the deal were hashed out during

weeks of sometimes torturous negotiations in Moscow. DanskOil CEO Magnus Larsen, a student of Russian history who spoke the language fluently, was often present. His hosts treated him to lavish dinners and showered him with expensive gifts, including several rare books. They also tempted him with beautiful young women, including one who spent a night in his suite at the Hotel Metropol. The FSB had the suite wired for sound and video, and recorded everything.

"I assume the FSB made Magnus aware of what it had in its possession," said Gabriel.

"It is my understanding the director hosted a proper screening party at Lubyanka, complete with cocktails and canapés. After that, Magnus signed his name to perhaps the most lopsided deal in the history of the petroleum industry. He also agreed to deposit one hundred million dollars in an account controlled by a close associate of Vladimir Vladimirovich."

"Which compromised him further still."

Sergei Morosov nodded in agreement. "Poor Magnus came to Moscow in search of Russian riches, and by the time he left he was burned to a crisp and fully under our control."

The FSB transferred the Magnus Larsen account to the SVR, which put the oil executive to good use. The Collector became an invaluable source of business intelligence, especially regarding future trends in the Western energy industry. He also provided the SVR with entrée to the highest levels of Western society and government, and pointed out numerous potential targets for recruitment and kompromat.

"He became a real self-starter, did Magnus. That's the beauty of kompromat. If someone is truly burned, you never have to remind them of their past transgressions. They do anything to stay in your good graces."

"Have you never tried to convince an asset that your system is better than your adversary's? That you are alone in a dangerous world and in need of their help?"

"I seem to recall that you employed a different approach when it came to my recruitment."

"You were a defector."

"Of the mailed-fist variety," said Morosov. "As for ideological recruitments, they went out of fashion with the end of the Cold War. Who in their right mind would willingly work on behalf of a country like Russia? We have two means of recruitment available to us. Kompromat and money. And in the case of Magnus Larsen, they went hand in hand."

"How?"

The Kremlin put its thumb on the scale of the RuzNeft deal, explained Morosov, and made certain it paid dividends for DanskOil's shareholders—and for Magnus personally. Not surprisingly, the Danish oil executive became one of Russia's most vocal advocates in the West. He said Europe had nothing to fear from its growing dependence on Russian energy or from Russia's tough-talking president, whom Magnus praised at every turn as a statesman who was leading his country out of its backward, repressive past and into a democratic future.

"As it turned out, Vladimir Vladimirovich was listening. He entertained Magnus at the Kremlin and at his various private residences, including his dacha west of Moscow. Because Magnus spoke Russian fluently, there was no need for a translator. He became one of Volodya's closest non-Russian friends. Not a member of the inner ring, mind you, but he was definitely part of Volodya's universe."

"How did he use him?"

"Mainly as a sounding board and adviser. But he also asked Magnus to carry out, how shall we say, sensitive assignments involving matters of Russian national security."

"What sort of matters?"

"The kind of jobs where Magnus's Danish passport and impeccable Danish manners were advantageous. He became Volodya's private emissary in everything but name. And when he got into trouble, it was Volodya who got him out of it."

"What happened?"

"Magnus got mixed up with another girl."

"In Moscow?"

"Denmark."

"How did Volodya help him?"

"He put his thumb on the girl," said Morosov. "And the girl vanished without a trace."

She was in her twenties, and Danish. Otherwise, Sergei Morosov knew nothing about her, including her name or the circumstances by which she ended up in a sexual relationship with the CEO of one of Denmark's largest companies. At some point—Morosov couldn't say when—she wanted out. She also wanted a significant amount of money to ensure her silence. Magnus agreed to pay. And when the girl came back for more, he raised the matter with his SVR handler, who told Magnus not to give it another thought.

"Death solves all problems," said Gabriel. "No girl, no problem."

"In Russia, this sort of behavior isn't necessarily frowned upon. A lot of girls who get mixed up with powerful men end up in the ground."

"Where did our nameless Danish girl end up?"

"I am not privy to the details, Allon. All I know is that she's still classified as a missing person."

"Who handled it?"

"The SVR. But the order came directly from the state president."

"I'm glad we cleared that up."

"Try to see it from Volodya's point of view."

"Do I have to?"

"Magnus Larsen was a valuable asset in more ways than one," said Morosov. "A messy scandal involving his private life would have led to his removal as CEO of DanskOil. Volodya was never going to allow that to happen. He'd invested too much money in him."

"How much are we talking about?"

"Several million a year in so-called consulting fees, payable to his account at TverBank, none of which he declares to the Danish tax authorities. He also has a house in Rublyovka, the billionaires' suburb west of Moscow. For all intents and purposes, Magnus Larsen is a Russian oligarch now."

"A Russian oligarch with a Danish passport and impeccable Danish manners."

"A Russian emissary in everything but name," added Morosov. "But why is Magnus Larsen of any interest to you, Allon?"

"Because he paid a Copenhagen rare book dealer to

steal a painting. And for the life of me, I can't figure out why."

"Perhaps you should ask him."

"I intend to, Sergei."

Morosov stood on the veranda of his dacha, his arm raised in farewell, as the SUV rolled through the camp's open gate and started back toward Rosh Pina. Only Ingrid, in the backseat next to Gabriel, returned the gesture, which brought a broad smile to the Russian's face.

"Who is that man?"

"I'm afraid I can't answer that question. Suffice it to say, he was very helpful."

"How so?"

"Peter Nielsen's client was the CEO of Denmark's largest oil-and-gas company."

"Magnus Larsen?"

Gabriel nodded. "And it gets better, I'm afraid."

"I'm not sure that's possible."

"Magnus has been a Russian asset for twenty years. And if my friend is to be believed, there's a dead girl in his past."

"Did Magnus kill her?"

"He didn't have to. The Russians did it for him."

"Was the girl Russian, too?"

"Danish, actually. It happened about ten years ago. My source wasn't able to tell me her name."

"It shouldn't be hard to figure out who she was. I'll have a look at the missing persons database."

"How about some dinner first? I know a place not far from here." Gabriel exchanged a look with Mikhail. "The view is extraordinary, and the food and ambience are very authentic. I think you'll find it interesting."

"More interesting than a secret detention center in the middle of nowhere?"

"Oh, yes," said Gabriel, reaching for his phone. "Much."

23
Tiberias

The voice at the other end of the cellular connection sounded strong and clear and resolute.

"When should Gilah and I expect you?"

"Twenty minutes or so."

"You'd better hurry, my son. Otherwise, I might not be alive when you get here."

"I suppose I deserve that."

"You do," growled the voice, and the connection was lost.

But how to paint an accurate portrait of such a man to an outsider like Ingrid? It would have been easier, thought Gabriel, to explain Bach's influence on the development of Western music—or the role that water had played in the formation and maintenance of life on earth. Ari Shamron was the captor of Adolf Eichmann and the twice-former director-general of the Office. He had given the service its identity, its creed, even its very language. He was the Memuneh, the one in charge. He was eternal.

His honey-colored villa stood atop an escarpment overlooking the Sea of Galilee. Gabriel prepared himself for the worst as the SUV scaled the steeply sloped drive—Shamron had been battling a litany of serious ailments for years—but the man waiting in the forecourt appeared in remarkably good health. He was dressed, as usual, in a pair of neatly pressed khaki trousers, an oxford-cloth shirt, and a leather bomber jacket with an unrepaired tear in the left shoulder. His right hand, the hand he had clamped over Eichmann's mouth, was clutching a handsome olive wood cane. His hated aluminum walker was nowhere to be seen.

"How long have you been standing there?" asked Gabriel.

"If you must know, I haven't budged since the day you left Israel." He looked at the woman at Gabriel's side. "Who's the girl?"

"Her name is Ingrid."

"Ingrid what?"

"Johansen."

"It's not a Jewish name."

"With good reason."

"Is she planning to convert?" asked Shamron. "Or is your relationship purely physical?"

"Ingrid was with me in Denmark last night when—"

"A Russian assassin tried to kill you."

"Actually," said Gabriel, "I'm convinced that she was the target."

"I'm relieved. But what did she do to irritate the Russians?"

"I'm still working on that."

"In the Upper Galilee?" Shamron's rheumy eyes settled on Mikhail. "With him?"

Gabriel smiled but said nothing.

"I don't suppose my niece knows you're here."

Shamron's niece was Rimona Stern, the first female director-general in the history of the Office.

"She's under the impression I'm in Jerusalem," said Gabriel.

Shamron's eyes narrowed. "You're not involved in some sort of palace intrigue, are you?"

"I wouldn't dream of it."

"You never fail to disappoint me, my son." Shamron raised a liver-spotted hand toward the front door. "Perhaps we should have something to eat. It's been a very long time."

The dinner that Gilah Shamron served that evening was not authentically Israeli but hastily ordered Chinese takeaway. Her husband fumbled with a pair of plastic chopsticks for a moment or two, then cast them aside and attacked his beef and broccoli with a fork instead. Never one for small talk, or to squander a captive audience, he delivered a sober lecture on the state of the world. As was often the case, he was worried—worried that the old postwar order was collapsing, that democracy was under siege, that China and Russia were displacing the United States as the Middle East hegemons faster than anyone might have imagined. He was hearing rumors that Beijing was attempting to negotiate a rapprochement between the Saudis and the Iranians, an unimaginable prospect even a year ago.

He asked Gabriel about his new life in Venice, and seemed pleased to learn that Chiara and the children were thriving. He was most intrigued, however, by the presence of a newcomer at his table, this beautiful young Danish woman named Ingrid Johansen who claimed to be a freelance IT specialist. It was clear that Shamron, a lifelong inhabitant of the secret world, didn't believe a word of it. He knew an operator when he set eyes on one.

Finally, he pushed himself to his feet and, with apologies to Ingrid and Mikhail, led Gabriel downstairs to the room that doubled as his study and workshop. The innards of a 1958 Grundig 3088 were scattered across his worktable. Tinkering with old radios was Shamron's only hobby. And when he had no radios at his disposal, he tinkered with Gabriel.

He settled atop a stool and switched on the lamp. "You first," he said.

"Where would you like me to begin?"

"How about the beginning?"

"In the beginning, God created—"

"Why don't you skip to the part about Ingrid?"

"She's a computer hacker and professional thief."

"Sounds like my kind of girl."

"Mine, too."

Shamron's old Zippo lighter flared. "Tell me the rest."

He waited until the conclusion of Gabriel's five-minute presentation before looking up from the radio. The expression on his face was one of profound disapproval. "You could be prosecuted, you know."

"For the unfortunate incident involving the Armenian gangsters in Antwerp?"

"For taking your friend into a secret Office interrogation facility. If I had pulled a stunt like that, I would have never heard the end of it."

"You know what they say about imitation, Ari."

"I'm inimitable, my son. But it is rather rich, don't you think? How many times did you berate me for keeping my hand in the game? How many times did you tell me that you were done with this life?" Shamron treated himself to a satisfied smile. "And now, as they say, the shoe is on the other foot."

"Are you quite finished?"

"I'm just getting started." He crushed out his cigarette and lit another, secure in the knowledge that Gabriel, now thoroughly on the defensive, wouldn't dare utter a word of protest. "And what have you concluded from this inquiry of yours thus far?"

"I was trained by a wise intelligence officer never to force the pieces."

"Because when we force the pieces, we sometimes see what we want to see rather than the truth—wouldn't you agree?"

"Sometimes," replied Gabriel.

"And then, of course, there is the problem of missing pieces. We don't know what we don't know. And I can assure you, my son, you don't have all the pieces."

"Which one am I missing?"

"The man who lived in the beautiful villa by the sea in Amalfi."

"Lukas van Damme?"

"Actually," said Shamron, "we used to call him Lucky Lukas."

"Van Damme was an Office asset?"

"For several years."

"Why?"

Shamron raised his hands in the shape of a mushroom cloud and whispered, "Boom."

24

Tiberias

South Africa's nuclear weapons program, among the most secretive ever undertaken, commenced in 1948—the same year that Israel declared its independence and three years after the United States brought a swift end to World War II by dropping a pair of atomic bombs on the Japanese cities of Hiroshima and Nagasaki. Initially, South Africa pursued a plutonium bomb, but in 1969 it switched to a uranium-enrichment program fed with domestically mined ore. By the late 1980s it had assembled a nuclear arsenal of six gun-type bombs, the last such weapons ever built.

A seventh bomb was under construction in 1989 when South Africa voluntarily agreed to surrender its nuclear weapons program—in part because the embattled White-minority regime, its days numbered, did not wish to leave an atomic arsenal in the hands of a Black-led successor government. The six finished gun-type bombs were dismantled under international supervision, and the weapons-grade uranium was stored at the Pelindaba Nuclear Research Center west of Pretoria. The facility experienced at least three serious security breaches in the post-apartheid era, the last in 2007, which the government initially dismissed as a routine attempted burglary. An independent probe of the incident, carried out by a former employee of the international investigations firm Kroll Inc., would later conclude that the raid was carried out by a disciplined team of heavily armed men who entered the facility in an attempt to locate and steal the nuclear explosives.

Among the most carefully guarded aspects of the South African nuclear program were the names of the scientists who enriched the uranium to weapons-grade strength and fashioned it into deliverable gun-type bombs. One of the scientists was a nuclear physicist named Lukas van Damme. With his life's work abandoned, and his country ruled by Blacks, he sought an escape hatch. He found one in his father's Durban-based shipping company, which he renamed LVD Marine Transport and moved to Nassau. Which was where, on a sun-blasted afternoon in

August 1996, he met a man called Clyde Bridges, the London-based European marketing director of an obscure Canadian software firm. "Bridges" was merely a flag of convenience. His real name was Uzi Navot.

"What was the occasion?" asked Gabriel.

"Panic at King Saul Boulevard," replied Shamron.

"Over what?"

"It turns out that Lucky Lukas wasn't so lucky at all, especially when it came to the shipping business. He stayed afloat by turning his company into a criminal enterprise. He was also hanging out with all the wrong people."

"Anyone in particular?"

"Representatives of countries that were seeking to duplicate South Africa's successful nuclear program."

"And we couldn't have that."

"Definitely bad for the Jews."

"But you skipped an important part of the story," said Gabriel. "The part about how the Office knew that Lukas van Damme, an ethically challenged shipping executive, was the brains behind South Africa's nuclear program."

"Van Damme? The brains behind the program?" Shamron shook his head slowly. "The South Africans never would have been able to build those bombs without our help."

"What was the nature of Uzi's conversation with Lucky Lukas that afternoon?"

"A friendly reminder of the perils he faced if he ever so much as considered sharing the family recipe with one of our adversaries."

"Negative treatment?"

"It wasn't necessary to go into specifics. Our reputation spoke for itself. Lukas practically recruited himself."

"How did you use him?"

"With my approval, Lukas sold his services to anyone who would pay for them, which gave us access to the nuclear hopes and dreams of our most implacable enemies, including the Butcher of Baghdad and his Baathist buddy in Damascus. I also turned LVD Marine Transport of Nassau, the Bahamas, into a subsidiary of King Saul Boulevard global enterprises of Tel Aviv."

"Brilliant."

"Quite," agreed Shamron. "The operation was an extraordinary success."

"But the Office's connections to the South Africans went far beyond a single nuclear physicist."

Shamron regarded him through a veil of blue-gray smoke. "*My* connections to the South Africans—isn't that what you mean?"

Gabriel was silent.

"If you are asking whether I helped the South Africans develop nuclear weapons, the answer is no. The Office under my leadership was capable of many things, but not that. But was I in favor of our efforts to assist the South Africans? Did I advise a succession of prime ministers from both the left and right to continue the program? I most certainly did."

"And when the South Africans decided to give up the nuclear weapons that we had helped them build?"

"I worked closely with my South African counterpart to ensure that there was no spillage of the weapons-grade uranium after the bombs were dismantled. I even toured the Pelindaba Nuclear Research Center."

"And?"

"Needless to say, I was deeply concerned about security. But I was also left with a nagging suspicion that the South Africans had misled the International Atomic Energy Agency and the rest of the global community about the number of weapons they had assembled."

"Why?"

"The assistance that we provided South Africa gave us unique visibility into the program. Our scientists were convinced that there were probably *two* unfinished weapons, not one."

"I assume you raised it with your counterpart."

"On several occasions," said Shamron. "And each time I did, he assured me that there were only seven weapons. Some years later, though, I was told by a trusted source that he had lied to me."

"Who was the source?"

"Lukas van Damme." Shamron resumed work on the Grundig radio. Absently, he asked, "How do you think we should handle my niece?"

"Given the fact that she possesses her uncle's volcanic temper, I think we should proceed with extreme caution." Gabriel paused, then added, "Perhaps even a bit of deception."

"My favorite word. What do you have in mind?"

"Someone should probably tell her that I conducted an unauthorized debriefing of Sergei Morosov."

"Yes," agreed Shamron. "Someone probably should."

25

Narkiss Street

S hamron's call went straight to her voice mail, and by the time she finally got back to him, the culprit was approaching Jerusalem. The hour was late, and her mood was brittle, which these days was its default setting. Her famous uncle wasted little time getting to the point.

"I'm going to kill him," was her reply.

"Another first," said Shamron. "But it would undoubtedly do irreparable harm to your career."

"Not if I make it look like an accident."

"It's only a rumor, mind you. You should probably look into it before you do anything rash."

"Where did you hear this rumor?"

"I'm not at liberty to say."

"You're not involved in something, are you, Ari?"

"Me? Never."

She rang the head of the Office's internal security division, who immediately raised the guards at the secret detention facility in the Biriya Forest. Yes, they admitted, the legend had arrived there unannounced earlier that evening. And, yes, he had questioned the prisoner for approximately an hour.

"Why did you let him in?"

"He's Gabriel Allon."

"You should have called me."

"He ordered us not to."

"Was he alone?"

"Mikhail was with him."

"Anyone else?"

"A woman."

"Name?"

"Didn't seem to have one."

"Describe her."

"Definitely not Israeli."

The woman in question, a hacker and professional thief named Ingrid Johansen, was at that same moment experiencing her first vision of Jerusalem. Shortly before midnight she followed Gabriel into an apartment located at 16 Narkiss Street, in the heart of the city's historic Nachlaot district. His phone rang as he was opening the French doors to the eucalyptus-scented night air. It was his successor on the line.

"I want you in my office tomorrow morning at half past ten," she said, and the call went dead.

Gabriel showed Ingrid into the guest room, then crawled into bed. By way of deception, he thought, thou shalt do war.

He was awakened at five minutes past seven by the thunderclap of an explosion. At first he thought it was only a dream, but the distant wail of sirens—and the sight of Ingrid standing anxiously in the doorway of his bedroom—told him that was not the case. In the kitchen they watched the breaking coverage on television while waiting for the coffee to brew. The bomb had exploded at a bus stop in Givat Shaul at the western entrance of Jerusalem.

"We drove past it last night," explained Gabriel.

"Are there casualties?"

"Several."

"Was anyone killed?"

"We'll know soon enough."

A second bomb exploded while Gabriel was in the shower—another bus stop, this one in north Jerusalem, so close it shook the apartment. He dressed in one of the dark suits hanging in his closet and returned to the kitchen to find Ingrid hunched over her laptop, her brow furrowed in concentration.

He filled a stainless-steel insulated tumbler with coffee and tightened the lid. "With a bit of luck, I'll be back in a few hours. Under no circumstances are you to leave this apartment."

"Actually," she answered, her fingers rattling the keyboard, "I wasn't planning to."

Downstairs, an armored SUV idled curbside in Narkiss Street. Ten minutes later, after clearing the snarled traffic around Givat Shaul, he was headed down Highway 1 toward Tel Aviv. His rediscovery, he thought, was nearly complete. All he required now was the consent of his successor. She was one of his better works. Girl with a volcanic temper. Girl with a will of iron.

One of the first directives that Gabriel had issued as chief of the Office was among his most enduring— his swift cancellation of a fully approved and Knesset-funded plan to move the service's headquarters from downtown Tel Aviv to an empty plot of land along Highway 2 in Ramat HaSharon. The colossal price tag was reason enough to kill the project, but Gabriel was also concerned by the proposed site's proximity to a busy shopping mall and cineplex. And then there was the name of the nearest highway interchange for which the area was known. "By what metonym shall we refer to ourselves?" Gabriel had lamented. "Glilot Junction? We'll be the laughingstocks of the intelligence world."

Besides, the drab building at the far end of King Saul Boulevard was not without its charms, beginning with the fact that it was actually a building within a building, one with its own power supply, its own water and sewer lines, and its own secure communications system. Analytical and support staff entered the premises through a door in the lobby, but division chiefs and field operatives came and went via the underground parking garage. So, too, did current and past directors-general, who also had use of a private lift to whisk them to the top floor. As Gabriel rose slowly skyward, he inhaled the previous occupant's cologne—Ébène Fumé Eau de Parfum by Tom Ford. Chiara had sent her a bottle of the stuff on the occasion of her last birthday, the hundred-milliliter size because fifty milliliters wouldn't do. Four hundred euros and change. International shipping not included.

The lift deposited Gabriel directly into the reception area of the executive suite, where a slender young man in a formfitting sport jacket and stretch trousers sat behind a barren desk. He indicated a pair of chairs and Gabriel sat down.

"What happened to Orit?" he asked.

"The Iron Dome? Director Stern thought it was time for a change."

Did she really? Gabriel would have paid serious money to see that one.

Just then the director's door opened, and out stepped Yaakov Rossman, the chief of Special Ops, otherwise known as the dark side of a dark service. With his steel-wool hair and pumice face, he looked like a cleaning implement for hard-to-reach areas—like eastern Syria and northern Iran, thought Gabriel.

"What are you doing here?" he asked, his tone accusatory.

"I'll find out in a minute or two."

"I'd love to chat, but I'm afraid we have a bit of a crisis on our hands."

"Really? Where?"

"Nice try," said Yaakov, and hurried out as though his crisis was taking place in a room at the end of the hall.

Gabriel looked at the receptionist, who was pondering the phone on his desk. A long moment passed before it emitted a two-note burst of tone, the signal that the director's office was secure. "She'll see you now, Mr. Allon."

"Lucky me."

Rising, he endured a wait of several seconds for the snap of the automatic locks. The room he entered was strangely unfamiliar. The desk, the seating area, the conference table: everything had been replaced and re-arranged. Even the video wall, which had received a significant technological upgrade, had been relocated. The decor was trendy and sophisticated, high finance as opposed to low cunning; the lighting was subdued. Somewhere beyond the tightly drawn shades was Tel Aviv and the Mediterranean, but you would never know it. The office might have been in London or Manhattan or Silicon Valley.

Rimona was contemplating something on a tablet computer. She wore a dark two-piece suit, the unof-ficial uniform of the Israeli espiocrat, and a pair of fashionable pumps. The demands of the job appeared to have melted a few kilos from her generous figure. Or perhaps her weight loss was intentional, thought Gabriel, part of an overall image reboot—like the new way she was wearing her sandstone-colored hair or the subtle change in her makeup. Somewhere under her suit of armor was the little girl whose left hip Gabriel had bandaged when she fell off her scooter while careening down her famous uncle's treacherously steep drive. But you would never know that, either.

Her silence was intentional, a shopworn technique used by Office operatives since time immemorial to make adversaries feel uncomfortable. Gabriel decided to seize the initiative.

"Yaakov seemed rather surprised to see me."

"I'm sure he was." She looked up from the screen and regarded him through a pair of cat-eyed spectacles, another new addition to her look. "I was hoping to keep your visit private, but my meeting with Yaakov ran longer than expected."

"Sounds like you have a real mess on your hands."

She didn't bite. "Yaakov would have never discussed an ongoing operation with someone who lacked the proper clearances. Such a violation of basic Office principles would have led to his immediate dismissal."

"Am I allowed to ask whether you two are playing nicely, or is that classified, too?"

"As you might imagine, Yaakov and I have had our ups and downs."

"He assured me that he was thrilled by your appointment."

"He's a liar by trade. We all are," she added.

"I hope I didn't leave you with a problem."

"It's nothing I can't handle."

"How much longer is he planning to stick around?"

"Yaakov will be leaving the Office in a few weeks to pursue opportunities in the private sector."

"Who gets Special Ops?"

"Mikhail. I'm giving Yossi my old job at Collections. Dina will take over as head of Research."

"It sounds as though you have your team in place."

"Who are we kidding? They're *your* team," said Rimona. "I just made a few minor adjustments."

Gabriel surveyed his old office. "More than a few."

"You cast a long shadow. For a month or so after you left, we all sat around staring at one another, wondering how we were going to carry on without you. The only way we could deal with it—"

"Was to pretend I didn't exist."

"We *did* keep your old chalkboard, though. It's still downstairs in 456C. It's like Churchill's underground war rooms down there." Rimona gestured toward the seating arrangement. "Won't you sit down?"

"Perhaps we should do this standing."

Her expression darkened. Girl with a volcanic temper. Her voice had a razor's edge. "How did my uncle know that you met with Sergei Morosov?"

"Because I told him."

"And did you also tell my uncle to tell *me* about it?"

"Yes, of course."

"Why did you do that?"

"To make you angry enough to take out a contract on my life."

"You succeeded." She placed a hand to her forehead as though taking her temperature. She was definitely running hot. "Why didn't you simply request authorization to meet with your old source?"

"Because sometimes it is better to beg for forgiveness than to ask for permission."

She lowered her hand. "Beg."

"I want to run an operation for you."

"Oh, you can do better than that."

"I *beg* of you to let me run an operation for you."

"What sort of operation?"

"It might be better if I had my old chalkboard."

"Why didn't I think of that?" Rimona reached for her phone. "You're a sneaky bastard."

"I was trained by the best."

"So was I, Gabriel. Never forget that."

26

Mount Herzl

The patient suffered from a combination of post-traumatic stress disorder and psychotic depression. Nowhere in her voluminous files, however, was there an accurate description of the terrible incident that had induced her condition, only a vague reference to a terrorist bombing in a European capital. Also absent was the name of the man, a former spouse, who continued to bear the cost for her round-the-clock care. As was often the case, he gave her doctor scant warning of an impending visit.

"I'll make the arrangements," said the doctor. "But I'd like a few minutes alone with you first."

"Is something wrong?"

"An encouraging development, actually."

The hospital was located in what was once the Arab village of Deir Yassin, where Jewish fighters from the Irgun and Lehi paramilitary organizations massacred more than a hundred Palestinians, including women and children, on the night of April 9, 1948. Several of the village's buildings remained standing, including the old Ottoman-era house where the doctor, a rabbinic-looking figure with a wondrous beard of many colors, kept his private office.

The former husband of his longtime patient sat on the opposite side of the cluttered desk. It had been several minutes since either man had uttered a word. In fact, the office was silent except for the occasional turn of a page. One page every minute, thought the doctor, who was watching the sweep of the second hand on the wall clock. Not fifty-eight seconds, and not sixty-four. One page every sixty seconds. The man must have been born with a stopwatch in his head.

"These are extraordinary," said Gabriel at last.

"I thought so, too."

"Whose idea was it?"

"Hers."

"You never encouraged her?"

The doctor shook his head. "In fact, given the disordered state of her mind, I was afraid of what she might produce."

"What happened?"

"I walked into the art room one day about six months ago, and there she was with a charcoal pencil in her hand. It was as if she suddenly remembered that she used to be a painter. She insisted I show them to you." He paused, then added, "No one but you."

The silence returned. The doctor stared into the cup of lukewarm tea he was holding in his hand.

"She's still madly in love with you, you know."

"I know."

"Most of the time she thinks the two of you are still—"

"I know," he said firmly.

The doctor addressed his next words to the window. "I've never judged you, Gabriel. But at this stage of her life—"

"And what about my life?"

"Is there something you want to talk about?"

"Like what?"

"Anything at all."

"I have a wife. I have two young children."

"You want to lead a normal life? Is that what you're saying? Well, some of us aren't meant to. You're not normal, Gabriel Allon. You will never be normal."

"Surely there's something I can take for that."

The doctor emitted a dry, quiet laugh. "Your sense

of humor is a defense mechanism. It prevents you from facing the truth."

"I face the truth every time I close my eyes. It never goes away, not for a single minute."

"That's the healthiest thing I have ever heard you say." The doctor placed his cup and saucer on the desk, spilling the remnants of his tea in the process. "You should know that when the bomb exploded in Givat Shaul this morning, it was very loud here at the hospital. I'm afraid she didn't react well."

"How is she now?"

"Five minutes ago, when I told her that you were coming to see her, she was overjoyed. But with Leah . . ." The doctor smiled sadly and rose to his feet. "Well, one never knows quite what to expect."

She was seated in her wheelchair in the sunlit garden, a blanket round her frail shoulders, the twisted remnants of her hands knotted in her lap. Gabriel kissed the cool, firm scar tissue of her cheek and sat down on the bench next to her. She stared sightlessly into the middle distance, as though unaware of his presence. He had endured periods of catatonia like this before. Her first had lasted thirteen years—thirteen years without so much as a word or a flicker of recognition in her dark eyes. It had been like communing with a figure in a painting. He had longed to restore her but could not. The woman in a wheelchair, oil on canvas, was beyond repair.

He opened her sketchpad and leafed through its pages.

"What do you think of them?" she asked suddenly.

He looked up with a start. *What do you think of them?* They were some of the first words she had ever spoken to him, long ago, when they were students together at Bezalel. Then, as now, he had been turning the pages of her sketchbook with unconcealed admiration—and perhaps even a trace of envy. She was eager to hear his opinion of her work. After all, he was Gabriel Allon, the talented only son of Irene Allon, perhaps the finest Israeli painter of her generation.

"Well?" she prodded him.

"I'm overwhelmed."

"It took some getting used to." She raised her contorted right hand. "Holding a pencil again, that is."

"It doesn't show."

He turned the pages. Landscapes, Jerusalem cityscapes, still lifes, nudes, portraits of her fellow patients, of her doctor, of her ex-husband at the age of thirty-nine. That was how old Gabriel had been the night a Palestinian master terrorist named Tariq al-

Hourani concealed a bomb beneath his car in Vienna. It was Leah, with a turn of the ignition, who had detonated the device. The explosion had killed their young son, Daniel, whom Gabriel had strapped into his car seat a moment earlier. Leah, despite suffering catastrophic burns and injuries, had somehow survived. The final minutes of their life together played ceaselessly in her memory like a loop of videotape. She was trapped in the past with no escape. And Gabriel was her constant companion.

Her eyes traveled over him, as though she were searching for a lost object in the cluttered closets of her memory. "Are you real?" she asked at last. "Or am I hallucinating again?"

"I'm real," he assured her.

"Where are we, my love?"

"Jerusalem."

She lifted her eyes to the cloudless sky. "Isn't it beautiful?"

"Yes, Leah," he answered, and waited for the familiar refrain.

"The snow absolves Vienna of its sins. Snow falls on Vienna while the missiles rain on Tel Aviv." She came back to him. "I heard an explosion this morning."

"It was a bus stop in Givat Shaul."

"Was anyone killed?"

There was no point in lying to her. Besides, with any luck, she wouldn't remember. "A boy of fifteen."

Her expression darkened. "I want to talk to my mother. I want to hear the sound of my mother's voice."

"We'll call her."

"Make sure Dani is buckled into his seat. The streets are slippery."

"He's fine, Leah."

Gabriel averted his eyes as her mouth opened in horror and she relived the explosion and the fire. Five minutes elapsed before the memory released her.

"When were you last here?" she asked.

"A few months ago."

She frowned. "I might be mad, Gabriel, but I'm not a fool."

"You're not mad, Leah."

"What am I?"

"You're unwell," he said.

"And what about you, my love? What is your condition these days?"

He considered his answer. "Satisfactory, I suppose."

"Trust me, it could be worse." She trailed a forefinger through his hair. "But you definitely need a haircut."

"It's the new me."

"I was rather fond of the old you." Her fingertip

moved down the ridge of his nose. "Are you working on anything?"

"An altarpiece by Il Pordenone."

"Where?"

"In Venice, Leah. Chiara and I are living in Venice again."

"Oh, yes. Of course. Tell me, do you and Chiara have children?"

"Two," he reminded her. "Raphael and Irene."

"But Irene is your mother's name."

"She's been dead for many years."

"You must forgive me, Gabriel. I'm unwell, you know." She tilted her face toward the sky. She was leaving him again. "Is she pretty, this wife of yours?"

"Yes, Leah."

"Does she make you happy?"

"She tries," said Gabriel. "But when I close my eyes . . ."

"You see my face?"

He made no reply.

"It seems we share the same affliction." She lowered her chin and gave him a shrewd sidelong look. "Does your poor wife know about this?"

"I do my best to hide it from her, but she knows."

"She must resent me terribly."

"She loves you dearly."

"Does she really?" She tried to smile, but the light was draining slowly from her eyes. "I want to hear the sound of my mother's voice," she said.

"So do I," replied Gabriel quietly.

"Make sure Dani is buckled into his seat."

"Be careful driving home."

"Give me a kiss, my love."

He knelt before her wheelchair and laid his head in her lap. His tears soaked her gown.

"Isn't it beautiful?" she whispered. "One last kiss."

It was dusk when Gabriel returned to Narkiss Street. He found Ingrid as he had left her, hunched over her laptop at the little café table in the kitchen. She had not changed her clothing or combed her hair, and there was no evidence she had eaten a bite of food all day. Indeed, it looked to Gabriel as though she hadn't looked up from her screen in the seven and a half hours he had been away.

She did so now. "You look positively dreadful," she said.

"So do you."

"But at least I have something to show for it." She rotated the computer and adjusted the screen. "Found her."

"Who is she?" asked Gabriel.

"The dead girl in Magnus Larsen's past."

27

King Saul Boulevard

Returning to the fold, even temporarily, was not as simple as flipping a switch. There were documents to sign, declarations to make, and dormant security clearances that required resuscitation. To that end, Gabriel was required to endure a session with the bloodhounds of Security, who were still seething over his unauthorized visit to Sergei Morosov's dacha in the Upper Galilee.

"Recent suspicious foreign contacts?" asked his inquisitor.

"Too many to count."

"Try."

"An art thief, an art forger, numerous art dealers, a crooked Antwerp diamond broker, the leader of a

Corsican crime family, a reporter from *Vanity Fair*, the head of security at the Pierre Hotel in Manhattan, a Swiss violinist, a British supermarket heiress who tried to murder her husband, the usual crowd at Harry's Bar in Venice."

"What about foreign intelligence contacts?"

"A friend from MI6. He used to work as a contract killer for the leader of the Corsican crime family."

"You neglected to mention the Danish woman."

"Did I?"

"We think you should put her on a plane, boss."

"Don't worry, I intend to."

The remaining rituals of his return to Office discipline were less contentious. The service doctors subjected him to a rigorous examination and, bullet wounds and fractured vertebrae notwithstanding, found him to be in remarkably good health. Identity supplied him with two new false passports—one Israeli, the other Canadian—and Technology gave him a new Solaris phone and a new laptop with the latest version of the Proteus hacking malware. Accounting did what it always did, which was implore him to hold down his operational expenses. He responded by giving Accounting a request for reimbursement for those expenses he had already incurred, and warned there was more to come.

Rimona offered him use of an empty office on the fifth floor, but to no one's surprise he headed straight for Room 456C instead. Once a dumping ground for obsolete computers and worn-out furniture, the windowless subterranean dungeon was now known throughout King Saul Boulevard only as Gabriel's Lair. He arrived there to find Dina Sarid, the future head of Research, gazing at the chalkboard. It was covered with Gabriel's impeccable script.

"I'm pretty good at spotting connections," said Dina. "But I must admit, I'm totally stumped."

"That makes two of us."

"Who is Magnus Larsen?"

"The CEO of DanskOil."

"And Lukas van Damme?"

"A former South African nuclear scientist who spent several years on our payroll."

Dina placed a fingertip next to the name of the Russian president. "His name I recognize, of course. His, too." It was the name of a Dutch Golden Age painter from the town of Delft. "But how are they linked?"

"Is there any chance you can help me find the answer?"

"My plate is rather full at the moment."

"But?"

Her dark eyes surveyed the names on the chalkboard. "Where should we begin?"

The headquarters of the Danish energy giant DanskOil was located in the Copenhagen district known as Frederiksstaden. The formidable building was among the most secure in Denmark—more secure, even, than most Danish government offices. Nevertheless, the company's computer network was no match for the hackers of Unit 8200, Israel's signals intelligence service. They slipped through the back door at dawn, and by midday they had the run of the place. Gabriel directed them toward the DanskOil–RuzNeft joint venture—and to the computer and telephones of the firm's chief executive officer, Magnus Larsen.

It took nothing more than a simple Internet search, however, to produce a mountain of material on this most public of men. Magnus Larsen was a colossus, a titan, a setter of trends, a visionary. He was brilliant and erudite, he was impossibly handsome. In company promotional videos, he was a man of action, never in the boardroom, always astride a pipeline or atop a drilling platform. Magnus of the chiseled jaw and piercing blue eyes. Magnus of the windblown blond hair. There was nothing Magnus couldn't do. There was no challenge Magnus hadn't met.

When asked by a fawning journalist how he would describe himself, he replied, "A businessman with the soul of a poet." A collector of rare books, he had somehow found time in his punishing schedule to publish four of his own. His most recent, *The Power of Tomorrow*, had been a major Scandinavian bestseller and gave rise to speculation he might seek elective office. Magnus dismissed the chatter as laughable. He was above politics. He dwelled on a higher plane.

He was also extraordinarily rich. His most recent annual compensation package was the equivalent of $24 million. His sprawling home in Hellerup, Copenhagen's most exclusive suburb, overlooked the Baltic Sea. His wife, Karoline, was a socialite and patron of the arts with a knack for getting her picture in the paper. His two boys, Thomas and Jeppe, were regarded as Denmark's most eligible bachelors—and determined, it seemed, to stay that way.

He had his detractors, though, especially on the environmentally sensitive left. Publicly, he made appropriate noises about a warming planet and transitioning to renewable sources of energy. But in private settings he was known as a climate skeptic who joked about extracting every last drop of oil and gas from beneath Denmark's territorial waters before it was too late. "A pipe dream" was how he described the

Danish government's much-heralded commitment to be carbon-neutral by 2050. "No pun intended."

And then there were those who found fault with his seemingly inexplicable attraction to all things Russian. It was public knowledge that he spoke Russian fluently, that he was acquainted with the Russian president, and that he owned a large home in the moneyed Moscow suburb of Rublyovka, where he rubbed shoulders with the oligarchs and members of the Kremlin inner circle. Unlike most Western energy companies, which had unwound their Russian deals after the invasion of Ukraine, DanskOil had stubbornly refused to walk away from its joint venture with RuzNeft, which accounted for nearly a third of the company's petroleum. Magnus claimed it was simply a question of the bottom line, that leaving Russia would result in a $12 billion write-down. His detractors, however, wondered if there was something more.

He was known to be something of a fanatic when it came to his schedule, which was laid out for him in fifteen-minute intervals by his longtime personal assistant, Nina Søndergaard. Unit 8200 located the schedule on her computer, along with numbers for Magnus's six mobile phones. His primary device was an iPhone. Gabriel attacked it with Proteus, and by midafternoon it was exporting the entirety of the data stored in its memory—emails, text messages, Internet browsing history, telephone metadata, GPS location data. It was also acting as both an audio and video transmitter, which allowed Gabriel and Dina to be remote participants in a meeting of DanskOil's senior staff.

Like most modern executives, Magnus Larsen was a dedicated user of encrypted email and text message services—namely, ProtonMail and Signal. He was also something of a shutterbug. Gabriel found numerous snapshots of Moscow and the Russian countryside. There were also photos of Russian business elites and Kremlin celebrities taken in casual social settings. Mad Maxim Simonov, the nickel king of Russia. Oleg Lebedev, otherwise known as Mr. Aluminum. Yevgeny Nazarov, the Kremlin's silver-tongued if mendacious spokesman. Arkady Akimov, the wildly wealthy oil trader who had recently fallen to his death from the window of an apartment on Baskov Lane in Saint Petersburg.

Gabriel likewise breached the mobile device of the late Copenhagen antiquarian book dealer Peter Nielsen, which produced a similar geyser of data. He appealed to Rimona for additional staff, and she reluctantly gave him Mikhail and his wife, Natalie Mizrahi, the only Western intelligence officer to have penetrated the insular ranks of the Islamic

State. They were soon overwhelmed, however, by the arrival of nearly one hundred thousand pages of DanskOil files, leaving Gabriel no choice but to take emergency measures. He needed someone who knew how to read a balance sheet, how to distinguish a clean transaction from a dirty one, how to follow the money. It was for that reason, and many others, that he picked up his phone and called his old friend Eli Lavon.

No one was sure exactly when he arrived—or even how he managed to get into the building—but then that was his special talent. He was a ghost of a man, easily overlooked, soon forgotten. Ari Shamron once said of Lavon that he could disappear while shaking your hand. It was only a slight exaggeration.

Like Gabriel, Lavon was a veteran of Wrath of God, the secret Office operation to hunt down and assassinate the perpetrators of the Munich Olympics massacre. In the Hebrew-based lexicon of the team, he had been an *ayin*, a tracker and surveillance specialist. When the unit finally disbanded, Lavon was afflicted with numerous stress disorders, including a notoriously fickle stomach. He settled in Vienna, where he opened a small investigative bureau called Wartime Claims and Inquiries. Operating on a shoestring budget, he managed to track down millions of dollars' worth of looted Holocaust assets and played a significant role in prying a multibillion-dollar settlement from the banks of Switzerland.

Against all better judgment, Lavon agreed to serve as chief of Neviot, the Office's physical-and-electronic surveillance division, during the five operationally intense years of Gabriel's term as director-general. And on the day of Gabriel's retirement, Lavon had retired, too. An archaeologist by training, he had planned to spend the final years of his life sifting through the soil of Israel's ancient past. "And now," he said, lighting a cigarette in spite of his old friend's well-known aversion to tobacco, "I am once again in this dreadful broom closet, staring at a mountain of documents."

The woman responsible for Eli Lavon's sudden recall to duty spent that day alone at Narkiss Street, as outsiders were strictly forbidden to enter King Saul Boulevard. During the next forty-eight hours, Gabriel saw little of her—a few minutes early in the morning, a few minutes late at night. He came and went from King Saul Boulevard as quietly as possible, but word of his return ricocheted through the building. Naturally, speculation abounded. Did he regret relinquishing the throne so soon? Was his chosen successor in trouble? Did she require his helping hand on the tiller? Was Shamron somehow involved?

Long ago, perhaps, when he recruited a wayward South African nuclear scientist named Lukas van Damme. Gabriel was convinced that the solution to the puzzle could be found somewhere in Van Damme's past. Dina found evidence to support his hypothesis on the third day of their investigation, in the location data stored in Magnus Larsen's phone—and in saved copies of his meticulous daily schedule. Evidently, Larsen had spent nearly a week in Johannesburg in August exploring the purchase by DanskOil of a South African mining company. He had flown there on a chartered aircraft and stayed at the Four Seasons Hotel. No other company executives had accompanied him.

Upon his return to Copenhagen, Magnus headed not for DanskOil headquarters but to Nielsen Antiquarian, where he remained for nearly two hours. Reason enough, thought Gabriel, to pull the CEO aside for an off-the-record chat. But where? Once again, they found the answer in Magnus's schedule. It seemed the DanskOil CEO would attend the Berlin Energy Summit in ten days' time. In fact, he was planning to deliver an address on Europe's energy future in the post-Ukraine world, with a book signing to follow.

Gabriel included Magnus Larsen's travel plans in the by-the-book request for an operational charter that he delivered to Rimona that evening at six fifteen. An analyst by trade, she read the file twice.

"For the record," she said at last, "you have no proof that Lukas van Damme's murder is connected to some phantom eighth South African weapon."

"Not a shred," agreed Gabriel. "But I know he wasn't killed over just a painting."

"Why would an advanced nuclear power like Russia be mixed up in a scheme to acquire two chunks of thirty-year-old South African highly enriched uranium?"

"I can think of several possibilities, none of them good. But I'm convinced that Magnus Larsen is involved."

"What makes you think you can turn him around?"

"The dead girl in his past."

Rimona removed a photocopy of Ingrid's passport from the file. "You're only going to get one bite at the apple. Are you sure you want her to take it?"

"She's perfect."

"At least let her spend some time with the instructors."

"Eli and I will work with her in Berlin."

Rimona exhaled slowly. "Who else?"

"Mikhail, Natalie, and Dina."

Rimona placed the file in her out-box. "If you so much as order Lebanese carry-out while you're in Berlin, I want to know about it. *Before* you order it, not after. You will seek permission for everything you do. Otherwise, you will be begging for your life. Do we have a deal?"

"We do."

Rising, he started toward the door.

"Why didn't you say my name?" Rimona asked suddenly.

Gabriel turned. "I'm sorry?"

"When I asked about personnel, you named everyone from the old team but me."

"You're the chief now, Rimona."

Her smile was brittle. "The chief who fell off her kick scooter."

Gabriel went into the antechamber and pressed the call button for the director's private lift. "And one more thing," she shouted from the office that once was his. "No Moscow."

28

Vissenbjerg

If there were two fringe benefits to Gabriel's unexpected return to the secret world, they were Travel and Transport, the Office units that moved field agents securely through airports and train terminals around the world and then supplied them with untraceable vehicles when they arrived at their destinations. Gabriel's Audi A6 sedan was waiting on the second level of the parking garage of Copenhagen Airport with the key taped inside the left-rear wheel well. He tore it loose, then, crouching, searched the undercarriage.

"Looking for something in particular?" asked Ingrid.

"My contact lens."

"I didn't realize you wore them."

"I don't."

He unlocked the doors and dropped behind the wheel. Ingrid slid into the passenger seat and frowned. "You could have rented a hybrid, you know."

"I'm a Venetian. I'm entitled to emit."

"Is that so?"

"I don't own an automobile, I walk or use public transportation everywhere I go, and my wife is allergic to air-conditioning. Furthermore, my daughter is something of a climate radical. If I so much as strike a match, I get an earful. My greatest fear is that she's going to glue herself to a painting in the Accademia."

He opened the glove box. Inside, wrapped in a protective cloth, was a Beretta 92FS.

"Membership obviously has its privileges," said Ingrid.

"I have a boatload of mileage."

"Where's mine?"

"I'm afraid that Office regulations strictly forbid issuing firearms to non-employees. Besides," said Gabriel, "we're just going to have a word with her, not shoot her."

He wedged the gun into the waistband of his trousers and reversed out of the space. Five minutes later he was headed west on the E20 into the blinding light of the autumn sun. He lowered the visor and took a long look into the rearview mirror.

"Are we being followed?"

"There are several dozen cars with Danish registration behind us. Whether any of them belong to the Danish police or the PET remains to be seen."

"How is it possible they didn't detain you at the airport?"

"It might have had something to do with the fact I was traveling on a Canadian passport."

"And if they figure out that you're back in the country?"

"My friend Lars Mortensen will read me the riot act. It will be one for the ages. An all-time showstopper."

"When are you planning to tell him that you're investigating one of Denmark's most prominent citizens?"

"At a time and place of my choosing."

The motorway carried them southward along the gentle curve of Køge Bay. Gabriel took a brief detour through the beach town of Karlstrup Strand, one that included a series of consecutive right turns.

Ingrid kept watch in her side-view mirror. "And what is my relationship to your service, exactly?"

"You're a temporary asset. We will use you for a single specific task and go our separate ways."

"I suppose you had a look at my background to make certain I wasn't a shady character."

"With all due respect, Ingrid, you *are* a shady character."

"Does that mean you didn't bother to run a check on me?"

"Did I say that?"

"Find anything interesting?"

"With the exception of Skagen CyberSolutions, remarkably little. In fact, you're a bit like that Russian who tried to kill us in Kandestederne the other night. You don't seem to exist."

"Plastering one's picture all over social media isn't a good idea in my line of work."

"No arrests?"

"Never."

"And you're not wanted anywhere?"

"Yes, of course. But the police are looking for the wrong version of me."

"How many are there?"

"I have more than a dozen different looks and identities that I use, but not all of them are women."

"I see."

"You've never?"

"Posed as a man? I do it all the time."

"As a woman," said Ingrid.

"I posed as a Catholic priest once. But never as a woman."

She looked at him carefully. "I have to say, you *do* look a bit like a priest, Mr. Allon."

"There's no one by that name in this car."

"What shall I call you?"

"How about Herr Klemp?"

"Klemp?" She was aghast. "No, that won't do."

"How about Herr Frankel instead?"

"Much better. But what's your first name?"

"Why not Viktor?"

"There was a German Expressionist painter by that name," said Ingrid. "His daughter survived the war and settled in Israel. She lived in a kibbutz called Ramat David. She was a painter, too. Irene Allon was her name."

"I knew her son," said Gabriel. "He was a real shady character."

The sun was an orange disk by the time they crossed the towering Great Belt Bridge. Vissenbjerg, population three thousand, lay another ninety kilometers to the west. It was dark when Gabriel and Ingrid arrived at their destination, a Q8 petrol station and convenience mart on an otherwise uninhabited stretch of road north of the town center. Next to the petrol station was a café with four outdoor tables. All were unoccupied, as were the tables in the brightly lit interior. Standing behind the counter, eyes on her phone, boredom on her face, was a magenta-haired woman in her mid-thirties.

"Perhaps I should make the approach," said Gabriel.

"Why you?"

"Because during your previous two visits to Jørgens Smørrebrød Café, you committed serious crimes, including the theft of an iPhone 13 Pro that belonged to a dead rare books dealer."

"But there's no evidence of my crimes."

"There is, however, a witness who undoubtedly told the police about a customer who was working on her laptop when the surveillance video magically disappeared."

"I can handle her," said Ingrid, and climbed out of the car without another word. When she entered the café, the magenta-haired woman behind the counter looked up from her phone and smiled warmly. The ensuing conversation was by all appearances convivial. Perhaps, thought Gabriel, he had been mistaken about the woman's recollections of the incident involving the faulty network video recorder.

After a moment the woman placed a cup of coffee and a Danish smørrebrød sandwich on the counter.

Ingrid paid for her order in cash and sat down at the table nearest the window—the same table, noted Gabriel, at which she had been sitting the night that Grigori Toporov of the SVR murdered Peter Nielsen and stole *The Concert* by Johannes Vermeer for a third time. But why didn't Grigori simply wait for Nielsen to deliver the painting to his client Magnus Larsen? Why a risky assassination in a fashionable quarter of Copenhagen?

Gabriel reprimanded himself for once again trying to force the pieces. Better to wait until he had a capable hand to guide him. Rimona was right; he would get only one bite at the apple. One chance to convince Magnus Larsen to see the error of his ways. An appeal to his conscience wouldn't do; Magnus, it seemed, hadn't one. Gabriel would have to break him, smash him to pieces, and then offer him a chance at redemption. The girl would be his ally. The dead girl in Magnus Larsen's past.

Volodya put his thumb on the girl. And the girl vanished without a trace . . .

The two women in Jørgens Smørrebrød Café were each gazing intently at their phones, though Ingrid was typing on hers with text-message intensity. Pausing, she glanced over her shoulder at the magenta-haired woman, who instantly looked up from her device with a start. Ingrid dispatched another text, to which the magenta-haired woman immediately replied. Two more exchanges of messages followed. Then the magenta-haired woman stepped from behind the counter and sat down at Ingrid's table.

Ingrid quickly sent one final text message. It landed on Gabriel's phone a few seconds later.

She gets off at 7pm. Go away.

Which left Gabriel nearly an hour to kill. He spent it driving back and forth along the same ten-kilometer stretch of empty road. Eight times he passed the little auto plaza, and eight times he glimpsed Ingrid sitting at the window table of Jørgens Smørrebrød Café with Katje Strøm, identical twin sister of Rikke Strøm, missing since September 2013.

When Gabriel turned into the auto plaza at seven o'clock, the interior lights of the café were extinguished, and the sign in the window declared the establishment to be closed for the evening. The door opened a moment later, and a man of perhaps forty emerged, followed soon after by Ingrid and Katje Strøm. The man set off toward a worn-out hatchback in the car park; Ingrid and Katje Strøm, toward Gabriel's rented Audi. Ingrid slid into the passenger seat, Katje climbed in back. She lit a cigarette and murmured something in Danish.

"Frankel," replied Ingrid. "His name is Viktor Frankel."

29
Helnæs

Their mother was a Greenlander Inuit, their father a commercial fisherman. Not long after the girls were born, he bought a plot of land on the island of Møn and tried his hand at farming. And when the farm failed, he drank. Their mother split when the girls were twelve and went back to Greenland. Their father killed himself a couple of years later in a single-car road accident. The first police to arrive at the scene said his blood reeked of akvavit.

Neither child wanted to join their estranged mother in Greenland, so the state looked after them until they finished their secondary education. Katje stayed down in Møn, but Rikke went up to Copenhagen and found work as a shopgirl and waitress. Eventually, she

landed a job at Noma, Copenhagen's three-star culinary mecca, where she delivered food to the tables of
Denmark's wealthiest citizens. While she was walking home one evening to the dungeon she shared with
four other girls, a good-looking man in an expensive
car lowered his window and asked Rikke whether he
might have a word with her.

"He said his name was Sten. Said he worked for a
rich and powerful man. Said this rich and powerful
man was interested in meeting Rikke. Said he could be
helpful to Rikke. Maybe get her a better job. You know
how these things go, Herr Frankel."

"Did Sten happen to mention the name of the rich
and powerful man who wanted to make your sister's
acquaintance?"

"No. Not that night."

They were parked on a deserted stretch of beach
on the island of Helnæs, not far from the lighthouse.
Ingrid and Katje were sitting on the hood of the Audi
drinking Carlsberg. Katje was chain-smoking, using
the stub of one cigarette to light the next. She was
under the impression that Herr Frankel was a freelance
German investigative journalist who had long been interested in her sister's case.

"How did she respond to Sten's generous offer?"

"She told him to fuck off."

"Did he?"

"Not for long. A couple of nights later, he was back again."

This time Rikke agreed to meet with Sten's rich and powerful employer—in an apartment in fashionable Nørrebro. Soon she was living in Nørrebro herself, rent free and alone. When Katje paid her sister a visit, she was shocked by what she found. The closets and drawers were filled with chic clothing, the refrigerator was stocked with expensive wine, and Rikke's wallet was stuffed with cash. The watch on her wrist was a Cartier. The diamond on her finger was at least two carats.

"How did she explain the sudden change in her standard of living?"

"A new job."

"Did she describe it?"

"Personal assistant to a wealthy businessman."

"That's one way of putting it."

"I said essentially the same thing."

"How did she react?"

"She told me the truth."

"Did she identify her patron?"

"Never. She said it was part of their arrangement."

"Total secrecy?"

Katje nodded and cracked open another Carlsberg.

"I told Rikke that she was making a terrible mistake. That she would end up like our mother. That she was little better than a prostitute." She flicked the stub of her cigarette into the darkness. "And guess what my sister told me?"

"I imagine she told you to fuck off and mind your own business."

"More or less."

"Did you?"

"Eventually. But we had a terrible quarrel first. It ended when her phone rang and she told me I had to leave at once. It was the last time I ever saw her."

Rikke had grown so isolated that for a long time no one realized she was missing. Finally, an old colleague from Noma contacted the police after receiving no response to dozens of calls and texts, and the police got in touch with Katje. No, she told them, she had not heard from her sister in several weeks. Was there anything unusual going on in her life? She was being kept by a wealthy and powerful man. Did Katje know this man's name? Her sister refused to divulge it. It was part of their arrangement.

When another week went by with no sign of her, the police declared Rikke missing and opened an investigation. There were stories on television and in the papers, and flyers posted all over the country. Katje couldn't go anywhere without being mistaken for her missing twin sister. She added streaks of crimson and purple to her coal-black Inuit hair and wore heavy makeup to hide her Inuit eyes.

"For the first time in my life," she said, "no one called me racist names."

Abandoned by her mother, orphaned by her father, lost without her twin sister, she decided to start a new life in a place where no one had ever heard of her. She chose Vissenbjerg because she saw a help-wanted advert for a counter job at Jørgens. She had three other part-time jobs as well and did volunteer work for a group called Enough, a feminist organization dedicated to the prevention of violence against women and children. She shared an old farmhouse with five other women. They were lost girls. Throwaway girls. Girls who had been disowned by their families. Girls who had been beaten by husbands and lovers. Girls who had been raped. Girls with scars. Girls with tracks on their arms. They never said an unkind word to one another. Never raised their voices. Never quarreled. They were a family. They had nowhere else to go.

And yet Katje never forgot Rikke—and never forgave herself for not dragging her out of that apartment in Nørrebro. She rang the police every Friday at 5:00 p.m. without fail and requested an update on the status of the investigation. Most of the calls lasted no more than a minute or two. Rikke, it seemed, had vanished without a trace.

"What about the man she was seeing?"

"The police told me they were never able to determine who he was."

"How hard could it have been?"

"Trust me, I asked the same question."

On the tenth anniversary of Rikke's disappearance, the Danish police appealed to the public one final time for help in finding her. And when no new leads were forthcoming, they gave Katje the last of the evidence they had removed from the apartment. Interestingly enough, there was no jewelry or money. In fact, the only item of any value was an old book.

"Which was odd," said Katje, "because my sister was never much of a reader."

"Do you still have it, by any chance?"

"The book?" She nodded. "I thought about selling it and donating the money to Enough, but I kept it instead. It's really quite beautiful."

"What is it?"

"*Romeo and Juliet.*" Katje Strøm shook her head slowly. "How pathetic is that?"

It was not truly a farmhouse but a cottage hidden away in a dense stand of trees on the road between Vissenbjerg and Ladegårde. Ingrid waited at the door while Katje went in search of the book. Two other women waited with her. Lost girls, thought Gabriel. Throwaway girls. Girls who had been raped and abused. Girls with scars.

Finally, Katje reappeared, clutching a leather-bound volume. She gave the book to Ingrid, and Ingrid handed Katje something in return—something she accepted reluctantly. Then the two women embraced, and Ingrid returned to the Audi. She waited until the cottage was behind them before switching on the overhead light and opening the cover of *Romeo and Juliet* by William Shakespeare.

"Hodder and Stoughton. Published in 1912."

"I don't suppose there's a sales receipt."

"No. But there's a lovely bookmark from the shop where it was purchased." Ingrid held it up and smiled. "Nielsen Antiquarian, Strøget, Copenhagen." She slid the bookmark between the pages of the century-old volume and switched off the light.

"How much did you give her?" asked Gabriel.

"Everything I had."

"That was very generous of you."

"I only wish I could have given her more."

"So do I," said Gabriel. "Starting with the name of the man who made her sister disappear without a trace."

"When are you planning to tell her?"

"Actually, I had someone else in mind for the job."

"Really? Who?"

"Magnus Larsen."

30
Berlin

The villa overlooked the Branitzer Platz in the leafy Berlin neighborhood known as Westend. It was solid and stately and hidden behind a high wall overgrown with ivy. Inside, there were two large drawing rooms, a formal dining room, and four bedrooms. Housekeeping, the Office division that acquired and administered safe properties, had put it on ice for a rainy day. Gabriel, before leaving King Saul Boulevard, informed Housekeeping that there was wet weather in the forecast.

Dina Sarid arrived a few minutes after nine o'clock the following morning, having caught the early El Al flight from Ben Gurion to Brandenburg. Bleary-eyed, she went into the kitchen in search of coffee. Ingrid was leaning against the counter, mug in hand, scrolling through the headlines on her phone.

Dina pointed toward the empty decanter resting on the warmer of the Krups automatic. "You're supposed to make a new pot."

"Says who?" asked Ingrid without lifting her eyes from the screen.

"It's proper safe house etiquette. Everyone knows that."

Ingrid took down a bag of Tchibo from the cabinet and placed it on the counter. "Just add water to the top of the machine and push the little button."

Mikhail and Natalie were routed through Frankfurt and arrived in the early afternoon. Eli Lavon, after spending three hours on the tarmac in Geneva because of a faulty cockpit light, finally showed up at six in the evening. He tossed his bag into the last remaining bedroom—not surprisingly, it was the smallest and darkest in the villa—and introduced himself to the new recruit.

"You must be Ingrid," he said.

"I must be," she replied.

"Gabriel tells me you're rather good at what you do."

"He says the same about you."

"He'd like me to show you some of our methods."

"Actually, I prefer to do things my way."

Over a dinner of takeaway Thai, they got to know

one another a little better. Gabriel shared a few details of the team's many operations together, all unclassified, and hinted at the horrors they had witnessed and the dangers they had faced. He made it clear that they did not judge Ingrid for the life she had chosen. The nature of their work oftentimes required them to break laws themselves and to occasionally utilize the services of professional criminals, including thieves.

"You possess a set of skills that make you uniquely suited to the task at hand. But you are part of an operational team now. A team that has slipped into Berlin without alerting the host service. Therefore, you have to follow certain rules."

"Such as?"

"You are never to leave the safe house alone or without telling us where you're going. And you must never drink the last cup of coffee without making another pot. There are some things," said Gabriel with a smile, "that are simply beyond the pale."

Ingrid turned to Dina. "Can you ever forgive me?"

"Bring us Magnus Larsen," replied Dina. "And I'll think about it."

He remained at DanskOil HQ in Copenhagen until half past seven that evening, with his compromised iPhone never far from reach. It was a chauffeur-driven ride of fifteen minutes up the Baltic coast to his home in exclusive Hellerup. The dogs were pleased to see him, but his wife, Karoline, scarcely acknowledged his arrival. Their strained dinner conversation required little translation on Ingrid's part. All was not well in the Larsen marriage.

He worked late into the night and sent and received numerous emails and text messages. Only one was related to Russia, a guided missile directed at DanskOil's VP for communications to formulate a new strategy for fending off public and political pressure to dissolve the RuzNeft deal. He turned in at midnight—without so much as a word to Karoline—and was up again at 4:00 a.m. for his morning exercise regime. Fifteen minutes on the treadmill. Fifteen minutes on the rowing machine. Fifteen minutes of weight training. Fifteen minutes of walking the dogs.

By eight o'clock he was back at DanskOil HQ, where his day unfolded in perfect fifteen-minute increments, scripted and timed by the industrious Nina Søndergaard. Shortly before lunch she presented Magnus with a draft itinerary for his upcoming trip to the Berlin Energy Summit. He would be arriving Tuesday morning and departing Thursday evening, with his remarks and book signing scheduled for Wednesday at 4:00 p.m. Like many of the attendees, he would be staying at the Ritz Carlton Hotel in the Potsdamer Platz. He would be dining with his fellow energy executives on both nights and planned to conduct twelve one-on-one side meetings, each lasting exactly fifteen minutes.

Not surprisingly, there was not a single spare minute in the entire document. There was, however, a personal errand that Magnus intended to run during his brief stay in Berlin—a visit to Lehmann Antiquarian on Fasanenstrasse at 2:00 p.m. Wednesday. A search of the CEO's private email account revealed that Herr Lehmann had recently come across a rare first edition of *Death in Venice and Other Stories* by Thomas Mann, Alfred A. Knopf, 1925. Near fine condition, original dust jacket, light restoration to the crown of the spine.

The venue for the summit was the Berlin Congress Center in the Alexanderplatz, in what was once East Berlin. The price of admission was five thousand euros, which granted patrons access to all speeches and panel discussions, as well as the marketing pavilion on the lower level, which was where the real work of any such gathering took place. Three partners from LNT Consulting, a newly formed company based in Berlin, were late registrants. Technology built the company's website, and Identity saw to the business cards. Mikhail would be posing as the firm's Russian-born CEO, Natalie as his trusted lieutenant. Ingrid's credentials and business card identified her as Eva Westergaard. Eva handled the IT.

She was also a professional thief who needed to be brought to heel before she could be dispatched into the field with a team of intelligence operatives. They subjected her to a crash course in the basics of their tradecraft, a tradecraft that had been perfected on the secret battlefields of the Middle East and Europe and handed down from generation to generation. They taught her how to walk and how to sit, how to speak and when to keep her peace, when to hold back and when to move in for the kill. She responded by telling them that everything they had told her was useless or, worse, mistaken. And when Mikhail objected, she stole the watch off his wrist. Eli Lavon would later describe it as one of the sweetest pieces of misdirection and sleight of hand he had seen in some time.

Leaving nothing to chance, Gabriel forced Ingrid to sit through several hours of dress rehearsals with her two colleagues from LNT Consulting. Afterward Eli Lavon took her into the streets of Berlin for a bit of pavement work. She dropped him on Friedrichstrasse in five minutes flat. Then, in violation of Gabriel's edict, she vanished for the remainder of the afternoon. When she finally returned to the safe house, she was clutching several shopping bags filled with new clothing.

"A little something to wear for the conference," she explained.

She also had gifts for each member of the team—Hermès scarves for the women, cashmere sweaters for Gabriel, Mikhail, and Lavon. They were boxed and wrapped. Even so, Gabriel insisted on seeing proof of purchase.

"I'm insulted."

"You're a kleptomaniac."

"I'm a professional thief. There's a difference." She handed over the receipts. "Satisfied?"

Technology had the website up and running on Friday, and the business cards arrived at the safe house Saturday morning. So, too, did three sets of tickets and credentials for the 2023 Berlin Energy Summit, one of which bore the name Eva Westergaard, an IT specialist from LNT Consulting. Ms. Westergaard was of the opinion that she should approach her target at Lehmann Antiquarian at 2:00 p.m. Wednesday, but Gabriel overruled her. It was a twenty-minute drive from the Alexanderplatz to Fasanenstrasse. Magnus would almost certainly be pressed for time. Indeed, he might well be on a phone call when he arrived at the shop, making conversation with a stranger impossible.

No, the book signing was the safer play. Ingrid would be assured of at least a moment or two of the target's attention, more than enough time to make a first impression on a man with a track record the likes of Magnus Larsen. The energy executive would doubtless find her charm and beauty difficult to resist. He might make time in his busy schedule to have a drink with her—or even dinner. And if he foolishly agreed to return to her home in the Berlin neighborhood known as Westend, he would find a terrible surprise waiting for him. The dead girl in his past. Or at least a reasonable facsimile.

31
Vissenbjerg–Berlin

The text arrived as Katje Strøm was assembling an arrangement of tulips and irises at the Blomsten flower shop in Vissenbjerg, the favorite of her four part-time jobs. She waited until the customer had left the store before plucking the phone from the back pocket of her jeans. The message was from Ingrid Johansen, the friend of the German journalist who was investigating the disappearance of Katje's sister, Rikke. It seemed the journalist had made an important discovery. He was wondering whether Katje would be willing to come to Berlin to review his findings.

She started to reply by text but on a whim dialed Ingrid instead. She answered instantly.

"When?" asked Katje.

"Immediately."

"Can't."

"Why not?"

Because it was a Monday, and she had her afternoon gig behind the counter at Jørgens. And because tomorrow was Tuesday, which meant she was pulling an 8:00 a.m. shift at Spar.

"Tell your employers you have a family emergency."

"I don't have any family."

"Tell them something, Katje. But please come to Berlin."

"How am I supposed to get there?"

"A car will pick you up when you get off work."

Only later did it occur to Katje that Ingrid had not inquired as to her whereabouts or the time her shift at Blomsten ended. Nevertheless, when she left the shop at 2:00 p.m., a car was waiting curbside in Østergade. There were two women inside. Both were dark haired, but the one behind the wheel had the olive-complected skin of an immigrant. The one in the passenger seat greeted Katje in German-accented English.

"I'm Dina," she said. "And this is my friend Natalie. We work with Viktor."

"What does he want to show me?"

"It would be better if we allowed Viktor to explain."

They stopped at Katje's house long enough for her to

pack a bag and grab her passport, then made the drive to Copenhagen Airport in record time. Their seats for the hour-long flight to Berlin were in first class. They were met inside the terminal by a tall, lanky man with skin like alabaster.

"This is Mikhail," explained the woman named Dina. "Mikhail, say hello to Katje."

Smiling, he led them outside to the short-term car park, where his Mercedes sedan was waiting. Thirty minutes later it drew to a stop outside a substantial walled villa. Katje assumed they were in Berlin but couldn't be sure. It was her first visit to the city.

"Viktor's place," explained Dina.

"I never knew journalists made so much money."

"His father was a wealthy industrialist. Viktor chose journalism to atone for his father's sins."

They all four headed up the garden walk to the entrance of the villa. Ingrid opened the door to them and, kissing Katje's cheek, drew her inside. The man she knew as Viktor Frankel waited in the drawing room. He was accompanied by a crumpled little figure who looked as though he was wearing all his clothing at once.

The little man averted his gaze as his companion rose slowly to his feet. His eyes were shockingly green. Katje hadn't noticed that the other night when they were parked along the beach on Helnæs island. His accent, when at last he spoke, was no longer German. It was something vague and indistinct that Katje couldn't place.

"Forgive me," he began. "But I'm afraid I've misled you. My name isn't Viktor Frankel, it's Gabriel Allon. And my friends and I need your help."

The name meant nothing to Katje. "What do you want me to do?" she asked.

He explained.

"Are you sure he's the one?"

"I have a feeling we'll know the instant he walks through the door."

Katje ran a hand through her magenta-colored hair. "But I don't look like Rikke anymore."

"Don't worry," he said. "Your friend Ingrid will take care of that."

It was Katje who had given the police the photograph they used for the missing person bulletin. She had snapped it, quite on impulse, on the day she saw her sister for the last time. Rikke was standing in the entranceway of her apartment in Nørrebro. Her smile was artificial and did not extend to her eyes; she was clearly annoyed with the person behind the camera. That was the image that had been plastered on billboards and lampposts around Denmark. That was how Katje recalled her sister's face.

A printout of the photograph was adhered to the mirror in the upstairs bathroom. Ingrid returned Katje's hair to its normal color, jet black, and trimmed it to the approximate style worn by her sister. Undoing the changes to her face required nothing more than removing her heavy eye makeup. Ten long years had passed, but the resemblance was startling nevertheless. She was the girl Magnus Larsen had spotted one night at Noma. The dead girl in Magnus Larsen's past.

That evening the girl shared a pleasant meal with Ingrid and her friends from Israeli intelligence. Their quiet laughter and easy camaraderie stood in stark contrast to the mood at Magnus Larsen's dinner table 450 kilometers to the north in the wealthy Copenhagen suburb of Hellerup. He worked late into the night and was up again at 4:00 a.m. for his usual morning workout. Five hours later he was seated comfortably aboard a chartered business jet, hurtling blindly toward his own undoing.

The protesters set out in a column from the Brandenburg Gate, led by the Swedish adolescent who was the new mascot of their movement. By the time they reached the Alexanderplatz, they were fifty thousand strong. The gods of oil and gas, their bank accounts swollen, their stock prices in the stratosphere, flowed past them in their petrol-powered limousines, unseeing. They were in the midst of the most profitable year in the history of their industry, a stroke of good fortune brought about by the war in not-so-distant Ukraine. As was often the case, human misery had been good for their bottom line.

The Americans came in force, the French in style. The Saudis wore western garb, the British were cloaked in gray. There were Canadians and Brazilians, Mexicans and Iraqis, but not a single Russian. For the first time since the summit's inception, there were no representatives from Russia's state-owned oil and gas companies. All were in agreement the gathering was better off for it.

But admission was not limited to the giants of the industry like Chevron and Shell. There were also delegations from hundreds of oil services firms, the drillers and explorers and manufacturers of platforms and pipelines. And then there were the smallest fish in the sea, the advisory firms that marketed themselves as spotters of trends and solvers of problems—firms like LNT Consulting of Berlin, a boutique outfit that advised legacy oil producers on how to transition from fossil fuels to renewables.

Their delegation was three in number, confident in demeanor, and striking in appearance—a tall gray-eyed man of Russian heritage, a woman who might or might not have been an Arab, and a beautiful Dane named Eva Westergaard. She dazzled at the morning coffee, lit up the booths in the marketing pavilion, and was the only thing anyone was talking about after the opening remarks by Germany's energy minister. "Westergaard," she said, pressing a business card into the outstretched paw of the chrome-haired Exxonite who approached her after the speech. "Have a look at our website. Let us know if you think we can help."

Lunch was served in the glassy atrium. While making her way down the buffet line, she passed within a meter or two of Magnus Larsen, the highly regarded CEO of DanskOil. Magnus, it seemed, was the only person in the room who hadn't noticed her. He was engaged in an unpleasant conversation with the CEO of BP PLC, who was wondering why DanskOil hadn't had the decency to walk away from its joint venture with RuzNeft.

"And spare me the drivel about your responsibilities to your shareholders," said the man from BP. "We lost twenty-five billion when we threw in the towel in Russia."

"But you made out rather well on the deal, didn't you, Roger? That was quite a bonus you gave yourself."

"Sod off, Magnus."

The highlight of the afternoon session was an altogether alarming speech on the global economic outlook by a former American treasury secretary. The team from LNT Consulting sat in the fifth row, two rows behind the CEO of DanskOil. At the conclusion of the program, they filed out of the auditorium and went their separate ways. The CEO of DanskOil headed off to a cocktail party at the historic Hotel Adlon; the team from LNT Consulting, to a stately villa overlooking the Branitzer Platz in the Berlin neighborhood known as Westend.

There they passed a quiet evening with the dead girl in the CEO's past. And they debated once again how best to make their approach. The woman called Eva Westergaard renewed her request to do it at 2:00 p.m. at Lehmann Antiquarian on Fasanenstrasse. Her colleagues, however, insisted she adhere to the plan that they, with their many decades of operational experience, had put in place. The CEO would be pressed for time at the bookstore and no doubt distracted by the volume of Thomas Mann. The book signing following his remarks was the better bet.

And so the woman called Eva Westergaard spent the remainder of that evening reading the CEO's most recent book, which, she had to admit, wasn't half bad.

It was in her handbag, pages flagged with sticky tabs, as she followed her colleagues into the Berlin Energy Summit at nine the following morning. She sat stone-faced through a panel discussion called "Oil as a Force for Global Change," turned heads at the midmorning coffee, and listened with interest to a presentation regarding the efficacy of carbon capture.

Lunch commenced in the atrium at one o'clock. The chrome-haired Exxonite invited the woman to join him, but she dined with her colleagues from LNT Consulting instead. At approximately one fifteen, she excused herself and set off unaccompanied toward the restrooms. It was nearly half past when her two colleagues, both veteran intelligence operatives, realized their mistake. They immediately rang the stately villa in the Branitzer Platz and explained the situation.

"What do you mean, you *lost* her?"

"I mean she is not among those present. Missing without a trace."

"She didn't."

"I think she did, boss."

A series of frantic calls to her mobile phone received no answer, but at 2:04 p.m. her whereabouts became clear. Eli Lavon would later call it one of the sweetest recruitments he had heard in some time.

32
Fasanenstrasse

The floor was scuffed and warped, the lighting subdued. There were books on shelves, books on tables, books under glass, and a single book—*Death in Venice and Other Stories* by Thomas Mann—resting on the desk occupied by Günter Lehmann, owner and sole proprietor of Lehmann Antiquarian. He regarded Ingrid unblinkingly through rimless spectacles. He wore a cardigan sweater and a burgundy-colored ascot. His cheeks were pink with windburn.

"Were you interested in something in particular?"

"Actually, I was wondering if I might just have a look round."

"Be my guest."

She lowered her eyes toward the volume lying on the desk. "It's in wonderful condition."

"I'm afraid it's spoken for."

"A pity." She walked over to one of the glass-covered cases. "Good heavens."

It was a first edition of *The Annex*, a work that would later come to be known as *The Diary of Anne Frank*.

"Have a look at the one lying next to it," suggested Günther Lehmann.

A first edition of *Ulysses* by James Joyce. "Is it really signed?" asked Ingrid.

"Jim," answered the bookseller.

Next to the volume of Joyce was a copy of *Atlas Shrugged* by Ayn Rand. And next to the Rand was *The Beautiful and Damned* by F. Scott Fitzgerald.

"One of my favorite books," said Ingrid.

Lehmann rose and unlocked the case. "The cover has been fully restored." He placed the book atop the glass. "Clean hands?"

"Spotless." Ingrid lifted the cover gently. "I'm afraid to ask the price."

"I might be willing to let it go for thirty-five." He pointed to the copy of *Ulysses*. "That one will cost you a million and a half."

A buzzer groaned.

"Will you excuse me?" asked Lehmann, and returned to his desk.

A dead bolt snapped, a bell chimed, a presence entered the room. Ingrid paid it no mind; she was staring at the signed first edition of *Ulysses*. A million, maybe, she was thinking. But only a fool would pay a million and a half.

The presence in the room was suddenly speaking to Lehmann. Something about the recent murder of a rare book dealer in Copenhagen. A terrible shock to us all, he was saying. Peter was a friend. I did a good deal of business with him over the years.

Ingrid turned to the first page of *The Beautiful and Damned* and read of Anthony Patch. She did not look up at the presence, did not acknowledge its existence. She waited for the presence to notice her. That was the way the game was played.

For now, the presence was entranced by *Death in Venice and Other Stories*. The photographs had not done it justice, he was saying. Yes, of course he would take it. Couldn't live without it.

Ingrid leafed through the pages of the Fitzgerald.

"I have a first edition of *Gatsby*," boomed a voice at her back.

It belonged to the presence. He had addressed Ingrid

in German. She counted slowly to five, then turned. Magnus of the chiseled jaw and piercing blue eyes. He seemed too large for the room.

"I beg your pardon?" she replied in the same language.

"*Gatsby*," he repeated. "I have a first edition. It was a very small print run, you know. Twenty-five hundred copies, if I'm not mistaken."

"Lucky you."

He indicated the copy of *The Beautiful and Damned*. "Are you going to buy that one?"

"Not at thirty-five." She closed the book's cover. "Too rich for my blood."

"You're Danish," he informed her.

"I'm afraid so," she answered, switching languages.

"Perhaps I should introduce myself. My name is—"

"I know who you are, Mr. Larsen." She drew the copy of *The Power of Tomorrow* from her handbag. "In fact, I'm coming to your speech this afternoon."

"Are you in Berlin for the energy summit?"

"I live here, actually."

"What sort of work do you do?"

"A consulting startup," she said, and then explained.

"We're doing extraordinary things with wind," said Magnus Larsen the visionary. "It's ten percent of our business, and growing."

"Yes, I know. DanskOil is the example we hold up to the rest of the industry." She offered him the book. "Perhaps you would sign it for me now and save me the trouble of having to stand in a line."

"I rather doubt you'll have to wait long."

"Does that mean you won't sign it?"

"Not if it means I won't see you later."

She slid the book into her handbag and started for the door.

"You didn't tell me your name," said Magnus.

She stopped and turned. "It's Eva."

"Eva what?"

"Westergaard."

"Give me a moment to pay for this, Eva Westergaard, and I'll take you back to the Congress Center."

"That's really not necessary, Mr. Larsen."

"Of course it is." He pointed toward the copy of *The Beautiful and Damned*. "That one, too, Günther."

She tried to object, but it was no use. The indomitable Magnus Larsen wouldn't hear of it. The deal was done, he declared. There was no going back.

"But it's thirty-five thousand euros."

"Would it make you feel better if I told you that I put it on my DanskOil expense account?"

"Heavens no."

The book was balanced on Ingrid's knees, wrapped in protective polypropylene, as they sped eastward across the Tiergarten in Magnus's hired Mercedes limousine. When they arrived at the Congress Center, she once again attempted to take her leave, but Magnus insisted that she accompany him to the green room where he would prepare for his appearance. It took place, as scheduled, at 4:00 p.m., not in the center's cavernous main hall but in a smaller auditorium on the second level. The audience was respectable; Magnus's remarks were well received. Ingrid sat in the front row. Her two colleagues from LNT Consulting were not in attendance.

She waited until the signing line had ebbed before approaching the table. Magnus's inscription was kind but not suggestive, nothing that might come back to bite him.

"Where are you off to?" he asked as he screwed the cap onto his Montblanc pen.

"Home."

"Husband?"

"Cat."

"Can the cat look after itself for an hour or two?"

"What did you have in mind?"

The summit's second-night cocktail party. The venue was the futuristic new headquarters of Germany's largest media conglomerate. They stayed for an hour.

"Hungry?" he asked as they were leaving.

"Surely you have plans."

"I canceled them. What are you in the mood for?"

"Your choice."

He chose Grill Royal. Perfect salads, perfect steaks, a perfect American movie starlet at the next table. Over espresso, the playful banter, the brushing of hands, the delicate negotiations.

"I couldn't," she said.

"Why not?"

"Half the summit attendees are staying there. They'll think I'm sleeping with you in order to drum up a little business for my struggling startup."

"Are you?"

"Actually, it was the thirty-five thousand you dropped on the first-edition Fitzgerald." She drew the volume from her handbag and placed it on the table between them. "Which one are you?" she asked.

"The beautiful or the damned? Somewhere in between, I imagine." He gazed thoughtfully into his wineglass. The businessman with the soul of a poet. "Aren't we all?"

The Branitzer Platz was not a proper square but a traffic circle with a small green park at its center. Ingrid directed the limousine driver to the correct address, and Magnus followed her through the gate. The key was in her hand when they reached the door. In the darkened entrance hall, she allowed him to kiss her, once. Then she led him into the half-light of the drawing room, where a girl gowned in white sat reading a copy of *Romeo and Juliet* by William Shakespeare, Hodder & Stoughton, 1912. Near fine condition, slight damage to the spine, some shelf wear.

33
Branitzer Platz

He stood motionless for a long moment, slack-jawed and silent, gazing in horror at the apparition before him. Finally, he wheeled around and saw Mikhail blocking the path to the door. "Who the bloody hell are you?" he demanded to know in his most convincing boardroom voice.

"I'm your past catching up with you at last."

Magnus Larsen's huge right hand became a clenched fist.

"I wouldn't, if I were you," said a voice at his back. "I can assure you, it won't end well."

Magnus pirouetted again and saw Gabriel standing next to the chair where Katje Strom, identical twin sister of Rikke Strøm, missing since September 2013, sat reading *Romeo and Juliet* by William Shakespeare.

The CEO retreated in fear.

Gabriel smiled coldly. "I suppose that means I don't have to go to the trouble of introducing myself."

Magnus froze and squared his shoulders.

"Nothing to say for yourself, Magnus? Cat got your tongue?"

The piercing blue eyes blazed in anger. "You won't get away with this, Allon."

"Get away with what?"

"Whatever game it is you think you're playing."

"Trust me, Magnus. This isn't a game."

He looked at Ingrid. "Who is she?"

"Her name is Eva Westergaard. She works for a boutique energy consulting firm called—"

"Who is she?" asked Magnus a second time.

"It doesn't matter who she is," answered Gabriel. "It's what she represents that's important."

"And what is that?"

"An opportunity for you to deal with this as an intelligence matter rather than a criminal one. If, however, you fail to take advantage of the situation before you, all the sewage from your despicable life will spill into public view." Gabriel lowered his eyes toward Katje. "Including her."

"I know who she is. And I had nothing to do with her sister's disappearance."

"That's because your friend Vladimir Vladimirovich handled it for you. You were so important to him they gave you a code name. They call you the Collector." Gabriel removed the volume of Shakespeare from Katje's hands. "It is undoubtedly a reference to your passion for rare books."

"Do you know how many times I've been called a Russian asset because of my friendship with Vladimir?"

"But I have the receipts," said Gabriel. "Including the one for your room at the Hotel Metropol in 2003 when you were negotiating the RuzNeft joint venture."

Magnus was silent for a moment. "What do you want from me?"

"I'd like you to tell Katje what happened to her sister. And then you're going to explain your recent interest in acquiring a South African mining company." Gabriel paused, then added, "Not to mention *The Concert* by Johannes Vermeer."

Magnus was incredulous. "What in God's name are you—"

"I would advise you," said Gabriel evenly, "to choose another path."

Another silence, longer than the last. "Why should I trust you, of all people?"

"Because I'm your only hope."

Magnus looked down at his wrist and frowned. "My watch is missing."

Gabriel exchanged a look with Ingrid. "I hope it wasn't expensive."

"A Piaget Altiplano Origin. But it had sentimental value as well."

"Your wife gave it to you?"

"Karoline? Goodness no. The watch was a gift from Vladimir." He looked at Ingrid again. "Who is she, Allon?"

"Perhaps I should allow Ms. Westergaard to answer that question for herself."

Ingrid returned the watch to Magnus.

"Ah, yes," he said. "That would explain everything."

34

Branitzer Platz

The origin story of Magnus Larsen had always glossed over his childhood. It was widely assumed, based on his aspect and appearance, that he was the flower of an old and prosperous Copenhagen clan of consequence. The truth, however, was that Magnus had been born into a working-class family in the town of Korsør, located on the western shore of the island of Zealand. His father did odd jobs, his mother did nothing at all. Neither one of his parents ever opened, let alone read, a book. Indeed, there was not a single book in the Larsen home save for the phone book and an old Bible.

Somehow young Magnus emerged from the circumstances of his birth with a formidable brain in his head.

A voracious reader and gifted student, he won admission to the University of Copenhagen, where he studied political science and Russian history. Then he headed off to Harvard for his business training. He joined DanskOil in 1985 and fifteen years later, at the age of forty, was promoted to the rank of CEO.

The company he inherited was profitable but by no means a major player in the industry. Magnus resolved to increase DanskOil's market share, which required additional petroleum—more petroleum than could be extracted from beneath Denmark's territorial waters. He found it in Moscow in the spring of 2003, when he reached an agreement with the Kremlin to embark on a joint venture with the state-owned energy company RuzNeft.

"And that," he added, "is when my life unraveled."

He was peering into the glass of vodka that Ingrid, after returning his watch, had thrust into his hand. They were seated together on the drawing room's dowdy formal sofa, the first edition of *The Beautiful and Damned* resting on the coffee table before them. Natalie and Dina, late arrivals to the gathering, wore the vacant expressions of stage extras in a café scene. Eli Lavon appeared to be contemplating a chessboard only he could see. Mikhail was pacing slowly, as though waiting for his flight to board. Gabriel stood next to Katje, the silent witness to the proceedings.

"Do you happen to remember her name?" he asked.

The CEO looked up from his glass. "Must we, Allon?"

"We're all adults, Magnus. Besides, we've heard it all before."

"Her name was Natalia. She was very beautiful. I made a dreadful mistake."

"I'm told that you were shown a video at FSB headquarters at Lubyanka."

"Let's just say that I was made aware of what the Russians had in their possession. If it had been made public, everything that I had managed to achieve would have been gone in an instant."

He had hoped it would end with the lopsided DanskOil–RuzNeft deal, that his life would return to normal, that he would never be reminded of the mistake he had made in Room 316 of the Hotel Metropol. But during a trip to Russia in the winter of 2004, it was made clear to him that wouldn't be the case.

"By whom?"

"Konstantin Gromov. At least that was the name he gave me. I'm sure it was a pseudonym."

"Konstantin was your new SVR case officer?"

Magnus nodded.

"What did he have in mind?"

"A long-term relationship."

"And you agreed, of course."

"What choice did I have?"

He was tasked with supplying the SVR with business and political intelligence, with providing the names of potential recruits, and with acting in ways that advanced Russian interests over the West's. He became a pied piper of a new Ostpolitik, reading lines from a script written for him by Moscow Center. He heaped praise upon the Russian leader at every opportunity, even after the vicious murder of Alexander Litvinenko in London in November 2006. Several friends stopped speaking to him. His wife, Karoline, who knew nothing of what had transpired in the Hotel Metropol, thought he had taken leave of his senses.

The pressure of leading a double life placed additional stress on their marriage, which had been strained for some time. And when Magnus noticed a beautiful half-Inuit woman at Noma one evening, he instructed his driver to make contact with her on his behalf.

"She rebuffed his first approach. Quite vehemently," he added with a fleeting smile. "But eventually she agreed to see me, and we entered into a relationship. I paid her rent and her expenses, bought her anything she desired, and made certain that she always had plenty of spending money. I made no demands regarding exclusivity. In fact, I encouraged her to see other men. But I insisted that she never tell anyone she was involved with me. She agreed she wouldn't."

"How long did this relationship go on?"

"Nearly a year. I treated Rikke with kindness and affection, and I thought she was happy with the financial aspects of our arrangement. That was why it came as such a shock to me when she demanded a large sum of money to maintain her silence."

"How much did you give her?"

"A million kroner, roughly a hundred thousand dollars. A few weeks later, she demanded a second payment, which I agreed to."

"And when she came back for more?"

"I happened to be in Saint Petersburg for a meeting at RuzNeft headquarters. I had a drink with Konstantin Gromov while I was there. He could tell that something was troubling me and insisted I confide in him."

"Which you did."

"I had nowhere else to turn."

"Did you give him Rikke's name?"

"I didn't have to."

"Because the SVR *rezidentura* in Copenhagen already knew that you were seeing her."

"Yes."

"And when she went missing?"

"I assumed that she was lying on a beach somewhere with all the money I'd given her. But when a few weeks went by with no sign of her, I began to suspect the worst."

"And you of course went straight to the Danish police," said Gabriel.

"And what exactly would I have told them, Allon?"

"The truth."

"I didn't know the truth." He looked at Katje. "You must believe me, Ms. Strøm. I was very fond of your sister, even after she blackmailed me. I had absolutely nothing to do with her death."

"Disappearance," said Gabriel.

"No, Allon. She has a right to know the truth. I have it on the highest authority that Rikke is in fact dead."

"How high?"

Magnus tapped the crystal of his Piaget wristwatch. "The very top."

Six months after his young mistress vanished without a trace, Magnus plowed another $5 billion into RuzNeft, increasing his stake in the company to twenty-five percent and earning himself a place on the Russian company's controlling board. Nearly a half billion dollars of that additional investment went straight into the pocket of the Russian president. Vladimir Vladimirovich rewarded his prized asset with a $6 million home in the gilded Moscow suburb of Rublyovka.

Magnus's wife visited once, declared the place grotesque, and refused to return. Magnus, however, found the life of a Russian oligarch to be intoxicating—the lavish parties, the private jets, the yachts, the beautiful women. His Russian friends started calling him Comrade Larsenov. His Western critics, too. He became romantically involved with a reporter from NTV. His marriage all but collapsed.

"Karoline and I have what I would describe as a very European marriage. She lives her life—quite well, I might add—and I live mine. As strange as this might sound, it wasn't my many dalliances and affairs that drove her away in the end, it was my friendship with Vladimir. Volodya was the final straw."

Magnus saw the Russian president frequently when he was in Moscow, usually in the company of other oligarchs, sometimes alone. One private meeting took place at Novo-Ogaryevo, his official dacha, on the day he signed a law that would allow him to remain in office until 2036, effectively making him a president for life.

"At the conclusion of our session, he handed me a gift-wrapped box." He held up his left arm. "'To Magnus, from Vladimir.' And then he asked me, as though it were the farthest thing from his mind, whether there were any developments in the search for the young woman with whom I had been involved. It never occurred to me that he knew of my situation. I was so shocked I could scarcely speak."

"Did he tell you that Rikke was dead?"

"Vladimir Vladimirovich? Of course not. He didn't have to tell me. He just gave me that smirk, the one that said he had taken care of that little problem for me. Not in order to protect me but to compromise me so totally and completely that I would do anything to stay in his good graces. He was reminding me that one day he would ask me to perform a service for him, a mission of great secrecy and sensitivity." Magnus lowered his voice and added, "Something that no one in their right mind would ever do."

Which brought them, shortly before midnight, to *The Concert*, oil on canvas, 72.5 by 64.7 centimeters, by Johannes Vermeer.

35

Branitzer Platz

It was Konstantin Gromov of the SVR, not Vladimir Vladimirovich, who gave Magnus his marching orders. The date was August 2, 2022, six months after the Russian invasion of Ukraine. The previous day, the United States announced it was sending another $550 million in military aid to Ukraine, including additional ammunition for the HIMARS mobile rocket launchers that had wreaked havoc on Russian supply lines and battlefield command posts. The Kremlin had largely crushed the internal antiwar movement, but there was grumbling among the oligarchs of the inner circle as the war began to take a toll on the economy and their lavish lifestyles. Most of the major Western energy companies—including ExxonMobil, Shell, and BP—had declared their intention to walk away from their Russian joint ventures. DanskOil, however, had refused to join the exodus.

"How did Gromov contact you?"

"The same way he always did, a chatty email to my private account about a book he thought I should see."

"Where did you meet?"

"Oslo."

"And the assignment?"

"Konstantin wanted me to travel to South Africa to negotiate the purchase of a small, undervalued mining company that specialized in rare-earth minerals. He thought it would be a nice addition to DanskOil's balance sheet."

"Did this company have a name?"

"Excelsior."

"And if I were to search for it online?" asked Gabriel. "What would I find?"

"Plenty of references to Excelsior *this* and Excelsior *that*, but nothing about a South African mining company. It was simply the cover story that Konstantin created to justify my travel."

"And the real purpose of your visit to South Africa?"

"It never came up."

284 · DANIEL SILVA

"Surely you must have had at least *some* idea."

"I'm not a complete fool, Allon." Magnus glanced at the girl in white and took a long pull at his drink. "Not all the time, at least. But I had no choice in the matter. Konstantin gave me a budget of a billion dollars and told me to get it done."

Magnus flew to Johannesburg a week later and checked into the Four Seasons. There was a message waiting. He rang the number and a man who called himself Hendrik Coetzee suggested they meet for drinks that evening.

"Where?"

"The hotel bar."

"Describe him."

"Typical Afrikaner. Tall, blond, too much time in the sun."

"Age?"

"Mid-sixties."

"A former soldier?"

"Intelligence, I'd say."

"Was he the current owner of this nonexistent mining company?"

"His representative."

"Did he know that you were acting as a cutout for the Russians?"

"His opening position suggested he knew full well who it was that I was representing."

"How much did he want?"

"Two billion dollars."

But over the course of several marathon sessions, Magnus managed to whittle the price down to a billion, payable to an anonymous shell company registered in Liechtenstein. The money would originate in the Cayman Islands, in an account secretly controlled by the SVR. Upon receipt of the funds, Coetzee would deliver a container to Pilanesberg International Airport in South Africa's North West Province, where a private aircraft would be waiting. Magnus was not privy to the details regarding the plane's route or destination. Nor did he know the exact nature of the material stored in the container. Nothing in the deal was in any way connected to him or his company. His hands were clean, his conscience clear.

An experienced negotiator, he anticipated a last-minute snag. Nothing, however, could have prepared him for the South African's astonishing demand.

"He wanted a painting," said Gabriel.

"But not just any painting. He wanted the most famous stolen painting in the world."

"Your response?"

"I laughed in his face. And when I stopped laughing, I asked him how I was supposed to find a painting that had been missing for more than thirty years. That was when he told me where it could be found."

"In the Amalfi villa of a wealthy South African shipper and art collector named Lukas van Damme."

Magnus nodded.

"If Coetzee wanted it so badly, why didn't he steal it himself?"

"He implied that he was a close friend of Van Damme's from the old days, that Van Damme would automatically suspect him if the painting disappeared. For that reason, there could be no South African connection to the theft."

"And when you told your SVR controller about the demand?"

"He gave me my next assignment."

"Commission the theft of *The Concert* by Johannes Vermeer?"

Magnus nodded.

"Thus providing the Kremlin the ability to claim with a straight face that it had nothing at all to do with any aspect of this wretched deal."

"I'm not a professional like you, Allon, but I believe the term of art is *plausible deniability*."

"But why would Konstantin Gromov think that you, a respected European energy executive, had the means to steal the world's most valuable missing painting?"

"Because Gromov is aware of the fact that I suffer from a condition known as bibliomania. He also knows that I have utilized the services of a Copenhagen antiquarian to acquire books that I could not otherwise obtain legally."

"An antiquarian," said Gabriel, "named Peter Nielsen."

"I think Peter was more shocked than I was," said Magnus. "He was also reluctant to take the commission. He said it was one thing to pinch a copy of Hemingway or Heller, quite another to get involved in an art heist on Italian soil."

"How did you convince him to change his mind?"

"Thirty million euros. Half up front, half on delivery. I told Peter to hire the best thief he could find, that there could be absolutely no mistakes." He glanced at Ingrid. "He said he knew someone who was up to the job."

"When was the next time you spoke to him?"

"The night he called to say the painting was in Denmark."

"I assume you knew that Van Damme was dead."

"Yes, of course."

"You must have been somewhat alarmed."

"That's one way of putting it. As you might imagine, I was quite anxious to complete the transaction."

"How were you planning to take delivery of the painting?"

"I wasn't. I told Peter that a courier would collect it at his shop."

"And where was the courier going to take it?"

"The Russian Embassy. From there, it was supposed to make its way to South Africa by diplomatic pouch."

"And when you learned that Peter had been murdered?"

"I knew that Konstantin Gromov and the SVR were killing anyone connected to that painting."

"And why would they do a thing like that?"

"I'm not a professional but . . ." He looked down at the copy of *The Beautiful and Damned.*

"Which one are you, Magnus?"

"I'll let you be the judge." He swallowed the last of his vodka. "What now, Allon?"

36
Berlin–Langley

Later that morning, two citizens of Denmark informed coworkers and loved ones that they would be extending their stay in Berlin for a period of forty-eight hours. One was the CEO of the country's largest producer of oil and natural gas; the other juggled four part-time jobs in the small town of Vissenbjerg. Both were untruthful as to the reason for the change in their travel plans, and neither disclosed their present whereabouts—a stately villa on the Branitzer Platz, in the Berlin neighborhood known as Westend.

The man responsible for their confinement, the recently retired Israeli spymaster Gabriel Allon, slipped out of the safe house shortly before dawn and took a taxi to Brandenburg Airport. Some twelve and a half hours later, he was in the hands of a CIA reception committee at Dulles International. It was approaching 6:00 p.m. when they escorted him through the iconic entrance of the Agency's Original Headquarters Building. Upstairs on the seventh floor, the director regarded him warily for a long moment, as though trying to decide whether he was real or a clever new piece of Israeli technology.

"What on earth are you doing here?" he asked at last.

"I was about to ask you the same thing."

"My president didn't give me much of a choice. What's your excuse?"

"You'll know in a minute."

The director glanced at his watch. "I'm supposed to meet my wife for dinner in McLean at seven thirty. Is there any chance I'm going to make it?"

"No," said Gabriel. "No chance whatsoever."

With his tousled hair, outdated mustache, and underpowered voice, Adrian Carter did not look like the world's most powerful intelligence officer. Indeed, he might have been mistaken for a therapist who passed his days listening to confessions of affairs and inadequacies—or a professor from a minor liberal arts college in New England, the sort who championed noble causes and was a constant thorn in the side of his dean. His unthreatening appearance, like his flair for languages, had been a valuable asset throughout his long career, both in the field and at Langley. Adversaries and allies alike tended to underestimate Carter, a blunder that Gabriel had never made.

They had worked together for the first time on a joint operation targeting a billionaire Saudi terrorist financier named Zizi al-Bakari. So successful was their collaboration that several return engagements would follow. Gabriel had willingly served as a clandestine auxiliary branch of the Agency, carrying out operations that, for political or diplomatic reasons, Carter could not undertake himself. Along the way, they managed to become the closest of friends. No one was more pleased by Adrian Carter's long-overdue ascent to the director's office than Gabriel. He only wished it had happened sooner. His five-year term as chief of the Office would have been much less contentious.

On that evening, however, Gabriel arrived at CIA headquarters as a private citizen with a most remarkable story to tell, a story that began when he agreed to undertake a quiet search for the world's most famous missing painting and ended, the previous evening, with the alarming debriefing of a Russian asset code-named the Collector. Adrian Carter, a man who was not easily surprised, sat spellbound throughout.

"Where is Larsen now?" he asked at the conclusion of Gabriel's presentation.

"Still in Berlin."

"And he's had no contact with the SVR?"

"Not unless he's telepathic."

"What about the Johansen woman?"

It seemed to Gabriel a peculiar line of inquiry, but he answered Carter's question nevertheless. The Johansen woman, he said, was under lock and key in Berlin as well.

"What are you planning to do with her?" asked Carter.

"I made a promise I intend to keep."

"No Italian police?"

Gabriel nodded.

"And Larsen?"

"Magnus will soon be a Danish problem." Gabriel paused, then added, "And yours, I imagine."

Carter did not take issue with the statement. "The question is," he said, "do you believe him?"

"He admitted to purchasing a quantity of South African highly enriched uranium at the behest of his masters in Moscow. It's not something a Danish energy executive would say in jest."

Carter made a church steeple of his fingertips and pressed it thoughtfully to his lips. "When the International Atomic Energy Agency certified that South Africa had given up its weapons, it explicitly said it had no reason to suspect that the inventory of fissile material was incomplete."

"If the IAEA had bothered to interview a nuclear physicist named Lukas van Damme, they might have reached a different conclusion. You should assume that the Russians are now in possession of the bullet and target of a crude gun-type weapon. And then you should ask yourself why a country with six thousand advanced nuclear weapons would go to the trouble of acquiring that material."

"Because the material cannot be traced to Russia's existing stockpiles. Which means it would be ideal for some sort of false-flag incident in Ukraine that Vladimir Vladimirovich could use as a pretext to bring the war to a swift and decisive nuclear conclusion." Carter frowned and added, "If he were so inclined."

"Is he?"

"The broader US intelligence community has concluded that Vladimir Vladimirovich, despite his irrational decision to invade Ukraine, is a rational actor who has no intention of using nuclear weapons. Our British cousins at the Secret Intelligence Service share our opinion."

"And what does the director of the CIA think?"

"He's troubled by the constant nuclear drumbeat he hears on Russian television. He's also alarmed by some of the things the Russian president's closest security and intelligence advisers, the so-called *siloviki*, are whispering into his ear. To describe the men around the Russian president as hard-liners is a dangerous understatement. The current director of the SVR is an unstable sociopath, or so my in-house shrinks tell me. But the real problem is Nikolai Petrov, the secretary of Russia's Security Council. Nikolai's wrapped around his own axle. He's a true paranoid ultranationalist radical. Nikolai thinks the war in Ukraine is part of a broader struggle between traditional Christian values and the decadent, homosexual West. Nikolai thinks Ukrainians are nonhumans and that Vladimir should have dropped the bomb on Kyiv a long time ago. Nikolai thinks Russia can win a nuclear war against the United States. Nikolai," said Carter, lowering his voice, "scares the living shit out of me."

"And how does the director of the Central Intelligence Agency know what Nikolai Petrov is whispering into the ear of the Russian president?"

"Sources and methods," protested Carter.

"Which is it, Adrian?"

The CIA director smiled. "A little of both."

37

Langley

C arter snatched up his phone and requested a pair of files. One was Nikolai Petrov's. The other was for someone named Komarovsky. They were delivered in short order by an earnest-looking young officer wearing a Brooks Brothers suit and striped tie. The covers of both files had distinctive orange borders and were labeled TOP SECRET//SCI, indicating they contained sensitive compartmented information, the highest level of classification in the American system.

Carter opened the Petrov file first. "Nikolai started his career at the KGB. No surprise there, they all did. But what sets Nikolai apart is that he cut his teeth in the Leningrad bureau in the 1970s along with you-know-who."

"Vladimir Vladimirovich."

Carter nodded. "Nikolai has been at Vladimir's side from the very beginning. He took over control of the Security Council in 2008, the same year his wife, for reasons that were never made public, decided to commit suicide. His office is in the Kremlin Palace, not far from Vladimir's. On paper he serves roughly the same function as our national security adviser. In practice, though, Nikolai wields far more power. The foreign and defense ministers report directly to him, as do the directors of the three major Russian intelligence services. Nikolai Petrov is the second most powerful man in Russia and is considered to be Vladimir's most likely successor. The very thought of it keeps me awake at night."

Carter handed Gabriel a photograph, a satellite image of a substantial English-style manor house surrounded by manicured grounds. The trees were in full leaf. A three-vehicle motorcade was parked in the drive.

"Not bad for a man who has never worked a day in the private sector," said Carter. "It's located west of Moscow in Rublyovka, the suburb of Russian oligarchs and Kremlin elites."

"And Danish oil executives," added Gabriel.

"Ever been?"

"Can't say I've had the pleasure."

"It's not an actual municipality," explained Carter. "It's a collection of gated communities, a bit like Florida-on-the-Moskva. Petrov lives in a development called Somerset Estates. Most of his neighbors are members of the *siloviki*. Therefore, the security is extremely tight."

"And how, pray tell, did a humble public servant like Nikolai Petrov afford a knockoff English manor house in the world's most expensive neighborhood?"

"Because Nikolai is a member in good standing of the inner ring. As such, he has access to an array of no-lose investment opportunities not available to ordinary Russian citizens. We imposed sanctions on Nikolai after the Russians went into Ukraine. His European bank accounts have been frozen, and the French seized his villa in Saint-Jean-Cap-Ferrat. His remaining wealth is ruble-based. Most of it is locked up in TverBank, which is also under sanction. Poor Nikolai," said Carter, "is in a bit of a pickle."

"How much is poor Nikolai worth?"

"At today's exchange rate? Just shy of three billion." Carter handed over another satellite photograph— the same English-style manor house, a different angle. He pointed out a window on the second floor. "That's his home office. He's a bit of a workaholic, our Nikolai. He usually leaves the Kremlin around nine p.m. and then works from home until long after midnight."

"Says who?"

"His personal computer." Carter extracted another photograph from Petrov's file. It was an unflattering close-up of a sunken-cheeked man of approximately seventy. The bags beneath his eyes suggested he had not been sleeping well of late. "Compliments of our friends at Fort Meade," said Carter.

Fort Meade, located in suburban Maryland, was the headquarters of the National Security Agency.

"The computer itself contains nothing of value," Carter continued. "But the camera and microphone allow us to eavesdrop on calls that Nikolai places on his secure phone, including calls to his friend Vladimir Vladimirovich. The camera also allows us to take photographs and videos of the office itself. Here's what it looks like when Nikolai isn't blocking the shot."

The photograph showed a chair and ottoman, a standing lamp, a drop leaf side table, and a government-issue safe.

"Combination?" asked Gabriel.

"Twenty-seven, eleven, fifty-five. Or thereabouts," added Carter.

"What's in the safe?"

"On any given day, it contains numerous Security

Council policy documents, some sensitive, others quite mundane. At present, however, the safe in Nikolai Petrov's mansion in Rublyovka contains the only copy of Security Council directive 37-23\VZ."

"Subject matter?"

"In short, it is Russia's plan to use nuclear weapons to win the war in Ukraine."

"Says who?" asked Gabriel.

Adrian Carter opened the second file.

Komarovsky was not his real name. It was a code name, borrowed from the pages of Boris Pasternak's epic 1957 novel *Doctor Zhivago*. Viktor Ippolitovich Komarovsky, a lecherous Moscow lawyer, was the novel's antagonist. The man behind the code name, however, was the CIA's most important Russian asset—so important that even the American president, who eagerly awaited Komarovsky's latest intelligence, did not know his identity.

In the lexicon of the intelligence trade, he was a walk-in, meaning it was Komarovsky who had made the initial approach. Carter did not say where or how the Russian made contact with the Agency, only that it had not been in Moscow. Indeed, the CIA's Moscow station chief did not know of Komarovsky's existence. A total of four people at Langley knew his identity, and the distribution list for his intelligence had just twelve names on it. Gabriel, for reasons he did not yet understand, had just been admitted to a very exclusive club.

The club to which Komarovsky belonged was the Russian president's inner circle of oligarchs and senior Kremlin officials. He claimed to be the leader of a network of Russian elites who were opposed to the war and the continued rule of the Russian president. He asked for nothing from the United States other than steadfastness. It was essential, he said, for the US and NATO to arm the Ukrainians with the advanced weaponry required to liberate every inch of Ukrainian soil, including the Crimean Peninsula. A Russian defeat on the battlefield, he predicted, would lead to widespread unrest and leave the Russian president no choice but to step down.

Carter was skeptical of Komarovsky's predictions, but he was impressed by the asset's intelligence, which gave Langley a window into the workings of the Russian president and the members of his inner circle. As the war dragged on, and the number of Russian casualties in Ukraine soared to unimaginable levels, Komarovsky grew alarmed by the prospect that the Russian leader and the hard-liners around him were considering the use of tactical nuclear weapons to turn the tide. The attack, Komarovsky told his case officer, would not be surprise in nature. It would be preceded by a crisis of the Kremlin's making, a crisis that would provide Russia with the pretext to use nuclear weapons for the first time since the United States dropped atomic bombs on the Japanese cities of Hiroshima and Nagasaki in August 1945.

"A false-flag attack?" asked Gabriel.

Carter nodded. "At first Komarovsky thought it would be something small. Something that would give the Russians an excuse to fire a couple of nuclear-tipped artillery shells and force the Ukrainians to come to their senses. He changed his mind, however, when he heard about Security Council directive 37-23\VZ."

It was a member of the council's staff who told Komarovsky of the document's existence. The source had not been allowed to read the directive—Secretary Petrov maintained constant control of the only copy—but he was familiar with its contents. It was the blueprint for an operation code-named Aurora, the name of the Russian warship that fired the opening shot of the November 1917 attack on the Winter Palace in Saint Petersburg. The directive contained multiple scenarios for how the manufactured nuclear crisis might escalate—and how Russia would respond, step by step, if attacked by the United States. The package of retaliatory measures included a preemptive nuclear strike on the American homeland.

"It was at this point," said Carter, "that Komarovsky made his first request of the CIA."

"Steal the only existing copy of Security Council directive 37-23\VZ."

Carter nodded. "He even offered to assist us."

"How?"

"By helping us gain access to Nikolai Petrov's home. As you might imagine, I gave the matter serious consideration. After all, what CIA director wouldn't want to know exactly how the Russians would respond if, say, we obliterated their forces in Ukraine with an overwhelming conventional attack?"

"And?"

"Komarovsky said he needed an operational team that wouldn't stick out like a sore thumb in Rublyovka. He was also quite insistent that we not send Americans who look like actual Americans."

"Not an unreasonable request given the fact that you're helping the Ukrainians kill every last soldier in the Russian army."

"But a difficult obstacle to overcome nonetheless." Carter paused. "Until you walked through the door with the perfect operational team in your back pocket."

"A pro-Russian Danish oil executive and a professional thief?"

Carter smiled. "One strives to avoid hyperbole in this line of work, but they might be the only two people in the world who could pull it off. With you looking over their shoulders, of course."

"It was my intention to drop this in your lap and go home to my wife and children."

"And now I'm dropping it in yours."

"Komarovsky is your asset. That means it's your operation to run."

"But Magnus Larsen belongs to you."

"I bequeath Magnus to the Agency. He's all yours, Adrian."

"You're the one who burned him. And you're the only one who can turn him around. Besides, you and your service are rather good at stealing sensitive nuclear-related documents, as I recall."

Gabriel lapsed into silence. He had run out of objections.

"How can you pass up the opportunity to help us avoid World War Three?" asked Carter.

"Who's engaging in hyperbole now?"

"Certainly not me."

Gabriel looked at the photograph of the safe in Nikolai Petrov's office. "Do you know what will happen if they get caught?"

"They will spend the next several years in a Russian penal colony. If they're lucky."

"Which means that one of us has to go on the record with the Danes."

"I'll leave that in your hands."

"What about Komarovsky?"

"We wait to hear from him."

"And then?"

"We let Komarovsky make the next move."

38
Berlin

Tell Adrian to find someone else."

"I tried. He says there is no one else."

"It can't be done."

"It has to be done, Eli. We have no other choice."

They were headed into central Berlin through a driving rainstorm. Lavon was behind the wheel of a Mercedes C-Class sedan. Gabriel was strapped securely into the passenger seat. There was a reason Ari Shamron had turned Lavon into a pavement artist. He was one of the world's worst drivers.

"Perhaps you should switch on the wipers, Eli. They really do work wonders in conditions like these."

The car drifted into the opposing lane of the motorway as Lavon searched the dashboard for the appropriate knob. Gabriel reached across the cockpit and adjusted their heading.

"Try turning the barrel at the end of the indicator arm."

Lavon followed Gabriel's suggestion, and the lights of the Berlin skyline came suddenly into focus. "Has it slipped your mind that Magnus Larsen was the one who acquired the nuclear fuel for this forthcoming false-flag attack?"

"Which makes him the ideal person to clean up the mess."

"He's a Russian asset. And not just any asset," added Lavon. "He's Vladimir's private plaything."

"Not anymore."

"Are you sure about that?"

"Did you listen to his interrogation?"

"Very carefully. And I heard a man who would say anything to save his skin."

"I heard a drowning man who was looking for a lifeline. And I intend to toss him one."

"What makes you think he'll grab it?"

"Kompromat," said Gabriel.

"And if he agrees?"

"All his sins will be forgiven."

"I think I'd take a deal like that."

"I'd kill for a deal like that."

"Poor choice of words." Lavon followed the exit for the Spandauer Damm. "The question is, will the Danes go for it?"

"Why wouldn't they?"

"A dead girl, a dead antiquarian, and a prominent energy executive who has been working for the Russians for twenty years."

"You forgot to mention the Russian that I killed in Kandestederne."

"Outside the home of the professional thief you intend to send into Russia."

"Your point, Eli?"

"There are some scandals that are too big to sweep under the rug."

"Name one."

"A dead Danish energy executive."

"It's one thing to bump off a dissident oligarch, quite another to kill the CEO of a Western oil-and-gas company."

"But why is the CEO going to make a sudden trip to Russia?"

"Because he has a seat on the board of the state-owned Russian oil company RuzNeft. At least for the moment."

"And the pretty young woman at his side?"

"These things happen, Eli."

"What do we say to Mrs. Larsen?"

"As little as possible."

Lavon sailed past the turn for the Branitzer Platz. "There is one serious flaw to the plan, you realize."

"Only one?"

"Komarovsky."

"The Americans seem to think he walks on water," said Gabriel.

"Surely you must have some idea who he is."

"Based on Adrian's description, I'd say he's an extremely wealthy businessman."

"That narrows the field considerably. But if he's really plotting against Vladimir and working for the CIA, why is he still walking the face of the earth?"

"Who's to say he is?"

"And if he isn't?"

"A cornered and humiliated Vladimir Vladimirovich will order the use of tactical nuclear weapons in Ukraine. And then . . ."

Lavon lifted his foot from the throttle. "I think I missed our turn."

"You did, Eli. Three turns ago."

Gabriel began his career as an assassin, but many of his greatest triumphs had been achieved not with a gun but with the power of his voice. He had convinced wives to betray their husbands, fathers to betray their sons, intelligence officers to betray their countries, and terrorists to betray their causes and even the laws of their God. Persuading DanskOil CEO Magnus Larsen to betray his puppet masters in Russia was, by comparison, a far less arduous endeavor.

The negotiations, such as they were, were conducted in the dining room of the safe house, with only Eli Lavon present. Magnus approached the matter as though it were nothing more than a business arrangement. He wanted a guarantee, in writing, that he would not face criminal charges and that nothing about his past conduct would leak to the press. Gabriel acceded to neither demand. It would be up to the Danish government, he explained, to determine the CEO's legal fate. He was confident, though, that he could convince the director of the PET to look the other way. As for leaks to the press, Magnus could rest assured there would be none from Gabriel or the CIA—unless, of course, they served an operational purpose.

"The DanskOil–RuzNeft joint venture?"

"The time has come, Magnus."

"Walking away from twelve billion dollars will do serious damage to my bottom line. *And* my stock price."

"You should have thought of that before you plowed all that cash into a Kremlin-owned oil company."

"I didn't have much of a say in the matter."

"And you won't have a say this time, either."

With that, Gabriel recited to Magnus a set of inviolable ground rules. He was to keep his phone with him at all times and was to immediately report any contact from his SVR controller or any other Russian national. Furthermore, he was to set aside two hours each evening for planning and training purposes. He was to say nothing to his wife or children about his activities. Any attempt to shield his communications, interpersonal or electronic, would be interpreted as a sign that his allegiance had once again tilted Moscow's way.

"You needn't worry about my loyalty, Allon. I'm with you now."

"But for the last twenty years, you've been with *them*. And that means your true loyalty will never be far from my thoughts." Gabriel tapped the crystal of the Piaget wristwatch. "You also happen to be a rather close friend of the Russian president."

"Along with several members of his inner circle, including Nikolai Petrov. Which is why I'm the only person in the world who can pull off this operation for you."

"How well do you know him?"

"Petrov? I'm not sure anyone really does—with the exception of Vladimir, of course. But I refer to him by his first name, and he calls me Comrade Larsenov."

"Is that supposed to make me feel better?"

"It should, actually. Nikolai trusts no one, especially Westerners. But he mistrusts me less than most."

"And why is that?"

Magnus smiled bitterly. "Kompromat."

The CEO returned to Copenhagen early the next morning aboard a chartered plane, accompanied by Mikhail and Natalie. Katje Strøm made the trip commercially with Dina and Eli Lavon, and by midday she was standing behind the counter at Jørgens Smørrebrød Café, gently fending off questions from coworkers and customers about her new hairstyle. Gabriel, however, elected to remain in Berlin for one additional day. He had a job he wished to offer the last member of his unlikely operational team. A mission of great secrecy and danger that would take her into the dark heart of a Russia gone mad. Something no one in their right mind would ever do.

39

Dübener Heide

W e had a deal, Mr. Allon."

"Did we?"

"Complete immunity in exchange for information leading to the recovery of *The Concert* by Johannes Vermeer. I can show you the letter, if you like."

"Not to put too fine a point on it, but we were never able to actually *recover* the Vermeer."

They were approaching Potsdam on the B1. Gabriel drove with one hand balanced atop the steering wheel, his eyes checking the mirrors for evidence of German or Russian surveillance. Ingrid was staring out her window.

"I'm a thief, Mr. Allon. I steal jewelry and cash, and once upon a time I pinched the occasional rare book for my friend Peter Nielsen. But I don't steal secret Russian government documents."

"Actually, we just want you to photograph it."

"In Nikolai Petrov's office? While he's downstairs?"

"Not long ago, you broke into a hidden vault room protected by a cipher-and-biometric lock and calmly removed the world's most valuable missing painting from its stretcher."

"I had a Glock 26 in my handbag, and the owner of the property was sleeping soundly. And if he had somehow managed to walk in on me, he would have been in no position to report me to the Italian authorities. It was a rather low-risk job."

"With potentially cataclysmic consequences."

"But I didn't know that when I accepted the commission, Mr. Allon. I thought—"

"That it would be an easy way to make ten million euros."

She frowned. "In case you're wondering, I kept exactly one million of the up-front money that Peter gave me. The remaining four million I gave anonymously to charity."

"So why do you do it?"

"Steal? Because I enjoy it."

"You're one of those, are you?"

"I suppose I am."

"How did you get your start?"

"The usual. Candy from the local market. Money from my mother's purse."

"She never noticed?"

"Yes, of course. Unfortunately, she locked me in my room with nothing but my laptop computer. She thought I was doing my homework. In a way, I was."

"I'm offering you a way out, Ingrid."

"That's very thoughtful of you, Mr. Allon. But I'm not asking for one."

Gabriel turned onto the E51 motorway and headed south. "Perhaps I'm going about this the wrong way."

"I'm certain you are."

"And what would be the right way?"

She gave him a sidelong look. "Explain to me how I would communicate with you without the Russians knowing."

"Genesis."

"What is it?"

"It was created by the same Israeli firm that designed Proteus. The current version looks and functions much like an ordinary iPhone 14 Pro Max. But the Genesis also acts as a secure clandestine satellite transmitter."

"How?"

"All you have to do is compose a text message to the proper phone number stored in your contacts, and the phone embeds it in your most recent photograph and squirts it securely to the bird. Once the message leaves your Genesis, the software eliminates any trace of it, so you don't have to worry about cleaning up after yourself."

"What would happen if the Russians were to get their hands on it?"

"We subjected it to the murder board of all murder boards. Not one of our technicians was able to spot the software."

"And if the Russians decided to break open the chassis?"

"They would find a great deal of Israeli technology, which they would undoubtedly attempt to reverse-engineer. Therefore, it is important that you never let your Genesis out of your sight."

"I haven't agreed to anything yet." She was picking at the polish on her thumbnail. "The Russians know what I look like."

"One version of you," Gabriel pointed out. "But I'm told there are several others. Besides, the last place they would ever expect to find you is at the side of Comrade Larsenov."

"They know my name, too."

"A new identity and passport will take care of that."

"Where am I going to get a new Danish passport?"

"From the director of the PET. Where else?"

"And when the director of Danish intelligence asks how we're acquainted?"

"I'll have no recourse but to tell him everything."

"If you do that—"

"Your career as a thief will be officially over. But not to worry, a fresh start at DanskOil awaits."

"A fossil fuel company? I'd rather go to jail."

Gabriel exhaled heavily. "We're really going to have to do something about your politics."

"There's nothing wrong with my politics."

"You're a woke social democrat and radical environmentalist."

"So are you, as far as I can tell."

"But I'm not sleeping with Magnus Larsen."

"Neither am I, just so we're clear."

"But that doesn't change the fact that he would never get involved with someone like you. And he certainly wouldn't introduce you to his Russian friends. You have to become a card-carrying member of the pro-Kremlin European far right."

"An asshole? Is that what you mean?" She made a show of thought. "You know, I wouldn't be in this mess if I hadn't stolen Peter's damn phone."

"Or the Vermeer," added Gabriel.

"Or the jewelry and money from your cottage in

Kandestederne. But it was great fun, wasn't it?" She was silent for a long moment. Then she asked, "How does the camera work on the Genesis?"

The 1,900-acre forest and heathland known as Dübener Heide lay one hundred kilometers south of Potsdam in the German state of Saxony-Anhalt, between the Elbe and Mulde Rivers. In the center of the nature preserve was a small hotel. Gabriel and Ingrid ate lunch in the dining room, then set out along a footpath into a dense grove of beech trees.

"Come here often?" asked Ingrid.

"I used to a hundred years ago."

"Why?"

"You'll see soon enough."

They followed the path for about two kilometers, then turned onto a secondary trail that delivered them to a small clearing. Gabriel stood stock-still for a long moment, listening. The forest around them was silent. It was just the two of them.

He walked some twenty paces across the clearing and stood before a thick-trunked beech tree. In his coat pocket was an index card and pushpin he had brought from the safe house. He laid the card against the white bark, level with his heart, and impaled it with the tack.

Ingrid watched him curiously from the opposite side

of the clearing. He rejoined her and handed over his Beretta. "Is a shot of that length in your repertoire?"

Frowning, she dropped her handbag to the damp earth and brought the weapon to eye level with a textbook two-handed grip. She fired a single shot. It caught the upper-right corner of the index card.

"Not bad," said Gabriel. "But this isn't target practice. You're trying to kill the man standing on the other side of the clearing."

"It's a tree, not a man."

"Never squeeze the trigger only once. Always twice. No hesitation, no delay. Tap-tap."

She did as she was told. Both shots missed the tree entirely.

"Try again."

This time both shots struck the tree, but neither found the index card.

"One more time. Tap-tap."

She raised the weapon to eye level and squeezed the trigger twice. Both shots pierced the index card.

"Much better." Gabriel drew an unloaded Jericho .45-caliber pistol from the small of his back and placed the barrel against Ingrid's right temple. "Try it now."

Both shots struck the index card.

Gabriel lowered the Jericho. "Very impressive."

"Your turn, Mr. Allon."

"I shouldn't think such a demonstration is necessary."

"The index card is a bit smaller than a man on a motorbike."

"But the man on the motorbike was moving. The little blue card is just sitting there."

"It sounds to me as though you're afraid you might miss."

He sighed. "The Beretta or the Jericho?"

"Competitor's choice."

He handed Ingrid the unloaded Jericho and rammed a fresh fifteen-round magazine into the Beretta. "Which quadrant of the index card would you like me to hit?"

"How about all four?"

Gabriel's arm swung up, and four shots rang out.

"My God," whispered Ingrid.

He fired the last round directly into the pushpin, and the index card fell to the earth.

"That was—"

"A parlor trick," he said, cutting her off. "Like your ability to steal someone's wristwatch without them knowing it. The problem is, the real world isn't like a shooting range. It looks something like this."

Without warning, he launched himself across the clearing, arm raised, firing on the run. Ten shots in rapid succession. Ten rounds into the flesh of the beech tree. The same spot. One atop the other. Breathing heavily, he swung round and saw Ingrid staring at him as though he were a madman. Together they collected the spent cartridges and started back to the hotel.

40

PET Headquarters

The headquarters of the Politiets Efterretningstjeneste, Denmark's Security and Intelligence Service, were located northwest of Copenhagen in the suburb of Søborg. The view from Lars Mortensen's top-floor office was tranquil and unhurried. Very little ever went wrong in Mortensen's world—except, of course, when Gabriel rolled into town.

"Surely," he said, "you must have had at least *some* suspicions about him."

"Were we troubled by his relationship with the Russian president? Yes, of course. Did we think he should walk away from his joint venture with RuzNeft? Without question. But this?" Mortensen shook his head, mystified. "Who could imagine he could be involved in something so despicable?"

"You never watched him? Never listened to his calls or opened his mail?"

"This is Denmark, Allon. And Magnus Larsen—"

"Has been a Russian asset for twenty years."

Mortensen allowed a moment to pass before speaking. "I assume there's a recording of his interrogation in Berlin?"

Gabriel gave a small shrug to indicate it was so.

"He confessed to all of it?"

"Everything."

"Rikke Strøm?"

Gabriel nodded.

"Do you believe his story?"

"That he had nothing to do with her death? If I didn't, I would have handed him over to your colleagues at the Police of Denmark and washed my hands of him."

"I should have been in Berlin, Allon. You had no right to question a Danish citizen without me being present."

"You're right, Lars," said Gabriel with false contrition. "That was a mistake on my part."

"One of many." The Danish spy chief looked down at the two photographs Gabriel had placed on his desk.

One showed an SVR assassin entering an out-of-the-way café on the island of Funen. The other showed the same SVR assassin lying dead on a narrow lane near the northern tip of the Jutland peninsula. "He was shot four times in the center of the chest and, inexplicably, once in the side of the knee."

"That's what he gets for trying to kill my dinner date."

"Where is she now?"

"In a safe house within walking distance of DanskOil headquarters."

"I want her."

"I don't blame you, Lars. But you can't have her."

"Why not?"

"Because we need her. Magnus, too."

"We?"

"Adrian Carter and I. We're working together again. You're welcome to join us, if you like. It will be like old times."

"What did you have in mind?"

"The heist of the century."

"Bigger than the job you pulled in Tehran?"

"Much less paper," said Gabriel. "But the stakes are considerably higher."

"I'm listening."

Gabriel gave the PET chief a brief outline of the operation he intended to plan and launch from Danish soil.

"Risky," said Mortensen. "What sort of promises did you make to Magnus to get him to do it?"

"I implied that you would look favorably upon his case if he were to help us."

"And the Johansen woman?"

"More of the same. If you had any sense, you'd hire her when this is over."

"The PET is part of the Ministry of Justice. We don't hire criminals." Mortensen returned the two photographs. "I insist on being a full partner. You and Adrian are to keep nothing from me."

"Done."

"I also want a promise that the video of Magnus Larsen's interrogation will never see the light of day."

"Never," repeated Gabriel.

"What do you need from me?"

"Countersurveillance for me and my operational team. Protective surveillance on Katje Strøm. Full-time physical surveillance on Magnus Larsen."

"What about electronic?"

"Don't bother. We own him."

"What else?"

Gabriel tossed four copies of the same photograph on Mortensen's desk. They were passport photos for a woman in her mid-thirties with short platinum-blond hair and cat-eyed spectacles.

"The Johansen woman?"

"One version of her."

"Name?"

"Astrid Sørensen."

"Date of birth?"

"Sometime in the late eighties. You pick the date."

"Address?"

"It doesn't matter, Lars. Just make it something I can actually pronounce."

The operation commenced three days later with an impassioned speech on the floor of the Danish Parliament by Anders Holm, founder of the Coalition for a Green Denmark, now a rising star in the Social Democratic Party. The firebrand environmentalist issued his demand at the behest of an old friend from Aalborg University, for what reason the friend refused to say, though she implied it was related to Danish national security. The phone call that Holm received from the director general of the PET made it abundantly clear that was indeed the case.

The authoritative *Politiken* piled on at midday with a blistering editorial—it included the words *shame* and *outrage*—and by that evening the usually cautious minister for business made it clear the time had come. Yes, he admitted, appearances could be deceiving. But by all *appearances*, Denmark's largest producer of oil and natural gas was helping to finance Russia's war in Ukraine. The situation, he said, was both intolerable and immoral. The sooner it ended, the better.

Not surprisingly, the commentary on social media was far less restrained. The general consensus seemed to be that DanskOil CEO Magnus Larsen was personally to blame for the tragedy that had befallen the Ukrainian people. That evening, as he departed DanskOil headquarters, a small but vocal group of protesters splattered his car with red paint. The organizer of the rally was a hitherto unknown group called the Ukrainian Freedom Federation. Curiously, the Danish police made no arrests.

If Magnus was troubled by the sudden renewal of criticism over DanskOil's ties to Russia, he gave no sign of it. Nor was there any indication he intended to knuckle under to the pressure. If anything, he seemed to relish the prospect of a fight. On the morning after the protesters attacked his car, he assured his senior staff that the work of the company would go on as normal and that no changes vis-à-vis the RuzNeft joint venture were imminent.

There was, however, a new addition to Magnus's team—an attractive woman in her mid-thirties, platinum-blond hair, cat-eyed spectacles, named Astrid

Sørensen. The sudden need for a second personal assistant was a mystery, especially to Nina Søndergaard, who had served Magnus faithfully for more than a decade. He gave her a splashy new title and a significant increase in salary, and all was forgiven.

The rest of DanskOil quickly fell into line as well. The HR department processed Ms. Sørensen's paperwork in record time, and the head of security issued her an ID and an all-access keycard. When the IT department offered her the standard guided tour of the company computer system, she declined it—Magnus, she claimed, had already taught her the basics. The IT department found the story implausible, as the businessman with the soul of a poet had yet to master the fine art of loading paper into his printer.

Her desk was located outside the CEO's fishbowl of an office. Her duties included answering his phone, greeting his visitors, reading and replying to his emails, and keeping his regimented daily schedule—in short, all the executive secretarial functions that were once the responsibility of Nina Søndergaard.

Inevitably, speculation arose as to the exact nature of the relationship between the embattled CEO of Denmark's largest energy company and his attractive new personal assistant. Those who stalked her online found photos of a fashionable, outgoing woman of no discernible sexuality or romantic status—proof, said some, that she was engaged in a relationship with a married man. Otherwise, the only noteworthy aspect of her various social media feeds was the distinct rightward tilt to her politics. This placed her largely in the mainstream of DanskOil's workforce. Extractors of fossil fuels in a nation of bicyclists, they were a politically self-sorting lot.

She resided, or so she claimed, in an apartment in Nørrebro. She spent most of her free time, however, in a safe house in the north Copenhagen neighborhood of Emdrup. The man for whom she purportedly worked was a frequent visitor as well, though his stays were shorter in duration—an hour or so each evening on his way home to his seaside mansion in Hellerup. Neither his wife nor his employees knew of his unusual movements, only his loyal driver, who assumed his boss was involved in nothing more interesting than another extracurricular romance.

Lars Mortensen of the PET dropped by most evenings to observe the training sessions. For better or worse, neither operative required much instruction when it came to the basics of tradecraft. One was a professional thief and confidence artist, the other a high-profile business executive who had been working as a coerced Russian asset for twenty years. Natural deceivers and dissemblers, they were a dream couple.

It was Gabriel, with help from Natalie and Dina, who wrote the story of their on-again, off-again romance. It seemed that young, vibrant Astrid desperately wished to wed wealthy, dashing Magnus and, unlike many of his other friends, was not put off by his descent into pro-Russian infamy—in large part because young, vibrant Astrid was rabidly pro-Russian herself. Regrettably, this was the least offensive of her political views. She also believed that Denmark needed to expel its Muslim minority, that the Covid vaccine was lethal, that global warming was a hoax, that homosexuality was a lifestyle choice, and that a cabal of blood-drinking liberal pedophiles controlled the global financial system, Hollywood, and the media.

An accomplished pickpocket, she possessed the nimble fingers of a virtuoso musician. Even so, she practiced dialing the combination of Nikolai Petrov's safe a thousand times at least—with the lights on, in pitch darkness, with her eyes open, while wearing a blindfold. Under any conditions, ten seconds was all she required.

But in order to reach the safe, she would first have to pick the lock on the door of Petrov's office. The PET's staff locksmith gave her a set of professional-grade bump keys and installed an array of common European locks on the internal doors of the safe house. Ingrid preferred to use the grip of a screwdriver—wrapped with tape to mute the sound—rather than a hammer to perform the actual *bump*. Extensive practice proved unnecessary. On her first attempt, she could open any door in the safe house in five seconds or less, a fraction of the time it took the locksmith from the Danish security service.

She was likewise proficient with the secure Office communications device known as the Genesis. Three test messages landed simultaneously at King Saul Boulevard and on Gabriel's secure phone within seconds of being sent. The photograph in which the final message was embedded depicted a smiling Ingrid with her arms wrapped around the neck of a delighted Magnus Larsen.

The camera of the Genesis looked and functioned like the camera of an ordinary iPhone, but the device's operating system had the ability to automatically hide and encrypt newly snapped photographs. Langley sent along an eighty-page mockup of the Security Council directive, complete with Cyrillic letters and numerals. Despite numerous attempts, Ingrid was never able to photograph the entire document in less than five minutes.

"An eternity," said Lars Mortensen.

"But necessary," replied Gabriel. "Under no circumstances can she steal the document itself. If that happens—"

"I will be negotiating with Nikolai Petrov to obtain the release of two Danish citizens from Russian custody."

"Better you than me, Lars."

With the help of an encrypted feed from the National Security Agency, Gabriel and his team were able to observe Petrov twice each day like clockwork—once at half past five in the morning and again around 10:00 p.m., when he arrived home from the Kremlin. On several occasions, the Russian stepped away from the desk when the door of the safe was open. There were two interior compartments. The lower was packed with gold ingots and bundles of cash. The classified documents were stored in the safe's upper chamber, arranged vertically like books on a shelf. They appeared to be fourteen in number, all with Security Council bindings.

The camera shot allowed Gabriel and Lars Mortensen to create a scale replica of Petrov's office inside PET headquarters. No matter which type of lock they used on the outer door, Ingrid was able to remove the mock directive from the safe and place it under the desk lamp in less than thirty seconds. Only once, however, was she able to photograph the eighty pages in less than five minutes. It was the same day that Adrian Carter informed Gabriel that he was on his way to Copenhagen. The time for preparation, it seemed, was nearly over. The Russian asset code-named Komarovsky had made his move.

41

Copenhagen Station

The American Embassy, perhaps the most hideous building in all of Copenhagen, was located on the Dag Hammarskjölds Allé, about a kilometer from DanskOil headquarters. Carter received Gabriel in the secure conference room of the CIA station, dressed in a blazer and a pair of crumpled gabardine trousers. The overnight flight from Washington had been unkind to him. He looked exhausted and under stress, never a good combination.

He extracted a cup of coffee from a pump-action thermos. "The president sends his regards. He wishes to thank you for undertaking this dangerous operation on our behalf."

"I'm not the one who's going to do it, Adrian."

"Is she ready?"

"As ready as she'll ever be."

"How long will it take her?"

"Too long for my comfort."

"Can you be more specific?"

"If the actual Security Council directive is eighty pages, it will take her approximately six minutes from beginning to end."

"And she knows that she can't remove it from Petrov's office?"

"She knows, Adrian."

Carter sat down at the head of the conference table. "I enjoyed your public campaign against DanskOil immensely. The red paint on the limousine was a lovely touch."

"More to come."

"Is Comrade Larsenov behaving himself?"

"It appears so."

"Russian surveillance?"

"My partners at the PET say not."

"We're go for launch? Is that what you're saying?"

"Do I have a choice?"

"Not really."

"Is there something you're not telling me, Adrian?"

"One of Russia's newest ballistic missile subs slipped out of Kola Bay the night before last, and their Tupolev bombers can't seem to stay out of our airspace off Alaska."

"Any other good news?"

"We think they might be moving some of their tactical nuclear weapons closer to the Ukrainian border."

"You *think*?"

"Low to moderate confidence," said Carter.

"What about the South African highly enriched uranium?"

"Our best guess is that it's somewhere between Russia's western border and the Kamchatka Peninsula in the Far East. The asset known as Komarovsky, however, is almost certain that Security Council directive 37-23\VZ will not only tell us where the material is but where it's going and how the Russians intend to use it."

"When did he make contact?"

"I'd rather not say."

"And I'd rather be in Venice with my wife and children."

"Two days ago. But don't ask where," Carter added. "I'm not going to tell you."

"Actually, I was planning to move straight to Komarovsky's real name."

"Don't bother."

"How is Magnus supposed to make contact with him if he doesn't know who he is?"

"Komarovsky will be the one to make contact with Magnus."

"How?"

"With this." Carter placed an old miniature paperback book on the conference table. The title and author were in Russian. "*Doctor Zhivago* by Boris Pasternak. The CIA arranged to have it published in 1958, and it circulated in Moscow and throughout the Warsaw Pact. I borrowed that one from the CIA museum. Komarovsky has a copy as well, a copy he will give to Magnus if he feels it is safe to proceed with the operation." Carter opened the novel. "This passage will be clearly marked."

"What does it say?"

"'And remember: you must never, under any circumstances, despair. To hope and to act, these are our duties in misfortune.'"

"How appropriate."

"Komarovsky sees himself as a man of destiny." Carter returned the volume of Pasternak to his attaché case. "Tell Magnus to accept every invitation he receives, even if it's an invitation to his own execution. It might just be from Komarovsky."

"Can he get them into Petrov's house?"

"Moderate to high confidence."

"And can he get them out again?"

"I suppose that depends entirely on your girl."

"She needs six minutes to photograph an eighty-page document, Adrian."

"How soon can they leave for Russia?"

"As soon as my Danish partners and I finish blowing up the DanskOil–RuzNeft joint venture."

"Get it done." Carter closed the attaché case. "I have a bad feeling about this one."

The prime minister's tone was offhand and unfailingly polite. She was wondering if he could drop by her office in the Borgen at five that afternoon to discuss DanskOil's situation in Russia.

"And not to worry, Magnus. Fifteen minutes will be more than sufficient."

She assured him the visit would be unpublicized, but several hundred angry protesters, and a large contingent of Danish press, greeted his arrival. The meeting was precisely three minutes in length. The prime minister gave him an ultimatum and a deadline and then sent him on his way. Outside, he found his limousine soaked with blue and yellow paint, the colors of the Ukrainian flag. The video of his departure was a global sensation.

The following morning, he informed his senior staff that he had no choice but to wind down DanskOil's position in Russia. He delivered the news to his board that afternoon but waited another day before calling RuzNeft chairman Igor Kozlov at the company's headquarters in Saint Petersburg.

"Is there really no way to resist the pressure?" asked Kozlov in Russian.

"I'm sorry, Igor. But I'm afraid I have a gun to my head."

"Why don't you come to Saint Petersburg? I'm sure we can come up with a solution."

"There isn't one."

"What's the harm in trying, Magnus?"

"When?"

"Next week?"

"I'm not sure I can hang on that long."

"In that case, how about the day after tomorrow?"

"I'll see you then," he said, and rang off.

His new assistant was hovering over his desk, notepad in hand. He instructed her to arrange private air travel from Copenhagen to Saint Petersburg and reserve two cathedral-view premium suites at the Hotel Astoria in Saint Isaac's Square.

"Two suites?" she asked, pointedly.

"You will be accompanying me, Ms. Sørensen. You should plan on being away for several days."

"Yes, of course," she said with a smile, and returned to her desk.

That evening, Gabriel and the team put her through the most grueling training session yet. She spent thirty minutes bumping locks, another thirty spinning the combination dial of the safe, and nearly two hours photographing the eighty-page directive. Afterward Mikhail led her upstairs for a Russian-accented mock interrogation while Gabriel and Eli Lavon briefed Magnus on the basics of making contact with a clandestine source. The CEO cast several glances at his costly Piaget Altiplano Origin wristwatch.

Annoyed, Gabriel asked, "Am I keeping you from something, Magnus?"

"This might come as a surprise to you, Allon, but I'm rather well versed in the etiquette of Russian tradecraft. And I'm not at all surprised that this Komarovsky fellow wishes to keep his identity secret from me. He's playing a very dangerous game."

"Any candidates?"

"I was about to ask you the same thing."

"He'll be the very last person you would expect."

"I suppose that would be Nikolai Petrov himself." Magnus was suddenly distracted by the sound of

Mikhail's shouted questions upstairs. "Is that really necessary?"

"For your sake, I hope it isn't."

"Is this the part where you threaten to destroy me if anything happens to her?" Magnus lifted his eyes toward the ceiling. "You needn't worry about Ms. Sørensen, Allon. I'll do whatever it takes to make sure she leaves Russia alive."

The next morning, a DanskOil spokesman announced that CEO Magnus Larsen would be traveling to Saint Petersburg to begin the discussions on winding down the company's joint venture with the Kremlin-owned Russian oil company RuzNeft. Nevertheless, Magnus's departure from DanskOil HQ that evening was once again marred by an ugly incident involving protesters. He dropped by the safe house for a final session and a communal dinner attended by several officers from the PET, including the director-general. Ingrid was clearly uneasy about what awaited her in Russia. She hid her fear beneath the far-right facade of her cover identity, holding forth on a range of incendiary topics, much to the delight of her audience.

"It's all scientific stuff," she said, borrowing a line from Tom Buchanan. "The idea is if we don't look out, the White race will be utterly submerged."

After dinner, Magnus returned home to Hellerup,

and Ingrid headed upstairs to pack. She went to bed around midnight, and by five the next morning she was gone. Gabriel waited until their chartered aircraft was airborne before entering her room to search for clues as to the true state of her emotions. Her farewell note was adhered to the wall, handwritten on an index card, impaled with a pushpin. "I won't let you down" was all it said.

PART THREE

The Contact

42

Saint Petersburg

In the broad square outside the old House of the Soviets, Lenin stood atop his plinth, his right arm stretched westward. Russians used to joke that the founder of the Soviet Union looked as though he were forever trying to hail a taxi. But one courageous social media dissident had hit upon a new theory, that Lenin was actually exhorting the young and able-bodied to flee Russia before they could be mobilized for the anticipated late-winter offensive in Ukraine. The dissident's video commentary had not found favor with Russian authorities, who dispatched her to a penal colony in the Ural Mountains after a summary show trial. Her husband and children had not heard from her since.

Ingrid snapped a photograph of the enormous bronze

statue with her new phone as their Mercedes limousine sat in late-morning traffic on the Moskovsky Prospekt. The car had been waiting for them on the tarmac at Pulkovo Airport. A reception committee from Ruz-Neft had eased their way through the arrivals process. No one had bothered to inspect Ingrid's passport, let alone her mobile cellular device.

She forwarded the photograph via an ordinary en clair text message to a friend in Copenhagen—a friend who did not actually exist—and included a few biting remarks about the European left befitting her new populist image. She also sent it to dashing Magnus, who was sitting next to her in the backseat of the Mercedes. This time her commentary was of a sexual nature. It brought a smile to the handsome features of his face.

"I'd love nothing more," he murmured in Danish. "But I'm expected at RuzNeft."

"Are you sure you don't want me to come with you?"

His response was well rehearsed. "Given the circumstances, it's probably better if you don't."

"What will I do with myself all afternoon?"

"Saint Petersburg is one of the world's most beautiful cities. Take a nice long walk."

"It's freezing."

"You're Danish." The playful squeeze he gave her hand did not go unnoticed by the RuzNeft security gorilla in the front passenger seat. "I think you'll survive."

"I certainly hope so," remarked Ingrid quietly, and stared out her window at the Orwellian Soviet-era apartment blocks clustered around Victory Park. Everywhere she looked, in shop windows and on the sides of cars, she saw the letter Z, the symbol of support for the war in Ukraine. Nowhere was there any sign of opposition, for even mild opposition, a shirt, a hand gesture, was no longer tolerated. The Russian president had recently referred to antiwar activists as scum and insects. It was rather tame in comparison to the standard Two Minutes Hate that appeared nightly on state-run television.

Finally, they reached Sennaya Square, and the thunderous Moskovsky Prospekt gave way to the imported European elegance of the tsarist city center. Magnus was on the phone with DanskOil HQ when they rolled to a stop at the red-awninged entrance of the historic Astoria Hotel. He muted the call as Ingrid was climbing out of the car.

"With any luck, I'll be back in time for dinner. I'll send you an update if I have a free minute."

"Please do," she said, and followed the porter into the lobby. The girl at Reception scrutinized Ingrid's Danish passport with a practiced sneer before surrendering two sets of room keys. As requested, their premium suites were adjoining. Ingrid snapped a photo of the view from her window and asked her friend in Copenhagen for advice on how she might kill a few hours in one of the world's beautiful cities. He advised her to visit the Hermitage. The Monet Room, he said, was not to be missed.

Ingrid had coffee and a pastry at Literary Café, the fabled haunt of Russian writers and intellectuals, then walked beneath the soaring Triumphal Arch to Palace Square, where a contingent of black-clad Thought Police were arresting several young antiwar protesters who had unfurled a banner at the foot of the Alexander Column. Several onlookers flashed Z symbols and shouted pro-Kremlin slogans as the protesters were led away.

Unnerved by what she had witnessed, Ingrid spent the next two hours roaming the endless rooms and galleries of the Hermitage, including Room 67, the Monet Room. Afterward, while walking past the garish palaces lining Millionaires' Street, she became convinced, based on nothing more than her well-honed professional instinct, that she was being followed.

She made no attempt to locate or evade the surveillance, for such countermeasures would not have been in keeping with her character. Instead, she paid her respects at the eternal flame in the Field of Mars. Then she toured the Marble Palace, which Catherine the Great had given as a gift to her lover Grigory Orlov, leader of the 1762 coup that removed Catherine's husband from power and installed her as empress of Russia.

Leaving the palace, Ingrid reached the conclusion that, had she been born in Russia in the late eighteenth century, she would have undoubtedly been among the crowds of starving workers who stormed the Winter Palace in November 1917 after hearing the shot fired by the warship *Aurora*. She also became certain that she was being followed by at least two men and a short-haired woman of perhaps thirty-five who wore a dark blue quilted down coat with a fur-trimmed hood.

It was the woman who accompanied Ingrid on a tour of the colossal Saint Isaac's Cathedral, where she watched the sun setting over the Baltic Sea from the cupola high atop the golden dome. Returning to her suite at the Astoria, she sent a message to her friend in Copenhagen about her visit to the Hermitage—and about the arrests she had witnessed in Palace Square. Then, having nothing better to do, she switched on the television and watched the late-afternoon fare on RT, Russia's English-language network. War is peace.

Freedom is slavery. Ignorance is strength. Two Minutes Hate.

It was nearly nine o'clock when Magnus finally returned to the hotel. He came upstairs to his suite long enough to remove his jacket and necktie and pull on a woolen sweater. Ingrid had reserved a table at the Italian restaurant in the neighboring Angleterre Hotel. The worn-out pensioner standing behind the bar looked old enough to remember the siege of Leningrad. The rest of the floor staff were women. They were staring dully at the television, which was tuned to NTV.

"Dmitry Budanov," said Magnus. Then he added gloomily, "My neighbor in Rublyovka."

"What is he saying?"

"Evidently, Russian forces are advancing on all fronts. The Nazi regime in Kyiv will soon be liquidated, and Ukraine will be wiped from the map like . . ." Magnus's voice trailed off. "I won't translate the rest, if you don't mind. Dmitry shares the Russian president's love of scatological political rhetoric."

They were seated at a table against the window. Outside, a steady snow was falling on Saint Isaac's Square. There was no one else in the restaurant. Ingrid maintained her cover identity nonetheless. She placed her hand atop Magnus's and gazed at him with devotion.

"I was afraid they were never going to let you leave."

"So was I," he answered quietly. "As you might imagine, it was a rather tense afternoon. The minute I withdraw from the joint venture, Russia's international isolation will be complete. For all his talk about a new world order, Vladimir doesn't want that to happen. He's placing enormous pressure on RuzNeft chairman Igor Kozlov to find some way of salvaging the deal."

"Personally?"

Magnus nodded. "And Igor Kozlov is placing enormous pressure on me."

"What kind of pressure?"

"The kind that can get quite unpleasant. But he also offered me a rather large financial incentive to remain in the deal. If I were to accept it, I will be among the most reviled men on the planet. I will also be quite rich, as will DanskOil's largest shareholders."

"You already are rich, Magnus."

"But I'll be Russian rich. Trust me, there's a difference."

"Are you considering it?"

"I'd be a fool not to. Igor would like me to remain in Russia for a couple of days while they crunch the numbers."

"What about the prime minister's ultimatum?"

"A sticking point, but hardly insurmountable. She has much less power than she thinks she does."

"The press are clamoring for a statement."

"Perhaps we should give them one."

Magnus reached for his phone and composed a tweet. Ingrid smoothed a couple of the rougher edges but otherwise left the original language intact. The first day of talks between DanskOil and RuzNeft regarding the future of their joint venture had been fruitful and would continue. She tapped the little blue bird and waited for the reaction.

"Well?" asked Magnus after a moment.

"The Twitterati do not approve."

The waitress arrived with their wine. Ingrid handed the woman the Genesis and asked her to snap their picture, which she sent to her friend in Copenhagen.

"Are we going to stay here in Saint Petersburg?" she asked.

"Actually, I was thinking we should spend a couple of days in Moscow instead. I'd love for you to see my place in Rublyovka."

Ingrid took up her phone again. "Plane or train?"

"Train."

"What time?" she asked, but received no answer.

Magnus was staring at the television, his face ashen. "What is your neighbor saying now?"

"He's reminding his many millions of viewers that Russia has the world's largest nuclear arsenal. He's wondering why Russia bothers to build and maintain such weapons if it is afraid to use them."

Ingrid snapped another selfie and forwarded it to her friend, along with a chatty update on their itinerary. Then she opened her menu and asked, "What do you recommend?"

"The linguini with crabmeat and cherry tomatoes. It's absolutely divine."

43

PET Headquarters

A promising beginning."

"It's early, Lars."

"I've always believed in the power of positive thinking."

"That's because you're Danish," said Gabriel. "I find it comforting to prepare myself for a calamity and to be pleasantly surprised if it turns out to be a garden-variety disaster instead."

They were seated in the back row of the PET's op center. They had been there, side by side, since the moment the chartered aircraft carrying Ingrid and Magnus Larsen touched down in Saint Petersburg. Mortensen had spent much of the day enraptured by the wizardry of Proteus, which allowed them to securely monitor Ingrid and Magnus's every word and movement—including the meeting, many hours in duration, that had taken place at RuzNeft headquarters on the Makarov Embankment. Mikhail and Eli Lavon had provided a simultaneous translation. Lars Mortensen, appalled by the conduct of one of Denmark's most prominent businessmen, ordered his technicians to immediately delete the recording of the meeting from the PET's computers.

At present the prominent businessman was sharing a quiet dinner at Borsalino, one of Saint Petersburg's better restaurants, with his attractive personal assistant. When the meal concluded, they returned to their adjoining suites at the neighboring Astoria Hotel. As instructed, they left their phones powered on. Their familiar, playful banter made it abundantly clear that they were involved in a torrid if entirely fictitious extramarital affair.

By midnight Saint Petersburg time, both were sleeping soundly. Lars Mortensen headed home to his wife, and Eli Lavon and Mikhail returned to the safe house in nearby Emdrup. Gabriel, however, decided to spend the night on a couch at PET headquarters in the event there was glass that required breaking.

Shortly after 7:00 a.m., while drinking coffee in the staff canteen, he received a text message from the prominent Danish businessman's assistant. Attached was a photograph of a sleek Russian bullet train awaiting departure at Saint Petersburg's Moskovsky Station. The next photograph arrived at 11:20 a.m. and showed the same train at the Leningradsky rail terminal in Moscow. It was followed two hours later by a photograph of the prominent businessman and his assistant standing outside a mansion in the moneyed Moscow suburb of Rublyovka.

"Was the house really a gift from the Russian president?" asked Lars Mortensen.

"Trust me, it was the least Vladimir could do."

"How much is it worth?"

"Thanks to the war, considerably less than what it once was."

Mortensen contemplated the photograph. "You have to admit, they do make an attractive couple."

"Let's hope Magnus's Russian friends feel the same way."

"Why must you always be so fatalistic, Allon?"

"It prevents me from being disappointed later."

The gated community was called Balmoral Hills—a curious name, for the land upon which the forty dwellings stood was as flat as the Russian Plain. The house itself was the smallest on the street, a Carraway cottage amid the palaces of the grotesquely rich. Even so, the opulence was tsarist in scale. Ingrid, stiff and restless after the long train journey, spent three hours in the world-class fitness center. Afterward she headed upstairs in search of Magnus. She found him in his office on a conference call with RuzNeft brass. He tapped the mute button and allowed his eyes to wander over the toned, sweat-soaked body leaning against the doorjamb. It was a performance on his part. The house was undoubtedly littered with hidden cameras and microphones.

"Good workout?" he asked.

"It could have been better." Ingrid treated him to a flirtatious smile. "How much longer are you going to be on that call?"

"At least another hour."

She gave a playful pout.

"Why don't you have a hot bath?"

"Only if you promise to join me later."

She ascended the fairy-tale double staircase to the second floor. Once again, their suites were adjoining, with separate master baths. Ingrid opened the spigot for the oversize Jacuzzi tub and peeled off her sodden workout clothing. She was slow in reaching for the monogrammed toweling robe that hung from the back of the door. She only hoped the voyeurs at the FSB were enjoying the show.

When the tub had filled, she switched on the jets and allowed the robe to slip from her shoulders. The water she entered was scalding. She cooled it a few degrees and closed her eyes. Gradually, her fear receded, the fear that had been stalking her since the instant her foot touched Russian soil. She had been tempted to let off a little steam on the train—a woman of means, an unattended handbag—but for the sake of the operation she had refrained. Besides, she reminded herself, she was no longer that person. She worked for the counterintelligence division of the PET, Denmark's small but capable security and intelligence service, and was posing as the personal assistant and mistress of Dansk-Oil CEO Magnus Larsen, who was now standing in the doorway.

Ingrid gave a start, and a wave of water washed over the side of the tub. Magnus spread a towel over the marble floor and poked at it with the toe of his loafer.

"Forgive me," he said, his eyes averted. "I didn't mean to frighten you."

"I was just daydreaming, that's all."

"About what?"

"You, of course." She smiled. "How was your call?"

"More of the same. RuzNeft is so desperate to preserve the joint venture that they're upping the ante."

"How high?"

"Another seat on their board and a significantly better split on the profits. I told them that my hands were tied."

"If only," said Ingrid, and climbed out of the tub. Magnus lowered his eyes to the floor as he handed her the robe. She took her time pulling it on. "I'm famished, Magnus. What are we going to do about dinner?"

"Actually, we received a last-minute invitation from a friend."

"Do we have to?" said Ingrid with mock apathy. "I'd rather spend some time with you alone."

"He's throwing a small dinner party at his place," said Magnus as he hastened toward the door. "Just a few people from the neighborhood. Very casual."

44

Rublyovka

The neighborhood friend was Yuri Glazkov, the much-sanctioned chairman of the Kremlin-controlled VTB Bank. Yuri was the proud owner of two private aircraft, though his superyacht, the 214-foot *Sea Bliss*, was rather modest by Russian standards. Shortly after the invasion of Ukraine, the Italian government had seized the vessel in Capri, where Yuri owned not one but three multimillion-euro villas. The Italians had seized those, too, based on their well-founded suspicion that the real owner was Yuri's friend Vladimir Vladimirovich.

The target of a Western travel ban, Yuri was marooned at his miniature Versailles in Rublyovka. Magnus decided to drive there in his Range Rover, the

Bentley Continental GT being unsuitable for the heavy snow forecast for later that evening. Beneath his over-coat he wore a cashmere sport jacket and a rollneck sweater. His phone lay next to Ingrid's on the Range Rover's center console.

"Are we *really* going to have this discussion again?" he asked wearily in Danish.

"You made me a promise."

"And I intend to keep it."

"When?"

"A date certain? Is that what you're demanding? Christ, Astrid. You're beginning to sound like the prime minister." He fell silent as they passed the flash-ing blue lights of a police checkpoint. "Do you know how long Karoline and I have been married? Thirty-three years. It will be easier to unwind the RuzNeft joint venture than disentangle our marital finances."

"I won't be your mistress any longer."

"That sounds like an ultimatum."

"Perhaps it is."

"This was obviously a mistake."

"Obviously," she repeated.

"Bringing you to Russia, I mean. You can leave to-morrow, if you like."

"I want to stay with you, Magnus." Then she added pointedly, "Alone."

"Do you think you can behave yourself tonight?"

"Unlikely," she answered, and brushed a fleck of imaginary lint from the leg of her designer black pantsuit.

They passed two more police checkpoints before finally reaching the outer walls of Yuri Glazkov's gated community, the name of which promised French baronial splendor. The flotilla of luxury motorcars and SUVs lining his circular drive—and the small army of heavily armed security men keeping watch over them— suggested it was no casual dinner party to which they had been invited. Magnus found a place to park and switched off the engine. Ingrid hesitated before opening her door.

"Who do you want me to be tonight?"

"Astrid Sørensen, I imagine."

"Personal assistant or girlfriend, Magnus?"

"Both."

"Isn't that sort of thing frowned upon?"

"Not here. I assure you, mine is the least complicated love life in Rublyovka."

Ingrid placed her lips against his ear. "In that case, you should probably look at me the next time I get out of the bath."

It was Anastasia, Yuri Glazkov's twenty-nine-year-old third wife, who opened the towering golden door to them. The hand she offered Ingrid in greeting was long and slender and jeweled. Ingrid held it lightly for fear of breaking it. Young Anastasia didn't eat much.

Nor did she speak a word of any language other than Russian. Magnus handled the introductions, and Anastasia bobbed her head agreeably before turning her attention to the newest arrivals, Kremlin spokesman Yevgeny Nazarov and his wife, Tatiana. Mrs. Nazarova, a former Olympic sprinter turned kleptocrat, flung her arms around Magnus as though he were a long-lost relation while her polyglot husband spoke a few words to Ingrid in his Radio Moscow English. A lifelong government employee, he wore a limited-edition Richard Mille timepiece worth in excess of a half million dollars. The watch was still on his wrist when he pulled Magnus aside for a tête-à-tête about the RuzNeft situation—but only because Ingrid had passed up a perfect opportunity to steal it.

Anastasia was not the youngest wife in attendance. That honor went to the child bride of the robber baron whose close relationship with the Russian president had cost him his Spanish football club. His latest wife, the daughter of an oligarch herself, launched into a blistering invective against the Ukrainians and NATO within a minute of shaking Ingrid's hand—all in the American-accented English she had acquired while earning her degree in sunny San Diego. Ingrid reciprocated with a tirade of her own, which met with the girl's approval. She suggested they exchange numbers, and they drew their phones. The girl's device was gold-plated. Ingrid somehow managed to resist.

She took a selfie with the girl and, turning, realized she had become separated from Magnus. She spotted him across the crowded formal drawing room chatting with Gennady Luzhkov, the much-sanctioned founder and chairman of TverBank. In close proximity were Oleg Lebedev, the much-sanctioned aluminum tycoon, and Boris Primakov, the much-sanctioned owner of Russia's largest chemical company.

Indeed, Ingrid was hard-pressed to find an oligarch in attendance who *hadn't* been sanctioned by the United States and the European Union over the war in Ukraine. Just four hundred miles to the south, ill-equipped Russian conscripts were dying horrible deaths in the frozen trenches of the Donbas. But here in Rublyovka, the kleptocrats who had become wildly rich through their association with Russia's new tsar were sipping French champagne and nibbling on caviar canapés. The comparisons to November 1917 were too delicious to ignore.

Magnus beckoned with a subtle wave, and Ingrid moved discreetly to his side. Gennady Luzhkov, a trim figure with a sharply angled face and white hair combed carefully over his pate, was in the midst of making a point in Russian. He stopped midsentence and waited for Magnus to introduce him to the beautiful young woman who had joined their conversation. Magnus did so in English.

"What brings you to Russia in the middle of a war?" asked Luzhkov.

Ingrid slipped her arm around Magnus's waist.

"I see," said Luzhkov. Then he looked at Magnus and murmured something in Russian.

"What did he say?" inquired Ingrid.

It was Luzhkov himself who answered. "I was telling Magnus that some men seem to have all the luck."

"Have you seen my most recent viral video?" asked Magnus.

"But you have an adoring young woman on your arm," replied Luzhkov. "And you also have a rather lucrative offer to maintain your joint venture with Ruz-Neft. At least that's the rumor."

"Is there anything you *don't* know, Gennady?"

Luzhkov's smile was inscrutable. But then there was nothing about him that wasn't. He was one of the former KGB officers who had engineered the Russian president's rise to power, and he had been richly rewarded as a result. His bank was Russia's fourth-largest privately owned house of finance—and one of its most corrupt. The US Treasury Department had imposed crushing sanctions on TverBank on the day Russia invaded Ukraine. Luzhkov had lost three-quarters of his net worth virtually overnight, along with his private plane, his superyacht, and his Swiss and French estates. His ties to the Russian president, however, were as strong as ever.

"You've been a great friend and partner of Russia for a very long time, Magnus. No one realizes that more than Volodya."

"I hope he understands that I am under enormous pressure to terminate the relationship with RuzNeft."

"Trust me, he knows."

"When did you last speak to him?"

"I had lunch with him today at Novo-Ogaryovo. I'm one of the few people he still agrees to see in person. He's quite isolated at the moment." Luzhkov paused, then added, "Perhaps too isolated."

He was interrupted by a round of applause that swept through the room. It had been prompted by the arrival of Dmitry Budanov. He was wearing a designer olive-drab field jacket with a large Z on the left shoulder, the one that faced the camera during his nightly broadcasts.

"He looks like he just returned from the trenches

of Bakhmut," said Luzhkov beneath his breath. "With the exception of the makeup, of course. I suppose he didn't have time to remove it after taping tonight's inspiring message to the Russian people."

"Last night's broadcast was rather unsettling."

"His insistence that we use our vast nuclear arsenal against our Ukrainian cousins? Unfortunately, it's not as farfetched as it sounds."

"You don't really think it could happen, do you?"

"I'm afraid that even I'm not privy to such information. But I have a feeling *he* might know."

Luzhkov pointed out the overcoated man who had just entered the room. It was Nikolai Petrov, the secretary of the Security Council of Russia.

The tolling of a bell summoned the guests to the chandeliered banquet hall for dinner. The table at which they gathered was the length of a rail car and ablaze with the light of a hundred candles. Waiters in traditional *kosovorotha* tunics charged their wineglasses with Château Margaux, and their host made a fiery toast about the war in Ukraine that Magnus quietly translated into Danish for Ingrid.

As luck would have it, she had been seated next to the English-speaking child bride of the robber baron, who spent the remainder of the evening lamenting her family's reduced circumstances. There were other tales of sanctions woe around the table—tales of yachts and homes seized, of bank accounts frozen, and of Western travel bans and residence visas summarily revoked. None blamed the Russian president; they didn't dare. A dozen of their ilk who had criticized the war had died under mysterious circumstances, with "apparent suicide" being the most common explanation. A slip of the tongue at a Rublyovka dinner party could well prove fatal.

Dmitry Budanov, for one, found the talk of lost luxuries unseemly. One of the world's richest television journalists, Budanov had lost a yacht and both of his villas on Lake Como to sanctions. But they were a small price to pay, he said, for the restoration of Russian greatness and the destruction of NATO and the decadent, gender-confused West.

"All of which can be achieved," he droned on, "if we take the steps necessary to prevail in Ukraine."

"And what steps are those, Dmitry Sergeyevich?" asked a male voice from somewhere along the table.

"The steps of which I speak nightly on my program."

"The nuclear option?"

Budanov nodded gravely.

"And when the Americans destroy our army in Ukraine?" It was the chemical mogul, Boris Primakov.

"Then we will have no choice but to respond in kind."

"And when they retaliate?"

"They won't."

"How can you be so sure, Dmitry Sergeyevich?"

"Because they are cowards."

"A game of Russian roulette?" asked Gennady Luzhkov. "Is that what you're suggesting?" Receiving no answer, he turned to Nikolai Petrov. "And what does the secretary of the Russian Security Council have to say on the matter? Does he share the opinion of our esteemed television host that the Americans would never use their nuclear arsenal against us?"

"What I think," said Petrov, rising slowly to his feet, "is that it is time for me to take my leave."

"Perhaps you could give us a brief update on the fighting before you go," suggested Yuri Glazkov.

Petrov's terse response provoked a round of rapturous applause. Ingrid, however, had no idea why; Magnus had stopped translating in order to reply to a text he had just received.

"What did he say?" she asked over the din.

Magnus slipped the phone into the breast pocket of his jacket before answering.

"Evidently, Russian forces are advancing on all fronts."

It was after midnight when the party finally ended, and the roads of Rublyovka were slick with newly fallen snow. Magnus drove at moderate speed with both hands on the wheel. Ingrid unlocked his phone and read his most recent text messages. Then she thumbed the phone to sleep and watched the snow falling on the beech trees lining the road.

"Who were you texting with during dinner?" she asked indifferently.

"No one important."

"Was it your wife, Magnus?"

"A friend, that's all."

"What's your friend's name?"

"It's none of your affair, Astrid."

The ensuing quarrel began courteously enough, but by the time they reached Magnus's home it was Russo-Ukrainian in intensity. Inside, young, vibrant Astrid stormed up the fairy-tale staircase and locked herself in her suite. She waited until she was in bed, buried beneath two thick comforters, before sending the message to the appropriate number in her contacts. It stated that DanskOil CEO Magnus Larsen had received a second invitation. This time it was for lunch at Moscow's famed Café Pushkin, at one o'clock the following afternoon. His host would be the chairman of TverBank, Gennady Luzhkov.

Or words to that effect.

45
Café Pushkin

The snow fell throughout the night, but by mid-morning the traffic was flowing normally along the A106, the two-lane artery connecting Rublyovka to the Moscow Ring Road. The thirty-kilometer highway was the shortest in Russia but doubtless the most pampered. The commuters who used it daily included the country's wealthiest and most powerful citizens, many of whom traveled by motorcade and worked behind the walls of the Kremlin. Keeping the highway clear of snow and ice was a priority, regardless of the drain on manpower, which was increasingly in short supply.

By the time Magnus set out from Rublyovka, the morning rush had ended. He reached the busy Kutuzovsky Prospekt at twelve thirty and arrived at Café

d on the Boulevard Ring in the historic
ict of central Moscow, fifteen minutes
edule. Inside, he was escorted to a small
he restaurant's second floor. The decor and
were pre-revolutionary Russia. Only one
he tables was occupied—by Gennady Luzhkov,
founder and chairman of TverBank, friend and confidant of the Russian president, and a former colonel in the Committee for State Security, otherwise known as the KGB.

Magnus lowered himself into the chair opposite and placed his phone on the white tablecloth in plain view. Gennady summoned the waiter, who filled their glasses with Dom Pérignon champagne.

"What's the occasion?" asked Magnus.

"Since when does a rich Russian like me need an excuse to drink champagne?"

"Are you still rich, Gennady?"

"Not as rich as I used to be. But at this stage of my life, money isn't as important as it once was." Gennady raised a pale fist to his mouth and coughed quietly. "Tell me more about this delightful woman named Astrid Sørensen."

Magnus repeated the story he had memorized in the safe house in Emdrup, that he and Astrid had been involved in an on-again, off-again affair for some time.

"It's obviously on again," said Gennady.

"Obviously," repeated Magnus.

"What are your intentions?"

"I was given an ultimatum on the way to last night's dinner party."

"What are you going to do?"

"Pursue the only sensible course of action."

"I can't say I blame you. She's quite beautiful."

The waiter placed an assortment of appetizers on the table and withdrew. Magnus helped himself to one of the meat-filled pelmeni. "And Raisa?" he asked, changing the subject. "How is she?"

"Living in Dubai with every other Russian who has the means to flee. I bought her a villa on the Palm Jumeirah. It only cost me twenty million."

"How often do you see her?"

"Once or twice a month. In fact, I was there a few days ago. Dubai is becoming more Russian by the day. It's a bit like Moscow with the thermostat set on high."

"How long can the economy withstand the sanctions and loss of so many talented young workers?"

"Not as long as the Russian people have been led to believe. Which is just one of the reasons why it is so important that you continue your joint venture with RuzNeft."

"Is that why you invited me to lunch, Gennady? To pressure me to stay in the deal?"

"Were you expecting something else?" The banker rotated his champagne glass between his thumb and forefinger. His bespoke suit fit him to perfection, but there was an unsightly gap between his throat and the collar of his handmade shirt. His skin was as white as the tablecloth. He looked unwell.

"No," said Magnus quietly. "I suppose I wasn't."

"If it makes you feel any better, it wasn't my idea."

"Whose was it?"

"Who do you think?"

"Vladimir?"

Gennady nodded. "The preservation of the DanskOil joint venture with RuzNeft is of the utmost importance to him. He would like you to know that there will be serious repercussions if you back out of the deal."

"Repercussions?"

"He didn't go into specifics. But then he rarely does."

"He intends to destroy me? What good would that do?"

"In case you haven't noticed, Volodya isn't terribly concerned about collateral damage these days. You would be wise to heed his warning and do everything humanly possible to continue the joint venture."

"Message received." Magnus seized his phone and

stood abruptly. "It was wonderful to see you again, Gennady. Please give my love to Raisa."

"But we haven't finished our lunch."

"Forgive me, but I've lost my appetite."

"At least allow me to give you this." Gennady opened his attaché case and removed a small rectangular object covered in gold wrapping paper. "It's a little something from Vladimir. A token of his esteem."

"Thank you, no," said Magnus, and started to leave.

"You're making a grave mistake, Magnus." Gennady placed the object on the table. "Open it."

Magnus reclaimed his seat and removed the gold wrapping paper. Beneath it was a dark blue gift box, and inside the box was a miniature Russian-language edition of *Doctor Zhivago* by Boris Pasternak. Magnus opened the volume to the bookmarked page and read the passage indicated by the red arrow flag.

To hope and to act, these are our duties in misfortune . . .

"Wouldn't you agree?" asked Gennady.

Magnus closed the book without a word.

"It's customary here in Russia to thank someone when they give you a gift." Gennady nudged the plate of pelmeni across the tabletop. "And you really should eat something, Magnus. Forgive me for saying this, but you look worse than I do."

———

Directly opposite Café Pushkin was a small square where Napoleon's soldiers, after entering Moscow in the autumn of 1812, had pitched their tents and burned the lime trees for warmth. The woman seated on the bench overlooking the dormant fountain was sorely tempted to do the same. Having arrived in Moscow the previous day, she was unused to the frigid Russian weather. The phone in her ungloved right hand felt as though it were a block of ice. It looked like an ordinary iPhone 14 Pro Max. It was not.

Two of the woman's associates were inside the iconic Moscow restaurant, feasting on beef stroganoff and pan-seared Muscovy duck. She knew this because she had received a photograph of their succulent meal at 12:47 p.m., when Magnus Larsen had arrived for his luncheon date with the Russian oligarch Gennady Luzhkov. The maître d' had immediately shown the Danish energy executive to a private room on the second floor. The woman's two associates had not seen him since.

Finally, at one fifteen, she received another photograph—blini with ice cream, piping hot coffee—with an accompanying update. Gennady Luzhkov was on the move. The woman, whose name was Tamara, spotted the oligarch a moment later, stepping from the restaurant's doorway. He was trailed by two body-guards. They helped him into the back of an armored Mercedes sedan and then climbed into an SUV. Both vehicles made a quick right turn onto Tverskaya Street and disappeared from Tamara's view.

Another five minutes elapsed before Magnus Larsen left the restaurant. Behind the wheel of a flashy black Range Rover, he made the same quick right turn onto Tverskaya Street. So, too, did a beleaguered Škoda hatchback. The driver was another one of Tamara's associates, a young surveillance specialist called Noam. He had been chosen for the Moscow op because, like Tamara, he was a fluent speaker of Russian.

Twenty minutes later, Noam sent her a photo. She immediately fired it to King Saul Boulevard, which in turn bounced it to Gabriel at PET headquarters in the Copenhagen suburb of Søborg. Smiling, he showed it to Lars Mortensen, his operational partner.

"Where are they?" asked the Dane.

It was Mikhail Abramov, a child of Moscow, who answered. The Collector and Komarovsky had gone to Novodevichy Cemetery to walk among the dead.

46

Novodevichy Cemetery

It was all his fault, you know."

"Not all of it, Gennady. You and your friends from the KGB certainly didn't help matters."

They were standing before the grave of Boris Yeltsin. Two of Gennady's bodyguards had followed them through the cemetery's redbrick entrance and were hovering out of earshot. Otherwise, they were alone.

"The West adored Yeltsin because he promised to magically transform Russia into a Western-style democracy," said Gennady. "And then they averted their eyes to the fact that he and the members of his inner circle were robbing Russia blind. He chose Volodya as his successor only because Volodya promised not to prosecute him. And then Volodya raised corruption to an art form."

"You did quite well for yourself, as I recall."

"We all did. But these days one needn't start a business to become rich in Russia. All one has to do is secure a job at the highest reaches of our government. The Kremlin spokesman is worth hundreds of millions of dollars. But he is a pauper in comparison to the secretary of the Security Council. Nikolai Petrov has spent his entire career working in government, and yet somehow he is worth approximately three billion dollars. I should know. The bulk of Nikolai's fortune is hidden in my bank."

They pondered the memorial for a moment in silence. It was, without question, the cemetery's most unsightly, an undulating Russian tricolor that critics had dismissed as a giant, wobbly birthday cake.

"It's hideous," declared Gennady finally.

"Quite."

"Where's your phone?"

"I seem to have left it in my car."

"It appears I've made the same mistake."

They walked along a snow-covered footpath beneath towering elm and spruce. There were graves to the left and right, small plots surrounded by low iron fences. Poets and playwrights, murderers and monsters: they lay side by side behind the walls of Novodevichy.

Gennady was coughing into his gloved hand.

"How much time do you have?" asked Magnus.

"I'm free for the remainder of the afternoon."

"To live, Gennady."

"Is it that obvious?"

"It is today, but last evening you concealed it rather well."

"I have good days and bad."

"Lung cancer?"

"And heart failure as well. My doctor has informed me that my account is already overdrawn."

"Which is why you suggested we come here."

"I find it very peaceful on days like this. It gives me a chance to think about how I wish to be remembered. Will I be a hero of Russian history or just another villain? Will I be celebrated for my courage or condemned for my greed and corruption?"

"What's the answer?"

"If I were to die this minute, I would be scorned as a greedy villain. A man who used his proximity to power to enrich himself. A loyal lapdog who did nothing when hundreds of Russian boys were being slaughtered each day in the killing fields of Ukraine. That portrait, however, would not be entirely fair."

"Because you're Komarovsky."

"And you," said Gennady, "are the Collector. Your controller is Konstantin Gromov of the SVR, but your original recruitment was a domestic matter handled by the FSB. Needless to say, you did not volunteer to become a pawn of the Russian government. There was a girl involved. Her name was—"

"You've made your point, Gennady."

They walked in silence for a moment. "There's no reason to be embarrassed, Magnus. These things happen all the time in Russia. This is the crowning achievement of Volodya's rule. He has turned Russia into a kompromat state. No one has clean hands in this kleptocracy of ours. Everyone is compromised. Some of us more than others."

"Not you, Gennady?"

"Most of my sins are financial," he admitted. "But the worst mistake I ever made was helping to make Volodya the president of the Russian Federation. He has brought us to the brink of disaster, and he needs to be stopped before he can do any more damage." He lowered his voice. "Which is why I told the CIA about a Security Council of Russia directive regarding the use of nuclear weapons in Ukraine, a directive so alarming that only a single copy exists."

"The one in Nikolai Petrov's safe."

Gennady nodded. "It is essential that the Americans and the rest of the civilized world know what Volodya and Nikolai Petrov are planning. I told the Americans that I would help them acquire the document. All I needed, I said, was a team of experienced operatives." He addressed his next remarks to the grave of the composer Shostakovich. "Imagine my surprise when they told me they were sending the CEO of DanskOil and his pretty young assistant."

"Mine as well," said Magnus.

"Who is she?"

"A professional thief."

"And what about you?" asked Gennady. "How did you get mixed up in this?"

"Kompromat."

"Theirs or ours?"

"Both."

"What in God's name have you done?"

"There's a bomb, Gennady. That's all that matters. It's a low-yield device made from South African highly enriched uranium acquired on the black market. Volodya is going to use it as a pretext to launch a nuclear strike against the Ukrainians."

"All of which is spelled out in the directive."

"Can you get us into Petrov's home?"

"Actually, we're expected tomorrow evening at ten o'clock."

"How on earth did you manage that?"

Gennady smiled. "I'm a professional."

Tamara found her way to Novodevichy in a gypsy cab driven by a fuzzy-cheeked boy of eighteen or nineteen. His battered old Kia reeked of cheap Russian tobacco and was bedecked with the letter Z. So was the boy. He wore a Z hoodie, a Z pendant round his neck, and a Z woolen hat pulled low over his eyes. The Ukrainians, he volunteered, were subhuman Nazis who needed to be exterminated. His older brother had been killed in the war, as had many of his friends. It was his profound wish, he insisted, to die for the motherland as well. Tamara shoved a wad of greasy rubles into his hand—it was tattooed with the letter Z—and wished him the very best of luck.

Across the street from the cemetery's entrance stood two hulking apartment blocks with a courtyard and car park between them. Noam was sitting on the hood of the Škoda, chatting with a couple of local skateboard hoodlums—about the war, of course. What else? Tamara declined to take part. Instead, she berated Noam for failing to pick her up at her mother's apartment. Never mind that her mother now lived in Ashdod in southern Israel.

On the opposite side of the street, the same two bodyguards were once again helping Gennady Luzhkov into the back of his armored Mercedes sedan. He looked fatigued, frail. Not so the tall Scandinavian who emerged from the cemetery five minutes later; Magnus Larsen was the very picture of health. And in good spirits, observed Tamara. It seemed his meeting with the oligarch had gone well.

His Range Rover was around the corner in a streetside space. He made his way to the Kutuzovsky Prospekt and joined the river of late-afternoon traffic flowing west. Tamara and Noam had been forbidden to follow him into the gated, high-security suburb of Rublyovka. But the Barvikha Luxury Village, located a few hundred meters beyond the first police checkpoint, was an entirely different matter. Magnus paid a brief visit to one of the few Western jewelry retailers still willing to do business in Russia. The four-carat cushion-cut diamond ring was a steal at six million rubles.

Tamara thought the purchase sufficiently noteworthy to warrant a secure satellite message to King Saul Boulevard, a message that landed a few seconds later on Gabriel's phone at PET headquarters. He received a photograph of the diamond ring in question shortly thereafter, sent to him by the woman who was now wearing it. The accompanying en clair text message, exuberant in tone, provided a wholly inaccurate explanation.

It seemed that wealthy, dashing Magnus had at long last asked young, vibrant Astrid to marry him. Astrid, of course, had agreed, provided that Magnus divorce his wife, which he had pledged to do. They were planning to celebrate their engagement that evening at the home of TverBank chairman Gennady Luzhkov. "More details to come," she wrote. "I'm so very, very happy."

47

Rublyovka

G ennady lived in a billionaires-only subdivision of Rublyovka called Mayendorf Gardens. His twelve-bedroom home, a glass-and-timber chalet once valued at more than $80 million, was among the development's least offensive. He answered the door himself, dressed in a pair of tailored flannel trousers and a cashmere sweater. The handshake he gave Magnus was perfunctory, but Ingrid he greeted warmly with Russian-style kisses on each cheek.

In the light of his soaring entrance hall, he admired the ring on her left hand. "A new addition, if I'm not mistaken."

"You don't miss much, Mr. Luzhkov."

"Nor do you, Ms. Sørensen. Or so I'm told." He

looked at Magnus. "Why such a small ring for so beautiful a woman?"

"It's four bloody carats."

"Here in Rublyovka we refer to such diamonds as accent stones."

The interior of the home was thoroughly modern. Gennady led them into the great room and with an unsteady hand filled three glasses with Domaine Ramonet Montrachet Grand Cru, one of the most expensive white wines in the world. The small talk he made was for the benefit of any listening devices that the FSB—or perhaps one of his business rivals—had managed to slip past his defenses. He seemed in no hurry to get to the business at hand.

"I hope you realize, Magnus, that I was joking about the ring. It really is quite lovely."

"I would have preferred to purchase it at Tiffany or Harry Winston, but they've closed their stores in Moscow."

"So have Hermès, Louis Vuitton, and Chanel," said Gennady. "Another unintended consequence of our so-called special military operation in Ukraine."

"I'm afraid DanskOil is next."

"I'm told you had a rather unpleasant conversation with your minister for business this evening."

"Told by whom?" asked Magnus. "Volodya?"

"Actually, it was Nikolai Petrov."

"Petrov?"

Gennady closed his eyes and nodded once.

"Why is the secretary of the Security Council monitoring my phone calls?"

"Because the secretary requires your assistance on a sensitive personal matter, and he wants to make certain you're trustworthy." Gennady turned to Ingrid and regarded her carefully for a moment. "Do you play billiards, Ms. Sørensen?"

"I'm afraid not."

"I don't believe you."

She smiled. "You shouldn't, Mr. Luzhkov."

The game room was on the lowest level of the chalet. The door, when closed, emitted a solid, coffinlike sound. Ingrid checked her phone and saw there was no service.

The room was a safe-speech facility.

Gennady was racking the balls on his billiards table, a beautiful William IV mahogany model with a red baize playing surface, perhaps early nineteenth century.

"Is this really necessary?" asked Ingrid.

"Essential."

"Why?"

"Because I have no intention of placing my life in your hands unless I know you're up to the task at hand."

"What does billiards have to do with stealing a document from a safe?"

"Everything." Gennady carefully lifted the antique wooden rack. "Care to make things interesting?"

"Trust me, Mr. Luzhkov. They already are."

"Financially," he explained.

"What did you have in mind?"

"If you can clear the table without a miss, I will pay you one million dollars."

"And if I can't?"

"Magnus will pay me the same amount."

"That hardly seems fair. Or interesting," added Ingrid. "How about three racks for ten million?"

"Done," said Gennady, and sat down next to Magnus.

Ingrid selected a cue stick and pocketed three balls on her break. Six more fell in rapid succession.

"Where did you find her?" asked Gennady.

"She found me," replied Magnus.

"Is she going to miss?"

"I can't imagine."

She cleaned the rest of the first rack, calling each shot quietly before executing it, and then moved on to the second rack, which she dispatched with equal speed and assurance. Gennady didn't bother with a third. He had seen quite enough.

He unlocked a cabinet and removed a gun. "You're quite good with a cue stick, Ms. Sørensen. But what about something like this?" He laid the weapon on the red baize surface of the table. "It's a Russian-made SR-1 Vektor, the standard-issue firearm of the FSB, the GRU, and the Presidential Security Service. It has an effective range of one hundred meters and is capable of piercing multiple layers of body armor. The magazine holds eighteen rounds. Despite its enormous power, the suppressor is quite effective."

Ingrid took up the Vektor and confidently made the weapon ready for firing.

Gennady was suitably impressed. "I don't suppose you've ever killed someone before?"

"I'm afraid not." Ingrid engaged the safety and laid the Vektor on the billiards table. "And I certainly don't intend to kill anyone tomorrow night."

"You might not have a choice. Not if you still want to be alive the following morning." Gennady returned the weapon to the cabinet and withdrew a glossy real estate brochure from the Moscow office of Sotheby's International. "Not long after Nikolai's wife died, he put his home on the market, anonymously, of course. The asking price was ninety million, and there was little interest. The Sotheby's brochure includes floor plans and photos of every room in the house, with the exception of Nikolai's office. It's located—"

"On the second floor of the mansion, overlooking the rear garden."

Gennady opened the brochure and pointed to a spot on the floor plan. "The door is located here, at the top of the main staircase, a few steps to the right."

"What about the lock?"

Gennady pointed toward the door of the game room. "Nikolai and I used the same builder. Our locks and hardware are all the same. It's a German model. Quite difficult to pick, or so I was led to believe."

Ingrid reached for her handbag. "May I give it a try?"

"Be my guest."

She went out and closed the door. Gennady locked it internally.

"Ready when you are, Ms. Sørensen."

There were two faintly audible thumps, and in she walked.

"So much for the locks being difficult to pick," said Gennady.

"Some are," said Ingrid. "Most aren't."

"What about safes?"

"The safes in most hotel rooms are a joke, but the one in Nikolai Petrov's office is the real thing."

"How are you going to get into it?"

"With the combination. How else?"

"How did you—"

"Sources and methods, Mr. Luzhkov."

"You're a quick study. But are you sure you have the right combination?"

"Within one or two digits to the left or right of each number. It won't take me more than a minute to work it out."

"What do you *think* the number is?"

She answered truthfully.

"Don't bother trying another combination. I'm certain that's the correct one."

"Why?"

"The numbers correspond to his late wife's birthday. But unlocking the safe is only half the problem. Once you're inside, you have to choose the *right* Security Council directive. There are likely to be copies of several others."

"Last time we checked, there were fourteen. But don't worry, I'll get the right one. Security Council of Russia directive 37-23\VZ, dated the twenty-fourth of August, eyes only the state president of the Russian Federation."

"I'm told it's approximately fifty pages in length. Once you finish photographing it, return downstairs and wait for Magnus and me to conclude our business."

"And what business is that?" asked Magnus.

"It seems that the secretary of the Security Council is concerned about the stability of his assets here in Russia. For that reason, he's quite anxious to transfer the bulk of his net worth to the West as quickly as possible."

"He's on the Treasury Department's sanctions list. If he tries to move his money, the Americans and Europeans will seize it."

"Which is why he's so grateful that you, a trusted friend of the Russian people, have agreed to secretly hold the money on his behalf."

"How much are we talking about?"

"Approximately two and a half billion dollars. At the conclusion of our meeting, you and Ms. Sørensen will immediately set out for Pulkovo Airport in Saint Petersburg. A private jet will be waiting for you at the FBO in the morning. Leave your vehicle in the car park. You won't be needing it again."

"Where is the plane going?"

"Because of the sanctions and travel restrictions, our options are rather limited. I suppose we could send you to Uzbekistan or Kyrgyzstan, but Istanbul seemed rather more unappealing. Your friends from the CIA can meet you there."

"And what about you, Gennady?"

"I plan to take another walk in Novodevichy and think about how I wish to be remembered."

"Whatever you do," said Magnus, "don't think too long."

Gennady smiled sadly. "No chance of that."

48
Copenhagen

The audio transmissions from Ingrid's and Magnus Larsen's phones went silent at 7:36 p.m. Copenhagen time and resumed forty-nine minutes later. Their location had not changed in the interim; they were inside the home of TverBank chairman Gennady Luzhkov in the exclusive Rublyovka gated community known as Mayendorf Gardens. A dinner was in progress. The conversation was empty and banal, and contained no clues as to what had transpired earlier. Ingrid eventually sent along a photograph, en clair, of the wine they were drinking with their meal. It was Château Le Pin Pomerol. In the op center at PET headquarters, mouths watered.

Ingrid waited until she had left Luzhkov's home

before dispatching her next message, this time using the satellite feature of her Genesis communications device. It stated that she and Magnus were expected at the Rublyovka residence of Secretary Nikolai Petrov at ten the following evening and that they would be departing Russia early the following morning aboard a private aircraft chartered by Gennady Luzhkov. It would depart not from Moscow but from Pulkovo Airport in Saint Petersburg. Its destination, according to the message, would be Istanbul.

It was a remarkable achievement on Luzhkov's part. As promised, the oligarch had managed to gain access to Nikolai Petrov's home. But what were the circumstances of the late-night visit? Gabriel had no idea. And how did Luzhkov propose to keep Petrov occupied while Ingrid opened the safe and photographed the Security Council directive? Gabriel hadn't a clue. And what was Luzhkov's plan in the event something went wrong? In all likelihood, he hadn't one. Neither, for that matter, did Gabriel, which meant that the life of a woman he had sent into Russia was in the hands of a man he had never met.

He remained in the PET op center until midnight, then headed to the American Embassy, where he spent the next two hours on a secure line to Langley. It was nearly 3:00 a.m. when he finally returned to the safe house. He managed to get a few hours of badly needed sleep, and by midafternoon he was showered and dressed and stalking the rooms with a severe case of preoperational jitters.

Ordinarily, he would have taken comfort in the soundness of his plan and the care with which he had assembled and rehearsed it. But the plan for tonight, if there was one, was in the hands of Gennady Luzhkov. Gabriel would be nothing more than a distant observer, helpless to influence the course of events. For an operational mastermind of his stature, it was the equivalent of driving a car without a steering wheel or throttle.

He was certain, however, that he could not spend the rest of the afternoon pacing the floors of the safe house, so he rang Lars Mortensen and requested a PET security detail. At half past four, with the afternoon light fading, the two bodyguards were following him along Strøget, Copenhagen's famed pedestrian shopping street. Eli Lavon, in a fedora and a woolen overcoat, walked beside him. The watcher's eyes were restless.

"They're the happiest people in the world, the Danes. Did you know that?"

"Second happiest," said Gabriel.

Lavon was incredulous. "Who's happier than the Danish people?"

"Finns."

"I thought Finns were the most depressed."

"They are."

"So how can they be the happiest people in the world and the most depressed as well?"

"It's a statistical anomaly."

Gabriel slowed to a stop outside a sporting goods store. On the second floor of the building, its windows darkened, was Nielsen Antiquarian.

He looked at Lavon and smiled. "So much for some scandals being too big to sweep under the rug."

"We have a long night ahead of us."

They entered a café on the opposite side of the street. Gabriel ordered their coffees in German-accented English while Lavon took inventory of the patrons at the surrounding tables.

"Looking for something?" asked Gabriel.

"A Russian assassin preparing to kill you."

"They've already tried that."

"You know what they say. Fourth time's the charm."

"That's not what they say, Eli."

They carried their coffees to a table outside in the street. The two bodyguards stood watch nearby.

Lavon lit a cigarette. "How long do you think it would take them to draw their weapons from beneath their coats?"

"Several seconds longer than it would take me to draw mine. Unless, of course, I'm overcome by smoke."

Lavon slowly crushed out his cigarette. "You realize, I hope, that you're engaging in displacement activity."

"Am I?"

"It's a psychological defense mechanism in which—"

"I know what displacement activity is, Eli. I was paying attention that day at the academy."

"So what's really bothering you? And don't tell me that it's my one bad habit."

"I'm worried about Ingrid."

"She knows what she's doing," replied Lavon. "And we trained her to within an inch of her life. We also reminded her, over and over again, to walk away if necessary."

"She has a stubborn streak."

"But she's more disciplined than you realize. And she has talent that only nature can bestow."

"Or a mental disorder," said Gabriel.

"You have a similar disorder. It just manifests itself differently."

"Please tell me more, Dr. Lavon."

"Your childhood left you with a textbook case of second-generation Holocaust survivor syndrome, which in turn instilled in you an almost uncontrollable need to repair things."

"Or to prevent the Russians from unleashing Armageddon."

"I was there a few weeks ago."

"The Tel Megiddo dig?"

Lavon nodded. "I'm relieved to report that I saw no sign the end times are at hand."

"You must not have been looking in the right place."

Gabriel's phone pulsed. Ingrid was hitting the gym in preparation for tonight's festivities at the home of the secretary of the Security Council of Russia. The accompanying photograph depicted her left hand wrapped around the grip of a dumbbell.

"Nice ring," remarked Lavon.

"Nice girl."

"She's a thief."

"So am I," said Gabriel. "I spent my entire career stealing secrets and lives."

"For your country, not for money."

"She gives it away."

"Except for the money she used to buy her beachfront home in Denmark and her holiday villa on Mykonos."

"Where she will spend the next several years in hiding because of her work tonight."

"She doesn't strike me as the sort of person to lie low for long. Needless to say," added Lavon, "you suffer from that disorder as well."

"Leah's doctor informed me that I'm not a normal person and that I will never *be* a normal person."

"An astute observation. But then he did actually go to medical school." Lavon watched the pedestrians filing past them in the street. "They certainly *seem* happy."

"But not as happy as the Finns."

"Ever been?"

"To Finland?" Gabriel shook his head. "What about you?"

"Once."

"Office?"

"An archaeology conference in Helsinki. I have to say, the people didn't strike me as particularly cheerful."

"It probably had something to do with the fact that their city was overrun with archaeologists."

Lavon lit another cigarette. "What is it now?"

"The note that Ingrid left in my room the morning she left for Russia."

"The one that said she wouldn't let you down?"

Gabriel nodded.

"She won't," said Lavon.

"That's exactly what I'm afraid of, Eli."

49

Rublyovka

At the conclusion of her workout, Ingrid swam a few laps in Magnus's indoor pool, then headed upstairs to shower and dress. Her clothing for the evening was laid out on the bed. Stretch jeans, a black pullover and jacket, low-heeled suede boots. Her black Givenchy handbag, which she had purchased earlier that day at the Barvikha Luxury Village, was large enough to accommodate an extra ring of keys, a screwdriver with a tape-wrapped grip, and a Russian-made Vektor pistol and suppressor.

At present the weapon was locked in the cabinet in Gennady Luzhkov's game room. He was expecting Ingrid and Magnus at eight o'clock for a light supper and a final run-through. Ingrid wasn't looking forward to it. She didn't believe in last-minute rehearsals, and she never ate before a score. Food weighed her down, doused the flame. It had been building in her all afternoon. Her skin felt feverish, her fingertips were tingling. She took no steps to alleviate her symptoms. They would subside when the document was hers.

The mundane chores of drying her hair and applying her makeup usually provided some relief, but not tonight; she was possessed. Afterward she regarded the finished product in the looking glass. Her shoulders and thighs were taut and hard. Her honey-colored skin was flawless. Not a drop of ink anywhere. Nothing that could be used to identify her. The invisible girl.

She dressed without a sound, then took up her handbag and went downstairs. She found Magnus in his woolen overcoat, pacing the rooms of his Russian palace for a last time. His hand shook as he checked the time on the Piaget wristwatch given to him by the Russian president.

He remembered to say a few words for the sake of the Thought Police. "Are you ready, Astrid? Gennady is probably wondering where we are."

Magnus had already loaded their bags in the back of the Range Rover and topped the tank with petrol. A few flakes of snow fell through the glow of the headlamps during the drive to Gennady's timber-and-glass chalet. Inside, he led them straight to the game room and closed the heavy door. The Vektor pistol was lying on the red surface of the billiards table with the suppressor screwed onto the end of the barrel. Next to it was an aluminum-sided attaché case.

"Open it," said Gennady.

Ingrid popped the latches and lifted the cover. Inside were tightly packed bundles of crisp hundred-dollar bills.

"A half-million-dollar down payment on the money I owe you," explained Gennady. "I'll wire the remaining sum to a bank of your choosing."

"It wasn't a real bet, Mr. Luzhkov."

"That's what the loser of a ten-million-dollar wager is supposed to say, not the winner. If nothing else, please accept the money as payment for what you are about to do. You deserve every penny."

"In my line of work, we generally get paid at the end of the job. And only if we're successful."

"Nevertheless, a bet is a bet, Ms. Sørensen."

"Banca Privada d'Andorra. My account manager is a man named Estevan Castells."

Gennady smiled. "I know him well."

Ingrid closed the attaché case and checked the combination settings on the locks. The latch on the left was set to 2-7-1. The latch on the right was 1-5-5.

"Do you recognize the numbers?" asked Gennady.

They were the same six digits as the combination for Nikolai Petrov's safe. Twenty-seven, eleven, fifty-five. Ingrid locked the briefcase and scrambled the dials. Then she unscrewed the suppressor from the barrel of the Vektor and slid both into her handbag.

"Please place the bag over your shoulder," said Gennady. "I'd like to have a look at it."

Ingrid did as he asked. The gun weighed nearly a kilo, but the bag was sturdy enough in structure to conceal its presence.

"Most people would never be allowed to get near Nikolai Petrov with a gun," said Gennady. "But because this is a social call, and because you will be with me, a trusted member of the Russian president's innermost circle, I'm confident Nikolai's security detail won't insult you by demanding to search your bag."

"Is he expecting me?"

"Actually, he insisted you come. For all his ultranationalist bluster, Nikolai can be quite charming, especially in the company of attractive young women. But under no circumstances will he discuss business in front of you. Nor will I, for that matter. After a few minutes of pleasantries, I will suggest that we find a quiet place to talk, leaving you free to make your way to his office."

"And you're sure there are no cameras?"

"Inside his private residence? Nikolai would never dream of it."

"What about the members of his security detail?"

"The guards will be outside the house, including in the rear garden. Therefore, it is essential that you make certain the blinds are closed in Nikolai's office before you switch on the desk lamp to photograph the document."

"Security Council of Russia directive 37-23\VZ, dated the twenty-fourth of August, eyes only the state president of the Russian Federation."

"That's the one." Gennady checked the time. "We should leave for Nikolai's in a half hour or so. Why don't we have something to eat and try to relax?"

Gennady's staff had left a tray of traditional Russian sandwiches and salads in the kitchen. Ingrid had only black coffee to drink. She was tempted to steal something, anything, just to take the edge off. The fingers of her right hand were working the imaginary dial of Nikolai Petrov's safe. Four turns to the right, three to left, two to the right. Twenty-seven, eleven, fifty-five. Magnus and Gennady were oblivious to the fire consuming her. They were watching Dmitry Budanov's nightly tirade on NTV—with increasing alarm.

Magnus swore softly.

Ingrid's hand went still. "Is something wrong?"

It was Gennady who answered. "Dmitry Sergeyevich is hearing ominous things from his sources in Russian intelligence. Evidently, these sources are telling him that the Ukrainians have managed to acquire a crude, low-yield nuclear weapon. Dmitry Sergeyevich seems to think Russia should launch a preemptive strike against the Ukrainians."

"Does he know something?"

Gennady's phone rang before he could answer. He lifted the device to his ear, spoke a few words quietly in Russian, then killed the connection.

"Nikolai is running behind schedule. He's with Volodya at Novo-Ogaryovo. A matter of the utmost urgency. He'll call us when the meeting is over."

Ingrid quickly dispatched a secure satellite message on her Genesis phone, advising the recipient to watch NTV. Then she placed her hand on the imaginary dial of Nikolai Petrov's safe. Four turns to the right, three to the left, two to the right.

Twenty-seven, eleven, fifty-five.

50
Rublyovka

When another forty-five minutes passed with no word from Petrov, Ingrid broke into Gennady's game room with her bump key and shot pool to settle her nerves. She ran five straight tables and had a single ball remaining on her sixth when Magnus finally called down that it was time to leave. The last ball was the dreaded thirteen, but the shot was dead straight into a near corner, the kind she could drop nine out of ten times with her eyes closed. Rather than tempt fate, she laid the cue stick on the table and headed upstairs.

Magnus and Gennady were waiting in the entrance hall in their overcoats and gloves. Ingrid went quickly into the kitchen to fetch her things. She conducted a needless final inventory, just to put at least a portion of her mind at ease. The bump key was in the front-right pocket of her jeans. A screwdriver with tape-wrapped grip was in her handbag along with the gun and its suppressor. Her phone she would carry in plain sight. The clandestine camera function was engaged. She would wait until they were on their way to Saint Petersburg to transmit the photos securely to Gabriel.

She pulled on her overcoat and, taking up the cash-filled attaché case, followed Magnus and Gennady into the frigid night. The snow was coming down harder now, big downy flakes falling straight from a black sky. Gennady, head lowered, made for the open rear door of his Mercedes. Ingrid placed the attaché case on the backseat of the Range Rover and climbed into the passenger seat. Magnus slid behind the wheel and started the engine.

"Petrov was leaving Novo-Ogaryovo when he rang. We should arrive at his home at roughly the same time."

"What do you suppose they were talking about?"

"Nikolai and Volodya? Why don't you ask him?"

"I just might."

"I was only joking." He gave her a sideways look. "Can you at least pretend to be a little nervous?"

"I don't get nervous."

"I do," said Magnus. "Quite nervous, in fact."

"Don't be." She gave his hand a reassuring squeeze. "Everything is going to be fine."

But only if she was able to pick the lock on the door of Nikolai Petrov's office, open his safe, find the correct Security Council of Russia directive, photograph the directive, and return it to the safe without Petrov or his security goons noticing. They were all former Spetsnaz soldiers and would be armed with the same type of sidearm presently hidden in Ingrid's handbag, an SR-1 Vektor purportedly capable of piercing thirty layers of Kevlar body armor. Her black pullover and jacket would provide little defense. If she were forced to draw the weapon, she thought, she would be dead. And so would Gennady and Magnus. Their deaths, however, would be slower than hers—and exponentially more painful.

They followed Gennady's motorcade along the tranquil private lanes of Mayendorf Gardens and out the development's front gate. The high-security community known as Somerset Estates was located on the westernmost fringes of Rublyovka along the banks of the Moskva River. Residents referred to it colloquially as "the Kremlin." Its defensive outer wall was the color of terra-cotta and at least six meters in height. The only entrance was flanked by two Gothic-style clock towers with green spires. All that was missing, thought Ingrid, were the luminous red stars.

Magnus slowed to a stop behind the Mercedes SUV

containing Gennady's bodyguards. The oligarch had assured them that the security check at the compound's entrance would be cursory. But when a minute passed with no movement, Ingrid removed the gun and suppressor from her handbag and slid it beneath her seat.

Another minute passed before Gennady and his bodyguards were granted admission to the compound. A security guard with a PP-2000 submachine gun slung across his chest beckoned Magnus forward, then raised a gloved hand. Magnus braked to a halt and, lowering his window, bade the guard a pleasant evening.

A conversation ensued, not a single word of which Ingrid was able to comprehend. Then the guard embarked on a slow walk around the vehicle. The beam of his powerful torch lingered for a moment on Ingrid's face—and on the aluminum-sided attaché case lying on the backseat. Returning to Magnus's open window, he inquired as to the contents of the bag. Of that, Ingrid was certain. Hearing Magnus's answer, the guard waved them forward.

Ingrid returned the gun to her handbag. "Did he ask you what was in the attaché case?"

"Yes, of course."

"What did you tell him?"

"The truth."

"He didn't think it odd?"

"In Rublyovka? You must be joking."

Gennady's two-car motorcade was waiting a few meters beyond the gate, tailpipes gently smoking. Magnus followed it past a parade of floodlit reproduction palaces, here Buckingham and Blenheim, here Élysée and Schönbrunn. There was also a miniature Kensington Palace, complete with an ornate gold-leaf gate, through which all three vehicles were allowed to pass without inspection.

The owner of the property was at that moment emerging from the back of a sleek Russian-made Aurus Senat limousine. It was a smaller version of the car used by the man with whom he had just finished meeting at Novo-Ogaryovo. He had a phone to his ear and was carrying his own attaché case. Because it was snowing heavily, he hurried through the front door of his home without first greeting his three late-night visitors.

The limousine rolled away with the slowness of a hearse, but a few members of Petrov's security detail remained behind in the forecourt. One of them was chatting with Gennady, who was clutching an attaché case of his own. Inside were financial documents related to tonight's after-hours gathering. The security man did not know that. Still, he appeared to have no interest in looking inside the bag. The man holding it was a former KGB officer and a trusted member of the Russian president's innermost circle. He was also Nikolai Petrov's banker and the manager of a significant portion of his ill-gotten wealth. He was above suspicion, as was his friend Magnus Larsen.

Magnus switched off the Range Rover's engine and opened his door. "Wait here," he said to Ingrid. "I won't be but a moment."

He climbed out and started across the forecourt toward Gennady. Ingrid, affecting irritation, lowered the visor and touched up her makeup in the lighted vanity mirror. A security man in cold-weather gear observed her efforts from his post on the snow-whitened lawn.

Judging her appearance satisfactory, she raised the mirror and saw Magnus walking back to the Range Rover. He opened her door and said quietly, "Let's go."

She seized her handbag and climbed out. Magnus draped an arm around her shoulders as they walked over to Gennady, who wore on his face a businesslike smile. The security men in the forecourt allowed them to approach the front of the residence unimpeded. The guard standing watch at the entrance opened the door for them and then stepped to one side.

They were in.

Gennady led the way into the foyer, and behind

them the door closed. Ingrid quickly took her bearings. The mansion's overwrought center hall was exactly the way it had appeared in the Sotheby's brochure. Arched passageways left and right, the curved main staircase straight ahead. The marble floor was the color of a gold bar, as were the appalling wall treatments. The light of the crystal chandelier was surgical white.

They followed the sound of Nikolai Petrov's voice through a passageway on the left, into a cavernous drawing room. It had been furnished expensively but without taste. Petrov was still on the phone and had yet to shed his overcoat. He had placed his attaché case on a credenza. It was a handsome leather model, black in color, with twin combination locks.

Petrov caught Gennady's eye and pointed out the silver drinks tray resting on one of the oversize coffee tables. Gennady removed the cap from a bottle of Johnnie Walker Blue Label and poured out three glasses. Ingrid accepted hers with a relaxed smile.

Gennady poured a fourth glass of the whisky and gave it to Nikolai Petrov. Two additional minutes went by before he finally ended his phone call. His eyes settled immediately on Ingrid. He addressed her in excellent English.

"Please forgive me, Ms. Sørensen. But as you can imagine, I'm rather busy at the moment." He slid his phone into the breast pocket of his jacket and extended his hand. "It is a pleasure to finally meet you. I'm only sorry we weren't introduced at Yuri Glazkov's dinner party. I might have been able to prevent you from making a dreadful mistake."

"What mistake is that, Secretary Petrov?"

"Marrying Magnus, of course. A woman like you could do much better."

At Petrov's suggestion, they removed their coats and sat down. Ingrid settled next to Magnus with the Givenchy bag at her side. Nikolai Petrov was eyeing her over his drink.

"I'm told you work with Magnus at DanskOil."

"That's correct, Secretary Petrov."

"Is there no way you can convince him not to dissolve his joint venture with RuzNeft?"

"I'm trying, but our woke prime minister is putting enormous pressure on poor Magnus to walk away from our Russian investments."

Petrov smiled. "Gennady tells me you're something of a populist."

"A populist? Oh, no, Secretary Petrov. I'm a true extremist."

"Please don't get her started," lamented Magnus. "Astrid makes me sound like a green social justice warrior."

"How refreshing," said Petrov. "Tell me something, Ms. Sørensen. How many genders are there?"

"There are two, Secretary Petrov."

"Can one choose one's gender?"

"Only in the leftist fantasy world that the West has become."

"And which gender are you? Or is a question like that a microaggression?"

"I'm a woman."

"Perhaps there's hope for the West, after all."

"Only if Russia wins the war in Ukraine."

"You needn't worry about that, Ms. Sørensen." Petrov shot a glance at his Tag Heuer wristwatch and hoisted himself to his feet. "I'd love to continue this conversation, but it's getting late, and I have business to discuss with my banker and your future husband."

"I understand," said Ingrid.

"Would you mind waiting here?" asked Petrov. "I promise not to keep Magnus long."

Ingrid smiled. "Take as much time as you need."

Gennady and Magnus rose in unison and, after a brief exchange in Russian, followed Nikolai Petrov into the adjoining room. The wood-paneled library, thought Ingrid, recalling the Sotheby's brochure.

Hand-crafted elegance, Old World style and grace. It was Gennady, with a mischievous wink, who closed the door behind them, leaving Ingrid entirely alone. Her skin felt feverish. Her fingertips were tingling.

51

Rublyovka

As Russian money laundering operations went, it really wasn't all that complicated. Gennady's explanation, however, was byzantine in its detail.

The process would begin, he said, with a series of wire transfers to a disreputable house of finance in Dubai with which TverBank was doing an increasingly brisk business. To avoid detection by FinCEN and other international watchdogs, the transfers would be on the smallish side, a few hundred million rubles, no more. The crooked Dubai-based house of finance would convert these rubles into dirhams, and the dirhams into dollars, all in the blink of an eye. Then the dollars would be fired to Argos Bank in the southern Cypriot town of Limassol, where they would be deposited in the account of a holding company clandestinely owned by Magnus Larsen, the CEO of Denmark's largest producer of oil and natural gas.

"I will oversee things from TverBank headquarters," Gennady continued. "But Magnus will have to fly to Cyprus first thing in the morning to sign the necessary paperwork at Bank Argos. He will remain in Limassol until the funds have been successfully offshored. I expect it to take no more than forty-eight hours."

"And when it's finished?" asked Nikolai Petrov.

"Magnus will secretly control a significant portion of your wealth. He will invest it wisely on your behalf using an array of anonymous shell corporations. Because he is a Danish citizen who is not currently under American or European sanctions, the money cannot be seized or frozen. He is the ideal wallet for a man in your position."

"I must have approval over all investments."

"Impossible, Nikolai. It is essential that you have no contact with Magnus whatsoever. For all intents and purposes, the money will be in a blind trust. Think of Magnus as your secret investment manager."

"The manager of a two-and-a-half-billion-dollar hedge fund?"

"In a manner of speaking, yes."

They were seated on opposing leather couches,

Gennady and Magnus on one, Nikolai Petrov on the other. On the low-slung table between them stood a nineteenth-century golden ormolu clock. The time was half past eleven. Seven minutes had passed since they left Ingrid and entered the library.

Petrov was contemplating his whisky. "And what sort of fee does my manager intend to charge for his services? The standard two and twenty?"

"The bankers in Dubai and Cyprus will take their cuts," said Gennady. "But Magnus has made it clear that he will accept no payment."

"How generous of him. But I require assurances nevertheless."

"What sort of assurances?"

"The kind one generally receives when entrusting a man with two and a half billion dollars."

"Magnus has been a great friend and supporter of Russia. And he has never done anything to violate our trust."

"That's because Magnus is a most compromised man." Petrov looked at Gennady's attaché case. "I assume you have some papers you'd like me to sign."

"That's putting it mildly."

"I intend to read every word of every document."

"I wouldn't have it any other way."

Gennady removed a thick folder from the attaché

case and laid it on the table next to the golden ormolu clock.

It was 11:35 p.m.

The door was where Gennady had promised it would be, at the top of the central staircase, a few steps to the right. Ingrid slid the bump key into the German-made lock and gave it a single tap with the handle of the screwdriver. A second strike wasn't necessary; the lock yielded at once. She turned the latch, and the door swung inward without a sound.

She stepped inside and closed the door behind her. From below she heard a baritone murmur of male voices, but otherwise there was no sound. There was no light, either. Petrov had left the shades drawn, a time-saving piece of good fortune.

She slipped the bump key and screwdriver into her handbag, then drew the Genesis phone. Using only the glow of the home screen, she illuminated her surroundings. The room was instantly familiar; she had entered another version of it several hundred times in an office building in suburban Copenhagen. The desk, the chair and ottoman, the drop leaf table.

The safe . . .

She crouched before it and laid a hand on the dialer. When Petrov had used it last, it had come to rest on the number forty-nine. She turned it counterclockwise five times to reset the wheels of the lock, then stopped on twenty-seven. The rest of the combination she entered as though it were second nature. The last step in the process was to turn the dial clockwise again until it stopped. The bolt retracted with a gentle thump.

The combination was accurate.

Ingrid opened the heavy door and shone the flashlight of the Genesis into the interior. Gold ingots, bundles of cash, Security Council of Russia documents stored vertically like books on a shelf.

She removed the first document, examined the cover page, then returned it to the safe. She did the same to the neighboring document, and the next one, and the one after that as well. And on it went, document after document, until she reached the end of the row. Then she closed and locked the door and reset the dial to forty-nine.

Security Council of Russia directive 37-23\VZ was not in Nikolai Petrov's safe.

The floor plan in the Sotheby's brochure had shown four large bedrooms on the second level of the mansion, all with private en suite baths. After slipping from Petrov's office, Ingrid turned to the right and made for a pair of double doors. The latch gave way, and she went inside. Exterior floodlight poured through tall, unshaded windows. Ingrid recognized the furnishings; photographs of the room had appeared in the sales brochure. By all appearances it was a guest room. There was nothing out of place, nothing personal—and no sign of a Security Council directive dated August 24, 2022, eyes only the state president of the Russian Federation.

Leaving the room, Ingrid headed toward the double doors at the opposite side of the landing. Beyond them was the bedroom of Nikolai Petrov. Once again, it was partially illuminated by exterior light. Ingrid peered around the edge of one of the windows and spotted two guards, silhouettes only, standing watch in the snow-covered garden below. Her search was rapid but thorough, the search of a professional thief—the bedside tables, the dressing room, the bath and commode. The Security Council directive was nowhere to be found.

She didn't bother to look in the other rooms; there wasn't time. Instead, she stole silently down the central staircase and reclaimed her seat in the drawing room. One of the baritone male voices in the library was now issuing what sounded like a threat of violence, an obligatory element of any gathering involving Russians and money. Fingertips tingling, Ingrid drained her glass of Johnnie Walker Blue Label and stared at the attaché case resting on the credenza. The attaché case that Nikolai Petrov had taken to his meeting that evening with the Russian president. A handsome leather model, black in color, with twin combination locks.

Nikolai Petrov did not make good on his vow to read every word of the documents, but he gave them a thorough review nonetheless, and even excised a few passages he found objectionable. Gennady had made certain to include a few extra needless declarations to sign, all of which required his own needless counter-signature. Magnus delayed matters further by taking issue with a clause regarding his liability for investment losses. He was more than willing to hold the client's money free of charge, but under no circumstances would he agree to make the client whole for a bad bet or two.

It was 11:52 p.m. when Petrov signed his name to the last of the documents. Gennady handed over a set to Magnus. He would need them to activate the accounts at Bank Argos. At least that was the explanation Gennady gave to Nikolai Petrov, not a word of which was true. Neither was Gennady's description of Magnus's travel itinerary—a predawn flight from Moscow to Cairo on EgyptAir, a midafternoon connection into Larnaca.

Petrov demanded to know where Magnus would be staying in Cyprus.

"The Four Seasons in Limassol," he answered, untruthfully.

"Alone?"

"Astrid is coming with me."

"She really is a remarkable woman," said Petrov as he rose to his feet. "It would be a shame if anything were to happen to her."

"Don't worry, Nikolai. I'll take very good care of your money."

"I certainly hope so. Otherwise, you will die a slow and painful death. A Russian death," said Petrov. "Trust me, Magnus. There's a difference."

They pulled on their overcoats and gloves, and Nikolai Petrov, having threatened murder only a moment earlier, showed them graciously into the night. In the snow-dusted forecourt, with the security guards looking on, Gennady shook Magnus's hand. The last of his three formal Russian kisses lingered on Ingrid's left cheek.

"Was it there?" he asked quietly.

"Run, Gennady," was all she said.

Expressionless, he lowered himself into the back of the Mercedes, and Ingrid and Magnus climbed into the

Range Rover. Two minutes later, after passing between the twin Gothic-style towers at the front gate, they were racing eastward along the most pampered highway in all of Russia. Their phones lay between them on the center console. Ingrid spoke as though the FSB was listening.

"How did your meeting go?" she asked with profound if contrived indifference.

"Better than I expected. Nikolai only threatened to kill me once. You, however, made quite an impression on him. He thinks you're a remarkable woman."

"I am, actually."

"What have you done now?"

"I got you a little something for our trip to Cyprus."

Ingrid reached into her handbag and removed the only copy of Security Council of Russia directive 37-23\ VZ. Magnus glanced at the document, then stared straight ahead, both hands gripping the wheel.

"It's beautiful," he said calmly. "But you really shouldn't have."

"I couldn't resist." Ingrid laid the document across her lap and reached for her phone. "What time does our plane leave tomorrow morning?"

"Five thirty, I'm afraid."

Ingrid groaned and photographed the document's

cover page. "We might as well go straight to Sheremetyevo."

"I have to say, I'm looking forward to spending a few days by the sea in Limassol."

"Not as much as I am," replied Ingrid, and photographed the next page.

52

Rublyovka–Copenhagen

Nikolai Petrov poured another two fingers of the Johnnie Walker Blue Label scotch into his glass and, snatching his attaché case from the credenza, headed up the stairs to the door of his office. The room he entered was in darkness. He placed the attaché case on the desk and switched on the lamp. Then he lifted the receiver of his secure phone to his ear and from memory dialed the number for the overnight duty officer at FSB headquarters in Lubyanka.

The officer's voice, when he came on the line, sounded heavy with fatigue—or perhaps alcohol. His tone changed abruptly when Petrov identified himself.

"Good evening, Secretary Petrov. How can I help you?"

Petrov told the officer what he wanted, a routine check of an airline passenger manifest.

"Which flight?"

"EgyptAir 725. Tomorrow morning."

Petrov heard the clatter of a keyboard. When it stopped, the duty officer said, "They're in first class. Seats 2A and 2B."

The next call Petrov placed was to the Four Seasons Hotel in Limassol. He did so from his personal cellular device. "Larsen," he told the switchboard operator. "Magnus Larsen."

"I'm sorry, but we have no one by that name staying in the hotel."

"Are you certain? I was told he was there."

"One moment, please." The operator placed Petrov on hold. She was back on the line a few seconds later. "Mr. Larsen and his wife are checking in tomorrow."

"My mistake," said Petrov, and killed the connection.

His wife . . .

Things had turned out rather well for Magnus. And to think that twenty years ago he was sitting in a room in Lubyanka watching a video of himself with a naked Russian girl less than half his age. He had never raged, never wept, never begged to be let off the hook. Instead, he had done everything they asked of him, no matter how demeaning or dirty—including the little errand he had run in South Africa. Petrov had to hand it to Magnus; he had played a rotten hand with considerable skill. And look at him now. A palace in Rublyovka, a beautiful young fiancée.

And two and half billion dollars of Nikolai Petrov's money . . .

A remarkable twist of fate, that. Still, Petrov was confident he held the upper hand. The woman was his insurance policy. Magnus would never do anything to place her life in danger.

Petrov took a long pull at the whisky, then, perhaps unwisely, poured the rest down his throat. He placed the empty glass on the drop leaf table next to his reading chair and checked the combination dial on his safe. It was set to the number forty-nine, which is how Petrov had left it that morning. The heavy-duty locks on his attaché case were likewise set to the proper numbers. These never varied. The left was set to 9-3-4, the right to 8-0-6.

He dialed in the correct combinations—2-7-1 on the left, 1-5-5 on the right—and popped the latches. He was about to lift the lid but stopped when his secure phone rattled. It was Semenov, one of his senior aides, calling from the Kremlin with the nightly casualty figures from Ukraine. The real numbers, not the pulp they fed to the Russian people through the likes of Dmitry Budanov. Today's fighting had been particularly costly. Another six hundred dead and wounded, most of them conscripts and convicts who had been cut to pieces by Ukrainian machine gunners in Bakhmut and Soledar.

It couldn't continue for much longer, thought Petrov as he hung up the phone. And if all went according to plan, it wouldn't. It was spelled out in granular detail in the document in his briefcase. The false-flag provocation, the measured tactical reprisal, the likely American and NATO response, the inevitable escalation that would push the world to the brink of nuclear annihilation for the first time since the Cuban missile crisis.

Petrov had war-gamed every scenario, calculated the mathematical probability of every potential outcome. He was confident the Americans would never use their nuclear weapons against Russia and risk the destruction of their cities and the loss of millions of innocent lives. Not in defense of a country most American citizens couldn't find on a map. The outcome of the crisis, therefore, would be a Russian victory in Ukraine, which would in turn lead to widespread civil and political disorder in the West and the collapse of NATO. The end result of this epochal upheaval would be a new global order, one with Russia, not the Americans, in charge.

And it would begin, thought Petrov as he extinguished the lamp in his office, in a few hours' time, with a single word. It wasn't until he was stretched out in his bed that he realized he had neglected to lock the Security Council directive in his safe. It was no matter; his home was located in the most secure gated compound in Russia and was surrounded by a small army of trained killers. The document wasn't going anywhere. Or so Nikolai Petrov assured himself, at 12:38 p.m. Moscow time, as he closed his eyes and slept the sleep of the dead.

The first photograph arrived at the op center at PET headquarters with the impact of an errant Russian ballistic missile. The Cyrillic numerals and letters 37-23\VZ were clearly visible; it was almost certainly the cover page of the Russian Security Council directive. But for reasons that were not yet clear, the document appeared to be resting on the knees of the woman who had photographed it. Even more troubling was her current location and heading, as depicted by the winking blue light on Eli Lavon's laptop computer.

"Please tell me she didn't," he said gravely.

"It certainly appears she did," replied Gabriel. "But maybe you should check the GPS data just to be sure."

Lavon extracted the coordinates embedded in the image. "She did," he said. "She definitely did."

Gabriel swore softly. Ingrid had removed the Security Council directive from Nikolai Petrov's mansion in Rublyovka. "How long do you suppose we have until he discovers it's missing?"

"Who says he doesn't know already?"

"She must have had a good reason."

"Like what?"

"We'll know in a minute, Eli."

Just then the next photograph hit their screens. It was the directive's opening page, a brief summary of what was to come. Lavon and Mikhail translated the material for Gabriel and Lars Mortensen.

"Dear God," said the Danish intelligence chief.

"And we haven't got to the good part yet," added Gabriel gloomily.

"No," said Lavon as the next page appeared on his computer. "But we're definitely getting warmer."

"What does it say?"

"It says that Ingrid needs to send us the rest of the document before Petrov finds her."

The images began arriving at regular intervals, one page of the directive every ten or fifteen seconds. Gabriel fired them securely to Langley, where they were set upon by the analysts and translators of the Russia

House. Within a few minutes, Adrian Carter's remaining hair was officially on fire. And with good reason; the directive left nothing to the imagination. It was a meticulously detailed blueprint for waging nuclear war in Ukraine, a war that would begin with a false-flag provocation code-named Plan Aurora. The hands of the Doomsday Clock, thought Gabriel, read one minute to midnight. Maybe less than that.

Nine minutes after they received the first photograph, they received the last. By then the winking blue light on Eli Lavon's computer screen had reached the Moscow Ring Road. Five minutes later, at twelve thirty local time, it was headed north on the M11, the Moscow–Saint Petersburg Motorway. Google Maps estimated the driving time to Pulkovo Airport to be seven hours. The chance of encountering snowfall along the way, according to the latest forecast, was one hundred percent. The odds that Ingrid and Magnus Larsen would make it out of Russia alive, calculated Gabriel, were somewhere around zero.

And they were about to get worse.

"What now?" asked Eli Lavon.

"Adrian wants me to get over to the American Embassy so we can have a word in private over Langley's network."

"About what?"

"Page thirty-six of the directive."

"Is it happening?"

"It might be."

"You don't think the Americans—"

"Yeah, Eli. I think they are."

With the exception of a brief diversion around the city of Tver and a zigzag through the lakes of the Valdaysky National Park, it was essentially a straight line radiating from the eleven o'clock position on the Moscow Ring Road and terminating at the southern gates of Saint Petersburg. Hiding was impossible; there were tolls to pay and cameras monitoring the flow of traffic. At 1:20 a.m. on a miserable winter's night, it was a trickle. Magnus was sailing along at 115 kilometers per hour and making excellent time.

Ingrid switched off his phone and removed the SIM card. "Pull over."

"Why?"

"Because you can't read while driving."

"Do you think that's wise?"

"Your phone is disabled."

"What about yours?"

"It's not connected to the cellular network."

Magnus guided the Range Rover onto the verge and

braked to a halt. Then he peered into the side-view mirror, his left hand resting on the latch.

"What on earth are you waiting for?"

A behemoth Russian truck thundered past in a swirling cloud of snow and road salt. "Does that answer your question?" asked Magnus, and climbed out.

Ingrid slithered over the center console and settled behind the wheel. Magnus, after passing through the glare of the Range Rover's headlamps, took her place in the passenger seat.

Frowning, he said, "I think I liked you better when you were my adoring secretary."

Ingrid quickly adjusted the seat and mirrors and pressed the accelerator to the floor. The road before her was empty and brightly lit. For now, at least, it was free of snow and ice.

Magnus switched on the overhead reading lamp and held up the Security Council directive. "First things first."

"It wasn't in the safe."

"Where was it?"

"His attaché case."

"Why didn't you photograph it?"

"There wasn't time."

"Your instructions were quite specific, as I recall."

"Nikolai Petrov took that document to his meeting with the Russian president tonight for a reason."

"And you can be bloody well sure he's wondering where it is now."

"Unless he doesn't realize it's missing."

"He'll find out soon enough." Magnus opened the Security Council directive and began to read. After a moment, he whispered, "Dear God in heaven."

"What does it say?"

"It says you did exactly the right thing tonight, Ms. Sørensen."

53

Copenhagen Station

Ordinarily, it took fifteen minutes to traverse the ten kilometers separating PET headquarters and the American Embassy on the Dag Hammarskjölds Allé, but Gabriel's driver made the trip in less than ten. Paul Webster, the CIA's Copenhagen station chief, was waiting in the lobby. His leather oxfords squeaked as he led Gabriel down a deserted corridor to the entrance of his secure realm. Inside, he fired up an encrypted video link to Langley. Adrian Carter appeared on the screen a few minutes later, his face taut with tension.

"You were saying?" asked Gabriel.

"Page thirty-six," repeated Carter. "The part about how these crazy fuckers are planning to erase one of their own villages with a false-flag nuclear attack. It's a nothing little place about an inch from the Ukrainian border called Maksimov."

"But the crazy fuckers didn't say *when* the attack was going to happen."

"That's true. But they were very specific about the staging point."

"Sokolovka."

"A real garden spot," said Carter. "Paul has a satellite image to show you."

The station chief was sitting in front of a computer just out of camera range. With a few clicks of his mouse, he brought up the photo.

"What am I looking at?" asked Gabriel.

"That little farmhouse in the bottom-left corner of the image."

"It looks like an ordinary farmhouse."

"That was how it looked the day the war began. But this is how it looked yesterday."

Webster brought up another image on his computer. This time there were two giant Kamaz military trucks parked outside the farmhouse in the rutted yard. They were surrounded by a dozen or so heavily armed men.

"It doesn't look so ordinary now, does it?"

"No," agreed Gabriel. "And neither do those Russian soldiers."

"My guys feel the same way. They think they might

be Spetsnaz GRU." The Spetsnaz GRU were the elite special forces of Russia's military intelligence service. "If you look closely, you can see that they've established a perimeter around that corrugated metal outbuilding. There's another Kamaz truck in there. Interestingly enough, it looks like a commercial truck. That's the one we're worried about."

"If you hit that building—"

"That's not the plan," interjected Carter.

"What *is* the plan?"

"We're keeping a very close eye on it."

"How's the satellite coverage?"

"Suffice it to say we have more assets in the region than we have publicly acknowledged. If that truck leaves the farm, we're going to be watching. And if it makes a stop in Maksimov, the Ukrainians are going to light it up with several HIMARS missiles. With our considerable assistance, of course."

"Driving time from Sokolovka to Maksimov?"

"Approximately two hours. Which means we'll have plenty of warning."

"How long will it take the missiles to reach the target?"

"Ten minutes. We're confident they can destroy the weapon without triggering a secondary nuclear detonation."

"You will, however, trigger a Russian response. A response," added Gabriel, "that will include an assessment of how it was that the Ukrainians knew about the plot."

"All the more reason you need to get your friends out of the country as quickly as possible."

"They're trying, Adrian."

"Where are they now?"

"Approximately halfway between Moscow and Saint Petersburg."

"How's the weather at the airport?"

"You're the director of the CIA. You tell me."

"I think there's at least a fifty percent chance they should consider alternative travel arrangements."

"I'd say it's closer to like seventy-five."

"Options?"

"Ask the Ukrainians to light up Nikolai Petrov's place in Rublyovka, preferably before he realizes his directive is missing."

"Be careful what you wish for," said Carter, and the screen went dark.

Gabriel stared at the satellite photo. A busted-down old farm in the middle of nowhere. Two giant Kamaz trucks in the rutted yard, another Kamaz in the outbuilding. That was the truck Langley was worried about. That was the one with the bomb.

The sixteen men billeted at the farmhouse in the hamlet of Sokolovka were attached to the 3rd Guards Spetsnaz Brigade, an elite reconnaissance unit of the GRU. Their commanding officer was Captain Anatoly Kruchina, a veteran of the wars in Chechnya and Syria, and one of the mysterious "little green men" who had seized Crimea in 2014. Thus far, Kruchina's most significant contribution to the so-called special military operation had come in Bucha, where he had helped the 234th Air Assault Regiment slaughter several hundred innocent civilians. It had been a nightmare, the worst atrocity he had ever witnessed. But war was war, especially when it involved Russians.

Kruchina and his unit were ordered to take up residence at the farmhouse in late November. The white Kamaz truck had arrived two days later. In the back was a cylindrical object about three meters in length, mounted to a steel frame and connected by a coiled wire to an external power source. Kruchina had not been told the nature of this peculiar-looking object, only that he was to allow nothing to happen to it—and that he must never, under any circumstances, throw the switch on the external power supply. As instructed, he had placed the truck in the farm's corrugated metal outbuilding and padlocked the door. And there the thing had sat for the better part of the last two weeks, watched over by sixteen of the GRU's most highly trained operatives.

The only break in the monotony had come the previous afternoon, when they received a surprise visit from the director of the GRU himself, General Igor Belinsky. He had been dressed in the uniform of a lowly colonel and accompanied by two engineers in civilian garb. They had inspected the object in the back of the truck and checked the battery level in the external power supply. Then the director of the GRU had told Anatoly Kruchina that he had been chosen to carry out the most important mission of the special military operation in Ukraine, perhaps the most important in the history of the GRU itself.

It was not a complex assignment. All Kruchina had to do was drive the truck to the village of Maksimov, leave it at a Lukoil petrol station, and throw the switch on the power supply. Detonation would occur thirty minutes later, but by then Kruchina would be long gone; another GRU operative would be waiting to spirit him safely out of the blast zone. Upon the successful completion of his mission, Kruchina would be promoted to the rank of colonel and awarded the GRU's highest citation. His future, the director assured him, was luminous.

"How many will die?"

General Belinsky had shrugged. They were only human beings, after all.

"But they're Russian citizens."

"So were the people in those apartment buildings back in ninety-nine. Three hundred were killed, just to make certain that Volodya won that first election."

At the conclusion of his briefing, General Belinsky had given Kruchina a parcel of civilian clothing. He was to remain in place at the farm until receiving the order to proceed. It would come from General Belinsky himself and would be preceded by the code word Aurora. Belinsky anticipated the transmission would occur sometime after six in the morning. He suggested that Kruchina try to get some rest. It was essential that nothing go wrong. He would need to be at his very best.

But it was now nearly 5:00 a.m., and Anatoly Kruchina had not slept a minute. He was seated at the wobbly linoleum table in the kitchen, dressed in the civilian clothing, a lethal *papirosa* burning between the first and second fingers of his right hand. His eyes were fixed on his secure satellite radio, which was resting on the table before him, next to the key for the padlock on the corrugated metal outbuilding. His thoughts were focused on a single question.

Why Captain Anatoly Kruchina, the grim reaper of Grozny, the butcher of Bucha? What had he done to deserve this great honor? Why had General Igor Belinsky chosen *him* for this most sensitive mission? The answer was obvious. They had chosen him because he had followed every order, and carried out every shit assignment, they had ever hurled at him. And yet he was certain, as certain as a man could be, that his director had misled him. There would be no promotion, no citation, no GRU operative waiting in a parked car at the Lukoil station—and no thirty-minute delay before detonation. War was war, thought Anatoly Kruchina. Especially when it involved Russians.

54

The Kremlin

There was nothing unusual in the way the morning began, no omen or inkling of what was to come. The president's chief of staff entered the Grand Kremlin Palace at his customary time, 6:00 a.m. sharp, and was his typical malevolent self. Silver-tongued Kremlin spokesman Yevgeny Nazarov sauntered in a few minutes later, looking as though he hadn't a care in the world, which wasn't the case. He had spent the entire forty-minute commute from his mansion in Rublyovka batting away reports that Russia had kidnapped thousands of Ukrainian children and locked them away in a network of reeducation camps. The official in charge of the program—she just happened to be Russia's commissioner for children's rights—was already hard at work in her office on the second floor.

Nikolai Petrov, the secretary of the Security Council, was running a few minutes behind schedule, but only because there was a backup at the Borovitskaya Tower, the business entrance of the Kremlin. Normally, Petrov might have upbraided his driver, but Plan Aurora required of him a deceptively serene demeanor, so he carried on reading his daily summary of global news as though untroubled by the delay. His attaché case rested on the opposite side of the backseat. The lid was open, but the internal compartment where he stored sensitive documents was tightly zipped.

Finally, the logjam broke, and Petrov's limousine rolled through the tower's arched passageway and into the courtyard of the Grand Kremlin Palace. Attaché case in hand, he headed upstairs to his office, which was presidential in size and grandeur. Pavel Semenov, his aide-de-camp, relieved him of his coat. As always, a traditional Russian breakfast awaited him. Semenov, ever attentive, poured the first cup of coffee.

"A restful evening, Secretary Petrov?"

"Yes, Semenov. You?"

"Not terribly. My son has a dreadful cough."

"I'm sorry to hear that." Petrov placed the attaché

case on his desk and popped the latches. "Nothing serious, I hope."

"I don't think so, but Yulia is quite worried." Semenov draped Petrov's coat over his forearm. "Is there anything you require for the morning staff meeting?"

"Some breakfast and a few moments to gather my thoughts."

"Of course, Secretary Petrov."

Semenov withdrew, closing the door behind him. Alone, Petrov sat down at his desk and lifted the receiver of his secure phone. With the press of a button, he rang General Igor Belinsky. The director of the GRU emitted his standard monosyllabic greeting.

"How was your trip yesterday?" asked Petrov.

"I couldn't get out of that shithole fast enough."

"You have a good man to handle the delivery?"

"A very good man. He's waiting for the order."

"Then perhaps you should issue it."

"Are you sure, Secretary Petrov?"

"I'm sure."

"And the state president?"

"He gave his approval last night."

"In that case, Secretary Petrov, please give me the proper code word, just so there are no misunderstandings later."

"Aurora."

"I beg your pardon?"

"Aurora," repeated Nikolai Petrov, and hung up the phone.

In the hamlet of Sokolovka, the wind was raging, and there were gritty pellets of snow in the air. Head down, Anatoly Kruchina trotted across the frozen mud of the yard to the door of the corrugated metal outbuilding. The two men guarding it were half dead with cold. Kruchina informed them that they were relieved of duty, then rammed the key into the padlock.

The damn thing was so frozen it took Kruchina a minute to wrench the shackle from the body—and another minute to roll aside the rusted door. The flat-nose cab-over cabin of the KamAZ-43114 filled nearly the entire opening. Kruchina shimmied past the heavy-duty bumper, slamming his left eye into the mirror in the process, and opened the driver's-side door.

There was a built-in step at the front of the cab, about three-quarters of the way up the wheel. Kruchina put his left foot on it and, swearing softly in anger, hoisted himself into the cabin. His eye was throbbing painfully. His first wound of the entire campaign. Hardly an auspicious start to his historic mission. What was next? An empty fuel tank? A dead battery?

He managed to close the cabin door without causing

further injury to himself and placed his satcom radio on the passenger seat. The key was in the ignition. Kruchina gave it a twist to the right, and the engine roared to life. A moment later he was headed west along a frozen single-lane road, bound for the Ukrainian border.

It took only five minutes for word of the truck's departure to reach Gabriel in the PET's op center in suburban Copenhagen. It was Adrian Carter, in veiled language, who delivered the news. The truck had left the farmhouse at 6:12 a.m. If the border town of Maksimov was its destination, it would arrive sometime between eight and eight fifteen. The instant the truck stopped, the HIMARS missiles would go up. And ten minutes after that, they would come down again.

"At which point," Gabriel told Lars Mortensen after the call, "Nikolai Petrov and his friend Vladimir Vladimirovich will go positively apeshit."

"They might assume the device malfunctioned."

"Unless Russian air defenses detect the Ukrainian missile launch. Then they'll know exactly what happened."

Eli Lavon was staring at the winking blue light on his computer screen.

"Where are they now?" asked Gabriel.

"About an hour and fifteen minutes south of Pulkovo."

"Which means they'll be on board their plane before the missiles come down on that truck."

"I rather doubt that." Lavon pointed toward the computer screen. Pulkovo had just put in place a complete ground stop. "Might I suggest an alternative?"

"There are none, Eli."

Lavon glanced at Lars Mortensen. "We could use the Danish consulate in Saint Petersburg as a lifeboat."

"We might get them into the consulate," said Mortensen, "but it will take years to get them out again."

"Then I suppose we're left with only a single option." Lavon enlarged the map on his computer screen and pointed out a spot northwest of Saint Petersburg.

Gabriel looked at Mortensen. "I need a plane."

55
Maksimov

The Lukoil petrol station was about a thousand meters from the now meaningless border between Russia and Ukraine's Donetsk Oblast. Anatoly Kruchina arrived at 8:19 a.m. Not bad given the terrible road conditions, he thought, but a few minutes behind schedule. He parked the truck at the edge of the broad tarmac and killed the engine, reveling in the sudden silence. Not for the first time, he thanked God that he did not earn his living by driving a truck.

He lit a *papirosa* and surveyed his surroundings. Two customers were filling their tanks at the pumps. One was a weather-beaten old man, the other a gum-chewing teenage girl. A third car was parked outside the entrance of the convenience mart. That one had a couple of kids in

the backseat. Kruchina had two of his own. They lived
with their mother in Volgograd. He hadn't seen them
since the beginning of the war. They thought he was a
hero, his kids. A defender of the motherland, a fighter
for Uncle Vova. Kruchina had begged their mother to
smash the television.

He checked the time. It was 8:22. He climbed out of
the cab and went into the convenience mart. The mother
of the two children was standing at the checkout counter. She looked to be in her late twenties, a war widow,
no doubt. They were everywhere. She gave Kruchina a
glare of disapproval, as though wondering why he wasn't
in uniform. Kruchina, for his part, wondered whether
the woman and her two children would soon be dead.

He wandered the aisles for a couple of minutes, ac-
cumulating food and drink, and returned to the checkout counter. The woman on the other side looked as
though she hadn't slept in a month.

"What time do you get off?" he asked.

"When the war is over," she joked, and scanned his
items.

Kruchina paid in cash and went out. The two kids
in the backseat of the car stuck out their tongues at him
as their mother pulled away. Leaving the petrol station, she headed eastward into Russia. Keep driving,
thought Kruchina. Whatever you do, don't stop.

He opened the door of the Kamaz and hauled himself into the cab. His encrypted radio chirped as he tore open his first bag of potato chips. The man at the other end of the distant connection didn't bother to identify himself.

"Have you arrived at your destination?" asked General Igor Belinsky, director of the GRU.

"I have."

"Is the device armed?"

"Not yet."

"Why not?"

"My ride home must have lost his way."

"He'll be there any moment. Arm the device immediately."

"Of course," answered Kruchina. "Right away."

He set aside the radio and gazed eastward down the highway. There was not a car in sight. There never would be, he thought. At least not one meant for him.

He made a final check of the time. It was 8:28 a.m. Then he unscrewed the cap from an American soft drink and, raising the bottle to his lips, ceased to exist.

On the southern fringes of Saint Petersburg, Ingrid had reattached her Genesis phone to Russia's MTS cellular network long enough to consult the online departure board at Pulkovo Airport. Not surprisingly, given the dreadful weather conditions beyond her window, it showed that no flights were landing or departing. She received additional confirmation of this fact a few minutes later via a secure satellite text message from Gabriel, who instructed her to proceed to the Finnish border instead. At present it was closed to Russians without valid EU visas, but Ingrid and Magnus, as citizens of Denmark, were free to make the crossing. Provided, of course, their Russian hosts allowed them to leave.

They skirted the center of Saint Petersburg on the high-speed toll road and made their way to the E18, the primary motor link between Russia and Finland. Magnus was at the wheel. He had been there since their last stop for fuel and caffeine, some four hours earlier, at an all-night petrol station in a hellhole called Myasnoi Bor. Ingrid had planned to stuff the Russian nuclear directive into the rubbish bin of the women's toilet, but she fled in horror the instant she opened the door.

The document was now locked in Gennady Luzhkov's attaché case, along with the half million in cash. Gennady's powerful Vektor pistol was still in Ingrid's handbag. As for the whereabouts of Gennady himself, Ingrid and Magnus knew nothing. They did not know whether he had been arrested or even whether he was alive or dead. If he wasn't dead yet, she thought, he would be soon—all because she had stolen the Security Council directive.

She looked down at Magnus's disabled phone.

"Don't even think about it," he said quietly.

"I have to know."

"Assume the worst."

"Do you know what they're going to do to him?"

"The same thing they're going to do to me if we're arrested. Besides, Gennady knew what he was getting into. I only hope that when the story of this affair is written, he'll get the credit he deserves."

"And what will they write about us?" asked Ingrid.

"I suppose that depends on whether the Russian border guards allow us to leave." Magnus rubbed the fogged windscreen with the sleeve of his overcoat. "It occurs to me that you know everything there is to know about me, and I know next to nothing about you."

"Yes," she said.

"Tell me *something*, at least."

"I grew up in a little town in Jutland near the German border."

"Good start. What does your father do?"

"He's a schoolteacher."

"And your mother?"

"A saint."

"You're obviously intelligent. Why did you become a thief?"

"Why did you become an energy executive?"

"Don't tell me you're an environmentalist."

"Devout."

"I suppose you're very green. Carbon neutral, that sort of thing."

"And if I was?"

"I would advise you to get professional help."

"It's all a hoax?"

"Look at the snow falling around you."

"We're in northern Russia, you moron."

"I will concede that the climate is warming. But the burning of fossil fuels has nothing to do with it."

"That's not what you wrote in an internal DanskOil memo in 1998. In fact, you said exactly the opposite."

His head swiveled to the right. "How could you possibly know that?"

"What do you think I was doing all that time I was sitting outside your office?"

"Find anything else interesting?"

"Numerous safety violations on your drilling platforms and several unreported spills."

"These things happen when one is extracting oil from beneath the North Sea." He stared straight ahead. The wipers were working at full speed. The defroster was roaring. "What are you going to do when this is over?"

"I thought we were getting married."

"Actually, there's something I've been meaning to tell you."

"Cad," she whispered.

"Guilty as charged. But I have to try to repair my marriage before it's too late."

"Do you think she'll have you back?"

"When I tell her what you and I did here in Russia, I have a feeling she just might."

Ingrid removed the ring from her finger.

"Keep it," said Magnus. "It will give you something to remember me by."

The weather was growing worse by the minute. Ingrid switched on the radio. The hosts of the program sounded apoplectic. "What are they talking about?" she asked.

"The Ukrainians just fired several missiles into a Russian village near the border."

"Did they?" Ingrid slid the diamond ring onto her finger. "What a shame."

56

The Kremlin

The news of a Ukrainian missile strike on the Russian border village of Maksimov surprised no one more than the secretary of Russia's Security Council, Nikolai Petrov. At first he assumed that the reports were mistaken. His opinion changed, however, when he saw the cell phone video on NTV. It was clear that the damage was the result of conventional weapons and not a low-yield nuclear device assembled from decades-old South African highly enriched uranium.

Most alarming to Petrov was the apparent target of the attack, a Lukoil station about a thousand meters from the Ukrainian border, the exact spot where Plan Aurora was to commence that morning. It suggested to Petrov that operational security had been breached, that there had been a leak. But how? Aurora had been closely held—so closely held, in fact, that only a handful of senior *siloviki* knew of the plan's existence. Petrov himself had maintained personal control of the only copy of the directive authorizing the operation.

It was in his attaché case, which was lying open on his desk. He unzipped the internal compartment where he stored sensitive documents and looked inside.

Security Council of Russia directive 37-23\VZ was gone.

The Royal Danish Air Force maintained a fleet of four Bombardier Challenger jets for the use of the prime minister and other senior government officials, but Lars Mortensen arranged for a chartered Dassault Falcon business jet instead. It departed Copenhagen Airport at 6:30 a.m., and ninety minutes later it was on the ground in Helsinki. Mikhail and Eli Lavon entered Finland as citizens of Poland, Gabriel as a Canadian. Had the Finnish immigration officials subjected him to a search, which they did not, they would have discovered that he was carrying a loaded Beretta 92FS and two extra magazines of ammunition. Mikhail had the .45-caliber Jericho.

A CIA officer named Tom McNeil met them in the lounge of the FBO. McNeil looked more Finnish than the Finns and spoke the language like a native. He addressed Gabriel in English, with the accent of a native New Yorker.

"We put three HIMARS missiles directly on the target. There was no secondary detonation of the fissile material and only limited collateral casualties."

"Any Russian reaction?"

"Not yet."

The FBO had arranged for a car, an Audi Q5 crossover SUV. Mikhail slid behind the wheel; Tom McNeil, into the passenger seat. Gabriel climbed into the backseat next to Eli Lavon. Five minutes later they were headed east on the E18. Mikhail's speed was entirely ill suited to the conditions.

Tom McNeil checked his seat belt. "Do you have much experience driving in snow?" he asked.

"I was born in Moscow."

"Now ask him if his parents owned a car," said Gabriel.

"Did they?" inquired McNeil, but Mikhail made no reply.

Gabriel looked at Lavon, who was staring at the screen of his laptop. "Where are they?"

"North of Saint Petersburg."

"How long before they reach the border?"

"In this weather? Three hours at least."

"And us?"

"That depends on whether Mikhail can keep the car on the road."

Gabriel stared out his window. It was nearly nine thirty in the morning, but it looked like midnight. "Do you think it will ever get light today, Eli?"

"No," he answered. "Not today."

TverBank Tower, once Moscow's tallest skyscraper, now a distant fourth, loomed over Bolshaya Spasskaya Street just beyond the Garden Ring. Cylindrical in shape with a tapered apex, it resembled a giant phallus. Or so complained the critics when TverBank chairman Gennady Luzhkov unveiled a scale model of the building at a glitzy press event attended by several Kremlin luminaries, including the Russian president.

Gennady's office was on the top floor, the fifty-fourth. He was seated at his desk shortly after 9:00 a.m. when his assistant informed him that Secretary Nikolai Petrov was on the line. Gennady, for any number of reasons, had been expecting the call.

"You treasonous bastard!" Petrov screamed. "You're dead! Do you understand me? Dead!"

"I will be soon," replied Gennady calmly. "But what seems to be the trouble?"

"She stole a document from my briefcase last night."

"Who, Nikolai?"

"The woman you brought into my home."

"Ms. Sørensen? Have you taken leave of your senses?"

"The document was in my briefcase when I arrived home, and it was *not* in my briefcase when I arrived at the Kremlin this morning."

"Tell me something, Nikolai. Was the attaché case in question locked?"

"Of course."

"Then how do you suppose Ms. Sørensen was able to steal it?"

"She must have picked the locks somehow."

Gennady exhaled heavily. "You really have to pull yourself together, Nikolai. The country is depending on you. Haven't you seen the news? The Ukrainians just attacked a village near the border. Though one can only wonder why they would waste precious missiles on a petrol station."

"Where are they, Gennady?"

"The Ukrainians? They're in Ukraine, Nikolai. If there are any left, that is."

"Magnus Larsen and the woman," said Petrov.

"In bed asleep, I imagine."

"Why didn't they go to the airport?"

"Because they had the good sense not to. Have you

seen the weather? Now if you'll excuse me, our man in Dubai is eagerly awaiting the first wire transfer."

"That money isn't going anywhere. Except to another bank," added Petrov. "I'm giving it to Yuri at VTB."

"You've already signed the transfer orders. I'm afraid it's too late. The bullet is in the chamber, so to speak."

"Tear up those transfer orders, you bastard."

"If you insist," said Gennady. "But I'll require your signatures on the cancellation order. It shouldn't take more than a few minutes. What time should I expect you?"

After enduring yet another torrent of abuse, Gennady rang off and immediately dialed Magnus Larsen. The call went straight to voice mail. Magnus, it seemed, had wisely switched off his mobile phone.

The manager of the FBO at Pulkovo Airport, however, answered Gennady's call without delay. The news was not promising. The weather had forced the airport to impose a full ground stop. The FBO expected conditions to improve around midday, but commercial flights would receive priority. It would be early evening, the manager predicted, before private aircraft received a departure slot.

Which meant that Magnus and Ingrid were now

trapped inside Russia. Gennady had bought them a few additional minutes, but surely not enough time to make their escape. What they required was a guarantee of safe passage from a powerful member of the *siloviki*—someone like the secretary of Russia's Security Council. Gennady was confident there was a deal to be made. All he required was a bit of leverage.

And so it was that Gennady Luzhkov, with a single phone call to an underling many floors below, transferred the lion's share of Nikolai Petrov's personal wealth—205 billion Russian rubles, none of it rightfully his—to an account held by one Raisa Luzhkova at the Royal GulfBank of Dubai. Petrov was automatically notified of the enormous transaction via email. He rang Gennady seconds after receiving it.

"Where's my money, you bastard?"

"Didn't you review the email, Secretary Petrov? Your money is at Royal GulfBank. But it won't stay there long. And when it's gone, you'll never find it. Unlike you, I'm very good at hiding things."

"What do you want?"

"A promise that you and your friends at the FSB will make no attempt to prevent Magnus Larsen and Ms. Sørensen from leaving the country."

"I don't suppose they're in their bed in Rublyovka."

"No."

"Where are they headed?"

"I haven't a clue."

"Best guess?"

"Kazakhstan," said Gennady.

"My money's on Finland."

"You don't have any money, Nikolai."

There was a long silence.

"Transfer the money to VTB Bank," said Petrov at last, "and I'll let them go."

"Other way around. Let them go, and I'll transfer the money. And then you can do with me as you please."

"Don't worry, I intend to."

The connection went dead.

Gennady dialed Magnus's number again, but there was still no answer. He needed to tell them that it was safe to cross the border. He had only one option.

He found the main number online and dialed. A cheerful-sounding woman answered in American-accented English. "Embassy of the United States."

"My name is Gennady Luzhkov. I am the chairman of TverBank and an asset of the Central Intelligence Agency code-named Komarovsky. Now listen carefully."

57
Southern Finland

It sounded too crazy not to be true. At least, that was the conclusion of the embassy operator, who had heard a great deal of Russian-accented nonsense over the phone lines since the beginning of the so-called special military operation in Ukraine. She immediately passed the message to her superior—it was more or less a word-for-word transcription of what Mr. Luzhkov had said—and the superior ran it upstairs to the office of the deputy chief of mission. It meant nothing to the DCM, but he had the good sense to bring it to the attention of the CIA station chief, who put it in a flash cable to the Russia House at Langley, which bounced it back across the Atlantic to Helsinki.

It would be another five minutes before the news

reached Tom McNeil via an encrypted email. It stated that Gennady Luzhkov, the founder and chairman of TverBank and a CIA asset code-named Komarovsky, had somehow managed to arrange safe passage from Russia for Ingrid and Magnus Larsen—doubtless at enormous personal risk to himself. McNeil was elated by the news, Gabriel less so. Experience had taught him that deals with Russians invariably went sideways, oftentimes as a result of nothing more than blinding Russian incompetence. He would therefore refrain from any celebration or expression of relief until his two assets were safely across the border.

He did, however, inform them of the encouraging development—with a clandestine satellite message sent to Ingrid's Genesis secure communications device. Her reply was instant.

"Well?" asked Eli Lavon.

"She wants to know whether she should try to carry the directive across the border."

"Could be a deal breaker."

"It would be nice to have the real thing, though—don't you think?"

"Too risky," said Lavon.

Gabriel sent the message. His phone pinged with a reply a moment later. "She's inclined to keep it."

"What a surprise."

Another ping.

"What is it now?" asked Lavon.

"Apparently, she also has a half million dollars in cash."

"Really? Where do you suppose she got it?"

Gabriel slipped the phone into his pocket. "I'm afraid to ask."

McNeil had the private cell number for the director of Finland's security and intelligence service. He dialed it when they were about an hour from the border and informed the director that two blown CIA assets were headed his way.

"They're Russians, these assets of yours?"

"Danes, actually."

"Names?"

"I'd rather not identify them over an insecure connection."

"Since they're blown, Mr. McNeil, I don't think it's a problem."

McNeil recited the two names.

"*The* Magnus Larsen."

"In all his glory."

The Finnish intelligence chief, whose name was Teppo Vasala, wished to be accommodating. But he was also eager to keep his country out of a shooting war

with the Russians. These days it was his primary ob-
session. "And you're certain they've been granted safe
passage?" he asked.

"As certain as we can be."

"I'll believe it when I see it. But if the Russian Border
Service allows them to pass through the checkpoints on
their side of the border, we will of course allow them to
enter Finland."

"You have our gratitude," said McNeil.

"How close are Larsen and the woman to Finland?"

"Ninety minutes."

"I assume you'd like to greet them when they make
the crossing?"

"They've had a long and difficult night."

"I'll have to arrange it with the Border Guard. How
many in your party?"

"Four."

"Who are the other three?"

"Person A, Person B, and Person C."

"Americans?"

"I'll leave that up to you, Director Vasala."

The Finnish spy chief gave McNeil the location of a
suitable holding point about ten kilometers from the
border and instructed him to wait there until further
notice. It turned out to be a car park shared by a su-

permarket and a bed-and-breakfast. McNeil headed into the hotel in search of hot coffee and food, and returned to the Audi a few minutes later to find Mikhail ramming a magazine into the butt of a Jericho pistol.

"What is that for?" asked McNeil.

"Shooting Russians."

"Just to be clear," said the American evenly, "no Russians are going to be shot today."

"Unless they try something foolish."

"Like what?"

"Take a good look at the man sitting directly behind me," replied Mikhail.

Eli Lavon, eyes on his laptop, elaborated. "The goal of this morning's operation, Mr. McNeil, is twofold. The safe return of Ingrid and Magnus Larsen is our first priority. But equally important is that Gabriel Allon, the man the Russian president hates most in the world, remains in Finland. Frankly, he's too close to Russia as it is."

"We're ten kilometers from the border."

"My point exactly," said Lavon. "And in a few minutes, we'll be ten *meters* from the border. Which is why Gabriel and Mikhail will both be armed."

"Not you?"

"Oh, no," said Lavon. "I've never been one for the rough stuff."

McNeil handed Gabriel an insulated paper cup and a small sack. The cup was filled with milky Finnish coffee. The sack contained something crusty and dark. Gabriel regarded it dubiously.

"It's a Karelian pasty," explained McNeil. "Rye pastry filled with rice porridge. Very traditional."

Gabriel, famished, gave it a try.

"What do you think?"

"I think you should probably answer your phone."

It was Teppo Vasala calling from Helsinki. McNeil listened in silence for a moment, then severed the connection. "Let's go."

Mikhail slipped his Jericho into the pocket of his coat and turned onto the highway. A blue-and-white sign, scarcely visible through the falling snow, gave the distance to the border crossing at Vaalimaa.

"For the record," said Eli Lavon, "you are now nine kilometers closer to Russia than you should be."

They were waved through a pair of checkpoints and directed to the Border Guard command post. Waiting outside was a Nordic giant called Esko Nurmi. He wore a Glock on his hip and on his face an expression of disdain for lesser beings. After exchanging a few Finnish pleasantries with Tom McNeil, he thrust an enormous hand toward Gabriel.

"Which one are you?" asked the towering Finn. "Person A, Person B, or Person C?"

"Does it matter?"

"Only if something goes wrong."

"In that case, I'm Person A."

"Does A happen to stand for Allon?"

"It might, yes."

The Finn's contemptuous expression changed to one of admiration. "It's an honor to have you here in Vaali-maa, Director Allon. Follow me, please."

They entered the command post, where an officer in a smart-looking sweater sat before a bank of video monitors. They were fed by an array of surveillance cameras pointed toward the Torfyanovka complex on the Russian side of the border. One of the cameras was focused on an assemblage of Russian Border Service vehicles parked on the tarmac in front of the inspection lanes.

"They arrived about an hour ago," explained Nurmi. "They're not the typical passport inspectors we used to see when the border was still open. They're members of a special tactical unit. And quite well armed."

"How far are we from the actual border?"

"About a kilometer and a half." The Finn walked Gabriel over to a nearby window and pointed toward a couple of yellow lights burning in the distance. "We have a substation about a hundred fifty meters from the border."

"Anyone on duty?"

"A single officer."

"I'd like to join him, if you don't mind."

"Sorry, Director Allon. This is as close as you go."

They returned to the control room. The situation on the Russian side of the border was unchanged. Esko Nurmi checked the time on his wristwatch. "According to my calculation, your two agents should be about fifteen minutes away."

Gabriel glanced at Eli Lavon, who nodded his head in agreement.

"Is he Person B or C?" asked Esko Nurmi.

"He's C, I think."

The Finn looked at Mikhail. "Person B looks like trouble."

"Definitely."

"Is he armed?"

"Right-front coat pocket."

"You?"

Gabriel gently patted his lower back.

"How did you get it into the country?"

"I'm not in the country."

"Did you enjoy your stay?"

Gabriel stared at the Russian trucks waiting on the tarmac on the opposite side of the border. "I'll let you know in fifteen minutes."

58

Torfyanovka

The village of Chulkovo was the last place they saw a pair of oncoming headlights. A half kilometer to the west, they came upon a Russian Border Service patrol car parked along the tree-lined verge, its wipers beating a lazy rhythm, running lights aglow. The officer behind the wheel was on his radio. He made no attempt to impede their progress.

"An encouraging sign," said Magnus. "They're clearly expecting us."

Ingrid shot a glance over her shoulder, but there was nothing to see; the rear window was covered with snow and grime. "Surely they're not going to let us simply *drive* across the border."

"We'll know soon enough."

"How do you suppose they were able to get us out?"

"Knowing the Russians, I'm sure the deal involved money."

"Nikolai Petrov's."

Magnus nodded. "Gennady must have moved it offshore. I assume he'll return it once we're across the border."

"And then?"

"Gennady will suffer a mysterious fall from the top of TverBank Tower."

They spotted a second patrol car parked outside a used tire shop in the hamlet of Kondratevo, and a third outside the dreary Motel Medved. Once again, there was no attempt by any of the officers to prevent them from reaching an international border that had been effectively closed and militarized for many months.

Magnus negotiated a final series of gentle curves, and the enormous Torfyanovka crossing point emerged suddenly from behind a veil of falling snow. Before the onset of the war, two million cars and trucks had passed through the facility annually. Now it was deserted save for a few military-style Border Service vehicles and about twenty uniformed men standing on the brilliantly illuminated tarmac in front of the inspection station.

The Russian border guards, with shouts and hand

gestures, instructed Magnus to stop, then quickly surrounded the Range Rover. One of the men leered at Ingrid through her window, but she stared straight ahead—toward the distant lights of the Finnish border complex at Vaalimaa.

Yes, she thought anxiously, they were definitely expected.

In the Finnish command post four kilometers to the west, Gabriel watched the video images of the impasse on the Russian side of the border with increasing alarm. One of the Russians was pacing the tarmac, a radio to his jaw. The others were standing like statuary around the motionless Range Rover. Esko Nurmi was right; they were no ordinary passport stampers.

"Looks like there's a snag," remarked the Finn.

"There usually is when Russians are involved."

They watched the video transmission for another minute.

"Maybe we should run down the hill to the substation," said Nurmi. "Just to be on the safe side."

"It might be a good idea to bring along Person B as well," said Gabriel. "Just for good measure."

The one with the radio appeared to be in charge. Eventually, he moved to the driver's-side door of the

Range Rover and gave the window two firm raps with the side of his gloved hand.

Magnus lowered the window a centimeter or two. "What seems to be the problem? We were given assurances by friends in Moscow that we would be allowed to cross the border."

The remarks provoked a tirade from the Russian on the other side of the glass. Magnus provided a simultaneous Danish translation for Ingrid.

"He says that no one in Moscow could have given us such assurances because the border crossing is closed. He says we have entered a restricted military zone and are now subject to arrest."

"Try showing him your passport."

Magnus slid his dark red Danish passport through the narrow breach. "My name is Magnus Larsen. I am the CEO of DanskOil."

The Russian accepted the passport and with his heavy gloves turned clumsily through the pages. Then he handed the document to a colleague and said something to Magnus in Russian. He translated the instructions for Ingrid.

"He wants to see your passport as well."

Ingrid handed it over, and Magnus in turn slid it through the opening. The Russian's inspection of the passport was brief. Then he stepped away from the door and spoke a few more words in terse Russian. They required no translation. The border guard wanted Magnus to get out of the Range Rover.

"Don't even think about opening that door," said Ingrid. "If you do, you're dead."

And then they would kill her as well. But only after they'd had a little fun with her. She reckoned the one standing at her window would be the first in line. He was pulling at the latch, trying to open her door. Ingrid ignored him. She was watching a pair of headlights moving down the slope of the hill on the Finnish side of the border.

She removed the Genesis phone from her handbag and reconnected it to the MTS cellular network—all while the man at the window was screaming at her in Russian.

"He'd like you to put away your phone," said Magnus.

"I gathered that."

The Genesis had acquired a signal, weak but sufficient to make a call. She dialed a number from her contacts and lifted the phone to her ear. Gabriel answered at once.

"Is that you I see on the other side of the border?" she asked.

"Where else would I be?"

"Are you aware of our situation?"

"My view is distant and somewhat obstructed."

"They're telling us that there was never a deal to let us leave Russia. They'd like us to get out of the car so they can arrest us. I could be mistaken, but I think they have other plans."

"You're not mistaken, Ingrid."

"Any advice?"

The connection was lost before he could answer.

Ingrid returned the Genesis to her handbag and wrapped her hand around the butt of the Vektor pistol. Then she looked at Magnus and said, "Drive."

Gabriel slipped his phone into his coat pocket and drew the Beretta from the waistband of his trousers. Mikhail drew his gun as well, then looked at Esko Nurmi. "What are you waiting for?"

Nurmi went into the substation and emerged a moment later with a Heckler & Koch G36 assault rifle. Together they walked the one hundred and fifty meters down to the border. Nurmi carved a line in the snow with the barrel of his HK.

"If either one of you sets foot on the other side, you're on your own."

Mikhail placed a toe on Russian soil, then withdrew it to the Finnish side of the frontier.

"He's trouble," said Esko Nurmi.

"Yeah," agreed Gabriel. "But you haven't seen anything yet."

It was perhaps not surprising, given the catastrophic performance of Russian troops in Ukraine, that the sixteen Border Service officers surrounding the Range Rover at the Torfyanovka crossing point blundered in the dispersal of their forces, placing four men at the stern of the vehicle and only two at the prow. Magnus Larsen's sudden acceleration took both of the men unawares, and both soon found themselves beneath six thousand pounds of British-made automotive machinery.

Their colleagues didn't bother with a verbal command for Magnus to stop. Instead, they immediately opened up with their Russian-made assault rifles, shattering the Range Rover's rear window. Ingrid swung to her left and returned fire with the Vektor, sending the startled Russians diving for cover.

"You might want to hold on to something," shouted Magnus.

Ingrid spun round in her seat and saw that they were bearing down on the crossing point's inspection station. Magnus guided the Range Rover into the centermost lane and smashed through the lowered boom barrier.

It was the last obstacle standing between them and the Finnish border, which was two kilometers to the west. Magnus had the throttle to the floor. Even so, their speed had slowed to sixty kilometers per hour. The road was covered with unplowed snow.

"Faster!" screamed Ingrid. "You have to go faster."

"I'm going as fast as I bloody well can."

The Range Rover shook with the impact of several large-caliber rounds. Ingrid pivoted in her seat and saw two all-terrain vehicles gaining ground on them. The Vektor's double-stack magazine held eighteen rounds. Ingrid estimated there were about ten remaining. She distributed the fire equally between the two vehicles, but it was no use; they were still closing.

Another burst of incoming fire tore through the Range Rover. Ingrid ejected the spent magazine and, turning, groped in her handbag for the spare. She gave up the search for it, though, when she realized they were veering off the roadway at something like a forty-five-degree angle.

"Magnus!" she shouted, but there was no response. He was slumped forward over the wheel, dragging them to the right, his foot like a brick upon the throttle.

They plunged into a depression and slammed into a coppice of white-trunked birch trees. The airbag deployed in Ingrid's face. "Faster, Magnus," she mumbled as she slipped into unconsciousness. "You have to drive faster."

In the aftermath, a secret Finnish government inquiry would establish with certainty that Gabriel Allon, the recently retired director-general of Israel's secret intelligence service, crossed into Russian territory at 10:34 a.m. Eastern European Standard Time—the same instant the Range Rover veered irrevocably toward the birch trees lining the E18. He was followed by Mikhail Abramov, who soon overtook him, and by Esko Nurmi of the Finnish Border Guard.

The two Russian vehicles reached the crash site first, and nine men emerged. All were oblivious to the fact that Mikhail was bearing down on them with a Jericho .45-caliber pistol in his outstretched hand. He put two of the Russians on the ground from a distance of about thirty meters and killed two more at close range. Which left five for Gabriel. It was a bit like that morning in the woods of central Germany. One in each corner of the target, another in the pushpin. Five dead Russians in the blink of an eye.

Esko Nurmi never fired a shot. Instead, he opened the driver's-side door of the Range Rover and extracted Magnus Larsen as though he were made of papier-mâché. Gabriel went to the opposite side of the vehicle and hauled open the passenger door. Ingrid was crumpled on the floorboard, semiconscious, drenched in blood. Gabriel searched for a bullet wound but couldn't find one. The blood was Magnus's.

Mikhail joined Gabriel next to the Range Ranger and looked inside. "What a fucking mess."

"Help me get her out."

They lifted Ingrid from the car and propped her upright in the snow. "The directive," she murmured.

"Where is it?"

She gave him no answer.

"Where, Ingrid?"

"Attaché case."

Mikhail found it resting on the floor of the backseat. The weight of the bag suggested it contained more than merely a Russian government document.

"What about the Genesis?" asked Gabriel.

"My handbag," she said.

It was lying on the front floorboard next to the gun that Ingrid had used to fight for her life. The weapon was a Russian-made SR-1 Vektor.

"Where in the hell did she get that?" asked Mikhail.

"Gennady," she answered.

Mikhail held up the attaché case. "And the half million in cash?"

She managed a half smile. "Seven in the corner pocket."

Gabriel reached a hand into the Range Rover and removed Ingrid's bag. The Genesis was inside. He slipped the device into his coat pocket and looked at Mikhail.

"Carry her up to the border."

"No," she said. "I can walk."

Gabriel and Mikhail each threaded an arm around her waist, and they started up the slope of the hill. The Vaalimaa crossing point was awash in flashing blue emergency light. Esko Nurmi, with Magnus Larsen draped across his massive shoulders, was nearly across the border. Behind him stretched a trail of blood.

Mikhail carried the attaché case in his free hand. "You know," he said, "in all the years I've worked for the Office, I have never once walked away from an operation with a half million dollars in cash."

"Just make sure you're still wearing your watch when we reach Finland."

Ingrid laughed in spite of herself. "How can you make jokes at a time like this?"

"Practice," replied Gabriel.

Ingrid's step faltered. "Poor Magnus. None of this would have happened if I hadn't taken the directive."

"We were able to stop the attack. You saved tens of thousands of lives last night."

"But the Russians are going to kill Gennady." She

looked down at her bloodstained hands. "He's going to die a terrible death because of me."

"Gennady knew the risks."

Ingrid's head fell against Gabriel's shoulder. The toes of her suede boots were gouging parallel groves in the snow. "Am I still walking?" she asked.

"You're doing beautifully."

"Where are we?"

"Still in Russia."

"How long until we reach Finland?"

Gabriel looked at the flashing blue lights. "Just a few more steps."

59

Novodevichy Cemetery

When Gabriel and Mikhail finally dragged Ingrid across the border, it was 10:42 a.m. in Finland. Tom McNeil immediately alerted Helsinki, and Helsinki passed the news to Langley, which fired it to Moscow. The station chief conscripted the same switchboard operator to phone Gennady Luzhkov. She gave him a highly redacted version of the calamity at the Torfyanovka crossing point, enough to let him know it had not gone as promised.

Perhaps not surprisingly, Gennady heard a far different version of the events when Secretary Nikolai Petrov phoned twenty minutes later. In Petrov's telling, the crossing had been unremarkable in every way save for its cordiality. He then demanded that Gennady return the money he had transferred to Dubai earlier that morning. Gennady replied by telling Petrov that his money was gone for good.

"We had a deal."

"And you broke it, Nikolai."

"They made it across the border. That's all that matters."

"What went wrong?"

"Surely you must have some idea."

"I think you called the director of the FSB, and the director of FSB called Volodya. And then Volodya ordered them to be killed."

"Not bad, Gennady. By the way, you're next."

"How long do I have?"

"Volodya has agreed to refrain from killing you until you give me my money."

"How sporting of him. What is his cut?"

"A half billion."

"Is that all I'm worth? And what in the world does Volodya need with another lousy half billion?"

"It's not about the money, you know that. Volodya wants everything."

"Including Ukraine," said Gennady. "Or are you the one who's really to blame for this nightmare?"

"I want my money back," shouted Petrov suddenly.

"And you can have it, Nikolai. On one condition."

"You're in no position to make demands."

"Au contraire."

"What do you want?"

Gennady told him.

"How appropriate," said Petrov, and hung up the phone.

He had been putting his affairs in order for some time now—God, how he hated the phrase—so there was very little left to do. A few final papers to sign, a couple of letters to post, a half dozen telephone calls he had been meaning to make. He was careful about whom he rang and what he said; he didn't want anyone else to contract his illness. He even misled Raisa, promising to join her in exile in time for the winter holidays. How was his health? Never better.

He took a final walk around the perimeter of his circular office, with its panoramic views of Moscow below, and from his preposterous desk removed a single item, which he wedged into the pocket of his overcoat. His bodyguards were in the anteroom outside his office, flirting with the youngest of his three personal secretaries. She thrust a stack of telephone messages into his hand and reminded him about his 3:00 p.m. conference call with several of TverBank's biggest investors. He instructed her to cancel the call but didn't explain why. The messages he stuffed in a rubbish bin on his way to the lift. Dead men, he thought, didn't return phone calls.

The last ride in his Mercedes saloon car was pleasant enough, but the wrinkled woman at the ticket window of Novodevichy accepted his rubles with Soviet indifference. Behind the cemetery's redbrick walls, the incessant din of Moscow receded. The snow covering the footpaths was untrampled. As Gennady walked among the dead, he thought about his favorite line from *Zhivago*—the line that had inspired him to embark on his treacherous path.

To hope and to act, these are our duties in misfortune . . .

He arrived at the grave of Gorbachev, destroyer of the Soviet Union, and at the stroke of three o'clock heard a commotion, something that sounded vaguely like the beating of wings. Turning slowly, he saw Nikolai Petrov and his security detail coming toward him through the evergreens. Behind them was a contingent of black-clad FSB thugs, the sort who dealt with traitors like Gennady.

Petrov slowed to a stop about ten meters from where he stood. His security detail hovered, overcoats open. The FSB thugs were content to remain in the background for now—like jackals, thought Gennady. His hands were now in the pockets of his overcoat. It was bitterly cold, after all, and he was unwell. His right hand was wrapped around the item he had removed from his desk.

To hope and to act, these are our duties in misfortune . . .

Petrov, mastermind of the Ukraine invasion, enabler of the Russian president's worst instincts, was staring at his wristwatch. "Let's get on with it, shall we, Gennady? I've got to get back to the Kremlin."

"Still looking for that document you misplaced, Secretary Petrov?" Gennady managed to smile. "Security Council of Russia directive 37-23\VZ."

Petrov lowered his arm. "Why did you do it? Why did you throw away your life?"

"Because it was madness. And I was the only person in Russia who could stop you."

"You haven't stopped anything, you fool. I will do whatever it takes to win this war."

"And so must I, Nikolai."

It was Volodya whom Gennady wanted to kill, but Volodya was now unreachable, so Petrov would have to do. It would have been quite easy to shoot him through his overcoat—like some movie gangster, he thought— but he drew the weapon instead and eyed his quarry properly down the barrel. He never knew whether he managed to hit him or even if he was able to pull the trigger. It was no matter; for one magnificent moment he was a Russian hero rather than a Russian villain.

He had no idea how many times they shot him—it must have been a hundred, at least—but he felt nothing. He toppled to the flagstones before Gorbachev's grave, his cheek against the snow, and for an instant he thought he saw Petrov lying next to him. Then it grew dark, and some part of him rose and went for a stroll among the graves. He was a citizen of Novodevichy now; he had earned his place here. He had chosen to hope and to act. His misfortune required nothing less.

PART FOUR

The Conclusion

60

Moscow–Venice

I t began, like most matters of significance in Russia, with a rumor. Eventually, it reached the ears of two reporters from the independent *Moskovskaya Gazeta* who found sanctuary in Latvia after the Kremlin made journalism a crime punishable by death. Their story, four paragraphs of carefully worded speculation, resulted in an immediate denial-of-service attack that rendered the *Gazeta*'s website inoperable. The reporters had no doubt who was behind the attack—or that they were onto something.

But nothing could have prepared them for the news that Nikolai Petrov, the powerful secretary of Russia's Security Council, had been assassinated during a visit to Moscow's Novodevichy Cemetery. Also killed was Gennady Luzhkov, the chairman of Russia's fourth-largest bank. The two men, both members of the Russian president's inner circle, had been shot to death. The gunmen, according to the Kremlin, were operatives of the Ukrainian intelligence service.

Because the statement had been issued by Yevgeny Nazarov, one of the world's great liars, independent Russian journalists and their Western colleagues automatically assumed it was a fabrication. The state-run Russian media, however, reported it verbatim and with an outrage appropriate to the moment. The NTV propagandist Dmitry Budanov wept as he read the news to his millions of viewers, then demanded immediate retaliation. Within minutes, missiles were raining down on civilian targets in Kyiv. The barrage was short-lived. Russia, it seemed, was running low on munitions.

By morning, even the docile state-run Russian media were beginning to ask questions. Why had the two men gone to the cemetery in the first place? And how had the Ukrainian assassins known that they would be there? Dmitry Budanov, for his part, was most troubled by the fact that they had been killed near the grave of Mikhail Gorbachev, whose funeral the current Russian president had not seen fit to attend. Also suspicious was the timing of the incident, coming as it did on the same day that several missiles had fallen—inexplicably, it seemed—on the tiny border hamlet of Maksimov.

Adding yet another layer of intrigue to the unfolding situation was a report in the authoritative *Helsingin Sanomat* regarding an exchange of gunfire between Russian and Finnish border guards at the Vaalimaa-Torfyanovka crossing point. The Finnish president quickly denied the report, going so far as to call it dangerous and irresponsible. In the next breath, however, he announced that he was moving several hundred additional Finnish troops to the border, lest the Russians get any foolish ideas about widening their already disastrous war.

But the Finnish president soon found himself on the defensive when it emerged that Magnus Larsen, the CEO of the Danish energy company DanskOil, was fighting for his life in a Helsinki hospital after being shot once in the back. This was the same Magnus Larsen, the press pointed out, who had gone to Russia several days earlier to extract his company from its controversial joint venture with the Kremlin-owned oil company RuzNeft. The whereabouts of Larsen's personal assistant, thirty-six-year-old Astrid Sørensen, were not known. Her colleagues at DanskOil headquarters in Copenhagen, who knew little if anything about her, feared the worst.

Finnish authorities refused to disclose the circumstances by which the prominent Danish energy executive had arrived in Helsinki, leaving reporters no recourse but to fill in the blanks with speculation. The logical conclusion was that Larsen had been shot in Russia, perhaps as a result of his determination to sever DanskOil's ties with RuzNeft. DanskOil's spokesman was able to offer the press no guidance, for the spokesman knew far less than the Finns. RuzNeft issued a terse statement wishing the CEO a speedy recovery. Kremlin spokesman Yevgeny Nazarov, for once, had nothing at all to say. Russia experts described his silence as tantamount to an admission of Kremlin complicity in the attempt on Larsen's life.

Much of the subsequent coverage focused on the CEO's long and unseemly relationship with Russia's president. Such talk was put to rest, however, by a lengthy exposé in *Politiken* that revealed Larsen's long-standing ties to Danish intelligence and, by extension, the CIA. For two decades, said the newspaper, the Danish energy executive had been a clandestine asset operating at the upper reaches of the Russian political and business worlds. He had preserved the RuzNeft joint venture at the request of his handlers and had returned to Russia on a dangerous mission to gather intelligence regarding the Kremlin's intentions in Ukraine. The woman who had accompanied him was not his personal assistant but an undercover PET operative. She was alive and well, according to *Politiken*, and back in Denmark.

Neither the Danish intelligence service nor the CIA chose to comment on the story, which most observers regarded as ironclad confirmation that every word of the article was true. A week after its publication, Larsen was back on Danish soil as well. Owing to concerns over his security, there was no one on hand for his arrival at Copenhagen Airport other than his wife, Karoline. Thirty minutes later they were safely behind the walls of their home in Hellerup, surrounded by officers of the PET's protective service. Larsen referred all press inquiries to DanskOil's spokesman, who declined all comment. The matter, he said, was now closed.

The press, as usual, had other ideas. They wanted to know the precise nature of the mission that Larsen and the PET officer had undertaken in Russia—and the exact circumstances surrounding the CEO's shooting. Was it somehow connected to the deaths of the two members of the Russian president's inner circle? Had it happened at the Russo-Finnish border crossing? And what about that mysterious missile attack on a petrol station in the Russian town of Maksimov? Surely, the reporters reasoned, there had to be more to the story.

They were right, of course. But no matter how many calls they made or sources they badgered, they were never able to uncover it. Still, the clues were all around them—in a darkened antiquarian bookshop in Copenhagen, behind the counter of a café on the island of Funen, and at the Isabella Stewart Gardner Museum in Boston, where visitors to the second-floor Dutch Room gawked at an empty frame measuring 72.5 by 64.7 centimeters.

Another important clue was revealed in the first week of December, when General Cesare Ferrari, commander of the Carabinieri's Art Squad, announced the recovery of *Self-Portrait with Bandaged Ear* by Vincent van Gogh. The news sent shock waves through the art world, though some were troubled by Ferrari's distinct lack of candor regarding key details of the case, including his refusal to say where or how the iconic painting had been found. This gave rise to speculation that more missing paintings might soon resurface. General Ferrari declined to take part in it.

But was the painting actually the missing Van Gogh? The Art Squad said it was, as did the Courtauld

Gallery's esteemed director, who flew to Rome for the news conference. He was relieved to find the canvas in remarkably good condition. Nevertheless, a minor touch-up was in order before it could be returned to its place in the gallery. General Ferrari, as it turned out, had someone in mind for the job.

"Is he available?" asked the director.

"He's hacking away at the altarpiece in Santa Maria degli Angeli in Venice."

"Not the Pordenone?"

"I'm afraid so."

"It's beneath him."

"I said the same thing," said General Ferrari with a sigh.

"He's a bit on the pricey side," said the director. "I'm not sure I have the money in the budget."

"Actually, I have a feeling he'd be willing to do it pro bono."

Which was indeed the case—provided, of course, that he was able to secure the approval of his immediate supervisor at the Tiepolo Restoration Company. Much to his surprise, she agreed without hesitation. The painting departed Rome the following morning in a caravan of Carabinieri vehicles, and by nightfall it was propped upon an easel in his studio. He inserted a CD into his British-made audio system—Schubert's String Quartet in D Minor—and pressed PLAY. Then he wound a swatch of cotton wool around the end of a wooden dowel, dipped it into a carefully calibrated mixture of acetone, methyl proxitol, and mineral spirits, and went to work.

61

San Polo

G abriel believed the craft of restoration was a bit like making love. It was best done slowly and with painstaking attention to detail, with occasional breaks for rest and refreshment. But in a pinch, if the craftsman and his subject matter were adequately acquainted, a restoration could be done at extraordinary speed, with more or less the same result.

Gabriel was certainly on a first-name basis with Vincent—he had restored him, forged him, and even stolen him—but he deliberately worked at a snail's pace. The iconic self-portrait would soon be one of the most viewed paintings in the world. Not the *Mona Lisa*, mind you, but it would certainly draw a crowd. It was inevitable, given the gossipy nature of London's art world, that the name of the conservator who knocked it into shape would leak to the press. It was essential, reasoned Gabriel, they both put their best foot forward.

The surest way to impede his progress was to limit the amount of time he spent at his easel. He accomplished this by walking the children to school each morning, collecting them again each afternoon, and taking *un'ombra* or two during his coffee breaks. Even so, his daily time on task reached an astounding five hours. He trimmed it further by imposing on Chiara to drop by the apartment each day for lunch. Invariably, it included a discussion of his most recent operation.

"But what if she hadn't removed the document from Nikolai Petrov's briefcase?" Chiara asked one cold and rainy afternoon. "What would have happened then?"

"The Russians would have carried out a false-flag nuclear attack in the village of Maksimov, killing a few hundred of their own citizens in the process. Several hours of highly choreographed popular outrage would have followed, leaving poor Vladimir Vladimirovich with no choice but to use his massive arsenal of tactical nuclear weapons against the Ukrainian military."

"How would the Americans have responded?"

"By destroying the Russian military in eastern Ukraine with an overwhelming conventional strike, leaving poor Vladimir Vladimirovich with no choice but to wipe Kyiv from the map. At which point," said Gabriel, "things would have become really interesting."

"A nuclear exchange between the United States and Russia?"

"A distinct possibility."

"A professional thief saved the world? Is that what you're saying?"

"The world isn't out of the woods just yet."

"Could it happen still?"

"Of course. But the chances have been greatly reduced."

"Why?"

"Kompromat," replied Gabriel.

"The Security Council directive?"

"Exactly."

"Does the Russian president know you have it?"

"At my suggestion, Lars Mortensen of the PET presented a few pages of the document to the SVR *rezident* in Copenhagen. He also gave the *rezident* proof that the SVR was behind the disappearance of Rikke Strøm."

"Which is why the Russians haven't exposed Magnus Larsen as a longtime Russian asset."

Gabriel nodded.

"And Rikke's sister?" asked Chiara.

"Magnus made a rather large deposit recently in

Katje's bank account. He also made a substantial donation to a Danish organization that combats violence against women and children."

Gabriel managed to work on the Van Gogh for only two hours the following day, in part because an intelligence attaché from the Finnish Embassy in Rome insisted on coming to Venice to question him about the incident at the border crossing. Chiara continued the interrogation that evening as they finished the last of their wine on the loggia overlooking the Grand Canal.

"And exactly how far did you venture into Russia?" she asked, her head resting on his shoulder.

"A hundred meters, I'd say. Without a valid visa, of course."

"Did you discharge your weapon?"

"I might have, yes."

"How many times?"

"Five."

"And how many Russian border guards did you kill?"

"Five."

"You're lucky you didn't start a war between Russia and Finland."

"It wasn't for lack of trying."

The Finns managed to keep his name out of the press, as did the Danes and the Americans. A part of him was disappointed; he would have enjoyed seeing the look on the Russian president's face upon learning that it was Gabriel Allon who had put a stop to Plan Aurora. Still, it was better that his role in the affair remain hidden from view. The last thing he needed at this stage of his life was yet another confrontation with the Russians.

Besides, as was usually the case, he was running behind schedule on a restoration. The director of the Courtauld, after taking delivery of a progress report, implored Gabriel to quicken his pace. So, too, did the general manager of the Tiepolo Restoration Company, who informed him that there would be no more lunch dates until he resumed work on the Pordenone altarpiece. His time on task immediately leapt to an appalling eight hours a day.

In the late afternoon, when he longed to gaze upon his mother's face rather than Vincent's, he had only to look down at the child lying at his feet, a workbook open before her, a pencil in her fist. Only once did she attempt to ascertain the reason for her father's weekslong absence from Venice. His answer, that he was attempting to prevent a cataclysmic release of greenhouse gases, met with a reproachful glare.

"There's no need to be patronizing," she said.

"Wherever did you hear a word like that?"

She licked the tip of her forefinger and turned to the

next page in her workbook. "Ultima Generazione is holding a protest in the Piazza San Marco this weekend. My friends and I are planning to attend."

"Isn't Ultima Generazione the group that blocked traffic on the Via della Libertà a few months ago?"

"They've assured the police that this protest will be entirely peaceful." Irene joined him before the canvas. "Why are his brushstrokes so thick?"

"He painted straight from the tube, wet-on-wet. Or, as the Italians would say, *alla prima*. Sometimes he even used a palette knife rather than a brush. It gave his paintings a unique texture. It also makes them somewhat tricky to clean." Gabriel pointed toward the button on Vincent's jacket. "The surface grime and dirty varnish tend to hide in the hollows."

"When will it be finished?"

"The director of the Courtauld Gallery is picking it up on Friday."

Which left Gabriel just three more days to make his deadline. Miraculously, the canvas had survived its theft and two illicit sales with only minor losses. He completed the inpainting on Wednesday and on Thursday applied a new coat of varnish. He also produced an exact copy of the work—if only to demonstrate his ability, were he ever so inclined, to earn his living as an art forger. The director of the Courtauld Gallery arrived at the apartment early Friday afternoon to find both paintings on display in Gabriel's studio.

"Which one is the real Van Gogh?" he asked.

"You're the expert. You tell me."

The learned art historian considered his answer at length. Finally, he indicated the canvas on the left.

"Are you sure?" asked Gabriel.

"Positive," replied the director. "The one on the right is an obvious copy."

Gabriel turned over the version on the left, revealing a pristine canvas and modern stretcher. "Don't worry, it will be our little secret."

The director placed the real Van Gogh in a purpose-built carrying case. "The press will want to know who handled the restoration. How shall I respond?"

"Tell them it was *that* Gabriel Allon."

"I was hoping that would be your answer." The director closed and locked the carrying case. "See you in London for the unveiling?"

Gabriel smiled. "I wouldn't miss it for the world."

62

Harry's Bar

General Ferrari accompanied the Van Gogh on its brief journey across the *laguna* to Marco Polo Airport. Once it was safely airborne and bound for London, he rang Gabriel and suggested they meet at Harry's Bar for a drink. Gabriel, who was sorely in need of a Bellini, agreed.

"Is there a more perfect beverage?" asked the general as the waiter delivered the first round to their corner table.

"No," said Gabriel. "Nor is there a more perfect place to consume the perfect beverage." He glanced around the deserted bar. "Especially in winter when we Venetians have the city largely to ourselves."

Ferrari raised his glass in salutation. "The director

of the Courtauld tells me that you had a little fun at his expense."

"The director of the Courtauld needs new eyeglasses."

"How many books on Van Gogh has he written? Is it three or only two?"

Gabriel smiled but said nothing.

"Perhaps I should take possession of the copy," said the general. "Just so there are no misunderstandings."

"I'll add a signature to avoid any possible confusion."

"Not Vincent's, I hope."

"Oh, no," said Gabriel. "I wouldn't dream of it."

The general laughed quietly. "I only wish you could sign your name to that business in Russia. The rest of the world needs to know that you were the one who saved us from a nuclear apocalypse."

"Actually, you're the one who deserves all the credit."

"Me? What did I do?"

"You dragged me down to Amalfi to authenticate the Van Gogh."

"A pretext on my part."

"And a rather obvious one at that."

"I have to admit, your theory of the case turned out to be more accurate than mine." General Ferrari drew a surveillance photograph from his attaché case and laid it on the table. It depicted a man of perhaps forty-five lunching in Amalfi's Piazza Duomo. He was accompanied by a fair-haired woman whose face was obscured by large sunglasses. "Recognize him?"

It was Grigori Toporov, the SVR assassin Gabriel had killed in Kandestederne.

"They entered Italy on Ukrainian passports," explained Ferrari. "Evidently, they were posing as well-to-do residents of Kyiv who had decided to flee their homeland rather than fight for it. They rented a rather substantial villa not far from Lukas van Damme's. Interestingly enough, they left Amalfi quite suddenly on the night of the murder."

"Thief came to dinner, thief stole painting, Russian assassin killed Van Damme."

"I'm afraid we can't prove it."

"Nor would we want to," said Gabriel.

"Because that would threaten to unravel your elaborate cover-up of what really happened."

"Thief stole painting, thief saved the world."

"With the help of the Danish energy executive who commissioned the theft on behalf of his masters in Moscow. And now the Danish energy executive is being treated like a conquering hero."

"And the thief is in hiding at her luxury villa on Mykonos."

"How much did she make on the deal?"

"Ten million for the job in Amalfi and another ten million shooting pool in Moscow."

The general frowned. "And who says crime doesn't pay?"

"You were the one who granted me the power of absolution."

"In exchange for information leading to the recovery of *The Concert* by Johannes Vermeer. Needless to say, the painting is still missing."

"What about Coetzee?"

"I gave his name and description to the South African authorities and asked them to quietly pursue the matter. They informed me yesterday that they've been unable to locate him." Ferrari shook his head slowly. "He and his partner made out rather well, didn't they? One billion dollars and one of the world's most valuable paintings."

"But the unaccounted-for eighth South African nuclear weapon has been taken off the black market. And the best part is that the operation was financed by the Kremlin."

"But what about the Vermeer?"

Gabriel made no reply.

"Is there no chance that you would consider going to South Africa to look for it?" asked Ferrari.

"I'm afraid I have pressing business here in Venice."

"Finding a buyer for your latest forgery?"

"Preventing my daughter from getting arrested at tomorrow's Ultima Generazione protest in San Marco."

"She's an activist, your daughter?"

"Irene? She's a true radical."

"And you?"

"I'm worried about the world we're going to leave her, Cesare."

"If anyone can repair it, my friend, it's you."

Gabriel raised his glass. "What do you think the carbon footprint of a Bellini is?"

"Quite small, I imagine."

"In that case, we should probably have another round."

General Ferrari signaled the waiter. "I suppose there are worse ways for a story to end. Wouldn't you agree?"

"Yes," said Gabriel. "Much worse."

Il Gazzettino seemed to think there was going to be trouble. The mayor agreed, and beseeched his citizenry to avoid San Marco at all costs. It was all the encouragement Gabriel needed to forbid his daughter to attend. His wife appealed to him to reconsider.

"Please, Gabriel? The child has her heart set on it."

"Is there no way I can talk you out of this?"

"Said the man who just returned from Russia."

"But I was saving the world."

"Now it's Irene's turn."

"Can't we just have lunch instead?"

"First, we'll let Irene and her friends save the world. Then we'll all have lunch."

"I'll make a reservation. Where shall we go?"

"We haven't been to Arturo in ages."

They rode to San Marco on a Number 1 and arrived at the piazza to find several thousand protesters gathered at the foot of the campanile. Chiara and Irene joined the brightly clothed throng, but Gabriel and Raphael wisely withdrew to a table at Caffè Florian, where they would have a ringside seat if things got interesting. Raphael had brought along his math homework, leaving Gabriel with nothing to do except imagine what would happen if a nuclear weapon were to land in the middle of the enormous square. Or on Independence Square in Kyiv. Or Freedom Square in Kharkiv.

He realized after a moment that his son was staring at him with his long-lashed, jade-colored eyes. "What are you thinking about?" asked the boy.

"Nothing at all."

"That's not possible," said Raphael, and resumed his work.

The mayor's warning notwithstanding, the demonstration was entirely peaceful. Speakers spoke, a chant was chanted, a song was sung, a beautiful rendition of John Lennon's "Imagine" that filled the piazza from the basilica to the Museo Correr. When it was over, Chiara and Irene made their way to Florian. So did four of Irene's classmates, all of whom, it turned out, would be joining the Allon family for lunch at Vini da Arturo.

It was located on the Calle dei Assassini. Gabriel telephoned during the walk from San Marco to alert the proprietor that their party of four had unexpectedly grown to eight. The confines of the cramped dining room required adults and children to sit at separate tables. The proprietor suggested a fixed menu for the children that sounded so enticing that Gabriel and Chiara ordered it as well. They scarcely spoke during the meal, preferring instead to eavesdrop on the conversation at the opposing table.

"Do you hear that?" asked Chiara. "Your children have lost any trace of an accent. They're Venetians now."

"Are they happy here?"

"They are now that you're home again. But they were miserable while you were away. Irene, especially."

"Is it my imagination, or does she have some idea what I was doing?"

"She's unusually observant, your daughter. And quite serious. They both are. I have no doubt they're going to lead lives similar to yours."

"I beg of you not to let that happen."

Chiara smiled sadly. "Why must you always make light of your accomplishments?"

"Because I'm endlessly bored by people who dwell on theirs. And because I sometimes wish . . ."

"That you had been born in Berlin and that your name had been Frankel instead of Allon? That you had attended the finest art academy in Germany and had become an important German painter? That your mother hadn't spent the war in Birkenau and that your poor father hadn't been killed in the Six-Day War?"

"You forgot to mention Vienna."

"But that's who you are, Gabriel."

"Eli says I have an uncontrollable need to repair things."

"Why do you think your daughter insisted on coming to the demonstration?"

"She's contracted my disorder?"

"Along with your brilliance and your decency and your sense of right and wrong."

"I worry about her."

"She worries about you, too."

"Why?"

"Because you're not as adept at hiding your grief from us as you think you are." Chiara squeezed his hand. "What was it like being back?"

"It's changed."

"Did you see Leah?"

"Yes, of course."

"How is she?"

"Her doctor chastised me for allowing nearly a year to go by since my last visit."

"I'm sorry."

"Don't be. It's not your fault."

Chiara tugged at a loose thread in the tablecloth. "Would you have told me if I hadn't asked?"

"Eventually."

"When?"

"Not while I was making love to you in our bed overlooking the Grand Canal."

Chiara's gaze was level and cool. "Now is the point in the conversation—"

"When I tell you that I'm the luckiest man in the world. You've made me very happy, Chiara. I can't imagine how my life would have turned out if we hadn't met."

"I do," she said. "You would have married the train wreck."

"I walked out on the train wreck."

Chiara dragged her thumbnail gently across the back of his hand. "And you were never in love with her?"

Gabriel looked at his two children and smiled. "Asked and answered."

Author's Note

The Collector is a work of entertainment and should be read as nothing more. The names, characters, places, and incidents portrayed in the story are the product of the author's imagination or have been used fictitiously. Any resemblance to actual persons, living or dead, businesses, companies, events, or locales is entirely coincidental.

Visitors to the *sestiere* of San Polo will search in vain for the converted palazzo overlooking the Grand Canal where Gabriel Allon has taken up residence with his wife and two young children. The business office of the Tiepolo Restoration Company is likewise impossible to find, for no such enterprise exists. Nor is there a London-based nonprofit organization known as the Venice Preservation Society. Vini da Arturo on the Calle dei Assassini is one of our favorite restaurants in Venice, and Adagio, located near the campanile in the Campo dei Frari, is a lovely spot to have a late-afternoon *cicchetto* and *un'ombra*. Deepest apologies to the staff of Hjorths Restaurant in Kandestederne for Gabriel's irritable mood at dinner. As for the dead Russian assassin at the end of Dødningebakken, well, these things happen.

The novel takes place during a span of several weeks during the autumn of 2022. The factual backdrop of that period—the battlefield situation in Ukraine, the sanctions and travel bans, the flight of Western oil companies from Vladimir Putin's Russia—is for the most part faithfully rendered. Where necessary, I have granted myself license. I have also fictionalized several companies and places. For example, there are no gated communities known as Balmoral Hills or Somerset Estates in the exclusive Moscow suburb known as Rublyovka.

Nor is there an eatery on the rue de Miromesnil in Paris known as Brasserie Dumas or a diamond brokerage in Antwerp named for a mountain in eastern Turkey. Jørgens Smørrebrød Café in Vissenbjerg is likewise fictitious, as are TverBank, RuzNeft, and the Danish energy company DanskOil. Indeed, I specifically chose to base my oil-and-gas company in Denmark because it could not possibly be confused with any other Western firm that has done business in Russia. The European Union's largest oil producer, Denmark has banned new exploration in the North Sea and intends to end all extraction of fossil fuels by 2050. At the time of this writing, the Scandinavian country of 5.8 million people derives 67 percent of its electricity from renewable sources, primarily wind.

The brief biography of the Dutch Golden Age painter Johannes Vermeer that appears in chapter 10 is accurate, as is the description of the March 1990 robbery at the Isabella Stewart Gardner Museum, the largest art heist in history. More than three decades after the theft, the whereabouts of the thirteen stolen works of art remain a mystery. Anthony Amore, the Gardner Museum's director of security, told the *New York Times* in 2017 that the missing works were probably within a sixty-mile radius of Boston. But the late Charles Hill, the legendary former Scotland Yard detective and art sleuth, was convinced they had made their way from Boston to Ireland. There is no evidence to suggest they were in the hands of the Kinahan cartel, a notorious Dublin-based criminal organization with links to Italy's Camorra and 'Ndrangheta. *Self-Portrait with Bandaged Ear* by Vincent van Gogh, which hangs in the Courtauld Gallery in London, has never been stolen—except in the pages of *The Rem-*

brandt Affair, my 2010 novel featuring Parisian art thief Maurice Durand.

The nuclear weapons program of South Africa's White-minority government is a matter of historical record, as is the regime's decision, taken during the dying days of apartheid, to relinquish its weapons. Israel has long denied reports that it provided assistance to South Africa, just as it has denied that it possesses a powerful nuclear arsenal of its own. The South African weapons—six finished, one under construction—were dismantled under international supervision, but the Black-majority government retains control of nearly five hundred pounds of highly enriched uranium. The Obama administration tried and failed to convince Pretoria to surrender its stockpile. The fissile material, which has been melted down and cast into ingots, is stored in a former silver vault at the Pelindaba Nuclear Research Center, where it remains an inviting target for thieves and terrorists. Nuclear experts say that slamming two pieces of the material together at high speed would likely result in a sizable nuclear explosion.

Russia, of course, is an advanced nuclear power, with the world's largest stockpile of nuclear weapons—weapons that Vladimir Putin and his favorite propagandists have repeatedly threatened to use in Ukraine. Among the most bellicose advocates of the nuclear option is Dmitry

Medvedev, the elfin former president, once regarded as a Western-leaning reformer, who now serves as deputy secretary of Russia's Security Council. When asked in March 2023 whether the threat of nuclear conflict between Russia and the West had receded, Medvedev replied, "No, it hasn't, it has grown. Every day they provide Ukraine with foreign weapons brings the nuclear apocalypse closer."

Such incendiary rhetoric is doubtless intended to weaken Western resolve and sow divisions within the pro-Ukraine alliance, but it is by no means empty. Or, in the words of Dmitry Medvedev, it is "certainly not a bluff." Russian nuclear doctrine has been modified to allow for a first strike in response to a perceived threat, and Russia's armed forces possess some two thousand tactical nuclear weapons, ten times the number of similar weapons in the US arsenal. Such smaller, lower-yield weapons could be used to achieve a limited battlefield objective—to capture the city of Bakhmut, for example—or to carry out a "managed" escalation of the Ukraine crisis in order to achieve Russia's territorial and geostrategic ambitions.

In the autumn of 2022, with Russian forces in retreat and casualties mounting, US officials grew alarmed that Putin and his military advisers were casting about for a pretext to use nuclear weapons in Ukraine—or that they might create such a pretext themselves with a false-flag operation. Tensions escalated after Russian defense minister Sergei Shoigu telephoned four NATO counterparts—including US defense secretary Lloyd Austin—to say that Ukraine was preparing to detonate a dirty bomb on its own territory and blame the attack on the Kremlin. Ukraine responded by accusing Russia of building the dirty bombs themselves using radiological material from a captured Ukrainian nuclear power plant. President Joseph Biden took the extraordinary step of publicly warning Vladimir Putin that he would be making an "incredibly serious mistake" if he were to use tactical nuclear weapons in Ukraine. At the White House and Pentagon, anxious national security and military officials reportedly prepared for a potential nuclear crisis by taking part in tabletop simulations.

But would Vladimir Putin actually pull the nuclear trigger—and risk a potentially cataclysmic confrontation with the United States and its NATO allies—in order to prevail in Ukraine? Most diplomats, intelligence officials, and military analysts insist it is unlikely, but opinion is far from universal. Indeed, one former senior US intelligence official told me the chances of a Russian nuclear attack in Ukraine were somewhere "between 25 and 40 percent." The threat level would increase significantly, the former official added, if Putin was confronted with a catastrophic military defeat that might lead to his removal from power and the loss of his ill-gotten billions.

Vladimir Putin now stands accused of war crimes in Ukraine by the International Criminal Court in The Hague. But longtime observers of the Russian leader say that what he fears most is a so-called color revolution—like the Orange Revolution that erupted in Ukraine in 2004 or the uprising in Libya that brought down strongman Muammar Gadhafi, whose brutal videotaped murder Putin watched obsessively. Increasingly paranoid and isolated, he has resorted to a level of internal repression not seen since the darkest days of Soviet communism. Dissent of any kind is no longer tolerated. Opposition to the war in Ukraine is a crime.

On the rare occasions Putin ventures into public, his speeches are increasingly divorced from reality. To justify the invasion of Ukraine after the fact, he has adopted the language of the European and American populist far right, recasting his unprovoked war of aggression as a sacred battle between Christian Russia and godless Western elites and globalists. The Russian people, however, know the truth—that Vladimir Putin alone is to blame for the calamity that has befallen Russia. If history is any guide, he might well get his color revolution, after all.

Acknowledgments

I am grateful to my wife, Jamie Gangel, who listened patiently while I worked out the plot of *The Collector* and then skillfully edited the pile of paper I euphemistically refer to as my first draft, all while breaking news almost on a daily basis on CNN. My debt to Jamie is immeasurable, as is my love.

I am forever indebted to David Bull for his advice on all matters related to art and restoration. One of the world's foremost conservators, David has restored works by both Johannes Vermeer and Vincent van Gogh. Unlike the fictitious Gabriel Allon, he has never had occasion to clean a painting by the ruthlessly ambitious Venetian school Mannerist known as Il Pordenone.

Mark Hertling, who served as the commanding general of the United States Army Europe, was an invaluable source of information about the war in Ukraine, as was James G. Stavridis, the sixteenth supreme allied commander at NATO and a bestselling novelist in his own right. Needless to say, any mistakes or literary license in *The Collector* are my doing, not theirs.

My super-lawyer, Michael Gendler, was a source of wise counsel and much-needed laughter. My dear friend Louis Toscano, author of *Triple Cross* and *Mary Bloom*, made countless improvements to the novel, and my eagle-eyed personal copy editor, Kathy Crosby, made certain it was free of typographical and grammatical errors. David Koral and Jackie Quaranto expertly shepherded my typescript through the production process on the tightest of schedules.

A heartfelt thanks to the rest of the team at HarperCollins, especially Brian Murray, Jonathan Burnham, Leah Wasielewski, Leslie Cohen, Doug Jones, Josh Marwell, Robin Bilardello, Milan Bozic, Frank Albanese, Leah Carlson-Stanisic, Carolyn Bodkin, Chantal Restivo-Alessi, Julianna Wojcik, Mark Meneses, Beth Silfin, Lisa Erickson, Amy Baker, Tina Andreadis, Diana Meunier, Ed Spade, and Kelly Roberts.

Lastly, I wish to thank my children, Lily and Nicholas, who were a constant source of love, support, and inspiration as I struggled to meet my deadline. The last sentence of *The Collector* was written with them in mind.

About the Author

DANIEL SILVA is the award-winning #1 *New York Times* bestselling author of *The Unlikely Spy, The Mark of the Assassin, The Marching Season, The Kill Artist, The English Assassin, The Confessor, A Death in Vienna, Prince of Fire, The Messenger, The Secret Servant, Moscow Rules, The Defector, The Rembrandt Affair, Portrait of a Spy, The Fallen Angel, The English Girl, The Heist, The English Spy, The Black Widow, House of Spies, The Other Woman, The New Girl, The Order, The Cellist,* and *Portrait of an Unknown Woman.* He is best known for his long-running thriller series starring spy and art restorer Gabriel Allon. Silva's books are critically acclaimed bestsellers around the world and have been translated into more than thirty languages. He resides in Florida with his wife, television journalist Jamie Gangel, and their twins, Lily and Nicholas. For more information, visit www.danielsilvabooks.com.

HARPER
LARGE PRINT

We hope you enjoyed reading
our new, comfortable print size and found it
an experience you would like to repeat.

Well – you're in luck!

Harper Large Print offers the finest in
fiction and nonfiction books in this same larger
print size and paperback format. Light and easy to read,
Harper Large Print paperbacks are for the book lovers
who want to see what they are reading without strain.

For a full listing of titles and
new releases to come, please visit our website:
www.hc.com

HARPER LARGE PRINT

SEEING IS BELIEVING!